Praise for Judith Tarr's *LORD OF THE TWO LANDS*

"The story of Alexander the Great has been pounded into dust, and I never thought to see it done fresh again, but Tarr's INSPIRED choice of heroines has given her a whole new slant on material so familiar that the names of even minor figures fall on the ears with a thousand echoes. Meriamon is a wonderful character, warm, potent, gentle, far-sighted, tough-minded, womanly to the roots. . . . Yet perhaps my favorite character is the man Niko—awkward, honest, splendidly sexy—and my favorite scenes are the lovely private moments between him and Meriamon. The ancients believed devoutly in the existence of a supernatural reality that utterly penetrated ordinary life and charged every act and word with meaning; Tarr gives this aspect of the ancient mind the expression and weight it deserves. The trip to Siwah was wonderful. All those demons, the malevolent earth, the sandstorm: I LOVED IT."

—Cecelia Holland, author of *The Bear Flag*

"Judith Tarr's LORD OF THE TWO LANDS moves away from her previous medieval efforts to the story of Alexander the Great. This is Alexander seen from a viewpoint similar to that in Mary Renault's *The Persian Boy*—someone who joins his campaigns in mid-course. . . .Alexander is as compelling as ever as a central figure for a novel, and Tarr has done her research and writing as well as ever."

—Chicago *Sun-Times*

"Judith Tarr's *Lord of the Two Lands* is an EXCITING story of Alexander the Great and his move into Egypt, told through the eyes of Pharaoh Nectanebo's daughter, Meriamon. Tarr has portrayed, in A REMARKABLY BELIEVABLE STORY, a rich sense of time and place. Since the plot does not turn on those elements, her use of oracles and the occult is entirely appropriate for the well-researched and entert
I SIMPLY COULD NOT
TURNED THE LAST PA

au

LORD OF THE TWO LANDS

JUDITH TARR

TOR

A TOM DOHERTY ASSOCIATES BOOK
NEW YORK

This is a work of historical fiction. Any references to real people, events,
establishments, organizations, or locales are intended only to give the fiction a sense of reality and authenticity. Other names, characters, and incidents are either a product of the author's imagination or are used
fictitiously, as are those fictionalized events which involve real persons
and did not occur or are set in the future.

LORD OF THE TWO LANDS

Copyright © 1993 by Judith Tarr

Cover art by David Cherry
Maps by Ellisa Mitchell

A Tor Book
Published by Tom Doherty Associates, Inc.
175 Fifth Avenue
New York, N.Y. 10010

Tor® is a registered trademark of Tom Doherty Associates, Inc.

ISBN: 0-812-52078-5
Library of Congress Catalog Card Number: 93-24635

First edition: March 1993
First mass market edition: January 1994

Printed in the United States of America

0 9 8 7 6 5 4 3 2 1

TO JEANNE

*For a clear eye,
a hard head,
and no compromises*

ACKNOWLEDGMENTS

A novel, particularly a historical novel, is seldom conceived or born in isolation. Particular thanks to: my agent, Jane Butler, who was present at the conception; Meredith Tarr, fellow Alexander enthusiast; the GEnie computer network, and particularly the members of the Science Fiction Round Table; Kathy Ferch, for the coronation in Memphis; Tom Doherty, Beth Meacham, and the staff of Tor Books, for the best going-away present a traveler ever had; and Jeanne Zimmerman, without whom this book would have been far less than it is.

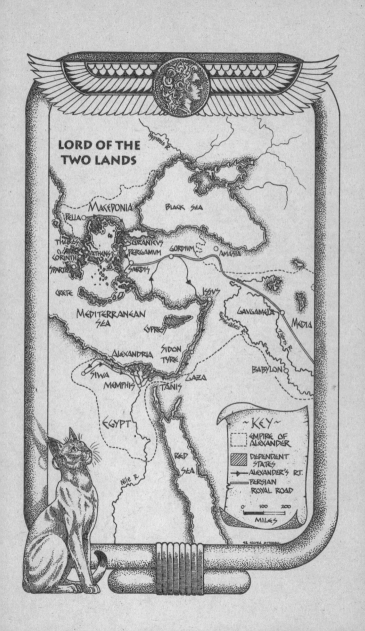

• PROLOGUE •

Nectanebo.

Nekhtharhab.

The power was in the name. The name was power.

Beloved of Amon, son of the Sun, Great House of Egypt, Protected of Horus, Lord of the Two Lands. Nekhtharhab. Nectanebo to the sea-peoples, the raw young Hellenes who served so well on all sides of the world's wars.

He stood on the horizon and looked down. It grew like the lotus flower, his land, kingdom and empire and heart of the world. Long slender stem of Black Land against the pitiless red of desert, great dark flowering of Delta on the edge of the Great Green that was the name and essence of the sea. Lifeblood of the lotus was the stream of the Nile, quiescent now, shrunk to its least extent, while its people tilled the black earth that was its gift. Almost, like a god, he could reach, touch. Almost, like a god, cup it in his hand.

The air sighed about him, a whisper like wings, a glimmer as of falcon-eyes. Memory touched, passed: sunlight, singing, the weight of the Two Crowns new and terrible upon his brows; and names on him, new names, strong names, god-names for a god-king.

Here in Amon's temple was silence and shadows, and the basin on its four clawed feet, and Egypt in it, the rich black land of Khemet, shadow-shaped in water of the Nile. The walls were alive with painted gods and kings and queens, beasts, birds, lotus, palm, papyrus, all the many-colored splendor of Egypt. Barbarians had not touched these. Not they, not the Parsa, though they had wrought horrors enough in other temples than this of Amon in

Thebes. They were gone. He had driven them out, he and his people; and if there had been more than simple human force in it, then that was no more than the enemy deserved. Their names would die with their memory, and they would be gone for all of eternity.

But they, being barbarians, did not understand what it was for a name to die. They were coming back. It was in the water: beyond the lotus that was Egypt, a red tide of blood, a blackness of war. Persia had held the Two Lands once. She would seize them again and grind them under her booted heel.

Nectanebo bent over the basin. The lappets of his headdress swung forward, nearly brushing the water. He thrust them back. One shoulder ached. A Persian mace had broken it in that last battle, just before he knew that he had won. The bone had healed well, but the ache had never wholly faded.

It was distracting him now, making the image waver, the power drain away. He drew a sharp breath, and the image steadied. It did not change. Persia was coming—not soon, perhaps; not for years, it might be—but inevitable, and inescapable. There was no power in Pharaoh, even in a pharaoh who was a great mage and master of the hidden art, to overcome an enemy so implacable. Their gods were young and few and eager for empire. His were old beyond telling and numerous beyond counting, and they had never willingly been gods of war.

"I can hold," he said, soft in the silence, "with the gods' help. But my body will die, and I become Osiris; and who will be Horus to defend my lands? I had a son. He is dead; the Parsa killed him. I have a wife. She is with child; and if it is a son, will his strength suffice for what I foresee? Who will defend my kingdom? Who will wrest it from the Persian's fist?"

The air sighed again, louder. The lamps flickered, casting long shadows. Painted kings seemed to stir, their eyes to kindle. Painted gods drew breath like living things. The ranks of hieroglyphs quickened, beasts and birds and stylized men shifting, stretching, yearning toward freedom.

Nectanebo breathed a word. The lamps ceased their swaying. The walls stilled. Something chittered away overhead. Bat; or spirit blown from its course and fluttering lost among the pillars. Nectanebo took no notice of it. The water blurred and rippled. A new vision grew in it.

Almost, he laughed. He had asked the gods, and they answered, from the very beginning. Lamplight limned it, granted it more shadow than light, but there was no mistaking the name of that dance. The man was as eager as a ram, and built like one, a heavy gleaming creature with muscles that rolled like water. The woman was nigh as tall as he, but if he was a ram, she was a tigress, turning suddenly in his clasp, locking legs about his middle and raking claws down his back. He grunted. She laughed, arched, sank teeth into his shoulder. Her face through streams of red-gold hair was wild, a little mad.

Her teeth had drawn blood. He took no notice of it, though it ran in the lamplight in streams the color of wine, or of the Tyrians' purple. Their shadows leaped and danced, a mingled shape of dark and light upon the wall. For a stretching moment it was a ram, a ram crowned with the sun, and a serpent coiled about him, locked in passion that was half war.

It broke, blurred, scattered. They dropped down in a tangle of limbs and bodies and coppery hair.

There was a silence. Nectanebo, trapped in the scrying, watched the wildness flow out of them. The man laid his head on the woman's breast. His hair was black and thick, cut as the Hellenes cut it, and he wore a beard like a Hellene, and that was a Hellene's face, though ram-heavy, ram-strong. She was slighter as befit a woman, but her beauty was as Greek as his, the full rounding of her body even in its slimness, the strong oval face and the long broad nose and the wide low brow: to an Egyptian, heavy and somewhat coarse, but striking for all of that. Her hands were long and strong, stroking the knotted muscles of his back, smoothing them one by one.

"A god was in us tonight," she said. Greek indeed, but not as it was spoken by envoys in the courts of the Two Lands: broader and softer, with the hint of an antique lilt.

"Not one of your damned snakes again?" His voice was deep, with the hint of a growl.

She laughed in her throat. "Not tonight, my jealous lord. Didn't you feel it? Didn't you see the light that was on us?"

"I saw you," he said.

"My lord." It was a purr. "My king. Were you Herakles tonight? Or were you more? Were you even—"

His hand stopped the name. His scowl was terrible. "I was myself. Or am I not enough for you?"

Over the heavy black-furred hand, her eyes danced with mirth. A gasp escaped him. His hand snapped free. She bared her sharp white teeth. "See, my lord, I prophesy. We've made a king tonight, you and I and—who knows? A god may pass where he will. I for one shall welcome him."

"Raving madwoman." His body was reviving. He rose above her. "We'll see if I need a god to do my rutting for me."

She smiled long and slow, and pulled him down.

Nectanebo straightened slowly. There was his answer. There, if he read it rightly, was his king: a spark in the womb of this woman, this wild barbarian creature who could not but be a queen. Her king was man enough, and strong enough, but Nectanebo was a mage, and he knew that this man was not what he was seeking.

Barbarians. Aliens. Foreigners. Had he wrested his lands from the Parsa, only to surrender them to the Hellenes?

He rose to his full height. He was aware as he had not been in a long while, that even in Khemet he was not tall; that in the world without, he was a small man. A little thin brown man with a scarred and stiffened shoulder, a suggestion of Ethiopia in the fullness of his lips and the broadness of his nose, but all Egypt in the long dark eyes made longer still with kohl. He was greater than he looked, and stronger. He was Lord of the Great House, master of the Two Lands. He had conquered the Parsa and freed his people, and restored the worship of his gods.

He did not kneel as even Pharaoh should before divinity. The mood was not on him. The power was in him still, though it had begun to ebb. "Why?" he demanded of the air.

It whispered, but it spoke no word that he could understand.

He stooped toward the chair that sat by the basin, caught up what lay there: the crook and flail of the Great House. He held them high. "Am I the last, then? Is the Great House to fall? Shall no man again be Lord of the Two Lands, but that he be the king of an alien people?"

Silence.

"Answer me!"

The echoes died unanswered.

He sank down. The floor was stone, and cold under the thin linen of his kilt. Crook and flail drooped on his knees. "At least," he whispered, barely to be heard, "at least, if ever you have loved me, let me know his name."

The stillness deepened. His shoulders sagged. The gods had forsaken him. Even his power was gone, drained away like water from a broken pot. He was mere man, and mortal, and deaf to aught that the heart could hear.

Alexander.

It was a whisper, fainter even than his own. It could have been the slap of bare feet on stone, the rustle of linen in a priest's robe, the hiss of a cat as it warred with shadows.

Every muscle stretched taut. He strained to hear.

Yes. Yes, he had heard it. A name—alien name for an alien king, but his king, his god, his hope.

Alexander.

·PART ONE·

ISSUS

• ONE •

"Alexander!"

The sea roared, crashing on stones. Louder by far were men's voices, the ring of bronze and precious steel, the neighing of horses, the mingled tumult of battle; and a name over them all, ringing up to heaven.

Meriamon had been walking since the world was made. She had had a horse, but the Parsa had taken that, farther back than she could remember. That they had not taken more was a mark not of their restraint but of hers. They would pay in their due time.

She crested the last, pitiless hill. The battle spread below, a seethe and clash of men and beasts, shouts and cries and the clangor of metal on metal. It sounded like nothing so much as a cattle market beside a smithy. But the drovers were Hellenes—Macedonians, she must remember to call them—and what they drove were Persians. Parsa. The enemy.

Her mantle heaved, struggling. A narrow tawny head thrust through the wrapping, opened eyes the color of minted gold, uttered a single, emphatic *mrrrrttt*. Meriamon gasped. Sekhmet's claws were wickedly sharp. The cat sprang free hissing her displeasure, shook from head to tail, and vanished behind a clump of scrub.

Meriamon drew the cloak tighter about her stinging breast. The wind plucked at her, whipping the muddied hem against her legs. She was wet with the unwontedness of water that fell from the sky, she was colder than she had ever been in her life, and there was a fire in her. The sun, sinking toward the sea, freed itself from its prison of cloud and thrust a long lance across the battlefield. It caught a splendor of scarlet and gold. God or man, she could not tell, so bright as it was: blinding her through all the shields of body and souls, down to the heart of her. Dimly in the afterblaze she saw a shadow, a quenched and stumbling thing that quailed before that shape of fire, and knew with a fierce dark joy that she looked on the Persian king. He turned, with his bodyguard all fallen and his enemies surging upon him; turned his glittering chariot and fled.

A roar followed him. The Macedonians surged in his wake. His people, loyal even in their shock, died defending his cowardice. His enemies laughed. The one who led them—flaming even in the last of the light, his little thick-set black horse prancing and snorting and flagging its tail—shouted something in a high fierce voice. The Macedonians shouted back. *"Alexander!"*

Meriamon smiled. Sekhmet returned from her errand, haughty and much displeased. "Walk with me, then," said Meriamon, "if riding warm and dry-footed is beneath your dignity."

The cat filliped her tail and started down the slope, picking her way delicately through mud and stones and scree. Meriamon sighed, half laughing, and followed her. A shadow followed them, a shadow within the woman's shadow, and its shape, if shape it truly had, was strange.

Meriamon knew about camps. She had lost her horse outside of one. This one was different, its people louder, dirtier, and infinitely more shameless, but men were men wherever they were. She kept her mantle wound tight and drew down a little of the twilight on herself, putting a twisting in it, willing eyes to slip aside. Macedonians were not like the Parsa, who brought their whole households to war as if it were a hunt for the court, though they had their servants and their camp followers. She did not care to be seen as she was: not only a woman but a stranger, and alien, and perhaps an enemy.

This camp was quiet, as camps went. All the noise and terror was in the other, among the Persians, as some fought and most fled and the women, trapped in their tents and their modesty, shrieked and wailed. Even over the sounds of battle and camp, Meriamon could hear them.

They had laughed and chattered while their kings made a mock of her gods. They had fluttered and cooed in the Great House of Egypt, and simpered as their men called themselves masters of the Two Lands. Now they would know what it was to be conquered.

Meriamon's jaw ached. She was grinding her teeth again. Hate was a fine fierce thing, but it was little enough to live on. And she had eaten the last of her bread yesterday.

Water at least there was in plenty. She would eat later, when she found what she had come for. People were beginning to mill and throng about her, soldiers coming back from the battle, the wounded limping or leaning on spears or carried on their shields. Their curses were a long drone, punctuated by cries of pain.

"You."

Meriamon drew still more shadow about her. The crowd had thickened, the tumult risen, surging from the battlefield. There was order in it, and purpose, however frantic it might look.

"You!" Something caught her cloak. She wheeled. A man stood over her. He seemed as high as the sky. He reeked of sweat and blood. "Go to the surgeons' tent," he said. "Tell them we've got one out here, and he's giving trouble."

She could understand him. Just. Macedonian, her teachers had told her, was Greek, but barely so. Her own Greek, gods be thanked, was where she needed it. "Why don't you tie him and drag him in?"

The man laughed: a sharp sound, with a catch in it. "Tie him? Tie our Ajax? Take a look at him!"

She had thought this man was huge. The one on the ground, in what looked to be a convulsion, stretched as long as a tree. There were two men on him, holding him. One fell away. The other rocked and swayed.

Her lips tightened. She stepped round the man who had spoken—commanding her like a servant: how dared he?—and approached the fallen giant. Even in dusk and fitful torches, she could see enough. "He has fits?" she asked.

"He got hit over the head. He keeps trying to go back and fight Persians." The lesser giant dodged a flying foot. "We'd clip his ear to keep him quiet, but we'd kill him if we tried."

"You had better not try," said Meriamon, evading flailing limbs, closing in on the man's head. He had lost his helmet; his hair was matted with something dark and glistening. Blood. She knelt, took the tossing, thrashing head in her hands. Lost it. Won it again, and held. She spoke a word, an ancient word, a word with power in it. *Peace*.

Little by little he stilled. Her shadow bent over him, enfolded him.

"Take him now," she said. Her voice sounded faint and far away. "Gently; jostle him as little as you may."

The Macedonians obeyed her. She was a little surprised, but dimly. So thin, her magic was, so far from the source of its strength. It was all she could do to quiet the man, to keep him so while his companions carried him to the surgeons.

Very likely he would die. She was no adept of Imhotep's temple, to work miracles with healing magic. She had only the one small gift of quiet, and knowledge enough if she were given light and space to wield it.

The man who had stopped her was still beside her, steadying the giant's shoulders with one long arm. The other two men had the rest of him. They were all wounded, she noticed. One limped. They all walked stiffly, with now and then a catch of breath.

The surgeons' tent was an image from the Persians' hell: dim lamps, leaping shadows, groans and shouts and howls of agony. The stink caught at her throat. "Over there," someone snapped, harried. 'There' being by the far wall, in a space barely large enough for a man of normal dimensions, and far from the nearest lamp. That at least Meriamon could remedy. She pointed with her chin. "Bring it here."

Two of the bearers were already gone, one at something like a run. The third looked ready to bolt. He brought her the lamp instead, and paused, swaying a little, frowning at her.

She was under him when he went down, catching the lamp before it fell, bracing the worst of his weight. But she was small even in Khemet, and he was Macedonian. They went down together, half on the giant, half in the passage between rows of bodies.

Meriamon struggled from beneath him. The lamp was safe. She used it to look at him. Not all the blood on him was his friend's. And his right arm—the one that he had kept out of her sight—did not look well at all.

The giant would keep. She attacked the smaller man's armor. It came free more easily than she might have expected, though it jarred him. She was glad that he was not awake to feel it.

There were no other wounds on him that mattered: cuts, bruises, one that might have been bad if it had been a little deeper. His arm was bound up roughly in strips torn from someone's tunic, stained solid with blood both dried and new-wet. With teeth-gritted care she peeled away the wrappings.

It could have been worse. A wound ran down the length of it, thin and not remarkably deep. Sword-cut, and a glancing one at that. It was little enough. The worst was what it ended in. The bone was broken at the wrist, the hand dangling like a dead thing. It seemed a clean break, no shards or splinters to foul the wound. But whatever had done it had crushed the flesh and ground the muscle into the tortured bone. A little more, and he would have lost the hand.

She could save it. Maybe. Care now, prayer, time and the gods' protection against fever—he would not be a one-armed man. Whether he could win back full use of arm and hand, only the gods knew.

Her eyes found a man hovering—no, boy, though he was bigger than most men in Khemet: wide curious eyes, idle hands. "Splints," she said. "Bandages, thread, needles. Water, as hot as you can get it. Herbs to wash a wound."

The boy was obedient, and quick about it. Maybe it was the weight of her shadow with its gleam of eyes.

When she had done all she might for the wounded man, she looked up. The tent stretched away in front of her. She blinked hard. It shrank somewhat. It was mostly a roof and poles, and sides that rolled up or down at need—all down now, closing in the sight and scent and sound of pain. Too much pain. She turned to the nearest man, awareness narrowing again, to focus on this one, endurable center. Little as she might know beside a healer-priest, she knew enough for this; more maybe than the Greek surgeons did. She could tell what needed stitching, what was broken and what was strained, when a limb could stay and when it had to come off; how to draw an arrow from a wound. People tried to speak to her once or twice. They might be asking what a woman was doing in the surgeons' tent. She did not answer. They had eyes. They could see what she did.

None of them interfered. Her shadow took care of that.

News came in with new waves of wounded: remnants of the fight, men returned from the pursuit, others who had taken wounds and only now troubled to notice them. The enemy was driven far away. The Persian camp was taken, and the king had taken the Great King's tent.

"And the Great King's women," said a man who had lost a hand. He had dropped his shield and used the strap to bind the stump and gone on fighting, crazy-mad as men could be when their blood was up. He was numbed now, part with wine, part with shock; and dizzy with victory. He grinned. He had excellent teeth, Meriamon noticed.

"Would you believe it? They take their wives to war. And their concubines. And all their slaves, and their brats, too. And a whole squalling pack of eunuchs."

He glanced at Meriamon and started, and fell suddenly silent.

She almost laughed aloud. She had forgotten the coat and trousers under her mantle. Parsa makeshifts, despicably barbarian, but warm. Was *that* why no one had named her female and cast her out?

The poor man was blushing. So was the one she was tending, who had a sword-cut the length of his side, shallow but bloody. She bound off the bandage and patted his shoulder. "Go on," she said, "and keep it clean. Come back here in a day or two; I'll give you a salve to help it heal."

He muttered what might have been thanks, and escaped into the night. All of them did who could; the ones who stayed were the helpless, the dying or the unconscious.

They were all being looked after. There was order in it, a rhythm born of long practice, a precision that should not have startled her: she had seen how this army fought. No magic here, no chanting of spells that had been old when the gods were young, but they did not do so ill without it, for barbarians.

She turned toward the door. She needed food and sleep; and Sekhmet was gone. Too much noise and stink here for a cat. Too much for a woman, too, worn as she was from the long road.

Something—maybe only the way the bodies lay, maybe the need to evade a knot of surgeons struggling with a writhing, screaming victim—sent her round the long way, back to where she had begun.

The giant was unconscious, but his breathing was steady and deep. The other was awake. Golden cat-eyes opened in the hollow of his side. Sekhmet yawned and sat up and began to wash her tail.

Somehow the Macedonian had got himself clean. From

the tautness about his lips, it had cost him more than he expected.

After all the men she had tended, he did not look quite so huge. He was taller than some but lighter in the bone, lean and rangy rather than bull-solid. Like most of the young ones she had seen, he wore no beard; the stubble on his cheeks was the color of barley straw, a shade or two lighter than his hair. His eyes even in the dimness were light, a clear pale grey like the sky in earliest morning. They shocked her a little. Light eyes—sky-eyes—were alien in Khemet.

He glowered at her. "I can't get up," he said, as if it was her fault that he had torn his arm to pieces.

"You won't, either," said Meriamon, "unless you want to set the bones awry."

"But I have to get up," he said with an air of sweetest reason. "I'm on guard duty."

"Not from here, you aren't."

He sat up. His face went grey. Meriamon lowered him down again, gasping a little: he was heavy.

And furious. "I was just bringing Ajax to the surgeons, damn it. You can't keep me here."

"I'm not," she said. "Your body is."

His good hand seized her coat. Sweat beaded on his brow, but he kept his grip, twisting. "Let me out of here!"

"There now," said a sharp voice behind Meriamon. "What's this—Nikolaos, is it? Let the boy go."

"Boy?" The soldier—Nikolaos—laughed, though he choked on it. "What do you mean, 'boy'?"

Meriamon looked over her shoulder. She had seen the man here and there about the tent, commanding the others when they seemed to need it. He was not young, but neither was he old; his hair was grizzled, his beard cut short. He wore a robe, much stained but respectably rich, and a mantle that had been crimson before it faded. He peered at Meriamon, frowning.

His frown deepened to a scowl. "Young woman, is this your idea of a prank?"

Meriamon drew herself up. Nikolaos' hand dropped. She straightened her coat with a sharp gesture and lifted her chin. "I come from Egypt," she said, "to serve your king. That service, now, seems best performed here." She paused. "Have I failed to provide satisfaction?"

"Egypt, you say?" The physician seemed interested in spite of himself. "How did you get in? Who sent you here?"

"I walked," she said. "These gentlemen brought me. They seemed to think I was a servant. That," she said, "I am not."

"So you say," the physician said. He rubbed his jaw. "We can't have you here."

"Why not?"

"Does this look like a place for a woman?"

She considered it. "It's cleaner than a birthing, mostly. Quieter, too. Have you looked at the man with the broken thighbone yet? I set it, but I could have used another pair of hands, to make sure the bones are lined up properly."

"*You're* the one who did that?" The physician looked her up and down. "You're no bigger than a kitten."

She smiled thinly. "I'm stronger than I look."

"Well," the physician said, rubbing his jaw again. "Well. If the men can keep their hands off you, and if you know what you're doing ... with Andronikos down with the flux, and Thrasikles, the blasted fool, running off with that boy from Pergamum ... Well. I won't say we can't use you. Egyptian, you say? Trained in a temple?"

"I was a singer in the temple of Amon in Thebes."

He eyed her narrowly. She did not look particularly august or terrible, she knew that, but she did not look like a Hellene, either. "I didn't think," he said, "that there were healer-priestesses."

"There aren't," said Meriamon. "I'm an oddity."

"Very odd," said the Greek. And yet he sounded comforted. A woman in his army—that was appalling. A woman who was a priestess, and probably a witch: that, it seemed, he could understand. It set her outside of normal reckoning, but it named her, too, and gave her a place in his world. Hellenes: they could endure anything, if only it submitted to their categories.

"So then," he said. "You've earned a bed for the night at least, if you don't mind a tentful of apprentices. Have you eaten?"

The thought made her head swim. She held herself erect by main force. "I . . . would be glad of a bite or two."

"You look it," he said. He raised his voice a fraction. "Kleomenes!"

A boy appeared at his elbow, owl-eyed but alert. Meriamon remembered him: he was the one who had brought her what she asked for, for Nikolaos. She admired his discipline. "Yes, sir?"

"Take this—boy"—the Greek hardly choked on it—"and see that he's fed. Give him a mat in the 'prentices' tent. If anybody lays a hand on him, give the fool a thrashing. I'll see you both in the morning."

That was a dismissal. Meriamon decided to accept it. Nikolaos was asleep or feigning it. Sekhmet had vanished. The physician bent to examine the soldier. Satisfied, Meriamon followed her guide into the startling quiet of the night.

Somewhere in the hours of her field surgery, the camp had settled to sleep. There was a little drunken singing still, the odd wail that marked a mourner, a murmur of men coming back late from pursuit or from securing the enemy's camp. The king was over there, they said, sleeping in the coward's bed. They did not leer at that as the earlier man had. He was alone, they said. He was odd that way, the night after a battle.

Her guide did not take her far. He roused a sleepy cook in one of the mess-tents, got bread and cheese and a skin of wine, and settled cheerfully to eat most of it. The bread was barley bread, fresh from the baking; it was good. The cheese was rank. The wine, even watered, gagged her with its sweetness.

The boy chattered without regard for her silence; or maybe it was his version of tact. It freed her from the need to speak, let her slide, warm and sated, into a drowse. She started awake when the boy lifted her in his arms. "You Macedonians," she said distinctly, "are all so big."

"You Egyptians are tiny," said Kleomenes. He grinned at her. They all had such splendid teeth. How did they do it? "Go to sleep, little Egyptian. I'll look after you."

She would not have trusted him. But her shadow was quiescent, and she so tired. She laid her head on his broad bony shoulder and sighed, and slid down into sleep.

• TWO •

Meriamon was in the surgeons' tent before the sun was up, with more of the good barley bread inside her, and a swallow or two of the horrible wine. She was clean, too: as clean as she could get without inviting rape. Hellenes did not wash if water was in short supply. They rubbed themselves with oil instead, rancid oil all too often, and scraped it off. She shuddered at the prospect, contemplated the grey and restless sea, shuddered again. But it was water, and she needed it, though it numbed her fingers and set her teeth to chattering.

The tent was warm with crowded bodies. The stink was worse, but she endured it. They were burning something pungent and oddly sweet, perhaps to cleanse the air. It made her think of incense and of temples, and an endless blue vault of sky, and a sun that never wavered or went out.

She swallowed past the ache in her throat. She had a

purpose here. Had not the gods themselves ordained it? If she must suffer this alien land, these barbarous people, then that was no more than her duty.

She thrust through the stink, found what needed doing, did it. Sekhmet, little harlot, was over by the wall again with Nikolaos. He lay and glowered and stroked the sleek tawny flanks. Sekhmet rolled coyly onto her back and wriggled.

He took the bait. He stroked the downy softness of her belly; and yelped.

After some considerable interval, Meriamon wandered by. The cat slept placidly beside his hip. Her purring was a distant thunder.

"Love-pats," said Meriamon, inspecting the wounds. "Not even halfway to the bone."

"Bitch of a cat," he muttered.

Meriamon laughed aloud. He was not at all amused. She folded back his blanket—it had the look and feel of a military cloak, and no doubt was. He was not modest, not as a Persian would be, but he was clearly unhappy that she should have appointed herself his physician. She took note that he was well though somewhat loosely made, with broad shoulders and big hands and feet. He did not have the whole of his growth. What would that make him? Eighteen? Twenty?

A child; and petulant at that. He bore pain well, to be sure; the bandages did not come off easily, but he clamped his jaw and moved when she told him and only then, and the only sound that escaped him was a long slow sigh when the wrappings were gone.

"You have a cracked rib," she said, "along with the rest. But healing well, that I can see. I'll strap the rib, and make you a sling for your arm."

"Then can I get up?"

"No," she said.

His glance was blistering.

"No," she said again, "you may not. Not for a while. I want to be sure I'm not missing anything vital."

"How long?"

She thought about it. "A day, maybe. Two. Then we'll see."

"A whole day? All I've *got* is a broken wrist!"

"You've got a little more than that," she said. "And I said two. Maybe. If the rib's not more than cracked. If the arm doesn't mortify. What did you do to it?"

He glowered, and he snarled at her, but in the snarl was an answer. "My horse took a fall and threw me. There was a chariot coming. I couldn't roll fast enough. A wheel went over my arm."

"Some god loves you, then," said Meriamon.

He shrugged, one-sided. "It had been raining. The ground was soft. I was up and fighting as soon as it went by."

Not quite as soon as that, Meriamon thought. He must have been in white agony.

It would be a red agony now, even with the dose she had given him. He was not paying attention to it. He was too busy being stubborn. "It's only my shield arm," he said. "I can still do guard duty. I can sling my shield over my shoulder."

"Not for a good while yet," said Meriamon.

He glared. "Tyrant."

She smiled. "I come by it honestly. My father was a king."

That stopped him. She left him with it, and with the cat, who seemed to have adopted him.

Meriamon was feeding gruel to a man who had got a spearbutt in the jaw, wishing that she had a barley straw and a boxful of medicaments from Imhotep's temple in Memphis, when a stir brought her eyes to the tentflap. People came and went often, soldiers coming in late with minor hurts that had kept them awake, or looking for friends among the wounded, or, now and then, walking away with the jaunty step of a man reprieved from the hospital. These were more than one, and coming in: young clean-shaven men in Macedonian cloaks, gold-bordered purple, and purple tunics. They were not all big men as Macedonians went, but they walked as if they were, with a look about them like lions in a pride. Young lions coming back from the hunt, glossy and sated, holding themselves like princes.

There was one whose cloak was different: purple unbordered. But for that, at first, she would not have noticed him. He was not as tall as the others. Not tall at all, unless in Khemet. His hair was lion-colored, cut like a lion's mane. He said something to the man nearest him—as tall as the tallest, that one, and darker-haired than most, like ruddy bronze. The tall one's face seemed carved in marble, so fine was it for a Macedonian face, and so quiet. Then he laughed, and he looked like a wild boy.

The other was more than wild. Even standing still, he seemed to flicker like a flame in a windowless room. He stepped away from the tall man into the light from the open tentflap. The sun caught his hair and flamed in it.

A murmur ran through the tent, rising to a roar. "Alexander!"

Meriamon had known in her bones, even before she heard his name. His presence was a fire on her skin. It drove out the pain that filled this place, lifted the shadows on it, even as it cleared her sight and sharpened it, and showed her the man beneath the king.

He raised a hand. The noise died down. "As you were," he said. Light, crisp, but laughing a little. His voice was high and rather harsh. He would have to work at smoothing it, Meriamon thought, but it would carry in a battle.

She went on with what she had been doing. The man under her hands was oblivious. His eyes were on the king. His king.

They were all like that. Even Nikolaos. They loved him.
They would die for him.

He knew what he was doing. Meriamon was trained to
see it; was born to it. But in him the knowing came after
the doing. It was what he was. He was as hot as a fire in
the forge, damped and gentled now, schooled to infinite
patience as he held the hand of a man who would not last
the day, and heard how the man had killed a Persian who
would have killed his friend. He asked after another man's
lover, traded banter with a grizzled veteran, dried a boy's
too-easy tears with the hem of his cloak. He seemed to be
everywhere at once, to speak to everyone at once, but each
one reckoned that the king had spoken to him alone.

"He's something, isn't he?"

Kleomenes had been trailing after Meriamon for a
while, fetching and carrying and adding an extra pair of
hands when she needed them. He had no illusions as to her
sex, and apparently no disillusion with it. He handed her
the roll of bandage that she needed, without taking his
eyes from Alexander. "I remember his father," he said.
"Now that was a man! Best king Macedon ever had, or we
thought ever would, till we got a look at Alexander."

She looked sidelong at the boy. Big as he was, he could
not have been more than fourteen. "You remember
Philip?"

"Everyone remembers Philip. He was like a hero, people said. Like Herakles, and a king. Alexander . . . Alexander is like a god."

She shivered a little. The boy's tongue ran independent
of the rest of him, for all that she could see. But he was
no fool, and he had a clear eye. She bent over the man on
the pallet. "Be ready with the salve," she said.

Alexander was mortal enough. He was walking stiff; she
heard a man whisper that he had got a sword-thrust in the
thigh, and ridden right on through it, and got merry hell
from Philippos the surgeon for it afterward. "And he still

half-staggering from the fever he got from swimming in the Kydnos," the man said. "Cold as Hekate's dugs, that was. But he doesn't stop for much, even for fever."

Meriamon suspected that he did not stop at all. Most of his followers had left, bored or called to duties. The tall man was there still, but as she watched, he said something to Alexander. Alexander smiled: a startlingly sweet smile. The tall man seemed dazzled by it. He turned away without obeisance or any mark of respect, but he needed none; it was in everything he did.

"That's Hephaistion," said Kleomenes. "His best friend in the world. They call one another Achilles and Patroklos. Gods know, they're as close as that. Closer." He sighed. "I saw them at Troy, sacrificing at Achilles' tomb. We all wept, it was so beautiful."

"I can imagine," Meriamon said. Her voice was dry. Children, she thought. Dreamers and children. And they wanted to conquer a world.

Did they know it yet? Even he, whose soul was fire— did he know what it was that he wanted?

He came round to her in his course. She did not try to avoid him. The man she tended was as besotted as any of the others, and he got his reward: a clasp of the hand, a word of praise for his bravery, a bit of banter to keep him smiling. There was nothing false in any of it.

One could not quite call him beautiful, even if one were a Greek. That full-lipped face with its flat cheeks and its firm jaw; the long strong nose growing straight out of the heavy brows; the broad forehead; the hair growing from a peak, lion-like, and falling as it would: they were too odd for beauty, too purely themselves. But the eyes were splendid. They were as restless as he was, and piercingly bright, yet they could still utterly, fixed far and dreaming on a horizon that only he could see. What color they were, she could not tell. Grey, blue, grey-blue, green, grey-green.

One was darker than the other. Or was that the angle of the light?

He shifted, and his eyes were clear grey, looking her up and down in curiosity and dawning mirth. "What in the gods' name are you?"

He asked it as simply as a child, with a child's arrogance, and a child's certainty that he would not be punished for it. She could not help but smile. "My name is Meriamon," she said, "and I was a singer in the temple of Amon in Thebes."

He frowned a little. She could see the swift mind flicking from thought to thought: his eyes changed with it, grey to green to blue to grey. " 'Was'?" he asked.

"Now I am here," she said.

"Why?"

Direct as a child, too, but that was no child's mind, weighing her, measuring her, taking in everything she was. "To serve you," said Meriamon.

His head tossed a little, impatient. Of course she had come to serve him, the gesture said. He was Alexander. He said, "You came a long way to wait on a barbarian king."

"My gods brought me here," she said.

"Why—" He paused. Someone was calling him, urgent, refusing to be ignored. He muttered something brief and shockingly vulgar, and grinned at her expression. "Mariamne"—his tongue did odd things to her name—"I have an army to look after and dead to bury, and a victory to celebrate. After that I'll talk with you. Will you come and see the rites of the savage Hellenes?"

No savage, this one, barbarian or no. She grinned back. "You Greeks are such children."

He laughed. "So we've been told. You'll come, then?"

"I'll come," said Meriamon.

• THREE •

Fool. Idiot. To forget this of all Hellene savageries.

They buried their dead. Oh, yes. But first they burned them. They marched in a vast glittering procession, every cuirass burnished, every spearpoint gleaming, horses in their finest panoply, chariot teams snorting and prancing and tossing their plumes. They circled the field of Issus; they massed in formation, wheeled, swung down the long broken level like one great shining creature, and halted in their ranks before the face of the king. He wore his golden corselet, his lion helmet. He sat on the back of his little black horse that was as much a legend as he was, and took their roar of acclamation and gave it back in the splendor of his smile.

And then they massed themselves round the tower that they had built of wood and flesh, and performed their sacrifices, and watched the priests pour oil over the pyre. The king cast the first torch. It arced high against the grey vault of heaven, crested and curved and fell, and caught on the summit of the pyre. Others came after it like a fall of stars. Then, so suddenly it singed the beards of those who lingered closest, it erupted into flame.

Meriamon could not watch the bodies burning. The wind carried the smoke away from her, or surely she would have disgraced herself. What would their souls do now? How would they cross the land of the dead, what judgment could they hope for, with no earthly home to anchor them?

People were wailing. It was part of the rite. She clamped her jaw on her own cry. So many bodies, so many souls lost—gods, how could they do it?

There were people near her on the slope. Most of them

were silent. One spoke beside her. "Did you lose someone in the battle?"

It was a woman's voice, and anything but Persian. Its owner seemed calm, dressed as a Greek woman with a veil over her hair and half-hiding her face. Meriamon took refuge in the sight of her—a curl of bronze-gold hair, a smooth ivory brow, a pair of great dark eyes. They were level on her, with sympathy in them, and curiosity: a peculiarly Greek expression. Her accent was as pure as any Meriamon had heard.

"How can they do it?" Meriamon asked. "How can they destroy the dead?"

"It sets their souls free," the Greek woman said. "Then we bury the bones, and they can rest."

"Is that rest? To destroy them?"

The Greek's brows drew together. They were strong, and elegantly arched. "If the soul is to be freed to cross the River into Hades, the bones must lie under the earth." She shivered in her fine blue mantle with its embroidered hem. "How horrible, to be fettered to the rotting flesh and forbidden passage to peace."

"Our faiths are very different," said Meriamon, thin and tight.

"You're Egyptian, yes? I heard that there was an Egyptian woman in the camp."

"I'm supposed to be a boy," Meriamon said.

"Someone has been chaffing you, then," said the Greek. "Believe me, a woman is safer than a boy where Hellenes are."

Meriamon looked at her. "Did some of the generals bring their wives with them after all?"

The Greek laughed, sweet and high. That was art, that swoop of mirthful notes; art worn to instinct. "Wife? I? Aphrodite forbid! No, my lady of Egypt, I am a camp follower, a *hetaira* they call me, which is a courtesan. Haven't you heard of Thaïs?"

"No more than you have heard of Meriamon."

Thaïs let fall her veil. She was not the raving beauty that Meriamon had expected. Her eyes were magnificent, and her skin was flawless. But her nose was long even for Greek taste, her mouth wide and somewhat overgenerous, her chin a shade too definite. Character. That was the name of it.

Meriamon had never spoken with a hetaira before. Concubines—men had those in Khemet. And there were women who sold their bodies for men's pleasure. But someone who seemed to glory in it, whose title meant "companion"—that was a Greek thing, and strange.

"We're a necessity, you see," said Thaïs in that bright, brittle voice. "For some men, boys are not enough, and their wives are good for little but spinning wool and bearing sons. We give them what their wives are hardly trained to give, and what boys lack altogether. We earn the title they give us."

"In Egypt," said Meriamon, "such women are called wives."

"Happy Egypt," said Thaïs. She half-turned, half-raising her veil, lowering her handsome eyes.

Meriamon had seen the man who came toward them. He had been with the king this morning, and he had ridden in procession with the men closest to the king. He was older than some of them, probably nearer thirty than twenty, with a strong bony face; long and loose-built, wide-shouldered, big-handed, but graceful as a fighting man has to be.

He greeted Thaïs with courtesy, as if she had been a lady. Thaïs kept her eyes down like a modest woman and returned his greeting in her pure Attic accent. "Ptolemy," she said, "do you know the Lady Mariamne?"

He inclined his head to her: greeting, courtesy, a flicker of—amusement? "The king has been talking about you," he said.

Meriamon raised a brow.

"He's fascinated," said Ptolemy. "Did Philippos really

let you walk right into his hospital and start working miracles?"

"About the letting," said Meriamon, "I don't think he had much choice. But I've worked no miracles. Plain field surgery is all I know."

"It's more than most of us do." Ptolemy rocked back on his heels. He grinned suddenly. "Herakles! I wish I'd seen his face when he saw you were a woman."

"It takes a bit of seeing," Meriamon said dryly.

"It does not." He was definite about it. Indignant, she might almost have said. "You've got a pup from the family litter in your lot. All he can howl about is that he's been cast into the hands of a female."

She narrowed her eyes. Loose bones, big hands, bony face. "That wouldn't be Nikolaos, would it?"

"Niko," said Ptolemy, "yes. Mind you now, he's a good soldier. Could be better, he's spoiled rotten and has been since he was a brat, but get him in a fight and he remembers his manners."

"He's polite about killing people?"

Ptolemy laughed. "Alexander said you had a tongue on you. So," he said, "did Niko." He sobered suddenly. "The doctors say he ought to have lost the hand. Now they say he'll likely keep it. If that's not a miracle, then what do you call it?"

"It wasn't as bad as it could have been," said Meriamon. "He lost a lot of blood to the rest of his wounds—that's why we've kept him down. Besides the pleasure of watching him sulk."

"Still," said Ptolemy. Then he grinned. "I like it, too, seeing him rolled up in bed and the doctors sitting on him. Time something slapped the nonsense out of him."

"I wouldn't care to wager on that," Meriamon said.

People had begun to scatter. The first fierce flame of the pyre had died to a long smolder. A shift in the wind brought the stink of it to her nostrils. Fire, burning, a sweet-savory roast-meat scent that brought the bile flooding.

The hands on her were a woman's hands, deft and cool, smoothing the hair out of her streaming face, holding her while she retched into the grass. Thaïs spoke over her, voice as cool as her hands. "This is no sight for an Egyptian. Whose fault is it?"

Meriamon gasped it out for herself, furious at her weakness. "Mine. I should have remembered—I should have known—"

"So should Alexander," said Ptolemy. And as her head came up, eyes wide with shock: "Yes, I heard him. Sometimes he just doesn't think."

"He is the king!"

"Why, so he is," said Ptolemy. "But there—you don't elect your kings, do you? You make them gods."

"They are gods," she said, "and sons of gods." Her stomach had settled a little. She drew herself up from her knees. She kept her eyes averted from the pyre; tried to breathe shallowly, though the wind had turned again and was blowing off the sea. "No. It was I who didn't think. I pay the price for it."

She looked up. He was looking down, frowning as if he strained to understand. His eyes were blue, startling in the bronzed and weathered face. For an instant her shadow flexed. Seeing—wanting—

He looked away. The moment passed. He helped her up with careful courtesy. "The king will want to see you later. Will you be in the hospital?"

"She will be with the women," said Thaïs. They both stared at her. "Lady Mariamne, I was going to speak with the Persian women. They may be glad of a woman's voice, even if it belongs to an enemy."

Meriamon stiffened. "I have no love for the Parsa," she said.

"Who does?" Thaïs drew up her veil. "Still, they are women, and probably they're terrified."

"I thought they were left alone," said Meriamon.

"That would make it worse." Thaïs slid a glance at Ptolemy. "Do we require a guard, my friend?"

Or, thought Meriamon, it might be *my love*. It was the same word.

"I'll send a man over," Ptolemy said. "It's quiet enough by now, I think, but let's not take chances."

One would never know that they were lovers. Or would one? They did not touch and their eyes seldom met, but there was a subtle tension in them.

It stretched taut, snapped. Ptolemy went back to his soldiering. Thaïs turned to go down the hill, walking as a dancer walks, erect and consciously graceful. It was a moment before Meriamon realized that she was speaking. "I met him in Athens when Alexander was there on embassy from his father, before he was king. I was a child then; my breasts were barely budded. My guardian thought Ptolemy a plausible prospect, Macedonian or no. I liked him myself: he was always pleasant, and he didn't either blush or act the bravo. Then he left, and I became a woman, and found patrons who would teach me in return for what I could give. Last year, when I heard that Alexander would cross into Asia, I decided to go with him."

"Not with Ptolemy?" asked Meriamon, walking in her wake.

"Certainly with Ptolemy. We met again, we were amenable, we sealed a bargain."

"Did your . . . guardian have any say in it?"

"My guardian was dead. It's not allowed in Athens for a woman to live for herself, free from a man's hand. My guardian's heir and I were not congenial."

"So you left."

"So I applied judicious pressure in the proper places, and was allowed to leave. I'll not go back soon, I don't think. I like this, this wild hunt against the Persians."

She was no tame thing herself. Trained, trammeled, shaped and pruned like a tree in a pharaoh's garden, still she was her own creature. She would not ride in battle like a man, she would hardly find that fitting, but she would watch with eager eyes and reckon every stroke. And when her man came back she would be waiting, a crown for his victory.

They walked wide round the funeral pyre. On the other side a soldier met them with crisp deference and his commander's compliments, and fell in behind them as they crossed the battlefield. It was empty, the earth torn and trampled but no body left to tempt the birds. The Greek dead were bones on a pyre. The Persians were gone to the care of their own people for rites that were no whit less horrible than burning, which they reckoned a pollution of sacred fire: set on high for the vultures to devour, then cast into a pit of nameless bones.

Meriamon felt the change as they forded the river, the guard walking ahead now and Thaïs kilting up her fine skirts and recking nothing of the water's bitter cold. The water was a barrier. The other side was the Persians', even in Macedonian hands. Their camp sprawled city-wide across the plain and up into the hills, with no order or reason in it that she could see, quite unlike the squares and straightways of the Macedonians.

What her shadow felt, what her heart saw, was a world both strange and bitterly familiar. The musk of their perfumes, the spice of their cookery, the hisses and gutturals of their language had ruled for far too long in her country. Even reft of its fighting men, reduced to slaves and the sick and the royal women, this could never be anything but a camp of Persians. Her nose wrinkled at a scent which she knew above all others. Faint yet distinct, like burning metal; a touch of heat on the shadow's skin, a suggestion of fire in the heart's eye.

The Magi had fled with their coward of a king. But their power lingered wherever they had been.

A sleek sand-brown shape sprang ahead of her, pouncing on shadows. Sekhmet, wise cat, had stayed away from the marching and the burning. She wove sinuous circles around Meriamon, startling passersby, winning an exclamation from Thaïs. "What in Hades' name is that?"

"Sekhmet," said Meriamon. She held out her linked arms. Sekhmet sprang into them and mounted to her shoulder, riding there with practiced ease. She was purring. Her incantation, Meriamon called it; guarding them both against the enemy's magic.

"Your cat?" Thaïs asked. She sounded bemused.

"Sekhmet belongs to herself," Meriamon said. "She chooses to go where I go. Mostly. When she has nothing better to do."

Sekhmet sank claws in her for that, but briefly, barely drawing blood.

"Remarkable," said Thaïs. She recovered herself quickly. "That should give the Great King's women something to talk about."

"Do you speak Persian?"

"Not a word," Thaïs said. "But we'll make do."

The Great King's tent was immense, a palace of silk and gold, so wide and so high that a hill rose inside it. Its walls were silk, and could be moved to make this room larger, that one smaller, or to make the whole one vast hall. Its floor was spread with carpets like meadows full of flowers. Its furnishings were gold and silk and jeweled furbelows, wagons' worth in every room, and none less than the best to be had.

Darius would not have liked to see them now. No one had looted them or damaged them unduly, once Alexander claimed them. But there were Macedonian soldiers where only princes had been allowed to come, lounging on the priceless couches, threatening the fragile silk with their armor.

The women were not here, they said. That was another tent behind this one. They offered, with much grinning and nudging, to guide the seekers to it.

Thaïs withered them with a glance, and went where they were pointing. That was out of the great tent across a courtyard walled in silk. No one lingered there. There were guards on the door, men who did not take their duty as lightly as their fellows seemed to. It might have been distaste, or it might have been the presence of another guard in Persian dress. A giant, a Nubian; and by virtue of his presence here, and his beardless face, a eunuch.

"We have come," Thaïs said in her clear uncompromising voice, "to speak with the royal ladies."

"The king said no visitors," said one of the Macedonian guards.

"The king wanted no men here." Thaïs' impatience was audible. "Come now, you know me. Would I rape or despoil a king's daughter? Even a Persian?"

The guard wavered. No one offered to back him. He shrugged. "All right. But if there's trouble, I'll say you were the start of it."

"So you should," said Thaïs. "Come, Mariamne."

Here still, unlike the Great King's tent, was Persia unsullied. No Macedonian faces here; no male at all who was not a eunuch. The silence lay heavy, punctuated at intervals by a smothered sound: a woman's weeping, a child's cry. The scent of mingled perfumes was overpowering, a thick, trapped scent with no strength in it to mask the stink of fear. The air did not move here, the light did not change. Always the same air, the same lamplit half-gloom, the same endless, monotonous sameness.

"Even a bird in the cage can see the sky," said Meriamon.

Thaïs made a sound. It might have been laughter. "It's a richer prison than Athenian wives and daughters know. These walls are silk, and the floor has carpets, whole kingdoms' worth. And they can travel with their man, though they travel in curtained wagons."

"If a prison moves, is it any less a prison?"

"Philosophy," said Thaïs, not quite mockingly, as a eunuch approached them.

He was old, thin-limbed but heavy-bellied, in a coat so rich it seemed to parody itself: deep crimson silk crusted with embroidery. He made Meriamon think of the baboon in Thoth's temple, irascible and holy, with his too-long arms and his withered face. He bowed to them, a bow carefully calculated, neither low enough to grant them sovereignty nor slight enough to offer insult. His greeting was faultless, and expressed in court Persian.

Meriamon did not speak it well, but she understood its meaning. Too well. Conquerors these interlopers might be, but they would speak the language of Cyrus and Cambyses, or not speak at all.

She inclined her head a meticulous degree. "We return your sentiments, O prince of servants. This lady who accompanies me is a friend of the king. Will the great royal lady deign to grant her audience?"

His lip curled the merest degree: at her accent, no doubt, as much as at her presumption. But he was a courtier. His face changed no line of its expression. "Is such a choice granted a prisoner?"

"A queen may always choose," said Meriamon.

"I will ask," said the eunuch. And went away.

Meriamon sat on a couch, finding it too soft, but better than nothing at all.

Thaïs stayed where she was, standing by the opening in the inner wall. "What did he say?"

"He's going to ask the queen if she will speak with you." Meriamon sat back. Sekhmet left her shoulder and walked along the back of the couch, prowling, relaxed but wary. Once she sneezed. Meriamon smiled. Sekhmet did not like Persian perfumes, either.

"He was rude," said Thaïs, "to speak Persian."

"So he was," Meriamon said. "And ruder yet to leave so abruptly, without a word of thanks or parting. He's not happy at all to be where he is now."

"He should be." Thaïs left the door and sat beside Meriamon. After a moment she tucked up her feet and reclined against the long curving arm. "In any war that ever was, a conquering king would have taken his enemy's women for his own. Alexander hasn't come here at all."

"Yet."

"When he comes," said Thaïs, "that's not what he'll come for."

"So," said Meriamon. "He's Greek clear through."

Thaïs let fall her veil, baring her face. "Greek enough, that's true. But he's Alexander. He won't ever take a lover by force. He likes his pleasure willing, and he likes to have love if he can get it."

"I can hardly see him wooing a Persian princess," said Meriamon.

"I can," said Thaïs. "He'd like the challenge."

"Not that she'd be worth it once he won her," said Meriamon. "Cage-birds seldom learn to fly."

"One with spirit, maybe," said Thaïs. "One who wants to be free."

"Spirit goes sour fast in a harem. It goes to wine or it goes to fat, or it takes to poisoning people."

"In Egypt, too?" asked Thaïs.

"Not in Egypt," said Meriamon, but softly. Sekhmet returned from her quartering of the room and curled in Meriamon's lap. She stroked the sleek fur, taking comfort from it. "Not . . . for a very long time."

Thaïs' eyes begged to differ, but she held her peace. She was like a cat herself, relaxed and supple, but ready to leap at a word.

They were not kept waiting long. Neither were they brought the cups of wine and the sweets that would have been proper.

The eunuch who came for them was another than the one who had taken their message, younger though still no youth, who looked as if he might have been beautiful once. His eyes were lovely still, great frightened doe-eyes, taking in the Greek woman and the Egyptian in Persian dress without seeming to comprehend them. His voice was strong and piercing-sweet as eunuchs' voices sometimes were. Meriamon wondered if he was a singer. "You will come with me, please," he said.

They followed him in silence. Sekhmet walked in Meriamon's shadow, quiet as a shadow herself, all but invisible.

The inner rooms were full of women. Meriamon could hear them through the walls like birds in an aviary, fluttering, murmuring, and once a sharp cry, abruptly cut off.

The room to which the eunuch took them seemed to be the centermost. A slender central pillar held up the roof, and its furnishings were like those in the king's tent, improbably, almost garishly rich. There were a handful of eunuchs huddled together as if for warmth, three or four veiled women who sat by the wall and did not speak, and in the center, the back of her chair set against the pole, a woman. Another stood beside and a little behind her. Neither was veiled. The one who stood was young, though not perhaps in Persian reckoning, and her face was pure Persian, beauty as flawless as a carving in ivory.

The other was old. Her bones were magnificent; she would have been a great beauty in her day. She was still handsome, with her haughty eagle's face and her deep eyes. She was still straight, and still, even sitting, imperially tall.

Darius the king was a giant among his people. It was clear to see where he had come by his height, if never his cowardice. Sisygambis his mother, Queen Mother of Persia, sat on what could only be a throne, and spoke a greeting in a clear strong voice. The woman behind her rendered it in Greek, speaking it well and with very little accent.

Thaïs inclined her head as if she herself had been a queen. "I greet you in return, great lady. And you, Barsine.

How is it that they left you here, and not in Damascus with the rest of the noblewomen?"

The Queen Mother understood. Meriamon could see it in her eyes. Barsine glanced at her, gained a flicker of permission. "I chose to stay," she said.

"You know that your father is fled with the king," said Thaïs. Calm, level. Not cruel. Not precisely.

"I know it," Barsine said.

"Barsine," said Thaïs to Meriamon, "is a satrap's daughter. Her father was a friend of Alexander in his childhood, and a friend of Greeks lifelong. Her first husband was a Greek. When he died she married his brother. That one died last year in the siege of Mytilene; and she went back to her father, and now she is here. She should have gone with the rest to Damascus."

"Alexander would simply have found me there," Barsine said. Her calm was a splendid thing.

The Queen Mother spoke in Persian and Barsine in Greek. "What does an Egyptian do in the following of the Macedonian king? Does she know that the satrap of her province is dead?"

"Is he, then?" asked Meriamon in Greek for Thaïs' sake. "No doubt his women will mourn him."

"You do not answer my question," Sisygambis said.

Direct, she, for a Persian. "Egypt is no province of mine or any other," said Meriamon. "I came here to serve Alexander."

"Why?"

"My father was Nekhtharhab, Nectanebo of Egypt," Meriamon said.

The Queen Mother's eyes hooded. Meriamon thought of cobras. And yet there was no enmity there. Necessity only, and indissoluble division. "Ah," said Sisygambis. There was a world of understanding in the syllable.

Meriamon almost smiled. "The rebel, yes. He died for it. But I live. I speak for him."

"That is your duty," said Sisygambis.

Sekhmet flowed out of Meriamon's shadow, approaching the Queen Mother. Sisygambis regarded her without surprise but with considerable interest. "That is a sacred cat?" she asked.

"Yes," said Meriamon.

Sekhmet considered the height of the silk-swathed knees and sprang. Sisygambis did not move. The cat preened against her, purring. Scent-marking her; seducing her.

She was proof against anything a human creature could send against her. But Sekhmet was the image of a goddess. Sisygambis yielded warily, touching a finger to the back that arched against her breast. Sekhmet slid under her hand, butting it with a hard round head.

Meriamon released a slow breath. One never knew with Sekhmet. "Be wary," she said. "Be respectful. Her claws are sharp."

"So they would be," said Sisygambis. She did not retreat. How unlike her son; how immeasurably more kingly.

A eunuch brought chairs at last, little silver cups filled with sweet wine, a box of appallingly sweet Persian confections. Thaïs was amused: her eyes glinted as they met Meriamon's. "Your cat is an excellent ambassador," she said.

"She is not my cat." As if to contradict her, Sekhmet abandoned the Queen Mother for Meriamon's lap and a pose of watchful interest, erect like an image in a temple. Meriamon smoothed the elegant gold-brown ear where it was pierced for a ring. That was left behind in Amon's temple, so much the less temptation for bandits on the road.

She eyed the cup of wine that had been given her, steeled herself to drink it. A flurry made her pause. A eunuch ran in, green with terror, and flung himself on his face before the Queen Mother. "Lady," he gasped. "Oh, lady, they have come, they are here, they want—they say—"

The Queen Mother's eunuchs froze. Fear, yes; and horror, not only of the news, but of the way in which it came.

Sisygambis regarded the messenger with massive calm. " 'They'?" she inquired.

"The enemy!" the eunuch cried. Then he seemed to master himself. "Great lady, the king, the Hellenes' king."

Sisygambis drew even more rigidly erect. "The king himself? He is here?"

"Yes, great lady. And—Ahuramazda protect us, Immortals defend us—he asks to speak with you."

"To speak with me?" She seemed to be thinking aloud. "But we are his. He won us. He can do whatever he pleases."

"He is a barbarian," said the eunuch.

"He is king." Sisygambis' voice was cold. "Tell him that he may speak with us."

The eunuch picked himself up and fled. Sisygambis sat still. Her long hands flexed on the arms of her chair, clenching, unclenching. Her voice was calm. Dismissing her daughters and their women to the sanctuary of seclusion, leaving herself and her companion and the eldest of the eunuchs. Deliberately, steadily, she drew her veil over her face. After a moment Barsine followed suit.

They could follow the king's coming in the sounds of the tent: sudden stirring, sudden stillness. Thaïs sat at her ease, not quite smiling. Meriamon was enjoying the moment much too much. To see the Queen Mother of Persia afraid and mastering her fear—that was sweet.

There were two of them who walked in behind the eunuch, side by side and easy with one another, even in this alien place. Hephaistion was a little ahead, on guard, scanning the room with wary eyes. Alexander was half-lost in his shadow. Walking so, he seemed smaller and much slighter than he was, a bareheaded boy in a simple chiton, keeping no ceremony.

Sisygambis rose. She was tall indeed, a fair hands-breadth taller than Hephaistion. As he paused, hand dropping to swordhilt, she went down in the prostration.

He stared, blank with astonishment. Then he flushed. "Lady," he said. "Lady, I'm not the king."

Barsine's voice echoed his, trembling a little itself, but clear, rendering the Persian of his Greek.

The Queen Mother rose. Her face was as calm as ever, but her lips were white. She saw Alexander then, starting slightly, then fixing on him. She began again to sink down.

He caught her. "No, mother. You don't have to do that to me."

"You are the king," she said, Barsine's voice her echo, a bare half-breath behind. "My error—your pardon— whatever penalty your majesty will exact—"

"That's all right, mother," he said lightly, helping her back to her chair. "He's Alexander, too."

She clutched his arm as if without it she would fall, and looked hard into his face. He gazed back, as intent as she.

Her eyes dropped first. She let go his arm. The marks of her fingers were scarlet on the fair skin; there would be bruises later. He did not seem to notice. Slowly Sisygambis lowered her veil.

Maybe Alexander understood what she was doing. He looked about for a chair, found one, pulled it up beside her. The eunuchs gasped. Not that he should dare, but that he should do it so completely without ceremony. He took Sisygambis' hand, direct as if no one stood between them, no mind but his and hers, no wall of speech or understanding. "There, mother. I'm afraid I've cost you no little anxiety, leaving you alone like this for so long. I'm sorry for that. I had too much to do, it got a bit ahead of me. Will you pardon me for it?"

"I do not think," said Sisygambis, "that anything gets ahead of you."

He smiled his sudden smile. Her eyes flickered, dazzled. "Oh, you'd be surprised. I do want you to know that you'll all be safe here; and the other ladies, too, when we catch up with them."

Again she studied his face. Not as if she doubted him. As if she needed to assure herself that he was real; that she had not dreamed him. "Why do you do this?" she asked.

He shrugged, boylike, tilting his head at that angle which was his and no one else's. "I don't make war on women."

"Then," she said with bitterness that was shocking, coming out of so calm a face, "you will not be fighting any longer against my son."

He did not seem surprised. "There are men in his army," he said. "They deserve a chance at honor."

"Perhaps," said Sisygambis.

He patted her hand where it lay in his. "I have to go, unfortunately. But I'll come back, if you'll receive me."

"I will always receive you," she said.

"Good!" said Alexander with every evidence of delight. "I hope you'll be more at ease now. You're in no danger as long as I have you in my keeping."

"I am no longer afraid," said Sisygambis, "now that I know what you are."

Alexander rose, laying her hand in her lap as gently as if it had been a new-hatched bird. "Good day, mother. May the gods protect you."

"May Ahuramazda and the good gods defend you," said Sisygambis, "my lord king."

• FOUR •

"That," said Thaïs, "was pure theater."

Meriamon was dizzy with her lungs full of clean air after the scented closeness of the harem, and silly with the freedom of sky over her head and clean earth under her feet. Sekhmet nipped her ear, bringing her back somewhat to herself. She glanced at Thaïs. "The king meant every word he said."

"Of course he did." Thaïs stepped round a soldier who had had a little more wine than was good for him. He grabbed for Meriamon, got Sekhmet's lightning-swift rake of claws for his pains. "That doesn't mean he didn't know what it looked like. Or the old queen, either. Isn't she impressive? She should have been king. Then we wouldn't be here, celebrating a victory."

"I for one am glad that she is a woman."

Thaïs laughed. "I could tell, even when you were being civil. Was it so bad in Egypt?"

"Yes." Meriamon wrapped herself tighter in her mantle. She did not want to speak of it, to be compelled to remember. "I should go back to the hospital. There are things I left undone."

"Not yet," said Thaïs. "They've put you with Philippos' boys, haven't they?"

"Yes."

"Not any longer. I've a bigger tent than I need now: Ptolemy gave me a present after the battle. It even has rooms, like the Great King's. You'll be quite comfortable in one."

"But—" said Meriamon.

"You also need clothes. And a place to keep them. Philippos should have you on the rolls and drawing rations; if not, you'd best speak to him. We all earn our way here, and draw our pay for it."

Slow heat crawled up Meriamon's cheeks. Mercifully Thaïs was not looking at her.

"I'll show you where my tent is," said Thaïs. "Phylinna is my maid, she'll look after you, too; she won't mind. She's always complaining that I don't give her enough to do."

There was no stopping her once she had set her mind on a thing. Meriamon found herself in a tent that was large enough for a tradesman's house in Thebes, divided into rooms: one in front, one in the middle, three small ones in the back. The furnishings must have belonged to a minor lord. There was even a chest full of clothing, plain stuff but beautifully made.

"His wives must have worked hard and long over these," said Thaïs, running a hand over an embroidered coat.

"Not his wives," said Meriamon. "Ladies of the Parsa never spin and weave. That would be beneath them. His slaves would have made these; or he bought them in the market."

"How odd," said Thaïs. "You aren't going to wear these, are you?"

Meriamon held a coat against her and laughed. "Hardly! It's big enough for three of me. But I do need a change of clothes."

"I can see to that," said the maid Phylinna. She was a little older than her mistress, and she did not act at all as one might have expected a slave to act. She said what she thought, and seemed to fear no reprisal. "What can we put you in? It's hardly proper for you to dress like a Persian, and a male at that. But a woman's gown might bring you trouble in the camp. Men," she said, "being what they are."

"And I can't wear what I wore at home," Meriamon said. "I'd freeze." She thought about it. "I suppose I'll have to go on being improper. At least until it gets warmer. Does it ever do that in this part of the world?"

"It's a furnace in the summer," said Phylinna. "Trousers, then. And a gown for when you want to dress up. Shall I see to it, mistress?"

"Do," said Thaïs. And when she had gone: "I should like to see you in a dress. I think you would be very pretty." Her hand reached to touch Meriamon's hair. "Such hair. And those eyes. Would you like a bath?"

Meriamon was growing used to Thaïs' quicksilver shifts. "I would give one of my souls to be clean."

"Then you shall be," said Thaïs.

Phylinna was only the chief of the hetaira's servants, and Thaïs seemed able to call on a fair few of soldiers as well. She had a great bronze basin brought in—more of the Persian plunder—and water for it, and everything else that one could possibly want for a bath. For the first time since she left Khemet, Meriamon shed her swathings of clothes down to the last bit of linen, and sank into steaming water scented with herbs and sweet oil, and felt deft servant-hands scouring away the weeks of her journey. Sekhmet, disgusted by the unnatural human obsession with water, took herself away from it. Even Meriamon's shadow was quiescent, sunk in the fragrant water.

It was cruelly hard to come out of it, even when it had begun to cool. Harder still to face her reeking and dirt-stiffened clothes with her skin singing *clean, clean, clean*.

Thaïs had gone out while Meriamon bathed. Now the hetaira came back, and her arms were full. She spread her booty on a table. "It's not perfect, of course. We'll need a little time for that. But will this do?"

Some prince must have brought his son with him. No grown Persian would be so small, and the quality of the garments was better even than what lay in Thaïs' box. Undergarments of linen so fine that it must have been woven in Khemet, soft trousers of crimson wool to tuck into doe-skin boots, coat of silk the color and sheen of lapis lazuli, embroidered with a frieze of lions, its belt inlaid with silver and clasped with lapis. There was a cap with it, rich green embroidered with silver. It all fit remarkably well, and it was warmer than what she had had, even without a cloak.

"Someday you'll have to tell me how you happened to come here in Persian clothes, with no baggage to speak of," said Thaïs.

"That's simple enough," Meriamon said. "I had a horse and a mule, and they carried me up from Egypt, and at good speed, too, with the gods' help. Then I met a riding of the Parsa, somewhere south of Tyre. They decided that I owed them tribute. They took me by surprise, and they were too many for me to fight. I gave them most of what they wanted. They would have taken more, but something scared them off."

Something, she did not say, had killed one of them as they fled, the one who had wanted more; and gained her her disguise. It was warmer than the thin linen she had had, and somewhat safer.

"You came all this way alone?" Thaïs was incredulous.

"Not . . . precisely alone," said Meriamon. She could feel her shadow behind her, rousing from its somnolence.

"I'd call you rash, if you weren't so obviously here, and no harm taken."

Meriamon shook her head a very little. Her shadow subsided unwillingly, but she was stronger than its wariness.

The hospital was much as she had left it. Two of the worst wounded had died. One was the giant whom they called Ajax—his given name, she gathered, was something else altogether. The prick of tears surprised her. She had never known him, and yet he had, in his way, belonged to her.

Nikolaos was very much alive. They had moved him from his solitary eminence and set him closer to the door. He had a book balanced on his knees, and read from it by the light of a lamp; some of the men near him listened. She did not recognize the verses—for they had to be that, melodious as they were, in a dialect that was not Attic, nor yet Macedonian.

" 'Immortal Aphrodite of the elaborate throne,
    wile-weaving daughter of Zeus,
    I beseech thee:

Vex not my soul, O lady,
with love's sweet torments.' "

He had a beautiful voice when he was not using it to complain. A surprising taste in poetry, too. Meriamon wondered whom he was thinking of as he dwelt on the liquid words.

Sekhmet's coming barely made him pause. He opened his elbow for her to slip between, and finished out the poem. Then he rolled the book and bound it, one-handed, with impressive competence. For a moment his face seemed almost pleasant, though his brows knit soon enough.

"If you keep that up," Meriamon said, "you're going to have a furrow deep enough to plant a row of barley."

"Then you can harvest it and make beer out of it," he said. His tone was nasty. "That is what you do with it, isn't it? Make beer?"

"Bread first," she said, "then beer. What was it that you were reading?"

"Sappho," he said. "She was a poet. She came from Lesbos—from Mytilene."

Mytilene was where Barsine's husband had died. Meriamon did not think that he would care to know that. "She wrote beautiful verses."

"It's my brother's book. Thaïs gave it to him. He lent it to me, to give me something to do." Since, he made it abundantly clear, he was not allowed to do anything else.

"He did well, then," said Meriamon. "I'm going to tell the servants to let you have a little wine. I don't think it will harm you; they'll put something in it to help the pain."

"I don't need anything to help the pain."

"Of course you don't," said Meriamon. "But the others might when you wake up screaming in the middle of the night."

"It doesn't hurt," he said stubbornly.

"Have you tried to walk about yet?"

He flushed. "No. They won't let me. Damn it, it's not my leg that's broken!"

"Tonight," she said, "for a little while, you may get up. But not now. Drink the wine when they bring it, and eat what they give you."

"Pap," he muttered.

"I shall be interested to see," she said, "what you are like when you're not exerting yourself to be unpleasant."

"I'm not—"

She patted him on the head. "Hush, child. It's for your own good, you know that very well."

If he could have bitten her, no doubt he would have. She was still laughing when she left him.

In a Persian bed in a conquered Persian tent, with Thaïs entertaining her patron at two rooms' remove and Sekhmet purring on her middle, Meriamon rested as she had not since she began her journey. She had her solitude, she was full of wine and meat and barley bread, in the morning she would have duties that she was glad of. She would have liked a proper headrest instead of these smothering cushions, and the blankets smelled faintly of horses, but she was comfortable, stroking the cat, half-dreaming in the nightlamp's flicker.

Her shadow moved softly about the room, part in time with the lamp, part in rhythm with her breathing. It wanted to be freed, simply to go its own way, apart from her. "No," she said to it, barely to be heard. "Not among strangers."

It reared up, a tall slender shape, upright like a man but longer-limbed, more sinuously supple. For an instant as it turned its head toward her she saw a long muzzle with a glint of fangs, sharp pointed ears, bright beast-eyes that gleamed in the dark.

"If that is the shape you wish," she said, "then you certainly may not go out. The Hellenes have killed or conquered all the Parsa. There's nothing left to hunt."

Not hunt, the eyes said. Walk. Run. Fly. Be free. Sun's rising would bring it back. That was its word. Would she doubt it?

"I don't doubt you," she said. "I fear for you."

It would take care that no one caught it, or even saw it. She was wavering. She firmed her will. "Tomorrow night. Maybe. If all is well."

It strained, resisting. After a moment, when she did not yield, it subsided. Its mood was so much like Niko's that she laughed, which pleased it not at all. Yet, like Niko, for all its sulks and sullenness it was obedient. As she opened her will to sleep, her shadow came and stood over her, guarding her against the night.

On the third day after the battle, the king summoned Meriamon. He gave her time to prepare: to finish what she had been doing in the hospital, to run to the tent, even to manage a hasty toilet. Thaïs was there to help her, barely awake after a late night but alert enough to play lady's maid. She insisted that Meriamon wear the peplos Phylinna had just that morning finished, folds of soft cream-colored wool with embroidery round the hem. The mantle that went with it was purple—true Tyrian, and where Thaïs had got it, or how she had been able to pay for it, Meriamon was afraid to ask. Not that she was given time. Thaïs had paints in plenty for lips and face and eyes, and she was determined that Meriamon use them.

It was strange to be a woman again, to look at herself in the little bronze mirror and see the Meriamon who had sung before the god in Thebes, but in the dress of a Greek lady, in wool that no priest would wear because he reckoned it unclean.

She had lost that compunction on the road south of Tyre. Still, she would have preferred a dress of fine Egyptian linen, a wig to cover her hair, and jewels to make her splendid. They would have been armor and banner before this alien king.

Thaïs could remedy that, somewhat. The earrings were Persian booty, beryl and carnelian set in soft pure gold. The necklace was from Athens, a collar of golden flowers. The bracelets were from somewhere far in the north, heavy gold with a dance of horsemen round a fabulous beast like a winged, eagle-headed sphinx.

"There," said Thaïs, stepping back to survey her handiwork. "You look like a lady of quality."

"Will that shock the king, do you think?" Meriamon asked.

Thaïs laughed. "Nothing shocks Alexander! Now go, you're keeping him waiting."

Even before Meriamon came into the king's tent, she could hear the raised voices. To her considerable surprise, the guard not only admitted her, he sent a man along with her, a dour Macedonian whose beard showed a sprinkling of grey. The anteroom was full of people, not all Macedonian by any means, and few of them soldiers. Their expressions ranged from squirming discomfort to unabashed curiosity. Not that they could have understood much of what went on within: the discussion was heated but the words indistinct.

Her guide led her past them to exchange words with the guard at the inner flap. The guard looked dubious, but he said, "Alexander told us to send her straight in."

Her guide nodded with a touch of impatience, as if the other was belaboring the obvious. "I'll take her, and answer for her if I have to."

She bit her tongue. This was no time or place to object to being discussed as if she were not there. Maybe it was her gown. Not only did she look like a woman, she looked respectable.

The king and his animated discussion—she would not say quarrel, not quite—were not immediately within.

There was another antechamber, a table covered with what looked like maps and dispatches and rolls of accounts, men sitting at it, busy and apparently unperturbed by the noise.

The room beyond looked like a council chamber. It was a moment before Meriamon realized that there were only a few people in it. Alexander, of course. Hephaistion, it seemed, inevitably. Ptolemy. One or two others whom she did not know, in what she had learned was the gold-and-purple cloak of the king's Companions. And facing the king, grey beard bristling, in armor that had seen much use, a gnarled tree-trunk of a man whose age might have been anywhere from fifty to eighty. He was not more than a palm's width taller than the king, but he took full advantage of it, bulking over the smaller, slighter man.

Alexander was angry, but controlling it. His lips were a thin line, his eyes as pale as water. They seized on Meriamon. She shivered: their touch was burning cold. "Ah, Mariamne. Will you sit down? I'll be done in a bit."

"You will not be done," gritted the man in armor, "until you answer me. We've had enough of your evasion. Will you or will you not—"

"Parmenion," said Alexander, light and deadly, "do you forget who I am?"

In the throbbing silence, Meriamon crept Sekhmet-quiet to a chair. There was someone else huddled near it, sitting on the floor, hugging knees to chest and staring with wide frightened eyes. Yet he was no child nor awed recruit; he was a man both tall and strong, bull-broad, bull-muscled, with a face that would have been handsome had not its features been so slack. As she stared at him, a trail of spittle found its way down his beard.

Addled, Meriamon thought. Someone took excellent care of him: his tunic was almost clean, his hair cut, his black brush of beard trimmed close to his jaw. He looked—she 'started. He looked like the portraits she had seen of Philip the king, Alexander's father.

This would be Arrhidaios, then, Philip Arrhidaios, Alexander's half-brother. She had not known that he would be here.

Something—maybe her shadow, maybe simple compassion—made her lay a hand on his shoulder. He started. "Hush," she said softly. "I won't hurt you."

He stared at her. His attention was abrupt and complete. The fear began to fade from his eyes. They were round and brown and moist like a dog's, with a dog's eagerness to trust.

She smiled. She did not need to pretend to warmth. Big as he was, he was a gentle creature. The smile he gave her in return was remarkably like his brother's. The same power, though dimmed and muddied. The same sweetness. "Pretty lady," he said. His voice was deep and rather muffled. "You come to see me?"

She could tell the strict truth, and confuse him. Or she could say what after all, at the moment, was true. "Yes, I came to see you. My name is Meriamon."

"Meri," he said. "Amon. Meri. That's a funny name."

"It's my name. Don't you like it?"

"Oh, I like it," he said. He frowned. She could see how formidable his father must have been, in what that knotting of brows did to his face. "My brother and Parmenion are fighting again. I hate it when they fight."

"Do you think they'd mind if you went somewhere else?" she asked.

He shook his head hard. "No. I want to stay. It's nice here. Except when they fight."

"You're very brave."

This smile lit up the whole of him. "That's what Alexander says."

Alexander was oblivious to him. The high voice had risen a notch or two higher. "I will do it when I am ready to do it!"

Parmenion slammed his fist into his palm. "And when

will you be ready? You must beget sons. You should have begotten a pack of them before you left Macedon."

"And had a war of succession raging behind my back?"

"You could die tomorrow. Then there would be a war because there *is* no succession. Look at your heir, by all the gods. *Look* at him!"

Arrhidaios shrank back. Meriamon reached without thinking, gathering him in, holding him. He was shaking.

"Alexander," said Parmenion, gaining control of self and voice with visible effort. "Alexander, listen to me. Yes, you are young. Yes, by the span the gods allot a common man, you have years yet to sire your sons. But a king is not a common man. In that tent yonder are the daughters of a king. You need not marry one or all of them— Macedon should have a Macedonian queen. But for the gods' sake, for the sake of your kingdom, at least consider taking a concubine. Even a half-Persian mongrel is better than no son at all."

Alexander said nothing. His nostrils were pinched tight.

"Alexander," said Hephaistion after a long moment. "I think he's right."

The king whirled. Hephaistion stood his ground. Meriamon, looking at him, saw for a moment as through a glass. Love, this was. Love so deep, and so certain, that it could endure even this: to surrender its beloved for a kingdom's sake. She blinked in the face of it. What she saw was not a man who loved a man. She saw a soul that loved a soul. Even beyond death. Even to the end of things.

Hephaistion's voice brought her back into the world: light, cool, fearless. He did not use his height to tower over Alexander, but neither did he allow Alexander's anger to diminish it. He set them on a level. "Think," he said. "For a change. It's only practical."

Alexander spoke through clenched teeth. "I will not soil my bed with a coward's get."

"They may be Darius' daughters," said Hephaistion, "but they're Sisygambis' granddaughters."

For a moment Alexander paused, taken out of his rage. "Sisygambis. Gods, what a woman!" Then his temper flooded back. "I won't be someone's heifer-tupping stud bull!"

"But, Alexander," said Hephaistion, almost laughing: laughter that, to Meriamon's ears, was half pain. "That's what a king is."

Alexander reared up. No one breathed. Hephaistion touched the king's shoulder lightly, daring the lion's claws. "Think about it," he said.

"I *am*—" Alexander drew a sharp, furious breath. He spun back to face Parmenion. "And if I take one of them—if I do that—will that be enough? Will you let me be?"

Parmenion opened his mouth, closed it.

Alexander's lip curled. "Look, Parmenion. Do you see that lady there? She's a royal Egyptian, Parmenion. Her father was their king, the last before the Persians overran them. Will you demand that I marry her, too? It would give me Egypt, wouldn't it? It would give me sons. Do you want that, Parmenion? Do you want me to take a foreign queen?"

"I want you," said Parmenion slowly, deliberately, "to consider the wisdom of begetting sons."

"I am considering it," Alexander said. "I am also remembering my father. Do you want me to be like him, Parmenion? He was a king of men, was my father. He could no more resist a woman than a dog resists a bitch in heat."

Parmenion went white.

Alexander smiled.

Meriamon was on her feet. She did not remember how she had got there. That was death, what was between those two: the old lord of warriors who had served the kings of

Macedon since he was a boy, and the young king who could endure no master.

Her shadow wrapped long arms about her. Open, it bade her. Open to the god.

"My father was a rutting bull," said Alexander, "and it killed him. I can learn from my elders, Parmenion. I can see which way lies disaster."

"A king without an heir is disaster to end them all."

"I will have one," said Alexander, "when I am ready."

"You young pup! You'll never be ready!"

Meriamon dropped walls and guards and shields. Her shadow rounded into substance: slender black-skinned jackal-man with eyes the color of sulfur. His breath was hot on the crown of her head. His hands, blunt-clawed, settled on her shoulders.

"Alexander!"

Her voice, the full trained voice of a singer of Amon, and in it the power of mage and priestess, daughter of the Great House of Khemet, voice of the gods.

"Alexander! This is no war for you now. What you fear, you have no need to fear. You are not as the one who ruled before you."

They stared, all of them: eyes like burning fingers on her flesh. She saw only Alexander.

"Alexander," she said, "for what you have failed to do, your people will pay. That shall be mended, or not mended, as the gods decree. But a battle now will destroy you all."

His eyes were wide, fixed. He saw what stood behind her. He was not afraid of it. He kept his fear for smaller things. "What are you, lady?"

"You yourself named me. I am Meriamon, daughter of Nectanebo, singer of Amon, blood of the Great House of Egypt."

"Is it your Amon who speaks in you now?" he asked, shaping the words with care, as if before an oracle.

Gods knew, she was hardly that. Simply a reed through whom the winds blew. "He is not *my* Amon, Alexander."

Alexander's lips twitched. "And yet he speaks."

"The gods speak. I am their instrument. That is why I came to you. Will you listen to them?"

His head bent. Reverence, and true, down to the heart of him.

"Make your peace now," she said. "You are king, and your name will live as long as names are remembered. But you must live in this world, among these people whom the gods have given you. They ask that you be a man, and more than a man, for your kingdom's sake."

"Must I yield, then?" he demanded with a surge of temper.

"Your heart knows," said Meriamon. "Listen to it."

He drew a breath. Not as quick, not as sharp as before. His eyes shifted from her face to that of the one who stood above and behind her. For a moment they seemed to blur: grey as rain, grey as mist above cold stones. They blinked. No anger in them, no longer. Only wonder, and dawning comprehension.

"I will make peace," he said, "for the moment. I will think on what I have been told. Is that enough?"

Parmenion might have spoken. Neither Alexander nor Meriamon heard him. "Enough," she said, "for a beginning."

Suddenly he laughed. It was light, free, and completely fearless. "It's all I'll get from you, isn't it?" He turned. "Very well, Parmenion. You heard the lady. You heard me. I'll think about it."

Parmenion did not look overjoyed. But when he would have spoken, his eye caught Meriamon's shadow and rolled white. He snapped a salute. "As the king wishes," he said.

•FIVE•

After Parmenion had gone, there was a long silence. The king's Companions stood like carven men, looking anywhere but at the king, or at Meriamon.

It was Arrhidaios who spoke, startlingly loud. "Meri, who is that? Where did he come from?"

Meriamon's breath caught. She felt her shadow's laughter, even as it shrank again into more-than-nothingness. Without its hands on her, its body against her, holding her up, she crumpled to the carpets.

The one who bent over her was the king. The one who brought wine was a blur, indistinct, but it was Alexander who held the cup to her lips. It was good wine, for once. Strong, only lightly watered. It steadied her.

He lifted her. He was strong, and not so slight after all: compact, all smooth muscle, like his little black horse. He laid her gently on one of the couches, though she would have resisted. "No," he said. "Rest a little. I know what you did."

She let her head sink back against the arm of the couch. He was dismissing the others, except for Arrhidaios, who came to peer worriedly down at her. "I'm all right," she said to him. "The god left me, that's all."

"Oh," said Arrhidaios. "It was a god. What was his name?"

"It's not proper to say it," she said.

He accepted that. He patted her clumsily. "He's a very nice god. He smiled at me."

She wondered what he had seen. The Anubis-face should have terrified him.

"Arrhidaios," Alexander said. His voice was gentle. "Will you sit down while I talk to Mariamne?"

Arrhidaios obeyed gladly enough, sitting close by her. There was an odd comfort in his presence.

A stir at the door brought them all about. A very large dog lolloped through it, flinging itself on Alexander in a paroxysm of delight.

Alexander laughed, engulfed in the beast; though he looked as if he wanted to snarl. "Peritas! Where did you come from?"

Something tawny-brown and hissingly furious streaked past man and dog and shot toward Meriamon. From the eminence of Meriamon's middle, Sekhmet yowled challenge.

"Alexander!" It was a boy, hovering in the doorway, looking disheveled and rather scared. "I'm sorry, sir, he got away."

"And what did he get away from?" Alexander wanted to know.

The boy swallowed. "He was on your bed, sir. Asleep. Then this . . . creature came in, and he went after it."

Sekhmet spat. Meriamon tried to smooth her bristling fur; got a claw-rake for her pains.

"That," said Alexander, "is a cat. Dogs chase cats. Didn't you know enough to head her off?"

"Sir!" The boy caught himself before he committed an indiscretion. "Sir, I tried. They tore through the whole tent, sir, and outside, and back in. By that time Peritas was in front. Sir," he said, "it was a very thorough chase."

"I can see," the king said dryly. He ruffled the great brindled ears, peering at the dog's muzzle. "She got in a stroke or ten, too. Never mind, Amyntas, I'll keep him with me. You can go."

The boy was happy to oblige. Peritas dropped to all fours, panting happily, seeming not the least perturbed by his battle-scars. Alexander inspected them, and shrugged. "He's had worse from brambles on a hunt."

"Don't insult Sekhmet," said Meriamon. The cat was subsiding slowly. She directed a final, contemptuous hiss at the dog and mounted to the back of the couch, arraying herself there with queenly disdain.

Alexander drew a chair close to Meriamon, but did not sit in it. He did not like to sit for long, she thought. He wanted to be up and doing. "Now," he said. "Tell me the truth. Why did you come here?"

"To serve you," she said as she had before. Her voice was steady. She was proud of that.

"How?"

"As you saw," she said. "I know enough medicine to be useful in your hospital. I have . . . other skills as well."

"Are you a sorceress?"

She considered the word. "Maybe," she said slowly, "as you would think of it. As I think of it, I am a priestess, a speaker for the gods. My father was a great mage. It helped him little, in the end, except to know that he was finished."

"That always seems to be the way with magic," said Alexander.

"Yes," said Meriamon. "It's fickle. When you think you need it most, it deserts you. But the gods are always there."

"They may choose to be silent."

"But they are there." She sat up, settling more comfortably. "They sent me to you. They, and my father's wish."

"I thought your father was dead."

"He is. He died when I was small."

"I'm sorry," said Alexander. He seemed to mean it.

"I remember him," said Meriamon. "He was very tired by then, and he knew what was coming, and he was completely unafraid. 'Years will pass,' he said, 'but one will follow me. That one will avenge my bones.'"

Alexander leaned toward her, intent. "He saw me?"

"From the moment you were conceived."

Alexander straightened. "What am I to Egypt?"

"Egypt is a Persian satrapy. It loathes the yoke. It longs to be free."

"And you think I'll free you?"

This was battle. It was heady, dizzying: face to face, force to force, and words flying swift and hard. "Haven't you come to free everyone from the Parsa?"

"The Hellenes sent me to end their long quarrel against Persia. They said nothing of Egypt."

"Egypt is part of Persia. Too large a part; far too unwillingly bound."

"Why do you hate them?"

"Why do the Hellenes hate them?"

"That is a very old war," Alexander said, "and a very long one."

"Ours is older," said Meriamon. "We were an empire before ever your people saw Hellas."

"Maybe it was time you withdrew in favor of a younger power."

"Maybe," said Meriamon with a delicate show of teeth. "Maybe we prefer to choose that power."

"Why would you choose me? I might be no better than Artaxerxes."

She laughed, hurting-sharp. "No one can be worse than Artaxerxes. No, king of Macedon. My father asked who would free us from the Persian yoke. You know what the gods answered."

"You would free yourselves."

"We tried," she said.

There was a pause. He began to prowl restlessly, like the lion he resembled. Abruptly he turned to face her. "You're telling me that I was made—that I was shaped—to be your gods' pawn."

Perceptive, that one. "You didn't know it?"

He raked back his hair, almost angry, almost laughing. "I thought I was *my* gods' instrument."

"Aren't they all the same," she asked, "in the end?"

"By the dog," he said. "I'm afflicted with an oracle."

"That's a better word than sorceress," said Meriamon. He looked hard at her, almost glaring. She stared steadily back. He blinked. Tilted his head. "I suppose, if I told you to go away, you'd simply keep on following me."

"You suppose rightly," she said.

The corner of his mouth twitched. "Then I won't subject myself to that. You're well situated, I've been given to understand. Would you rather be somewhere else?"

"No," said Meriamon, startled, and not a little for that it mattered. "No, I like sharing a tent with Thaïs."

"Do you?" He looked bemused. "Well, then. And Philippos has you on his roster—I approved that yesterday. All that's wanting is a proper attendant for you."

"I have one," she said.

His eyes slid toward her shadow, and slid away again. "I'm sure it—he—does very well. I was thinking of someone a little more conventional. How is Nikolaos coming along?"

She blinked. She hoped that that was a shift. "He's doing well. He can get up tomorrow. I rather lied," she confessed, "about how bad it was. To keep him from leaping up and heading straight back to the lines."

"With Niko," said Alexander, "that was a very wise thing to do." He paused, head tilted, thinking. "Good. He won't be able to do any fighting for a while, but he should be up for light duty. I'll see that he's assigned to you."

She realized that her mouth was open. She closed it. "He may not be happy about that."

Alexander laughed. "I know he won't be. It will be good for him. He's been spoiled, what with one thing and another. Time he learned to do something he doesn't want to do."

"I'm not sure I like being a punishment."

"You won't be," said Alexander, "once he stops to think. I almost wish I didn't have to be king. I wouldn't mind playing guardsman myself."

She stared at him. He was smiling at her. As if she were more than a voice. As if—of all things—he liked her.

That had not been in her reckoning, when she took this

duty to which she had been bred. That he would regard her as a friend. That she, who was nothing and no one in the gods' eyes, should be glad of it; should think of him, in her turn, with friendship.

Her tongue was in control of itself. It answered him coolly. It even managed, almost, to suppress the smile that rose from one of her more antic souls. "That would be interesting. The King of Macedon relegated to the post of lady's maid."

He grinned, unabashed. "Why not? Herakles did it, didn't he? And I'm his seed." His grin faded to a grimace. "I'd better go and be king now, before my kingdom gets away from me. You're welcome to stay here for as long as you like. My brother would like it," he added, with a glance at Arrhidaios.

"Oh, yes!" Arrhidaios said. "Stay with me, please, Meri? Will you make your god come out again?"

"If he wants to," said Meriamon.

Alexander smiled at them both, as proud as a matchmaker with a new match. "Good, then. I'll leave you to it."

Clever man. He gave her time to recover her strength, and kept his brother occupied in the bargain. Peritas, at least, went out with his master, to Sekhmet's vast relief. She spat once more to send him on his way, and promptly went to sleep.

Nikolaos was not amused. Nikolaos was loudly and lengthily displeased. He did not even notice that he was better. He had had one bad day and a wretched night; then, almost without transition, as such things sometimes did, his body decided to heal. He would be stiff for a while, and he would be in no condition to fight until his arm was knit, but he was mending. He could walk, with his ribs bound tight and his arm in a sling. He hurt, that was evident from the set of his jaw, but he did not speak of it. It was only pain. It was idleness that drove him wild.

Until he was informed of his new duties. The message came from his captain, no less. "King's orders," the man said. There was nothing that Niko could say to that.

After the man had left, Niko howled. Philippos himself cast him out of the hospital, roaring in his field-sergeant's voice. "Out! *Out!* You're making my sick sicker! Get out of my sight!"

That at least Niko was delighted to do. Meriamon did not pursue him. He would slow down soon enough, once his hurts caught up with him.

When she came back to her tent toward evening, he was sitting in front of it. He was white around the lips, but he was steady enough. He was in armor except for the corselet. That lay on the ground with his shield under it and a pack beside it. Sekhmet leaned against his thigh as if to give him comfort.

"Think of it this way," Meriamon said. "You get to stay with the cat."

He glared under his brows. "Did you put him up to this?"

"Who? The king?" She was ready to hit him, or Alexander, or both of them. "Gods, no! Do you think I'd have asked for you?"

That stopped him. He snapped erect, outraged; and gasped. He was not ready yet to move that quickly.

"I'm no happier than you," she said, "believe me."

"How can you—how can you dare—you—"

"There. Look what you've done to yourself. That's all you need to do, pop that rib and put yourself right back in the hospital. Philippos would not be happy at all."

His teeth clicked together. His rage was so vast, his outrage so profound, that for a moment she honestly feared that he would take a fit.

Instead he went cold. For the first time that she could remember, he controlled himself. Slowly, carefully, he drew himself to his feet. He swayed. She did not offer to support him, although she watched him closely. He steadied. He drew a very cautious breath. "Nikolaos Lagides of the Royal Squadron, Companion Cavalry, detached"—that was bitter—"reporting for duty."

She would never let him see that he had surprised her. She inclined her head as a royal lady should. "I accept your service," she said, though that was not what he had offered at all.

He might have objected. But something in him had broken; or perhaps it had mended. He saluted stiffly, and stood at attention as she walked past him into the tent.

• SIX •

Hellenes could do nothing without music. There was always someone singing or beating on a drum, or playing one of their infinite varieties of flutes. There was no better way to gather a crowd than to bring out a lyre and play it.

Meriamon, raised a singer before the god, had been mute since she left Khemet. Her music, like her magic, burned low in her, far from the land that was its source. Sometimes in the night as she lay listening to the sounds of the camp, voices of men and women, snorting of horses, flute and lyre and wine-sodden song, she knew that she was a flower cut from its root, withering slowly in this alien air.

The night before they were to begin the march away from Issus, Thaïs gave a dinner-party in the tent. Banquets in Khemet could be extravagant, and it was fully expected that every guest should give himself fully to the spell of the wine, but Macedonians made Egyptians seem abstemious. They would be drinking and roaring till dawn, and up with the sun, ready for a long day's march; if any of them was the worse for his night's debauch, he would die rather than show it.

She had been invited, of course. She had gone for a little while. But she was feeling ill: too much strangeness, too little sleep, and her courses were on her, stronger than anything the doctors had in their pharmacopoeia.

She lay in her too-soft Persian bed, curled about her aching middle. Sekhmet was warm against it, giving what comfort a cat could. Meriamon squeezed her eyes against the easy tears. She was always like that in the dark of the moon.

Her shadow had gone hunting. She had had no will to keep it back. It was a living thing, though magical. It needed to feed. Blood if it could get it, and the essence that was in blood. These hills were full of small wild things; and it took joy in the chase, running under the sky, silent ebon jackal-man with sulfur eyes.

A little of that joy came back to her now and almost comforted her. She was close at last to sleep. The singing nearest her had paused. There was a moment's silence; then the notes of a lyre, and a lone voice. It was a very good voice, with the marks of training in it: both depth and clarity, and a range that even she could marvel at. She let the words slide out of comprehension, blur into pure song, wine-song, love-song, sleep-song. On the very edge of the dark, the singer's name whispered itself to her. Nikolaos.

A smile went with her into sleep. Not so sullen now with wine in him and his unwelcome duty forgotten, and oh, but he could sing.

She was her shadow, running the hills in the night. Warm blood in her, a life taken with thanks and returned to the gods with its gift of sustenance.

She was herself, her ka, her spirit that was Meriamon in every line and essence. Meriamon as she was in Khemet: lady of the temple, clothed in white linen, eyes made beau-

tiful with kohl, intricate wig concealing her hair. A great
collar lay on her shoulders, gold and lapis, carnelian and
crystal, beryl and malachite. Gold twined about her arms,
swung heavy from her ears. A fillet of gold bound the wig
about her brows.

The air rustled as with wings. Somewhere a serpent
hissed.

A shape rose up before her, terrible and beautiful: a co-
bra, hood spread wide, tongue flicking, swaying as it rose.
Meriamon regarded it without fear. This was dream, and
holy beyond holy, if that one showed itself to her; and the
other, dark wings spread wide, vulture-head raised, cold
eye fixed on its companion. Edjo of the Delta, uraeus serpent, goddess of the Red Crown, enemy of the enemies of
Ra who was a face of Amon; Nekhbet of the White
Crown, vulture-goddess, guardian of Upper Egypt.

Meriamon bowed before them. They took no notice of
her. She was royal blood but not queen, nor would ever be.
That, she had known since she was small; she had never
been aught but glad of it.

High above her a hawk screamed. Horus-falcon, who
watched over the Great House, whose eyes were the sun
and the moon. His wings stretched from horizon to horizon. His voice filled the sky.

And yet the heart of it was silence. And in that silence,
presence.

Very slowly, very carefully, Meriamon lifted her head.
Amon, she thought. Hidden one. Wind-god, sky-god. Lord
of the ram, king of the gods, whose face was the sun.

No. A whisper, softer than wind in the reeds, gentler than
water lapping its banks. Nile water, Nile reeds, under a sky
that knew no cloud, and stars that never hid their faces.

No, child. Soft as a mother's voice, soft as sleep. It was
everywhere about her. It had no face, no mortal semblance
at all. It was simply, purely presence. It wrapped her
about. It cleansed her of grief. It comforted her; it gave her

strength. All that sleep could give, it gave her, and more than that. It made her, however briefly, whole.

Meriamon opened her eyes. The nightlamp had spent its oil. The camp was not quiet, it was never that, but its clamor had muted. Even in her walls of silk she could sense the coming of dawn.

She lay on her back and stretched, arching against the cushions. Sekhmet walked the length of her body, light-footed, lambent-eyed. Meriamon swept her up and laughed, and stopped, startled. She felt—by every god and goddess, she felt as if she could sing.

The rags of her dream frayed and vanished. There had been wings in it, serpent-eyes, a voice—

She sat up, shaking her hair out of her face. The air was cold. She sprang shivering out of her warm blankets, snatching boots and cloak. It was early for her bath, but she was in no mood to wait for it. She pulled on trousers and shirt, blowing on icy fingers to warm them, wrapping herself tightly in her mantle.

It was an hour yet till sunrise. Those who had to be up were moving quickly, muttering at the cold. Those who could afford to sleep were doing it, cherishing the last bit of warm darkness before the trumpets called them to the light.

At the door of the tent, Meriamon paused. The lump of blankets just inside it was snoring in Niko's rhythm. Her toe itched to dig into his side, to rouse him to his king-given duty.

She took pity on him. She stepped over him into the cold still air. Even the sea was as quiet as it could ever be, the stars fading, the wind asleep.

A shadow filled her shadow. Jackal-teeth gleamed; sulfur-eyes laughed. It was strong as she was, replete with running and the hunt. It brushed her back with warm fingers. She smiled over her shoulder.

Something loomed behind it. She started. Her shadow bared its teeth.

She quelled it, though her heart beat hard with shock. Niko's eyes were huge, his voice a croak. "What—what in the name of—"

It was all she could do not to burst out laughing. He looked like a half-fledged bird: all limbs and eyes and startlement, with his hair standing up in tufts and his blanket trailing behind. He shivered convulsively, but never thought to cover himself. She did it for him.

He shied, and stopped, eyes rolling white. She tucked in the edges of his blanket, careful of his splinted arm. "There," she said. "Now you won't freeze."

His teeth clicked together. "What in the name of Hades was that?"

"What?" she asked.

Her eyes dared him to press her. He looked as if he was going to; but he was stronger than that. Or more prudent.

"I'm going for a walk," she said. "You needn't come with me. I'll be quite safe."

For answer he stepped out past her, picking up his spear as he went by it, and stood waiting.

He stayed out of her shadow. Wise man. She did not feel any better protected for that he was there, but neither was she displeased. Her shadow, like Sekhmet, found him fascinating. Great tawny-furred creature like a yearling lion, with his odd light eyes and his rough-carved face. He was not so ill to look at when he was not sulking; and he had a long-limbed grace, even with his arm in splints.

There was no one by the privies, which was a mercy. Niko did his business apart from her, and kept his eyes to himself. When she was ready, he was waiting, expressionless. Better than a scowl, she thought. She wondered if his head was aching. He did not look it; but then Macedonians all drank like sponges.

"I heard you singing," she said, "last night."

He did not say anything.

"You have a very good voice."

Nothing still. She slanted a glance at him. He had shouldered his spear and drifted a little apart from her, keeping to the outside as she skirted the camp's edge. Guarding her.

Temper rose, subsided. He was only doing his duty.

"Someday you'll have to sing for me," she said.

"If my lady wishes," he said. His voice, like his face, held no expression at all.

Her lips thinned. She did not speak to him again.

If Meriamon had not seen how swiftly Alexander's army broke camp, she would have refused to believe it. Every man knew his place and each had his task, meshed and mingled like the great battle-beast of the phalanx. If there was confusion, if horse ran loose or hound escaped its tether, it confused only those whose duty it touched upon; and they were quick to settle it.

They laughed as they did it, joked and sang, and some of the young men danced. By full daylight the whole army was formed in ranks and the march began, and at its center the long train of the booty, horses and mules and the shaggy Persian camels, and the lumbering wagons of the women. The hospital had vanished early into its own string of mules and its single light cart for the worst wounded. Meriamon was satisfied to walk behind the cart. Niko, of course, was not.

He had tried to retrieve his armor and his weapons and carry them as his fellows did, even of the cavalry, who kept their horses to ride in battle and marched like common soldiers. Meriamon had let him go. His commander was no fool. He sent him back promptly. "I can carry my own gear," Niko muttered loudly enough for her and anyone else to hear. "I've got two arms, haven't I?"

"Not at the moment," Meriamon said. And when he glared at her: "Would you prefer to play packhorse now,

simply to prove that you can do it? Or would you like to
have the use of that arm when the bone sets?"

"I won't anyway, will I?"

His bitterness was deep, and so honest that she stared.
"What ever makes you think that?"

He curled his lip. "Oh, come. You've all been jollying
me along so nicely—do you think I'm that stupid? I know
I'm lucky to have anything attached to my shoulder. I
could lose it yet. Couldn't I?"

"Not if you take care of it," said Meriamon.

"What for? So it can dangle prettily and give people
something to stare at?"

She blinked. That was real pain, and real fear, strong
enough to catch at her heart.

He spat in disgust. "Never mind. I'll shut up and play
invalid."

"You do that very badly," she said, sharper perhaps than
she had meant.

"Good," said Niko.

The column wound out of the valley and ascended the
hills, going down the way Meriamon had come: southward, with the sea on their right hands. The Parsa were
driven far away. Inland, the scouts said, north and east, all
the way to Cappadocia. The king did not deign to follow
them. His eye for the moment was on the sea and its cities.

Parmenion was gone. Meriamon could imagine Alexander's relief to be freed of that potent and censorious presence. The general had accepted the charge of securing
Damascus. It was a gate, and a great one, between Persia
and the sea; and the lords of the Parsa had sent their
women and their treasure there, a rich prize for
Parmenion's taking.

Meriamon climbed up onto the back of the cart. The
men in it were silent, drugged or unconscious. One of
them did not look to last the day. She did what she could
for them, and made her way carefully to the front. The

mules kept a brisk walk, pulling the rattling, rocking thing; she could almost reach out and touch the thick-muscled haunches. She thought about getting down again. The mules would be happy to lose even her little weight, but she was more comfortable than she might have expected, and tired enough, for a moment, to indulge it.

As she braced herself to slide down, swift hoofs came up behind. She glanced over her shoulder. The king had runners going up and down the line, mounted and afoot. He was in front himself, being a banner for the rest to follow.

This was not one of his white-chitoned pages. It was a Persian in trousers on a Persian horse, a delicate beauty like a gazelle, its rider matched to it with an artist's eye. He brought his mare to a neat, prancing halt beside Meriamon's wagon and bowed in the saddle. "If your highness will be so gracious," he said in excellent Greek, "my lady would speak with her."

Meriamon raised a brow. "Your lady?"

The eunuch flushed; or perhaps it was only the wind on his cheeks. "My lady Barsine."

Meriamon inclined her head. He offered a hand. She swung lightly from wagon-front to horseback. The eunuch wheeled his mare about and sent her cantering back down the line.

A horse, thought Meriamon. She would have to ask for one, or find a way to buy one. It would drive Niko wild to see her mounted and himself forbidden it. She almost laughed at the prospect; then hated herself. He was hurt, that was all, and afraid. Some men bore it in silence. Some screamed without shame. A few, like that one, grew angry at it, and hated their weakness, and were conspicuously nasty to everyone who saw them in it.

She settled to the mare's stride. It was smooth, its rider as skillful as all the Parsa seemed to be, as if born to a horse's back. She was not as good as that. She had come to it later, though young still, and she had not ridden enough while she was in the temple. Horses were not a common thing in Khemet. Boats for the Nile, feet for the land, those her people knew. But she was royal, and her father had wanted her trained in that as a prince was; knowing, or foreseeing, what need she would have of it.

She wondered what Barsine could want with her. Maybe it was the Queen Mother who asked, and Barsine but a pretext. No danger threatened: her shadow was quiet, gliding at the horse's heels, making it skitter and fret.

The Persian women's wagons were as magnificent as their tents, great wheeled land-ships brilliant with paint and gilding, hung with leather as supple as cloth, and silk within in the rich deep colors the Parsa loved. Dark to Meriamon's eyes; ornate and overwrought, too many curves and folds and no clean angles.

She was sorry to leave the horse's back and the bright air, cold though it was with the wind blowing, but clean. Perfumed dimness reached out for her and sucked her in.

Not the Queen Mother, then. Her wagon was larger by a good measure, and all gold. This one was not quite bursting with women and eunuchs; was, Meriamon suspected, all but empty compared with the others. The one who was their focus sat propped with cushions. She was wearing Persian mantle and veil, but the gown under it was Greek, and her hair was knotted in a fashion Thaïs too was fond of, caught with a silken fillet.

She was still, for all of that, pure high-nosed Persian. Her beauty seemed the more brilliant for its presence in this rocking, swaying box; her eyes were almost hungry, watching Meriamon as she clambered in.

Meriamon narrowly avoided falling into the lap of a huge-bellied eunuch, lurched forward, dropped down in front of Barsine with nothing resembling grace. No one laughed. Meriamon took a moment to get her breath back. Her hair was in her eyes. She shook it away, pulling off her Persian cap, not troubling to put it on again.

"Lady Mariamne," Barsine said gravely.

"Lady," said Meriamon, not too breathlessly. "Barsine."

There was a pause. Meriamon was not in a mood to fill it. So many ears; so many eyes. It was worse than the novices' court in the temple, when a new one came in and everyone watched and whispered and wondered if she could sing, or would she be a dancer, and how long would it be before she learned to do either?

Meriamon could sing. She was not an ill dancer, though there were better before the god. She did not intend to do either here. She sat and let her breathing slow, and waited.

Barsine smiled slightly. "You are welcome in my palace," she said. "I had hoped that you would bring your cat."

"If I had known," Meriamon said, "I would have asked her if she would come."

"She accepts no command?"

"She is a cat," said Meriamon.

Barsine's smile widened. "We had cats in our house when I was small. I never managed to tame one."

"Cats aren't tame creatures," said Meriamon.

"So my father said." Barsine leaned back against the cushions, propped on her elbow. She was slender, slim-hipped and high-breasted like a young girl, though she could hardly be less than five-and-twenty. Boyish, Meriamon thought. Even her face—in a cap, over a man's coat, it could have been a young man's, with its arched nose and its firm chin. Persian youths could be as beautiful as this, and often were; they prized their beards the more, perhaps, for that they made it clear who was a man and who was not.

"Your Greek is very good," said Meriamon. "Better than mine."

The lids lowered over the great eyes. "My thanks," Barsine said. "I had good teaching. I was a child when I was married to Mentor the Rhodian, who served the Great King but who never forgot that he was a Hellene; and when he died, I was given to his brother. They wished me to speak their language. I was a good wife: I obeyed them."

There seemed to be no mockery in her tone. Her eyes

were lowered, and unreadable. "Did you take no pleasure in it for yourself?" Meriamon asked her.

She shrugged minutely. "Obedience is pleasure."

"Not," said Meriamon, "in Egypt."

Barsine looked up then. "Not even for a wife?"

"I've never been a wife," Meriamon said.

"No?" Barsine looked down again. Parsa manners: they thought it the height of rudeness to stare. "How interesting."

"Shocking." Meriamon tucked her feet under her. The wagon was not swaying so much now. They had come down from the hills to a brief level. If she listened over the manifold sounds of the army on the march she could hear the sea, more distant now but clear. "Did you summon me to ask if I had ever been married?"

Barsine's cheeks flushed, delicate as a Damascene rose. "You must think me unpardonably rude."

"Only foreign," said Meriamon, "and interesting. Is there something I can do for you?"

Her briskness calmed the Parsa woman a little. "You talk like a man," Barsine said.

"I dress like one, too. It's warmer."

Barsine smiled as if she could not help it. "Everyone says that you are ... unique. Now I believe it."

"You may also believe that I have duties waiting. Pleasant as this is," Meriamon said, "it's keeping me from my work."

She heard the hiss of breath caught. More than one; and that was anger, tainting the air. Her shadow drew closer about her.

Barsine's smile did not waver. "They say," she said, "that the king reckons you a friend."

"Not to me," said Meriamon.

"They do," Barsine said. "And they say that you could have been more than a friend."

"They say much too much."

"Only if it is a lie."

Meriamon's eyes narrowed. That word, that sin, was the

worst of any the Parsa knew. To ride, to shoot, to abhor the Lie—that was all the learning a Persian lord expected to need; and if it was simpler in the saying than in the doing, then that was only the way of the world.

She spoke very carefully. "What I could have been, the gods know. What I am, you see before you. The king is not a lover of women."

"The king—" Barsine paused. "The king has asked me . . . to be . . ."

Meriamon bit her lip. That, coiling in her—that was jealousy. And laughter: at herself, at the king, at Barsine. Who surely was not devious enough to do this to wound, Parsa though she was. Meriamon kept her eyes half-lidded, lest they betray her. "And you ask my advice?"

"I ask the one who could—who should—have been the one he chose."

"Why do you think that?"

"It should have been one of the Great King's daughters. We know that, all of us. But he refuses, of his courtesy, and because he dreams of a kingly gesture. You are as royal as they, as he would think of it, and worthy of him."

"And you're not?"

"I am old," said Barsine, who could not have been more than a handful of years older than Meriamon; and Meriamon was a bare season older than Alexander. "And I am no maiden, and no princess royal."

"Maybe that's why he wants you."

Barsine looked up, startled.

Meriamon smiled. It was not difficult, once she began. "And you're very beautiful, but it's a beauty he can approach. He likes to talk to people, you know. That could be hard when the lamps are out, to have an interpreter lying between you."

Barsine pressed her palms to her cheeks. She looked as if she could not decide whether to laugh or to be outraged.

"And of course," said Meriamon, "there's Parmenion.

He has all Macedon behind him, and Macedon wants its king to get heirs. Its king will get them when, and only when, he chooses. Was he always so stubborn about having his own way?"

"Always," murmured Barsine. She lowered her hands from her cheeks. "How did you know that I knew him?"

"I guessed. Your father took you with him, then, when he went to exile in Macedon."

"He took us all. The Great King would have killed us else."

"So," said Meriamon, "you knew Alexander when he was small."

Barsine smiled. "Small he may have been, but his will was a giant's. He was into everything. They had me running after him, because I was quick, and small enough to go where he went, but strong enough to pull him out if coaxing failed. It usually did. He could never bear to be told what to do."

"I can believe it," Meriamon said dryly. "Now you see why he asked for you. You know him, and maybe he remembers you; and it's *his* choosing. Since he must choose at all."

Barsine smoothed a fold of her gown, refolded it, pressed it into a pleat. "He came to me himself. He was very abrupt. 'I should like you to be my mistress,' he said. 'If it suits you.' "

"Does it?"

"Do I have a choice?"

"Yes." Barsine smoothed another fold, refolded it, pressed another pleat. Meriamon spoke more softly. "Did he insult you? Not asking you to be queen?"

"No!" Barsine seemed shocked at the thought. "Oh, no. I never wanted to be a queen; nor expected it. But for him to pretend that I can choose ... it's cruel."

"Not cruel," said Meriamon. "Simply Alexander. He's better at wooing armies than women, I think. And he's used to men, who can say no."

"If I did," said Barsine, "what would he do?"

She was frightened. Meriamon could see it clearly. But brave, and trying hard to understand.

"What would he have done," asked Meriamon, "when you were children?"

"He's no child now," Barsine said. "He is the king."

"He's still Alexander."

Barsine pondered that. A faint line deepened between her brows. "Probably," she said at last, slowly, "he would do nothing." Her voice grew stronger, her words more certain. "He might try to persuade me, but he'd never force me. That's not his way."

Meriamon waited, listening.

"I've known him so long," murmured Barsine, "yet you know him so well."

"There's nothing here that isn't known to everybody."

"But you understand."

"My gods understand," said Meriamon.

Barsine sat up. She could hardly be shocked at alien faith, she who had been wife to Hellenes. "I shall think on what you have said. They were right, who called you wise, and friend to the king."

Meriamon's gods were wise. As for friendship, that was part of it. She did not say it. The woman had needed someone to talk to, that was all, so that she could decide what she would do. There were greater ironies than a Parsa woman seeking wisdom from an Egyptian and an enemy, but at the moment Meriamon could not think of any.

The gods were wise, and incalculable in their wisdom. Her shadow only laughed. It saw nothing strange in that she should want to like a Persian, even a Persian who was half a Hellene.

She would like the Hellene, then, and hate the Parsa. Since the gods wished it. No matter what it did to mind and wits and sanity, or to good clean hate.

•SEVEN•

Alexander's army came down into Phoenicia with the sea on the sunset side and the mountains of the Lebanon against the morning sky; and snow on them when cloud did not veil them, blinding white and alien to eyes that were born in Khemet.

This was a strange narrow country, mountain-walled, sea-bound: deep ravines and gorges, sudden rivers, brief levels where they could rest themselves and their wearied animals. Hellas was like this, they said, if never so narrow. Macedon was wider, but its men knew mountains and called them home. They laughed at the steepest ascents, went bare-armed, bare-legged, even bare-bodied in the cold.

There were people here, clinging to the sea-cliffs, making their living out of the little land and the greater sea. They fled in their boats when the army came, and left their villages unguarded but for the dogs and the frantic fowl.

Alexander would not let his army plunder the villages. They took the fowl, those who were quick enough, but left the dogs alone. The more antic of them danced on the sea's edge and sang to the boats, mocking or comforting, or sometimes both together.

Marathos was different. Marathos was a city, and not a small one, perched on its rock with its ships in harbor below. Alexander took it without a blow struck. The prince of that country surrendered to the rumor of his army, and crowned him with gold in token of it.

Alexander took it as his due. His army—wild boys, the lot of them, even those who should have known better— celebrated the bloodless conquest with a festival, and

Straton the king's son gritted his teeth and paid for it. Marathos was prosperous, a traders' city, and could win back its losses; and his own city was safe, Arados on its lofty island where Alexander's army could not go.

"Not without ships," Niko said. He was not talking to Meriamon. She had gone to look at the market and maybe buy a frippery, and one or two of the king's Companions had fallen in with her and her guardsman. She was well guarded, walled in by big ruddy Macedonians, and Niko for once seemed almost happy.

Not that he had been at first. She had seen how he braced himself for mockery of his ignominious new duty. But his friends were like every other Hellene with sense: they looked at Meriamon and saw a woman and a foreigner, and that was worth a frown, but beyond that they saw the priestess and the oracle. They accorded her careful respect, because it was safest, and greeted Niko with honest pleasure. He eased quickly after that, and now he was talking about ships.

"If we had a fleet," he said, "we'd be twice as dangerous as we are now. The Persians are strong on the sea; as long as we're not, we're vulnerable to a fleet at our backs."

"Well, but when have we ever been a sea power?" one of the others wanted to know.

"We've never needed to be," Niko said. "Our grandfathers were shepherds and hunters. They dressed in skins and counted themselves lucky to have a stoup of wine at festival time. Philip changed all that. He raised us up; he made us a power. He built the best army in the world. Now Alexander's using that army. But if it's going to do him any good at all, it has to have a fleet to go with it."

"What for, if he's just out to get Greek cities back from the Persians? They've got their own ships if he needs them."

"But they're not *his*," Niko said. "What did the gods

give you eyes for, if you can't see what's right in front of your face?"

"I see a wineshop," the other said, "and a potboy I'd give a fleet for. Hai! Sweetcheeks! Wait for me!"

He was gone, with the others galloping after. Niko watched them go. "Infants," he muttered.

"You make perfect sense to me," said Meriamon.

He started. He had forgotten all about her. His face closed in; he stiffened to attention.

She sighed. He would never let her forget that she was duty, and no pleasure. "I don't suppose you know where I can find a goldsmith."

"That way," he said. "We passed it as we came."

She had been too busy listening to notice. "Show me," she said.

She bought a ring for Sekhmet's ear, and wavered over something for Thaïs. Gods knew, the hetaira had gauds enough, and for her they were wages. Something else for her, then: something different.

Meriamon's mood when she came out had been bright enough, but it had darkened to storm-color by the time she left the goldsmith. He was an Egyptian, and he had offered her beer of his wife's own brewing. The sight of his thin brown face, the taste of his thin brown beer, struck her heart with longing for home. She hated to leave him, but hated worse to stay, and remember that she had cast in her lot with barbarians.

She did not go back to the market after that. She went straight to the camp outside the city's walls and took refuge with the surgeons. The hospital was all but empty of wounded now, the last and worst either dead or recovered enough to escape. There were a few men too sick with ordinary mortal ills to walk about, a malingerer or two being dosed with preparations as horrible as they were harmless, a horseboy who had got kicked, a servant who had burned himself in a cookfire. There was nothing for her to do. She could have made herself useful by combing the market for herbs and healing drugs, but she did not want to go back. She went to her tent instead and thought about sulking in it.

Thaïs was there with Ptolemy and a whole army of revellers. They could not even wait for a decent hour; or had they stopped at all since last night? Someone had got hold of a barrel of apples, and someone else said Alexander would come when he was done with kinging it in the Great King's tent, because Alexander loved apples with a rare passion. "Remember when we had boats on that river—was it the Kydnos? And we had an apple war, Alexander's boat against Nearchos', and Alexander won by a core?"

Nearchos himself, slender-waisted Cretan with his long lovelocks and his clever eyes, laughed with the rest of them. "Right to the heart, it went, and slew me fair. That was a rare sea-battle!"

Meriamon had no laughter in her. She was as cross-grained as Niko at his worst, and for no reason that she could think of. She escaped under cover of their merriment, little caring where she went, if only it was quiet.

She went clear to the horselines, in the end. Hellenes thought it the height of indignity to ride a gelding or a mare. Their stallions were fierce creatures, kept muzzled on strong leads and well separated from the captured Persian mares. But stallion-noise was beast-noise, comforting in its way; most of them were sensible enough, for stallions, standing hipshot and slack-eared and amenable to a moment's tribute.

Alexander's own horse had a tent of his own and an army of servants like a king, and like a king he ruled them with a fine and haughty air. He had guardsmen too, royal pages who did turn and turn here as with Alexander.

The two on guard did not seem to mind that Meriamon walked past them to the stallion's run. Maybe it was the sight of Niko in his Companion's cloak, which they had yet to earn. Maybe they welcomed the diversion. One even ventured to smile at her. She smiled back, discreetly.

The king's horse was hobbled but not muzzled, with a long enough tether that he could almost roam free. He was nothing remarkable to look at compared with the Persians' slender beauties, though he was said to be of Nisaian blood himself: not quite fifteen hands, Meriamon judged, a bit bow-nosed, heavy-necked and short-coupled. But even in a hobble he moved well, and the eye he turned on her was bright and wicked.

She approached him with respect. He watched her, ears up, nostrils flaring to catch her scent. She could see the brand on his shoulder, the oxhead that had given him his name.

"Boukephalas," she said. He snorted. She smiled. She was close enough to touch. She laid her hand on his neck, cupped the velvet of his muzzle. He lipped her palm delicately, as if to belie every tale of warhorses that she had ever heard.

He was not a young horse. The hollows were sunk deep above his eyes; the flesh clung tightly to his skull. But he moved like a youngling, and rolled his eyes like one, informing her that yes, he was quiet for courtesy's sake, for after all he was a king; but that was purely of his choosing.

He was the king's age almost exactly—her own within a season. Her shadow felt the power in him. He was part of Alexander, part of the legend that had been building since the king was born. The king still rode him in battle, still chose him above younger and finer mounts, because he was Boukephalas.

He threw up his head and neighed. Meriamon clapped her hands over her ears. He tossed his head and sidled, snorting.

Mares. New mares coming in in a herd, with grooms and servants and hangers-on, and Persian trappings on every one of them.

Her shadow reared up. It knew the hot-iron scent of Parsa magic, Magi setting wards, guarding—who knew what. Doing gods knew what behind the walls, closing in on the king.

Meriamon did not remember bidding farewell to Boukephalas. Her shadow was all but gone; but for the sun knitting it to her, it would have sprung free. When she ran, it spread wings and flew.

A small supple person in Persian trousers could go where an obvious woman or a Macedonian soldier could not. Straight through the crowd that had gathered to watch the Persian embassy ride in, under arm and spear of the guards who held them back from the king seated under a canopy that had been the Great King's, in an elaborate gilded chair that had belonged to Darius. Alexander had had warning, and he had taken advantage of it. He was in his golden corselet, and he wore the heavy golden fillet of a king. The ends of its purple ribbon stirred in a restless wind, but he was perfectly still.

Meriamon stopped on the inner rim of watchers, between a great ox of a Macedonian and a slender nervous Persian. The highest of the Persians stood in front of the king—stood erect; did Alexander know what an insult that was?

She did not need eyes to find the Magi. There were three of them in white from head to foot, one white-bearded but the others younger, perhaps his sons.

They were not aware of her. She was a shadow with eyes, a power outside of their power, and maybe their gods did not speak to hers. They claimed the one and only Truth, which had served them very ill in Khemet.

The wind boomed in the gold-woven canopy. There was silence under it: a pause, in which the king's voice was soft but very clear. "So. Darius has a message for me. What is it?"

One of the glittering personages crooked a finger. Another produced a roll hung and clashing with seals. Yet another presented it, bowing, to the king's interpreter.

That dignitary could not be troubled to break the seals with his own hand. Another did it for him, with ceremony. "It is written," the interpreter said, "in Greek."

Alexander was amused. Maybe. "Read it, Thyrsippos," he said. It was polite, but it was an order.

The interpreter drew a breath and began. " 'Philip of Macedon rejoiced in the friendship of the Great King Artaxerxes; yet when Artaxerxes' son succeeded him, Philip the king assaulted him without cause, and made war against him. Now Alexander rules in Philip's place, and yet he has sent nō word of alliance or of friendship. Rather, he has led his army into Asia, and wrought much harm to the king and the people of Persia. Thus Darius the king has ridden to war to defend his realm and the throne of his ancestors. A god willed that the battle end as it ended. Now Darius the king asks of Alexander the king that he free from captivity his lady wife and his mother and his children, and grant friendship and alliance. Thus he beseeches Alexander to send to him an embassy in the company of these his trusted servants, Arsimas and Meniskos, that they may exchange pledges of honor and of friendship.' "

The interpreter lowered the letter. The silence was deeper even than before.

Alexander sat under all their eyes, as still as if cast in bronze. When he moved it was startling, like a mountain shifting. He leaned forward, held out his hand. Thyrsippos set the letter in it. He read it quickly, his lips barely moving; Meriamon could not hear the whisper of the words.

He rolled the letter and held it so, tapping it lightly against his palm. His eyes were dark, liquid, almost drowsy.

"Thyrsippos," he said. "Get your pen-box."

One of the scribes hastened to offer one; and, at the interpreter's command, to use it as it was meant to be used.

"Write this," said Alexander, speaking slowly, then more quickly as the words came together in his mind.

"Alexander of Macedon to Darius in Persia. Your forefathers brought war and invasion against Macedonia and Hellas and wrought havoc among our people without incitement or provocation. As commander of the armies of Hellas I crossed into Asia to avenge that act of war—a war for which Persia, and Persia alone, is to blame. I defeated your satraps and your generals. Now I have defeated you yourself and all your armies. By the gods' will I rule in your country, and I have taken into my charge those of your people who sought sanctuary with me. No force constrains them; they serve me of their own will and gladly, as they themselves will testify."

Alexander paused. The Persians said nothing, did nothing. They seemed powerless to move. He leaned toward them. His voice rose by a careful degree. "Come to me, Darius. Come to me as to the lord of Asia. Do you fear that I shall harm you? Then send your friends, and I will pledge their safety. Ask me for your mother and your queen and your children and whatever else you can wish for, and I will give them to you. Only remember that I am king of Asia, and you are not my equal. All that was yours is mine; ask for it fittingly and you shall have it, but fail in that and I will give you the recompense of a thief. Or would you contest your throne? Stand then and fight for it. Do not run away. For wherever you may hide, be sure of this: Alexander will find you."

Alexander sat back. "Write it fair," he said, "and you, Thyrsippos, take it to Darius. You will be safe. My word on that."

No one asked him how he could give pledges for Darius. Even his own men were speechless. King of Asia! Had he gone mad?

Hardly. He was laughing behind those limpid eyes. Light wild boy-laughter, daring the lion in his pride; dancing with the whirlwind.

The Persians would not stay to suffer the madman's courtesy. They asked only that they be assured of the royal ladies' safety. When they had seen it, though night was coming winter-swift, they took their horses and the small company of the king's embassy, and went back the way they had come.

"Pity," said Alexander. "They missed some good apples."

And some very painful humiliation; but Meriamon did not say that. She was too richly pleased to have seen their faces as they learned what Alexander was. Mad, yes, but as a god is, or a king whom the gods have made.

•EIGHT•

From Marathos to Sidon was a triumphal procession. Sidon, that ancient city, opened its arms to Alexander and called him King of Asia.

It had a king of its own, who sailed in Sidon's fleet under the Persian king. His son and heir was nowhere in evidence when Alexander sent for him; he had wisely made himself scarce. If he had any sense, he would have put to sea where Alexander could not get at him.

Alexander was not inclined to go after him. He went hunting instead. They were a small party, as a king's following went: a company of the Bodyguard, some of the older pages, a friend or two, even a few of the more intrepid nobles from Sidon. It was a glorious, yelling, blood-and-sweat chase, and a lion at the end of it for the king to kill.

"Better than battle," one of the Sidonians said in traders' Greek, grinning through his tangled beard.

Hephaistion looked down at the man whose head came just to his shoulder, and returned the grin with one somewhat less broad. He had got a clawing when the lion turned at bay, going in too close; but it had laid the beast's heart open to Alexander's spear. Alexander would have something to say about that, come evening. Now he was in the lead with the lion's skin for a cloak and its cleaned skull for a helmet, leading the hunt back to the city.

Hephaistion lengthened his stride a fraction. The wounds were nothing to fret over—spectacular but shallow, and bound tight. The bandages across the ribs were a nuisance: they made it harder to breathe.

"He is . . . impressive," the Sidonian said.

Hephaistion glanced at him again. His grin had faded. Another had come up beside him, younger and neater-bearded but obviously his brother: little red-brown curly-bearded man, hawk-faced and quick-eyed. Artas the elder and Tennes the younger were his guest-hosts in Sidon, and apt for almost anything.

"Your Alexander," Tennes said, "is somewhat more than tales make him."

"The boy king," Artas explained. "The young fool who's mad enough to take on Persia. One doesn't expect him to be so . . ."

"Brilliant," said Tennes. "Striking."

"Capable," said Artas.

Hephaistion wondered if he should be offended, or should pretend to it. He shrugged to himself. Sidonians chattered. It was their nature. Alexander never minded if people talked about him, as long as they gave him due respect. As these did, after their fashion.

. They were already talking about something else, and doing it in Greek which was their courtesy, or maybe their cleverness. "Sidon's king is no Alexander," Tennes said.

"Straton?" Artas snorted. "Straton is the Persian king's toady. His son hasn't seen fit to linger, now that Alexander's in the city."

"Sidon needs a king," said Tennes.

"It has Alexander," Hephaistion said.

That should have quelled them. But they were Sidonians. "Alexander is a king of kings," Artas said. "And what king can he be king of here, if the one who wears the crown is out commanding a fleet in Darius' name?"

Hephaistion felt his eyes narrow, his smile go hard. "Why? Does one of you want it?"

Their jaws dropped. It was something for the ages, to see a Sidonian struck dumb.

Artas found his voice. It came out strangled, but that passed. "One of us?"

Hephaistion halted. They were last in the procession, and had got behind as they talked. Now the rest were round a bend in the track. They might have been alone in this steep and stony place, with a tree crouching over them and a dry streambed marking the way down to Sidon. "That's what you're asking, isn't it? For me to talk to Alexander, and for him to name you king."

Artas drew himself up. He did not have much height, but he had dignity enough when he needed it. "I cannot be king. Nor can my brother. Our blood is ancient, and noble beyond question. But it is not royal."

Now Hephaistion was speechless.

"Isn't that so in Macedon?" Tennes asked. "Mustn't a king be of the royal line?"

"Yes," Hephaistion said. He was tempted, perilously, to laugh. They had him neatly in their ambush. He could fight his way out of it, he supposed. Or stay and see what they were getting at.

"There, you see," Tennes said. "Neither of us can be king."

"That wouldn't stop most people," said Hephaistion.

Tennes laughed. Artas smiled. "We're not philosophers," he said, "or altruists. We're merchants. Why should I want to be king, and live mewed up in the city, and never go out trading? I'd run screaming into the hills."

Hephaistion's eyes flickered to the hill on which they stood, and the mountain behind. "So would I," he said. He shifted his feet. There: better. Less ache under the bandages.

"Still," said Tennes, "somebody has to be king. A city needs a head; someone to look to when there's trouble, and to talk to the king over him as king to king."

"And what do you think I can do?" Hephaistion asked. He put an edge in it, to warn them.

They caught it. Artas let the lightness drain out of his face. He looked older for it, and solider. More like a spokesman for his people—which, no doubt, he was. "We know that Alexander listens to you. We think—"

"We?" asked Hephaistion.

"Tennes and I." Level, that, inviting no argument. Hephaistion chose to let it pass. Artas went on. "We think that you have a good eye for people, and a clear head for judging them. We've seen how you keep the army fed and provisioned, and things running smoothly. You're good at what you do."

Hephaistion raised a brow. "So? What does that have to do with choosing a king for Sidon?"

"Everything," said Tennes. "We know who might do. But we need someone to convince Alexander."

"Just Alexander? Not your own people?"

"That's our side of it," Artas said.

"I can't help feeling," said Hephaistion, "that I'm being taken for a fool. Why don't you simply send an embassy to Alexander and ask him to approve your choice?"

"We're doing it," said Tennes with an air of perfect innocence. "We're asking you to be our embassy."

Hephaistion began to walk again. The rest of the hunt was long gone. He did not hurry for that, but he did not drag his feet, either. The others had to trot to keep pace.

They picked their way down the last steep slope, out upon the open road. Sidon's fields stretched in front of them, and the city up against the sea. The hunt was well ahead, almost to the walls. Even at that distance Hephaistion knew Alexander: there was no mistaking that quick gait or that angle of the head in its exotic new finery.

After a while the brothers stopped trying to coax him to say anything. They dropped out of Greek then and into their own language. He took no notice. It was almost peaceful, like the chatter of birds.

He got his talking-to, over wine, very late. By then there was no one near to listen, except one or two of the Companions who had fallen asleep on the couches. Pages would carry them to bed in a little while.

Alexander had drunk less heavily than some; even at that, he could hold his wine as well as anyone Hephaistion knew. His humours burned it up. He moved more slowly, that was all, and fidgeted less. His words were clear, precise, and cutting, on the theme of idiots who walked up to lions as if they were the Egyptian woman's cat, and risked their necks for nothing but to set up a kill for a friend who was perfectly capable of setting up his own, and if that was not enough, came ambling back hours late—

"Not hours," Hephaistion said. "I was talking to Artas and Tennes."

Alexander's teeth clicked together. He hated to be interrupted in the middle of a speech.

Hephaistion had been nursing the same cup of wine for most of the evening. It had stopped being shameful long ago, that he had a poor head for it. He met Alexander's glare over the rim of the cup and sipped, savoring the taste. "You weren't beside yourself with fear for me, either. You were telling the tanners exactly how you wanted your lionskin cured and fitted. Are you really going to wear it?"

"Why? Do you think I'll look silly in it?"

That was real worry, and real vanity, but it had a dangerous edge. "You'll look magnificent, of course," Hephaistion said. "You always do."

"You looked magnificent in front of the lion," said Alexander. "Magnificent, and bloody reckless. Whatever possessed you to go in that close?"

Hephaistion shrugged. It hurt. "It wasn't supposed to be quite so dramatic. Damned thing lunged before I expected. I learned my lesson, believe that. I'll be walking stiff for a week."

"At least," Alexander growled. But the worst of his temper was gone. He left his couch, staggering only a little, and sat down on Hephaistion's. "So what were you talking about with your two magpies?"

Hephaistion grinned. "They do go on, don't they?"

"They all do in Phoenicia. They're almost as bad as Celts." Alexander lowered his brows. "Well?"

Hephaistion told him.

"Clever," Alexander said when he was done. "Using you to get at me. Do they think I'll do whatever you say?"

"I doubt it," said Hephaistion a little wryly.

"It can't be someone popular," Alexander said, "if they cornered you on a mountainside instead of tempting you with ease and comfort and good wine under a roof like a properly civilized being."

"And servants listening, and people coming in and out, and rumors all through the city before the hour was out. No," said Hephaistion, "they didn't want that. I wonder why?"

"You didn't think to ask?"

Hephaistion's cheeks were warm. "I never do, do I?"

"No," said Alexander, not too impatiently. "Go on, then. Find out for me what this kinglet of theirs is like."

"And if he looks like making a king?"

"Make him one," said Alexander. Lightly, but meaning it. Trusting him as far as that. It was half pain, to know it, and half sweetness; and all honor, as of a king to a lord and friend.

Artas and Tennes were not unduly cocky, at least to Hephaistion's face. "After all," said Tennes, "we can name whomever we please, but Alexander has to approve of him."

"And Sidon," said Hephaistion. He did not speak of himself. Some weapons were best kept in the arsenal for when one needed them.

"We'll see to Sidon," Artas said.

"So then," said Hephaistion. "Who is this man who should be king? Do I know him?"

"I doubt it," Artas said. "He's not in the city much. If I know him, he doesn't even know about Alexander."

Hephaistion's brow went up.

"He's not a fool," Tennes said quickly. "He's poor, that's true, but it's not his fault. His blood is as royal as you could ask. He's honest, which isn't a virtue in a merchant. But in a king—if it doesn't get him assassinated, it should serve him very well."

"That depends," said Hephaistion. "There's honest, and then there's tactless. How do I know that he can be a king?"

"Come and see for yourself," said Artas.

They sent the servants to fetch a necessity or two, and had horses readied: riding horse for Hephaistion, carriage team for the brothers, since they had a fair distance to cross.

"His name is Abdalonymos," Artas said when they were on their way. "He keeps a garden outside the walls, and lives on what he gets from it."

Hephaistion's stallion bucked under him, protesting the slowness of the pace. He sent it into a sidewise prance, keeping more or less level with the carriage, and said, "He sounds like something out of a book."

He looked like something out of Hesiod: another of these little brown men, but browner than some, and broader, strong with years of heavy labor. His tunic was ragged and his trousers threadbare, and the earth of his garden was thick on him as he knelt in it, clearing away a tangle of weeds.

The brothers picked their way toward him, with Hephaistion following and the servant behind, carrying a bundle wrapped in faded wool. He was aware of them: he glanced over his shoulder, but he went on with what he was doing. His face was pure Phoenician, with a nose like a knifeblade. His eyes were clear but preoccupied; they widened not at all to see the Macedonian looming behind his countrymen. "Wait just a bit," he said in quite decent Greek. "I'm almost done."

They waited. The brothers glanced at one another and at Hephaistion, with a glint of mirth. Hephaistion grinned back. "Alexander should see this," he said, making no effort to keep his voice down. "He'd love it."

Abdalonymos kept on with his work, methodical but quick. At last he stood straight. The plot was clear, the weeds in a neat pile to the side of it. He dusted his hands on his shirt. It did little but add to the stains that were there already. "Well," he said, looking from one to the next. "What can I do for you?"

Tennes crooked a finger. The servant came forward. He laid the bundle on the cleared ground and folded back the covering. Gold gleamed within, and the deep splendor of purple. "This is yours," said Tennes, "as King of Sidon."

Hephaistion stiffened. This went far beyond any authority he had given. But he kept his tongue between his teeth, and watched Abdalonymos narrowly, and waited.

Abdalonymos looked at the glittering things in their dull wrappings, and then up at the men who offered them to him. His face was flushed, maybe, under its weathering. "Now," he said. "Now look here. I'm not taking any of your pranks. Not in my garden."

"Not a prank," said Artas. He pointed with his chin. "This gentleman is a prince of Macedon, King Alexander's friend. He's looking for a king for Sidon. We told him that you would make a good one. Are you going to make liars of us?"

No more, Hephaistion thought, than they were making of themselves.

Abdalonymos yielded not a fraction. "King?" he said. "Alexander? What is this?"

"Sidon has a new overlord," Artas said patiently. "His name is Alexander. He comes from Macedon. He defeated the Persian king in a battle, and now he is king of Asia."

"What's a king to me?" the gardener asked. "The earth is the same, no matter who calls himself lord of it."

"But if the lord is bad," said Hephaistion, "the earth suffers."

Abdalonymos looked at him. His eyes were not quick and glancing-shallow as Phoenician eyes were wont to be. They looked deep; they took careful measure. It was almost a Macedonian look, level and shrewd and suffering no nonsense. "And who might you be?" he wanted to know.

"King Alexander's friend," said Tennes.

That was not what Abdalonymos wanted. Hephaistion had known that before Tennes spoke. A smile wanted to conquer his face, but he held it still: his tragedy-mask, Alexander called it, smooth and inhumanly serene. "I am a king's friend," he said, "but that's not the whole of me. My father's name was Amyntor; he was a lord of men and horses in Macedon. When he died I took over his lands."

"Why didn't you stay in them?"

A shrewd blow, that. It almost cracked the mask. What woke behind it, whether grief or homesickness or rueful mirth, or a mingling of all of them, Hephaistion could not tell. "My friend was given a great trust," he said. "He asked me to share it with him."

"That would be the conquest of Asia," said Abdalonymos. Oh, no, no fool at all, though he did not know a king's name when he heard it. Nor was he an ignorant man, with his good Greek and his hard questions. "I can't say I have much love for the Persians. They burned us out, back in King Ochos' day, and we were a long time building again. I'll be glad if I see that they're gone for good. But why should I be glad of a new overlord? He could be worse than the old one."

Quick anger tightened Hephaistion's jaw, but he did not burst out at once with it. He took a long breath, careful of his bound ribs. He counted heartbeats in the marks of the lion's claws. He said, "A good and honest king can do much, even under a bad Great King. A bad king can wreak havoc in despite of a good overlord. Though," he said, "not for long, if Alexander hears about it. Alexander has infinite patience in most things. But he has none at all for cowards and thieves."

"I'd like to see him," said Abdalonymos.

"So you shall," Hephaistion said, "if you'll be king. He'll set you on your throne himself, and crown you with his own hand."

"No," said Abdalonymos. "That won't sit well with people here. They'll want a say in it. They hated it when the Persians got too obvious about being our masters. That's what made them turn rebel."

"We can speak for the people," Artas said. "You know us; you know what influence we can bring to bear. Will you be king in Sidon?"

"Well," said Abdalonymos, looking at the crown and the robe and the staff where they lay in their wrappings. The sun made them shine; the black earth of his garden brightened their splendor. He raised his mud-blackened hands. "I'm no princeling," he said.

Hephaistion held out his own hands. They were clean enough, but roughened and calloused with years of riding and hunting and fighting. "Soft hands would blister fast," he said, "if they had to hold the reins of kingship."

"I suppose," said Abdalonymos. He looked about him. His garden was grey and forlorn in its winter sleep. Overhead, sudden and sharp, a seabird cried.

Abdalonymos stiffened his shoulders. "All right," he said. "All right. Get me to a bath and tell me what a king does, and let me see how I like this Alexander. If we look like getting on, I'll do it."

Hephaistion let the smile bloom at last. "Oh, you'll get on. Believe me, lord king. You'll get on famously."

Meriamon was not there to see the new king's meeting with Alexander, but she heard about it afterward. Abdalonymos was blunt and completely unawed, and Alexander, people said, was delighted with him. They did, indeed, get on; and Sidon settled to it, though its elders were not pleased to be ruled by a man of low estate. "So I'll give him a great one," Alexander said, and gave him all that the old king had had, and a share of the Persians' booty, and a great estate outside the city, with his old garden in the middle of it. After that, will they or nill they, the elders held their peace.

Meriamon was tired of traveling about, of living on strangers' sufferance, of being rained on and windblown and shouted at in languages that were not her own. Worse than that, she could not sleep, for when she did, her dreams were haunted.

It was not the Parsa. The Magi had gone with Darius' ambassadors, and they had not come back, openly or in secret. This was something else. As if the gods wanted to speak to her, but the distance was too great, her strength too little, so far from its source.

It was always the same dream: the dark country, the vulture and the serpent, the shadow-dancers, the voice speaking, gentle and low. She always woke before she understood the words. It was not the dream of comfort that she had had at Marathos. Its darkness was the darkness behind the stars. Its gods wore demons' faces. She lay there always in that bed which was not an Egyptian bed, and breathed air that was not the air of Khemet, and knew, in the dark before the dawn, that if she did not see her home again, she would die.

She was growing thinner. Her Persian trousers were loose, folded thick under the belt. Her face felt bony and haggard; when she glimpsed it in the side of a silver cup, there were hollows under her eyes.

"You look awful," said Niko.

They had been the better part of a week in Sidon, and the army was starting to settle in, as armies will if given opportunity. Where they would go next or what they would do, no one was sure of, although there were rumors in plenty. Meriamon dragged herself out of bed before sunup, dressed in what came to hand, came out to the central room to find Niko there alone, mending a shield-strap. It should have been impossible for a man with one good hand and one in splints, but he was making do.

He no longer glared quite so terribly when she came out in the morning, but his greeting was pure Niko. She knotted her hands together before they could rise to her face, and went to look at the breakfast laid on the table by the brazier. Greeks would never eat anything but dry bread till midday at least, but Phoenicians were more sensible. They ate well before the day began, to make it begin properly. Here was flat bread fresh from the baking, a bowl of dates, a jar of watered wine, even a dainty: something savory that smelled of spices. Her stomach clenched.

"You look as if you haven't slept since Issus," he said. "Are you sick?"

"No," she said, not quite snapping it. She poured a cup of wine, choked down a sip.

He stood up. At first he had made heavy going of it, between pain and the unbalance of his splinted arm, but he was mending now, and he had his grace back. There was a surprising quantity of it. "You're homesick. Aren't you?"

She did not like to be loomed over. She moved out of his shadow, aiming for the door.

He was there, broad as a wall and quite as immovable. "Go back and eat, and then I'll take you to Philippos."

"I'm not hungry," said Meriamon, "and I certainly don't need a doctor."

"You can't see yourself," said Niko.

She glared up at him. "I'm not sick!"

"Tell that to your mirror."

She drew a long, careful breath. "Yes, I am homesick," she said. "Yes, I have been sleeping badly. No, I am not ill, or haunted, or mad—unless you give me reason to be."

"So eat," he said. "Maybe you don't mind if you die on me, but I'm fond of my hide. I'd rather the king didn't have it for a carpet."

"I won't die on you."

"Prove it."

She glared. He glared back. She stalked to the table and snatched a round of bread, and bit into it. It was still warm, fresh and fragrant. It tasted like ashes.

She ate it. Niko counted every bite. Damnable, maddening man. He disliked her intensely, she could see it in every line of him; but she was his duty, and he would look after her if it killed him.

He was supposed to fall in love with her. Guardsmen did, in stories. Particularly if what they guarded was a princess, and a maiden at that, and no man but the king to answer for her.

Not this guardsman. When the bread was gone, he set a bowl in front of her and filled it with the spiced meat. It was goat, probably. She tasted it. Yes, goat. If she could have had goose or duck, or the flesh of a fat ox . . .

Somehow she ate it. Her stomach wanted to cast it up again, but she was stronger. The wine went down a little more easily, both dizzying and steadying her.

She set down the empty cup. "Now, tyrant. May I have your leave to go?"

"Now you may," he said. Was that a flicker of a smile?

Of course not. Niko never smiled at her.

· NINE ·

There was a boy waiting when Meriamon came back to her lodging, one of Alexander's own pages. The king would like her company, the boy said, if it pleased her ladyship.

For a moment she was sure that Niko had had something to do with it. But he had been with her all morning, treading on her shadow till it was sorely tempted to snap at him, and he had not spoken to anyone who belonged to the king. He seemed as surprised as she, even with Sekhmet to distract him, draping her loudly purring self over his shoulder.

"The cat, too," said the page. "Alexander said she should come. And dress for riding, if you will."

Meriamon stifled a sigh, and shrugged inwardly. Why not? Her clothes were clean, and she was presentable enough, though Phylinna was hovering and signaling broadly toward the bath.

"I'm ready," Meriamon said. "Shall we go?"

When Meriamon came out of the house with Sekhmet riding on her shoulder, another of Alexander's messengers was waiting for her: a redheaded, freckled, gap-toothed Thracian savage, holding the bridle of a bay mare. She was Persian booty beyond a doubt, but smaller than the Persians were accustomed to breed. Desert stock, Meriamon saw, and very fine, and if her blood ran true, as hardy as she was beautiful. There was fire in her, in the flare of her great nostrils and the roll of her great eyes, and yet she looked to have sense.

She was a kingly gift in her trappings of silk and gold, with plainer gear for the march, and the horseboy to look after her. And, he said half in signs and half in abominable Greek, there was a mule in the lines as well, with pack and driver, and if she wanted a cart she could have that, though the king thought she might be well enough suited as it was.

"That, I am," said Meriamon, running a hand down the silken neck, blowing softly into the mare's nostril. The mare blew back more softly still. She saw Meriamon's shadow: her ears pricked, quivered; her eye rolled. But she stood her ground. Meriamon smoothed the long black forelock, traced the shape of the star beneath it. "She is beautiful," she said.

The Thracian grinned. Meriamon could not help but grin back. Little thick bandy-legged lad with his gapped teeth: he looked like Bes, dwarf-god, luck-god, whose gift was laughter.

Even Niko could not take the edge off her pleasure. He was quite as unhappy as she had expected, to see that she would be mounted where he could not. "Soon," she said to him. "When you've mended a little more. Then I'll let you ride."

That was not enough for him, but it would have to do. Even Imhotep's priests could not make a bone heal faster than it wanted to, and her power was a dim candle to the great blooming fire of theirs.

Enough, she thought. She set Sekhmet carefully on the ground, grasped mane, swung up to the gilded saddlecloth. Sekhmet leaped to her lifted knee and thence once more to her shoulder, coiling about her neck. The mare stood rock-solid under them both. Meriamon gathered up the reins. The bit was a bar of simple bronze, none of the Greek cruelty that pried the jaws apart and held them rigid. But then, thought Meriamon, the Greeks insisted on stallions.

The Thracian let go the bridle. The mare was warm, supple, new-ridden from the lines. She tucked her chin and flagged her tail and danced. Everything in Meriamon yearned to clap heels to the sleek sides and plunge whooping through the city.

She turned the mare about instead. Niko had not moved. His jaw was set hard.

There was another horse waiting, and the page readying to mount it. It was a gelding, big for a Greek horse and heavy-headed, with a mild eye. From the slope of its shoulder, it would have a smooth gait. Meriamon looked from it to Niko. His eyes were fixed on a point somewhat to the left of the gelding's ears.

"You'll need help mounting," she said.

His shoulders stiffened. For a moment she thought that he would bolt. He moved, but not away. Toward the gelding. The page looked unhappy, but he offered his linked hands. Niko set foot in them and swung lightly astride. He took in rein, using teeth and sword-hand. He would have done the same, maybe, in full armor, with a shield on his arm.

His eye caught the page. The boy scrambled up behind him. Niko kicked the gelding into a walk.

The mare pawed the ground and snorted. Meriamon let her move into a dancing trot, passing man and boy and gelding, leading them down the winding street.

The king was waiting at the northward gate with a company of horsemen, and one without a rider: a fine snorting stallion, fighting the bit with its disks of bronze holding his mouth wide, shedding flakes of foam as he tossed his head. Niko's. Obviously.

"No," said Meriamon.

Niko showed her his teeth. "Think you can ride him?" he asked the page.

The boy shrugged. His nonchalance was elaborate. "If you like," he said.

"I don't like," said Niko. "But he needs his exercise. Get on with you. People are waiting."

Grinning, too. The page approached the stallion, calming as he moved, till he had the reins in his hands. He paused to let the beast inspect him, forestalled a lunge, mounted in a smooth long leap.

As they rode out of the gate, Meriamon found herself beside Alexander. That was intended: she could see it perfectly well. She could feel the eyes on her, too, and the pressure of scrutiny. There was less enmity than she might have expected, knowing courts, and this one most of all. Alexander's men were fiercely jealous of him, fought over a moment of his time, came to blows over a word or a glance.

She was not a man. That mattered. And she was not a Macedonian, which should have mattered, and did, until they remembered what else she was. Sometimes she suspected that they thought of her rather as they did of Sekhmet: the gods' creature, as uncanny as she was holy, and nothing human to hang their envy on. If anything, she proved what they had always known, that their king was not like any other in the world.

She shook herself. She was maundering, and time ran on. She glanced back. Hephaistion was directly behind, and Niko beside him. The two of them were talking easily, as if they were friends. Hephaistion was recovering well from his encounter with the lion. No stiffness in him that she could see. Or in Niko, either, though even a smooth-gaited horse could jostle hard enough if put to it.

"Don't worry," said Alexander. "If it gets to be too much for him, I'll send him back."

"You knew he'd come," Meriamon said.

"He's your bodyguard," said Alexander.

She considered answers to that. None seemed adequate. She shifted on the saddlecloth instead, getting more comfortable, feeling out the mare's gaits. They were like silk.

"Do you like her?" the king asked.

She glanced at him. His face was open, shining. He loved to give presents; it was the part of being king that, maybe, he liked best. Meriamon smiled. "She's fit for a queen," she said.

"I thought so."

Sekhmet uncoiled from about Meriamon's neck. Before Meriamon could stop her, she lofted smoothly across the arm's length of space onto Alexander's shoulder. He did not start or recoil, though his eyes widened. Sekhmet liked her new resting place: it was broad and level, and it barely moved with his horse's gait. Meriamon could hear her purring even through the thudding of hoofs and the murmur of men's voices.

Alexander reached up very carefully and scratched the cat under the chin. Her purring rose to thunder. She draped herself over his neck, giving herself up to bliss.

"Peritas would be appalled," Meriamon observed.

"Peritas is in disgrace," said Alexander. "He chased a certain cat through one midden too many. Or was chased. Accounts vary. I've confined him to quarters."

"Oh," said Meriamon. "Oh, no. She didn't."

"She did," Alexander said. "Peritas knows better, too. I know you'd never believe it, but he's as well trained as any dog in Macedon."

"I do believe it," Meriamon said. "I believe that he's immune to cats, too. Except for Sekhmet."

"Except for Sekhmet." Alexander rubbed the cat's ears. She, the harlot, leaned into the rubbing, eyes shut in ecstasy. "No wonder you named her that."

"That is her name," said Meriamon, "and her essence. Power and chaos, and the lioness' heart. Names are power, Alexander."

"So they are," he said. "Mariamne."

"Meriamon."

"Meri-Amon."

"Better," she said with a touch of a smile.

They rode on in silence. Meriamon was content to be quiet, to feel the sun on her face, to listen to the men talking behind. They were leaving the open fields now, riding up the track of a small swift river, coming to a wide grove that rose before them on the flanks of a mountain. Road and river passed into the trees under an arch of branches. A strong green scent blew toward her, a scent of earth and trees and holy places. Alien, and yet familiar: sanctity was sanctity, wherever one found it. This was a holiness that she knew, although it was not her chief power. A power of making and healing.

"Whose is this grove?" she asked. Her voice, though soft, was loud in the green stillness.

"It belongs to Asklepios," said Alexander. "Though here they call him Eshmun."

"In Egypt he is Imhotep," said Meriamon. "I feel him in the air; I sense him in the earth. This is his river, is it not?"

Alexander looked at her, not surprised, not exactly; but as if he had let himself forget what she was. "This is his river," he said, "and his temple where we're going. It's a great place of pilgrimage. People come from all over Greece and Asia to ask him for healing."

"Have you something to ask him for?" asked Meriamon.

"No," said Alexander, who still limped when he thought no one was looking. "I give him honor, that's all. I thought you'd like to do the same."

"I would," she said.

Under the peace of the trees, Sekhmet came back to Meriamon. A cat knew about peace, but healing was a thing that she did in solitude. She slid inside Meriamon's coat and lay there, warm and still.

Meriamon looked over her shoulder. No one was talking now, or laughing, or making the way light with a song. Niko was a little pale. There was no one else on the road, which was strange, if this was indeed a place of pilgrimage. Or maybe they came by another way; or the way was cleared for Alexander.

Whatever the reason, they were alone in the god's

wood, in the shade and the cool and the windless stillness. No bird sang. No leaf stirred. Only the river moved, flowing swift and eager to the sea.

The trees ended suddenly. The light was blinding bright, the wind breathtaking, cold as it was and strong, funneling down the narrow gap in the mountain. Up against the wall of it, set high on a dais of stone, stood the temple.

In Sidon they built, as in Khemet, for the ages. Huge blocks of pale stone piled one on another to form walls that rose up against heaven. There was an air of Khemet in the angling of them, and more of Persia in the winged bulls that stood atop them, but the crimson that shaded them was Phoenicia purely, the purple land, the place where all peoples met and mingled.

Twin pillars stood on either side of the gate, one bright gold, the other bright crimson. The gates themselves stood open on a wide columned courtyard brilliant with paint and gilding, alive with carving and limning and, somewhat drab among the images, a gathering of crimson-clad priests. Their heads and faces were shaven as in Khemet, startling in this country where men wore their hair long and grew their beards to their breasts. Their robes were thin and must have been cold in the winter chill, even with the sun imparting its whisper of warmth; caps on their bare skulls and stoles over their left shoulders did a little to warm them, Meriamon supposed, shivering in her heavy coat and her Persian cap.

There were women behind them, ranked and silent, and boys with softer faces than one saw in the city, fat and sleek, which was reckoned beauty here. What they did for the god, Meriamon did not need to ask. The body's pleasure was a kind of healing.

There were people to take their horses, others to offer ceremonial water for washing, wine for drinking. Each of them dipped his fingers in the bowl, sipped from the cup. When cup and basin had gone round, one of the priests came forward and addressed Alexander as lord and king.

Alexander was gracious. Seducing these people as he did everyone, with a word, a gesture, a flash of those remarkable eyes. Of course he would do honor to the god; of course he would tour the god's temple; naturally he was delighted to meet the priests, one by one and by name, and the priestesses, too, and the boys down to the least and shyest, a little dark thing who had not yet grown sleek with ease and good feeding. Alexander smoothed the blue-black curls with a light hand and coaxed him into a smile; then, with a word, into laughter. When Alexander turned away, his light lingered, shining in the boy's face.

"Whoring for the god," Niko muttered under his breath. "A good tumble in the grass, with both sides willing—that's rite and sacrament enough. This is disgusting."

"In Babylon they do it out in public," said one of the others—Peukestas, Meriamon reminded herself. The handsome one with the elegant hands, who was not at all as languid as he looked. "Right out in the sacred grove, where anyone can see. This is as circumspect as a Persian harem."

"Have you been in one, that you'd know?" Nearchos looked about. "Interesting work here. Is that Eygptian, there?"

"And Persian next to it," said Meriamon. "Everyone has been here at one time or another, and left something to show for it."

"That's like the Phoenicians," Nearchos said. He linked arms with Peukestas and wandered off, as most of the others were doing, as if by consent. The king was still occupied with the priests, getting ready to go into the sanctuary. Hephaistion was with him, of course, and Ptolemy, and after a little, Peukestas and Nearchos and black-bearded Kleitos and one or two of the others.

Meriamon had meant to go in with them. Now she did not want to. The god's image would be a Phoenician image, with maybe something of Khemet in it, or maybe not.

The hand of the Parsa was heavy here. She did not want to see a Persian face on Sidonian Eshmun.

She wandered instead. Niko followed her. The temple was a simple enough place, porch and hall and inmost sanctuary, but a city had grown about it, shrines and chapels, courtyards, colonnades, houses for the priests, granaries and treasuries, groves and gardens and, bound to the river by a stone-lined channel, the pool and fountain of the god. There the pilgrims came when there was no king to grace the temple with his presence; there they found healing, or not, as the god willed.

The fountain was surprisingly simple. A spout and a basin, that was all, with water bubbling into the basin and spilling over into the pool. The pool was big enough to swim in. There were weeds in it, and a flicker that might have been a fish, or maybe a coin cast in as an offering.

"Do you wish healing?"

Meriamon started and almost fell in. The person who had spoken to her must have been there all the while, sitting quiet near the fountain, the crimson robe faded to brown, blending into the shade of the wall. It was a woman by the voice, but old enough almost to be sexless, with white hair bound tightly under the faded veil.

Meriamon drew a long breath. Her heart stopped hammering. She bowed low, as low as if this had been a priestess of her own gods. "Holy one," she said.

"No holier than you," said the priestess. She moved slightly, into the light. Her eyes were on Niko. "No, priestess from the Two Lands. I spoke to this one."

He looked surprised, as if it had never occurred to him to connect his splinted arm and the god's healing. "Lady," he said. "Holy one. I don't know——"

"Of course not." The priestess was tiny, even standing: she hardly came to his breastbone. Even Meriamon was taller than that. She tilted back her head, birdlike, and fixed him with a bright hard stare. "Do you want to be whole?"

"Yes," he said, barely above a whisper. *"Yes."*

"So," said the priestess. "Sit down."

Meriamon thought that she should say something. Do something. But the god had brought them here, surely; and this priestess had been waiting for them.

Whatever else she was, she had a surgeon's eyes. She made Niko take his arm out of the sling—his lips went white as he moved it; whiter than Meriamon had seen them in days—and rest it on the curbing of the pool. Then she unwrapped the bindings. Meriamon moved closer, alert, but did not interfere. The gnarled hands were deft, sure of themselves.

It was not pretty to look at. The long muscles were shrinking with disuse, the flesh pale and withered, the stitched wound healing into a livid scar. The bone looked to have set straight, at least, and of late he had had some movement in his fingers, though the thumb was twisted still.

Niko's eyes were shut. He was hardly squeamish: he always insisted on watching when Meriamon changed bandages. She should not have let him ride so far.

Eshmun's priestess bent over the curbing, dipping water in her cupped hands. Her lips moved. Prayer, maybe, or incantation. She poured the water over the wounds.

He gasped. His eyes snapped open. His arm jerked; spasmed. His face went grey.

"Be still," said the priestess, soft, but there was iron in it.

"It's cold," he said.

"It's winter," said the priestess. She filled her cupped palms again, washed his arm again. And yet a third time.

"I don't feel anything," said Niko.

Nor did Meriamon.

Or—no. Something. It was faint, so faint that her shadow barely quivered. It was not the wind-rush of power that she knew in herself, nor the blaze of fire that was Alexander. It was almost not there at all.

The priestess dried Niko's arm gently with the edge of her veil. When it was dry she began to wrap it again, tight in its splints.

He could hardly resist her, with pain stiffening every move he made. But he said, "I see no miracle."

"No." The priestess was calm.

"I suppose," he said, "your god doesn't see fit to favor me."

"That is his privilege," the priestess said. She finished the binding, tucked in the end of it, arranged the sling about his neck. "Eshmun bless," she said, "and keep you."

That was a dismissal. Meriamon obeyed it without question. Niko, whose eyes were full of questions, followed her perforce. He was neither awed nor comforted. He was angry. "Mummery!" he said.

"No," said Meriamon. "It's not."

He glowered at her. He was tired, he hurt, of course he was cross. He would be blaming her for letting him do what he had wanted to do. If he had had his miracle, he would be doubting it. He was a Hellene. That was the way he was.

She was very tired, suddenly, of Hellenes. She turned from the way back to the temple, to a gate that opened on a little court. A man of stone stood in the center of it, solid, foursquare, and unmistakably of Khemet. His name was carved on the plinth, and his titles, and the rest of his immortality, preserved in this alien place.

She stopped in front of him. He was stone, not flesh to shiver in this alien cold; he strode out in his pleated kilt, clasping crook and flail to his breast, head raised under the crown of the Two Lands, eyes fixed beyond the horizon.

Her finger smoothed the carved oval that bound his name. Nekhtharhab. Nectanebo. The face was not a bad likeness: a face of Upper Egypt, long-eyed, broad-nosed, full-lipped. He had looked far more the Ethiop than she, whose mother had been born in the Delta.

Tears pricked, sudden and unwelcome. They said that he had fled to his kin in Ethiopia, running like a coward from the Parsa and their power. Parsa lies. He had died in the fall of Thebes, his last great working broken by the massed power of the Magi, no magic left in him, but strength enough to die under a Persian sword. His body lay in the Red Land in a secret tomb, strong-warded against thieves. His spirit was long gone under the earth.

She was his inheritance. She had a little learning, a little power. She dreamed dreams. She was never the mage that he had been. She would never wear the Double Crown. She was eyes and a voice, and a flicker of memory.

"Your father?"

She did not turn. She had felt his coming like a fire on her skin.

"My father," she said.

Alexander stood behind her. Looking up, no doubt, into the face of the man who had willed him into existence.

That was the gods' doing. She kissed the cold stone feet and moved away from them, letting the wind dry the tears on her face.

There was no one with Alexander. He had come here alone, led as she was led, by chance or the god.

"You weep for him," he said.

"I weep for myself."

"That too," he said.

"He was hardly ever there," said Meriamon. "He was always away, being king, being a mage, being our shield against the night."

"He was your father."

"Yes." She looked up again at the carven face. It had never been so still in the living man, nor ever so serene, even amid the great magics. He had been—formidable, yes. But quick, too; nervous in his movements; gifted with sudden laughter. He loved to ride his horses, and to laugh about it, saying that he was as bad as a Persian.

"He couldn't sing at all," she said. She did not know where the words came from. "He couldn't carry a note. It used to startle him that I couldn't not carry one. Even when, for laughter's sake, I tried. Gods-gifted, he called me. Amon's sweet singer." Her throat wanted to swell shut. She swallowed hard, a little painfully. "I can't sing at all now. I haven't sung since I left Egypt."

"You miss it so much?"

"It's more than that. Homesickness—you Hellenes have a word for that. Do you have a word for the heart that can't live anywhere but in its native country?"

"We know it," he said. "Exile is a bitter punishment, even for us who wander the world at will."

"But I'm not in exile. I wanted to come. I wanted to see another sky, and look on other faces. Only, when I did it, the music went away."

"Maybe it will come back."

"It will," she said, "when I go back to Egypt."

"Soon, then, for your music's sake."

She shrugged. "I am where the gods want me. The music is outside of it."

"Not if you're robbed of it."

"Are you robbed of anything," she asked him, "for being so far from Macedon?"

"I am Macedon." He said it simply, without even arrogance. "The land—that is where it is, and what it is, and when the time comes I'll go back to it. But not now. Here's all the world in front of me, and victories enough to give me wings; and yet I've scarce begun to fly."

"Will your army fly with you?"

"They'll follow me wherever I go."

They would. She had seen it. "Where?" she asked him.

Her heart was beating. This was what she had wanted; this was why she had come. To speak that one word.

He did not answer at once. She looked at him. He was looking at her father's image, as if he could find an answer in its face; as if, so strong the will he bent on it, it could stir and wake and speak. But there was no magic in him, not for him to use, whose whole self and kingship were the gods' doing.

He did not need it. He could see farther than any sooth-sayer, if he but thought of it.

"I have to secure the sea," he said after a while. "That's only wise, since Persia has always been strong there. So I take Phoenicia, whose ships fight for the Great King. After that, there will be Darius. He'll give me a fight—his princes won't let him do otherwise. From the sea, then, with my people ruling the cities at my back, I can turn inland and take the revenge my father meant."

"There's more to the sea than Phoenicia," Meriamon said, "and more to the empire than Asia."

Someone else spoke. Niko. She had forgotten him; and he was right by her, standing in her father's shadow. "You mean Egypt, of course."

"Of course," she said.

"But," said Niko, "if we take Egypt, what happens to Persia?"

"It waits," she said, "and after a while grows tired of waiting, and thinks that the barbarian has stomach only for the edges of empire. Egypt has always been rebellious. What matter if it rebels again? Time enough later to bring it to heel."

"Darius would think like that," said Alexander. "He was brave once—they made him king on account of it. But he's grown soft, and used to his comforts. He'd give up the sea, I think, if that were as far as I wanted to go."

"And Egypt?"

"Do I want Egypt?"

She stiffened. He was smiling. Testing her. She showed her teeth in what could have been a smile. "You want Egypt," she said. "Your strength is there."

"My strength is in Macedon."

"Is that why you left it?"

Now it was he who went stiff, who met her smile with

tightened lips and glittering eyes. "The tree grows high from a deep root."

"Deep," she said, "and wide. Who are you, Alexander? Who was your father?"

"Do you speak dishonor of my mother?"

Deadly, deadly. Her smile warmed and widened. "I least of any woman in the world. My father saw your begetting, clear in the water of seeing. But a god can wear many faces."

She was aware, almost too keenly, of Niko: of how he listened, taut and silent.

Alexander's stillness was deeper, but there was a quiver in it, the quiver of the flame that even motionless, still burns.

"Remember Tyndareus," said Meriamon, "and Herakles your forefather."

"No," said Alexander, barely above a whisper. "She told me once—more than once—but that was rancor. He could never hold to one woman alone. Even her. Especially her. She was always too fierce a fire."

"Fire calls to fire," said Meriamon. Soft, as soft as he. Her voice, and not her voice.

"No," he said. "No god sired me. None has ever claimed me. I'm Philip's get, and no one else's."

"No?"

He seized her in hands that were cruelly strong. "Then where was the god when I needed him? Where was he when they beat me and starved me to break me to their will? Where was he when my father took woman after woman, flinging shame in my mother's face, and laughed when she railed at him? Where was he when my father mocked even me with his bastard get, and cast me out for demanding what was mine? *Where was he when my father died?*"

Love, she thought in that bitter grip. Love, and hate so deep it twisted full round to love again, soured with envy, sweetened with pride. Great men so seldom begot great sons; and there was Philip, and here was Alexander, and which of them had ever endured a rival?

"They say that you killed him," she said, clear and calm and perfectly sane.

He did not snap her neck. Nor did he strike her. That was ingrained in him from his mother's teaching: never to raise hand against a woman.

He let her go. He drew back a step, breathing hard. He said, "I could have killed him. I wanted to—gods, more often than you can imagine. But not that way. Not through such an instrument."

"A fool," said Hephaistion. He had come to stand behind them, and clearly he had been listening for a while. "That was an honest idiot, lady. He thought himself scorned for a younger and prettier boy; he chewed on it for years, till there was nothing left but hate."

"He was mad," Niko said, like an echo of the king's friend. But his voice was his own, and his solidity at Meriamon's back. "There was nothing left of him but rancor. No, lady. Macedonians have always been inclined to kill their kings, it keeps the line strong. But not that way."

"I know it," said Meriamon. And if she had not, she would have known it when Alexander cried out to her of his father's death. His father in the blood. There was never any doubt of that. But his father in the spirit . . . "You are not flesh alone, Alexander. But gods have their own ways and their own times. Maybe you were tested, and tempered in the forge. Maybe you were meant to find your own way."

"Then why are you here?" he demanded of her.

"To guide you," she said. "Perhaps. If it is your choice."

"Do you mean I have one?"

His mockery made her smile. "I'll not blast you if you refuse me."

"No. You'll wear away at me till I give in."

She shrugged a little. "I can be very stubborn. It's a flaw in me."

"In all your race," said Alexander. "Tell me why I should go to Egypt." But before she could speak, he held up a hand. "No, don't give me gods and prophecies. Give me good common sense. What use is Egypt in my fight against Persia? Its satrap is dead; I saw his body. Its lesser overlords will be too caught up in fighting against me to keep your people down. They can rise by themselves and settle matters without me. Why do they need me at all?"

"For what you are," she answered. "For what the gods have made you. What do you want to do, Alexander? Do you want revenge, and only that, and assurance that Persia will stay away from Hellas while you live to defend it? You had that much when you left Issus."

"I won't have it as long as Darius is alive to remember his manhood."

"Well then. Suppose he does remember; suppose you get him to stand and fight. Suppose you even win. What then? Will you go back home and be king in Pella, and play at archon of the Hellenes? Is that empire enough for you?"

"It was for my father."

"Was it?"

Alexander's face was very still. "Are you telling me that I should conquer the world?"

"I am telling you that you can try."

"And Egypt?"

"Egypt is waiting for you."

"I know nothing of that," said Alexander.

"Then maybe you should learn," said Meriamon. "We can teach you, Alexander. Our land is very old, and our power runs deep. We can give you both."

"Can you give me the truth about what I am?"

"If you will come to us," she said, "we can."

" 'We'?"

"My gods," said Meriamon, "and my people."

"I don't believe you."

She smiled. "Of course you don't. You know so little, and yet you could have so much ... Do you know anything of oracles?"

He blinked at the shift, but his mind was quick. "Delphi?"

"Ah," she said. "Your bright god. No, I mean your father. He who speaks from your mother's country, from Dodona of the great trees."

"He is not—" Alexander shut his mouth with a click. Opened it again, speaking tightly. "Yes. I know Dodona."

"That is one of the world's ends," said Meriamon. "There is another. Deep in the deserts of Libya, beyond the horizon of the Two Lands, where the god's voice speaks out of the sand and the deep water. We call him Amon in my country, hidden god, sky-god, king of gods. He is your Zeus also, and his voice is the voice that speaks from the trees."

She had caught him. He leaned toward her, quivering like a hound on the scent. Behind him her father's image seemed to stand taller, its eyes to glitter. "That place too I know," he said. "They call it Siwah."

"Yes," said Meriamon. "Siwah. It waits for you, if you will come to it. It holds the truth of all that you are."

"But," he said, testing her even yet, because he was Alexander. "What good is truth, if Persia takes me from behind?"

"Persia can do nothing to an empire fairly won."

His tension eased a fraction. His brows were knit. "And so we come back to it. You want me to conquer the world."

"Are you afraid to try?"

The quick temper sparked. She smiled at it. "Maybe it's you who should be afraid," he said. "How do you know what I'll do with your country once I have it?"

"That is with the gods," she said.

"You're quite mad, do you know that?"

"Yes," said Meriamon.

He looked at her, at her calm under the gods' wings, and the shadow of her father slanting long across her.

Suddenly he laughed. "Well then, so am I. I'll do it. I'll be your king in Egypt."

·PART TWO·

TYRE

·TEN·

Meriamon should have been content. She had Alexander's promise and his army's readiness to march out of Sidon. They were going to Egypt. The king was coming to the throne which the gods had ordained.

Maybe it was the wine she had had at dinner with the king, little as she had drunk of it. She left early and exhausted, but she slept badly, and her dreams were dark. Even her shadow, set on guard, could not drive them away. "I did what you asked," she cried out to them. "I gained what you wanted. Why won't you let me go?"

They returned no answer. Only words she could not hear, promises, commands, remonstrance or reassurance that she could not catch.

She rose more tired than when she had lain down, to hear the word that had gone out. Tomorrow they left Sidon. Comfortable as some of the army had been, no one grumbled where she could hear. It was a fine clear day, if cold, with a keen wind off the sea. Good packing weather, and if it held, splendid for marching in.

She had little to pack, and that was taken care of. Phylinna and the servants had it in hand. There was nothing for her to do but hang about and watch and get in the way.

In the end she went up on the walls, looking for a moment's peace. The city was like an anthill stirred with a stick, but it was quiet up there, high over the harbor, with the sea beyond so blue it pierced the heart. Khemet had never been a country for seafarers. Yet here on the height of Sidon, with the wind in her face, she almost understood. No bitter Red Land here, no desert as far as the eye could see; no Black Land ever reborn from the Nile. Only wind and stones and changeful, changeless sea.

Her shadow did not like it at all. It stretched thin behind her, shivering. Sekhmet, wise cat, had stayed in the house where it was warm.

She sighed at them both. Niko at least looked happy. He stood apart from her, leaning on the parapet, and eyed the ships as if he had a mind to buy them. She would have to look at his arm later. Eshmun's priestess had worked no miracle over it, but there had been something there, in the words she spoke, in the water she washed it with. He was in a little less pain today, who by rights should have been in more, what with riding so far and going straight to dinner afterward, and never a thought of resting. Though whether even a god could give him back full use of his hand . . .

It was well for him that he was left-handed. His sword-arm was safe. He could fight, even, as long as he could manage a shield, though when it came down to fighting hand to hand, a man with two strong arms had every advantage over a man with one.

The worst of it, for him, was simple vanity. His face was forthrightly unhandsome, with its strong bones and its heavy jaw, but his body was well made, and he knew it. A scarred and withered arm, however proud a memory of battle, destroyed the symmetry that Hellenes prized so much.

One thing Meriamon could grant the older Macedonians: they did not hold with Greek nonsense about beauty. Scars were beautiful because they made a man. Scars taken in battle were most beautiful of all.

She rubbed her own smooth-skinned arm and shivered. The wind was growing no warmer, though the sun was high. Niko saw the movement, standing there without sleeves or trousers, with his cloak blowing out behind him. He reached up to his shoulder and undid the sunburst brooch. Before she could stop him, he had wrapped the heavy thing about her.

It was warm. It smelled of horses and of clean sweat. She would happily have curled up in it and let him grin at her, but he was still her charge. She struggled out of the cloak, which no more wanted to leave her than she wanted to leave it, and made him put it on again. "I won't be responsible for your death of cold," she said.

"But," said Niko, "if you turn to ice and shatter, my hide is forfeit."

"I'm not that fragile!"

"Oh, you're as tough as old leather. But you grew up in Egypt. This is a fine balmy day in Macedon."

"Gods forbid that I ever look on that country," she said through chattering teeth.

"It's beautiful," he said. "Wild, and sometimes even we find it cold. It makes us strong."

"I should like to see you on a fine balmy day in Thebes, when the sun sends his lances straight down and the sand sends its heat straight up, and even the desert falcon takes refuge in the shade."

He shuddered.

She reached up and patted his shoulder. "There now. You have something to look forward to."

"The king loves heat," said Niko. "He loves cold, too. Nothing ever stops him."

"Except idleness."

"Well," said Niko. "Then he finds something to do. Like conquer the world."

She laughed. He had lifted her spirits. Again. He made a habit of that. Not that she would tell him, or he would stop. He was as bad as Alexander about doing anything that anyone else wanted him to do.

The sun was shining when they left Sidon, and the strong wind blowing, making their armor glitter, whipping their cloaks behind them. The horses danced and snorted and flagged their tails. The men sang as they marched. Alexander, up in front of them all, led them in a song that must have reddened ears even in the prostitutes' quarter. The Sidonians, to their credit, cheered him on his way regardless, and some of them even rode beside him.

"They're not horsemen," Thaïs said, watching them. She spoke as one who knew. Her seat on the sand-colored mule was competent, and she would stay there for as long as she needed to, but it was plainly no pleasure.

"They'd rather be on shipboard," Meriamon agreed. Her mare was restive, not liking this crawling pace. When they came out to more open country, Meriamon would let her run for a bit. Others would be doing it, too. And Alexander might even try his trick for passing the time on the march: running alongside a chariot, now leaping in and riding, now leaping out and matching the horse's pace.

Niko was riding again on the same gelding he had had before. When she met his eye, he stared levelly back. He was not going to walk, it was clear, as long as anyone else was riding.

As long as he did not look ready to faint, she would allow it.

She looked over her shoulder. Sidon was no city of hers, but it had housed her for a while. And Eshmun had favored her cause with the king. She offered him a prayer of thanks. He had not healed her of anything that troubled her; but only Khemet could do that.

She faced forward. South, with the wind at her back. Southward to Egypt.

An hour out of Sidon, Alexander's cavalry transformed itself into infantry, freed the horses from their bits and returned them to the lines and swung into the rhythm of the foot-pace. Half a day out of Sidon, the clouds rolled in. Well before nightfall the rains came down. Wind drove them. Sleet edged them. Men wrapped their armor in leather and themselves in their cloaks and endured. Beasts lowered their heads and tucked in their tails and pressed on. Meriamon, in two wool cloaks and a leather one, was more exquisitely miserable than she had ever imagined she could be. The cold, the wet, the wind, conspired to leach her body of every spark of warmth. The cold sank swiftly into her bones, and there stayed. Nothing that she did could shake it free.

In camp that night they had the tent, and fire in the brazier, tended lovingly by the servants. It warmed the air a little. It warmed Meriamon's bones not at all.

She slept a little, shivering. Her dreams were the same dreams, but for once she welcomed them, because they were warm. She woke to cold and wet and endless rain. She ate what somebody gave her, but after a bite or two it gagged her. She found her mare—she would have to give the beast a name; names were everything; but there was nothing in her now but cold. She mounted. She rode. There was nothing to see but rain, nothing to hear but wind. She could not feel her hands or her feet.

Warm. Something was warm. She floated. No, her head floated. Her body was lost somewhere below, poor miserable heavy thing. There was ice in its bones.

"Mariamne!"

A name? But it was not hers.

"Mariamne!"

Another one. Another voice. Quick. Angry?

"Mariamne!"

Three times was power. But not over Meriamon. She laughed at it. It roared back. No words at all. No name. Only wind and falling water, and cold, but so warm, so sweet, so light . . .

"Damn it, she's not made for this!"

Words. Hurting-loud; piercing-sharp.

"The fever's broken." Someone else, softer, calmer. "She'll keep on sinking now, or she'll come out of it. Either one. The gods will decide."

"The gods?" Laughter, short and bitter. "You believe in them after all?"

"I believe that there is more to the world than what I can see."

"The king believes every word of them. Greek education or no. And he'll give me to any one of them who asks, if this woman dies."

"Why? What can you do? You're a guardsman, not a physician."

"I shouldn't have let her get sick."

The soft voice lilted with mockery. "Oh, then you could have stopped her? You could have told the rain to go away, and calmed the wind?"

"I could have made her ride in a wagon with some of the Persian women. They wouldn't mind. They like her."

"Maybe," said the other. The woman.

"Maybe that's still worth thinking of," the man said. "Their tents are warmer, with all those rugs and carpets; and quieter, too. She'd get good nursing there."

"Better than here?"

Thaïs. That was Thaïs talking. And Niko, rough in her ears, angry.

Scared.

No wonder, if he honestly believed that Alexander would punish him for her weakness.

He said, "She's too sick for me to look after. You, too; didn't you just say so? The hospital's wagon is no place for a sick woman."

There was a pause. Then: "I'll ask Barsine," said Thaïs.

"But—" said Niko.

A pause. A gust of icy air. "The rain has let up a little. I'll do well enough. Phylinna! Come with me, please."

The cold blast stopped. Warmth crept about Meriamon. She opened her eyes, heavy as the lids were, resisting.

Dimness. A lamp's flicker. A huge shadow danced and capered. It was not her own. Her shadow was gone. Gone—

Niko caught her and held her down. She struggled. "My shadow!" she cried to him. "My shadow—I can't—"

His face was empty of understanding. She could not make him understand.

Not in Egyptian.

Greek came back to her, poor stumbling snatches. "I can't find my shadow."

"It's right behind you."

She struggled in his grip. He was cradling her as if she were a child. To him she was no bigger than one. "That's not my shadow. My *shadow!*"

"It's here," he said. Not understanding. "It's right here. Hush now. Rest."

"It's not—" She broke off. He did not know. She clamped her lips shut and lay where she was, trying to breathe. Her lungs were not deep enough.

"I'm sick," she said. Startled. Not liking it at all.

"You're sick." Niko kept on holding her. Rocking her, even. His face was never as gentle as his arm was, holding her in its curve, cradling her in his lap. He looked furious.

"How long?"

He looked down at her. "You're not delirious."

"I am. Still. A little. Tell me! How long?"

"Since yesterday."

"Since—" Her head fell back against his chest. "Two days. Two—nights?"

"Just one."

A moan escaped her. "Gods. My shadow."

"Hush," said Niko.

She hushed. Her shadow was gone. There was nothing in her that could hunt for it. No strength. No power at all. The sickness had emptied her.

After a long while she found another word. "Sekhmet?"

"Here."

Soft paw, prick of claws. Murmur of inquiry: "Mrrrrttt?"

"Sekhmet," said Meriamon. The cat's light weight

lofted into the nest that Niko's arm and lap made of her body. She was not strong enough to gather the cat in. Sekhmet did that herself, butting against Meriamon's chin, purring.

Niko was grinning. It died as soon as Meriamon saw it, became his usual scowl. "You are awake. You really are."

"For a little while." Meriamon sighed, coughed. He tensed; his grip tightened to pain. "Please," she said.

He stopped hurting her. He did not lay her down. He was sitting on her bed. He looked tired, as if he had had too little sleep for too long.

"I should look at your hand," she said.

"You should not," he said. "Philippos looked at it yesterday, after you fainted. He said it was mending perfectly well."

"Not better than well?"

He did not understand that, either. She did not try to sigh again, since it scared him so when she did. He was warm, at least. And not in pain, that she could tell. There were worse places to rest her head. Maybe, if she kept quiet, he would sleep.

It was she who slept, sliding down into the long dreamless dark. And woke to moving and jostling and a babble of voices, someone asking a question and someone answering.

"Still alive?"

"Still."

"Thank the gods."

"Of course I'm still alive!" Meriamon snapped.

Strangers' faces stared at her. The voices were long gone. She breathed in the scent of Persian unguents and looked at Persian faces, and thought. *No.* And, *Out. Must go—out—*

They caught her and made her drink wine heavy with spices and thick with sleep, and held her until she succumbed to it. She struggled even then, battling captivity.

* * *

"How is she?"

This voice she would know when she lay in her tomb. This one would call her souls together and make her live again.

"Sleeping," said someone female, someone who hardly mattered. "Breathing—better than before, I think. We had to dose her. She went wild when she saw where she was."

"Nobody warned her?" he said sharply.

"Alexander," the woman said, respectful without servility, "as sick as she is, she would hardly remember."

"True enough," he said after a pause. When he spoke again, his voice was much closer. Right over her; and the weight on her middle was Sekhmet, purring. "Sweet Hygieia, she's shrunk to nothing! What have people been feeding her?"

"Whatever she will eat."

"Precious little, then, if she's been as sick as that. I'll have my cooks fix her a posset."

He touched her. His hand was fire-warm, even against her burning skin. It felt of her brow, her cheek. It rested over her heart, where her breast curved; more maybe than he had expected, bird-small as she was. He did not pull away. "Water, too," he said, "as pure as we can find. I'll make sure you get some. She's dried to a husk with the fever."

"We've been giving her what we have," the woman said, "but more would be welcome." She paused. "You value her."

His hand left Meriamon's breast. "Yes, I do. Does that disturb you?"

"No," said the woman in her Greek that was perfect but for the hint of a Persian lilt. Barsine. The name came, and with it the memory of her face. "No. You don't want her for what her body is."

"I might," said Alexander. Light. Almost bantering.

Barsine did not respond in kind. "I have all of you that I need."

"Do you?"

Meriamon could have opened her eyes. She did not. This was nothing that she was meant to hear.

"Will you come to me again?"

"Yes," said Alexander. Still light. Still easy. But there was truth in it.

"*He* doesn't mind?"

"Who? Parmenion?"

"Is he your lover, too?"

Alexander laughed. "No, Hephaistion doesn't mind. He knows who comes first."

"Yes," said Barsine. Her tone was level, calm. Colorless.

Maybe he heard it. Maybe he did not. He moved away from Meriamon. "Look after my friend. Help her to get well again."

He left. Barsine did not move. "First," she said to the air. "Yes. And those of us who are always second—what have we?"

Friendship, Meriamon could have told her. Goodwill. Protection.

She could not but know it. If it made her bitter, then that was her right, as well as her folly.

Meriamon was very ill. She knew that. Her head was light, her thoughts inclined to wander, but she could think clearly enough for brief stretches. She could reckon and count, and surmise. As far as she could tell, it was the third day out of Sidon. That meant that they were at Tyre, or close to it if the rain had slowed them. It was not raining any longer. There was wind above the tent, stirring the heavy walls, and sun beyond it, and the sound of the sea.

People kept talking over her head. Alexander went away, and after a while Barsine followed. The women who came to sit with Meriamon were given to chatter, and chatter they did, incessantly. "Sister, have you heard?" one asked the other. "Have you heard what he wants with Tyre?"

"What, the sacrifice in the temple?" her sister said. "It's one of his gods, they say. The one he claims to be descended from, who wore a lionskin, the way he does sometimes. Do you think he's handsome?"

"I think our lady is in love with him. She's not wise. Everyone knows about the other one, the one who's so beautiful to look at, but he never looks at women at all."

"That's a shame," the sister said.

"It's what is. It doesn't stop the king."

"Nothing stops the king."

They sighed together. "Did you see the envoys when they came to camp? They were so humble it must have hurt. With their king in the Great King's fleet, and this king at their doorstep, and nowhere to turn; and now he wants to pray to their god. I think he baffled them. They couldn't say yes or no. They had to go away and promise to come back."

"He wasn't happy about that. He hates to wait."

"He won't wait much longer. They were coming this morning, Sardates said when he brought breakfast."

"We could go," the other said. "And see."

"You wouldn't."

"I would."

"But," said her sister. "If our lady catches us—or if Sardates does—"

"They won't," the other said with sweeping confidence. "The mouse is asleep, look. She'll be well enough for an hour."

"She could die," her sister said doubtfully.

"She hasn't so far. Go on, get our wraps, before Sardates comes back and catches us."

They went, one striding strongly, the other still protesting, but following her.

Mouse, Meriamon thought. They called her a mouse. She would be angry, later. Or she would laugh.

It was better than some of the things they might have called her.

They were at Tyre. She had been right, then. And Alexander wanted to sacrifice to the god there. That would be Melqart, whom the Hellenes likened to their Herakles.

He did like to pay his respects to the gods wherever he went. It was a courtesy of his, and a piety. And he was king, and priest as well as king; it was for him to make the sacrifice.

She was sitting up. Her head reeled. She took no notice. She shivered convulsively. Parsa modesty had wrapped her in a robe under all the blankets and furs, but the air was cold. She fell getting out of bed. She stayed there on hands and knees, scraping together her strength. After a while she went forward, still on all fours, and found a cloak, and shoes that were her own. She had to rest when she had put on each shoe, and after she had wrapped the mantle about her.

Somehow she got to her feet. Once she was up, she found that she could stay there, if she kept moving and did not stop.

The sun struck her blind, but no blinder than the light that called her. The wind almost beat her down, but no harder than the force that drew her to the shore. She ducked her head and made herself small and pushed against it. Her sight came and went. She did not stop to wonder where she was going. The sea's scent was strong, its voice sighing through her. The sun was warm on her back, though the wind was bitter.

There were people. She did not see them, except as shadows. She did see where they were: the long white sweep of shore, the blue brilliance of the sea, the rock in the midst of it ringed in walls and crowned with towers. There were ships, black and crimson and Tyrian purple, and purple sails, and hawk-faced sailors with gold in their ears, leaning over the rails.

She was as close as that. Close enough almost to wet

her feet in the sea. Down the length of the shore she saw them, remote and clear as images in a scrying-pool: the Macedonians in their cloaks and their tunics and their scorn for wind and cold, the Tyrians in their long robes and their curled beards, smaller than the Macedonians, Egyptian-small, thin and dark and wily. They were polite. They even smiled. They yielded not a hair's width.

"Lord king," said the one who stood foremost, neither the oldest nor the youngest of them, but clearly the highest in rank. His robe was dyed with his city's famous purple and embroidered with gold. "The priests have spoken. The elders concur with them. There will be no Persian nor Macedonian within the walls of our city."

Alexander stood facing him, wearing the lionskin that he favored, with its head for a helmet. He looked odd to Meriamon's eyes, half man, half lion, yet all Alexander. His high color was up, between the wind and his temper, but his voice was quiet. "Even if I come alone, with only a friend or two? Even if I promise to touch nothing and offend no one, and worship the god as his priests prescribe?"

"The priests prescribe that there be no sacrifice," the envoy said.

"Herakles is my forefather," said Alexander. "I wish to do him honor in his own city."

"If honor is what you wish to give him," said the envoy, "then you may give it in Old Tyre, down the shore yonder. There's a temple to Melqart there; its priests would be pleased to receive you."

"New Tyre is Herakles' city," Alexander said, still quietly, still calmly. "He built it with his own hands; he sanctified it with his presence."

The envoy's head shook from side to side. "Lord king, we regret to oppose you, but we must. Our laws require it. We cannot permit a foreigner in our city. You are welcome here and in Old Tyre; you may sacrifice to your ancestor with our priests' blessing. But not in our city."

"I see," said Alexander softly, barely to be heard above

the song of the wind. He was bulking larger the more quietly he spoke, the fire in him rising higher. "The king makes sacrifice here as in our country. You will not have this king inside your walls. Will you not reconsider?"

"We cannot," the envoy said.

Alexander's head lifted. The color had left his face. His eyes were brilliant in it, open wide and fixed on the city. "I will make the sacrifice," he said. "You have my word on it."

"Then you will wait long," said the envoy. He too had gone pale under beard and bronzing. Alexander's pallor was rage. The envoy's was anger, and more than anger, fear. But he would not yield; no more than Alexander.

"I will wait as long as it takes me," Alexander said. "Nor will I move until I have made my sacrifice."

Even his own people gasped at that. They could see the city on its rock and the stretch of sea between, and the ships in it, tiny under the immensity of the walls. Twenty fathoms and five, that was the height of them. No one had ever scaled them. No one had ever taken them.

Alexander smiled at them. "I'll take you," he said. "I'll have my sacrifice."

• ELEVEN •

"It's not mad," said Ptolemy. "It makes perfect sense."

"Lunatic's sense." Niko was disgusted. "Have you taken a good look at the place? Half a mile of water between us and it, no fleet to our names, and our king is crazy-mad because somebody told him he couldn't have what he wanted."

"I'll say he's angry," Ptolemy said. "He always did hate to be crossed. But he hasn't lost any wits to speak of. Think, for once. Remember what we're doing here.

There's a whole fleet out there, taking its pay in Persian gold, and most of it built and crewed by Phoenicians. The Tyrian king is in it, and you can be sure he's near the head of it. He can come in here with a whole army, keep it supplied, land it when he's minded to fight and keep it nicely out of range when he's minded to rest, and kill any chance we have of breaking the Persians' yoke."

"I know that!" Niko snapped. "I'll wager I know it better than you. But he can't take Tyre. What's he going to do it with? Wings?"

"He has a plan," Ptolemy said. "You watch."

"Yes," said Niko. "And for how long?"

"As long as it takes," his brother said.

Meriamon did not remember coming this far down the shore. She had been up by the women's end of the camp. Now she was past the place where the king had been, leaning against a spear that someone had thrust into the sand and apparently forgotten, listening to Niko and his brother. There were other people about. They were all shouting, saying most of the same things that either Ptolemy or Niko had said. Most of them were of Niko's mind.

The king was gone. So were the Tyrians, rowing away in one of their boats, and no doubt glad to have escaped alive. The king's anger had a scent like hot iron, hanging in the air, making men's eyes roll white.

"He can't do this," she said.

Her voice was clear in a moment of silence. Niko spun about, quick as a startled cat. She met his eyes. "He can't do it," she said again. "He can't stay here. He'll have to move heaven and earth to take this city. What will happen to Khemet?"

"What in the gods' name are you doing here?"

His temper did not trouble her at all. Even with the spear to hold her up, she was swaying. Her knees had had enough. So, on reflection, had her hands. But she wanted an answer. "What of my country? What will become of it while Alexander salves his pride in Tyre?"

"Well," said Ptolemy. "It's been around for a while. It can wait a little longer."

"Months!" she cried. "Years. It's too long. It's—too—"

Niko caught her. She was surprised. She might have expected Ptolemy to do it, unhappy as Niko always was to be her nursemaid; and he had got out of it so neatly, abandoning her among the Parsa women. But he was there when she fell, keeping her from falling too hard, and then cursing because he did not have enough arms to lift her. His brother did it for him, making nothing of her little bulk.

"It's too long," she said.

"It cursed well might be," said Niko, "if you kill yourself fretting over it. I'll have those bitches' necks, by gods I will. Letting you out when you're half dead, burning up with fever, and how in Hades you walked this far—"

"I don't know," she said, "how I got here. Aren't you happy? He'll kill them instead of you, if I don't get better."

"*I'll* kill *you*," he gritted.

"There," said Ptolemy. He was worried; his brow furrowed when he looked at Meriamon. But he was amused, too. "There now. I'll get you back where you belong, m'lady, and as for you, Niko, maybe this time you'd better keep a watch on her. She's right, you know. You did dump her off on Barsine. I'd hate to hear what the king would say if he knew."

"He knows," said Meriamon. "He came. He didn't say anything. Except I'm too thin."

"You are." Ptolemy began to walk. His stride was long and firm, but he carried her lightly, nodding now and then to men who passed. They stared. She could feel their eyes, a raw pain, for she had no shadow to protect her. She had forgotten about her shadow. She struggled.

"No," she said. "Not back there."

"What, with the women?" Ptolemy frowned down at her. "You're best with them, you know. Barsine even studied medicine for a while, with Greek tutors. Thaïs can't take care of you as well as that."

"No," said Meriamon.

"Delirious," Niko said. "She was like that when she woke up and saw where she was. Wild. They had to dose her."

"No," Meriamon said again. "I won't go back there. Don't take me back there!"

She was weak, but she was stronger maybe than Ptolemy had expected. She almost broke his hold. He gasped: her elbow had caught his ribs.

His arms clamped tight. She could hardly breathe. Her hair was out of its plaits, snarled across her face. Her arms were trapped; she could not push it away. Shaking her head made her dizzy. Her stomach heaved.

Even for that he did not let her go. He would need a clean chiton.

"That does it," he said. "I'm taking her to Philippos. Unless," he said to her with an edge of irony, "your highness objects?"

She had no words in her. Nor fear; nor flight. Philippos was not the Parsa. More than that, she did not care for.

Meriamon should have not gone down to the water. She knew that very well. She did not need everyone telling her, repeatedly, whenever she was awake enough to hear it.

She almost died. They told her that, too. Often. Did they think she did not know? She knew the dark, and the long light, and the voices without words. She knew the dry land and the empty sky. She knew the shadows that passed there. She knew death. She had walked its edges all her life, in the silence behind the gods' commands.

They did not want her yet. Death and his demons would have taken her in spite of them, but Philippos was stronger than they. He would have been a priest in Khemet. He had the gift and the art, and the strength of will. He was a greater healer of bodies than she; what he might have been as a healer of souls, she could well see.

When he was not there, Kleomenes was. He never said much, and that was astonishing, for Kleomenes loved to chatter. He watched, he listened, he did what needed doing. Something about his touch woke a truth in her. Even on the edge of the dark she smiled. Why, the boy was in love with her. Poor thing, he should have had better sense.

Niko, now: Niko had sense. He slept by her pallet, when he slept at all. He gave what help he could, and neither Philippos nor Kleomenes was shy about asking for it. He was gentler than she would have believed, if she had not been the object of it. He was certainly not in love with her.

Kleomenes' adoration was like a hand on her skin, constant, unvarying, sometimes comforting, often uncomfortable. Niko was presence simply, no worship in it. Far down in the dark she was aware of him, standing like a stone among the shadows, guarding her. When Philippos fought his battle for her life, Niko was there. When Philippos went away to rest, Niko stayed. She was his duty. He had forsaken her once. He would not do it again.

He was there when she decided to wake. His presence was part of why she did it then. Philippos was too strong, Kleomenes too mutely worshipful. Niko was there, that was all. She opened her eyes on lamplight and said, "I'm hungry."

He was sitting by her bed with Sekhmet in his lap. He did not start or stare, but something in him eased perceptibly. He set the cat beside her, got up, went out. She heard him calling, and people answering. In a little while he came back. "You'll get a posset," he said. "For now, drink this."

He held her head while she drank sweet water from a cup. She was lying down again, dizzy with effort, before it struck her. One arm had held her, the other hand had held the cup.

He was still in bandages, but the sling was off, and the splints.

"That long?" she asked, staring at it.

"Yes." He sounded almost angry. Impatient, maybe. She was too weak to tell.

"How—"

"I'm not supposed to tell you."

She tried to sit up. She got her head up, but that was as far as it went.

"Half a month," he said, snapping it. "Don't get up. You'll kill yourself."

"No," she said. "I won't die now." But neither did she try to move. She lay for a while, simply breathing. She would never have believed that she could be so weak, or so tired for doing so little. And so long. Anything could have happened. Oh, gods—anything at all.

She clung to calm against the easy panic, the easier and far more frightening tears. "We're still in Tyre?"

"Still."

She sighed. Her heart ceased its hammering. Her eyes cleared. She looked about. "I'm in Thaïs' tent."

"You wouldn't stay in Barsine's."

Clearly he had no sympathy with that. She could not imagine why he would. Sekhmet stretched purring along her side, welcoming her back to the living. In a little while she would stroke the cat. She was too tired now. She would sleep, she thought. Real sleep, healing sleep, with no dreams in it.

It was slow, learning to live again. Sometimes she wondered why she bothered. Here was Alexander, and there was Tyre, and neither would give in to the other, though the stars fell. Alexander would never come to Egypt. He would live here and he would die here, because all men died, even men who were begotten of gods.

But life, having won its way with her, was not about to let her go. She slept, and sleep healed her. She ate, and strength came back. She learned to walk again, slow stumbling steps, leaning on Nikolaos or Kleomenes or Thaïs. The hetaira had been there in the dark, too, but not so often and not so strong as the others; healing was not at all her gift. Living was, and laughing, and making Meriamon remember both.

She was the one who saw to it that Meriamon had a real bath, well before anyone else might have allowed it, and salvaged her hair. "They wanted to cut it," she said, "but I wouldn't let them. Men. They'd never think of anything so simple as a pair of braids. They've got to hack and cut, and never mind the consequences."

Meriamon would not have minded it if they had. Her hair was filthy, and even braids had not kept it from knotting. Why it had not acquired a nest of vermin, she could not imagine. It was pleasant, she admitted, to lie in the warm water and be stroked like a cat, and then to lie in a soft robe while Thaïs and Phylinna between them combed out her hair. Wet, it came halfway to her waist. She was surprised. It had grown. The sickness had dulled it; it would probably come out in handfuls, and then she would have to cut it off in spite of Thaïs.

She rested her cheek on her arm. In spite of the effort of getting up and having a bath, she was not extraordinarily tired. Before Phylinna came to help Thaïs with the combing, she had opened the tent's flap and tied it there, letting in sun and a bit of breeze. It was warmer than Meriamon had expected. There was nothing much to see outside but the tent across the way, and a dog or two asleep in the sun, and now and then a soldier or a servant. Those might have lingered if her guardsman had not appeared, looming, saying nothing, but encouraging them to go about their business.

One of them came and did not retreat. He was almost as tall as Niko but even narrower, rawboned and gangling, coming in right over Niko's spear, and grinning down at

Meriamon. "Now I know you're well," said Kleomenes. "You've taken a bath."

"Was I so repulsive?" Meriamon asked.

"No," he said, taken aback. "Oh, no. Not at all."

She swallowed a sigh. She did not know that she was ready to be adored, even by Kleomenes. Fortunately for her peace of mind, he sat with every appearance of ease, ignoring Niko's lowering looks, and considered her with a physician's eye.

"You'll do," he decided. "I won't tell Philippos you got wet. You know what he would say."

Meriamon did. "Did he send you?"

"Well," said Kleomenes. "Yes. In a manner of speaking. He wanted to know how you were. I came to see. You're looking very well," he said, "considering."

Considering that she looked like a years-old corpse. There was no flesh on her bones at all. She had not tried to find a mirror. She would be all eyes and cheekbones.

"You should see what the king is doing," Kleomenes said. He had been talking for a while; she had slipped off, as she still sometimes did. It did not seem to trouble him. "He's going to take Tyre, you know. He's sworn it. He's got a whole army of workers out there, people from Old Tyre and people from the villages, and his engineers, and every soldier he can spare from guard duty."

She did not want to know. But she asked, because she could not help herself. "Why?"

"People say he's out of his mind," said Kleomenes. "Tyre is an island. Well enough, he says, but not when Alexander is done with it. He'll build a bridge. He'll make it a leg of the land. Then it will have to surrender like all the rest of this country, and be a part of it."

Meriamon closed her eyes. Mad. Indeed. Obsessed.

Thaïs spoke over her. "He won't have much trouble on this side. But the water is deep out toward the island, and the Tyrians won't sit still to wait for him."

"He'll do it," said Kleomenes, whose adoration of the

king was older and even stronger than his worship of
Meriamon. "He's got crews out in the mountains, cutting
down trees, and people tearing down Old Tyre for its
stones—they're huge; they must have been laid by giants.
You can already see what his bridge will be, from the beginning he's made."

"Show me."

At first Meriamon did not think that anyone heard her.
Then Kleomenes said, "What?"

"Show me what he's done," she said. "Take me to the
bridge."

"Maybe in a few days," said Kleomenes. "When you're
stronger."

"Now," said Meriamon.

She had her way. Kleomenes was not happy, but there
were uses for adoration. Thaïs shrugged, Phylinna fretted,
but to no purpose. Niko said nothing. He glared at the boy,
the worse for that Kleomenes had to carry her. Niko's arm
was hardly strong enough for that yet, if it would ever be.

They made a fair procession, with Sekhmet in the lead,
head and tail high, and the rest of them following.
Meriamon was wrapped like the dead, as thick and almost
as tight. One of the servants had a sunshade, which she did
not like at all; she wanted, needed, that warmth on her
face, that brightness in her eyes, though they burned and
teared with the strength of it.

It was Niko who understood. He got rid of the shade, if
not the servant. He set himself in the woman's place, still
without a word. Meriamon was glad of him. He was an
anchor in the turning of the world, even with a scowl on
his face.

The wind was cold but it was clean, once they came to
the sea. She breathed it in, drinking deep. She felt a little
stronger; as if, almost, she could get down and walk.
Maybe when she came to the bridge she would.

While she was sick the camp had moved south toward

Old Tyre, setting itself between the town and the shore opposite the island. It was a fair distance for Kleomenes, farther than she had expected, but he managed it. He was sweating in the cold and breathing hard as they followed the sounds of hammering and sawing and the beating of drums to the king's bridge. Men were shouting and some were singing, and there was a startling amount of laughter.

That was Alexander. He was in the middle of them in nothing much but a hat, lending a hand wherever they needed one. He seemed to be everywhere at once. Now far down the road urging on the team of mules that dragged in yet another great fallen cedar, now on the shore with a handful of his engineers, drawing with a stick in the smoothed sand, now out on the mole itself, clambering over the stones and timbers, perching at the very end with the water lapping his feet. It was a fair few furlongs already, though wider as yet than it was long, a blunt finger pointing toward Tyre.

Wherever Alexander was, people smiled wider, moved faster, worked harder. He warmed them like a hearthfire, just by being with them.

Kleomenes set Meriamon carefully on the sand, out of the way of the men but close enough to see what they did. He flung himself beside her and occupied himself with simply breathing. The others, after a moment's pause, wandered off toward the bridge. Except Niko. He stayed on his feet, spear in hand, on guard. Sekhmet rather spoiled the picture, draped as she was over his shoulder.

Meriamon watched Alexander's men build Alexander's bridge. So great a labor already, and so little of the whole; and the city waiting, silent behind its walls, haughty and impregnable. They would fight when the time came. Ships were running in and out of the harbors, the Sidonian north of the mole's line, the Egyptian south of it: bringing in provisions for the siege. Often their sailors mocked the men on the shore, laughing and jeering and even, more than once, relieving themselves in long arcs over the bows.

"We piss on you!" they shouted in gutter Greek. "Come up to the walls and see! Right in your faces, bully-boys. Right in your kinglet's eye."

"Want to bet on it?" That was Alexander's voice, high and sharp and unmistakable; and he was laughing.

"Surely," one of them yelled back. "What's the stakes?"

"Your hide," said Alexander, "and your city thrown in."

The ship had come far in in its captain's bravado, so far that it nigh ran aground. He had to scramble back out to deeper water, with the Macedonians jeering him on. No one thought to shoot, though it would have been a fair spearcast, or an easy shot with a bow.

Not yet, thought Meriamon. They would remember soon enough. Then the blood would flow.

She was very tired, but she had no desire to sleep. She lay in her nest of sand. Sekhmet stalked a flock of seabirds, sand-colored cat against sand-colored shore.

She closed her eyes for a moment. When she opened them, Alexander was striding toward her, windblown and ruddy-faced and sheened with sweat. He should have been reeking. There was no scent on him but salt and sea and clean wool. He looked as if he wanted to pick her up and hug her, or maybe shake her for daring so much so soon.

The strength of him was almost more than she could stand. It rocked her where she lay.

He dropped down beside her, boylike, half grinning, half frowning. "You shouldn't be here."

"No," she said.

The grin conquered the frown. "Of course you had to do it. I would. I did when I got sick swimming in the Kydnos. Philippos was beside himself."

"I'm not afraid of Philippos."

"Nor was I," said Alexander. "I should have been. I got sicker the first time I tried anything. But then I got stronger." He eyed her. "I've seen you looking better."

She laughed. It was weak, but it was honest mirth. "I

look like creeping death. I don't mind. Much. I never had any looks to lose."

"Don't say that," said Alexander.

"Why not? It's true."

"I'll never understand modesty," Alexander said. He stretched out, propped on his elbow. He was fully at his ease, but he could see everything that happened where his men were. His eyes never rested, no more than his mind.

"You were there," she said. "When I was sick."

"Once or twice," he said. "You had us worried."

She took no notice of that. "You were in the light. I didn't know it was you; and yet I did. Do you know how strong you are?"

She did not mean in body. His eyes narrowed a little; his brows drew together. "I prayed," he said. "I made sacrifice. I didn't think your Imhotep would mind that I called him Asklepios."

"Or Eshmun?" she asked.

He shrugged a little. "I sent to the temple in Sidon. The priests said that you had your own gods, and your own power against sickness."

"So I do," said Meriamon. She turned her eyes from him toward the work he had begun. "It seems you have forgotten them."

"No," Alexander said.

"This is not forgetting?"

He was still. His voice was soft. Not as it had been with the Tyrian embassy, not quite. But it was not a voice that one could argue with. "When I slept, the night before I came to Tyre, I dreamed. A man came to me. He was a big man, but not so big as I might have expected. He carried a club; he wore a lion's skin.

"Of course I knew his name. 'Herakles,' I said. 'Do I dream you, or is this a sending?'

" 'If you know my name, you know the rest of it,' he said.

"That made me laugh," said Alexander, "which was hardly respectful, but he laughed with me.

" 'You know what you have to do,' he said. 'This city is yours; I name you my heir.'

" 'Even if I have to take it by force?' I asked him.

" 'Even so,' said Herakles."

Alexander paused. Meriamon did not say anything. "You see," he said. "I dream, too; and I dream true. This I have to do. When it is done, I shall go on to Egypt."

She could argue with a god if she thought he needed it. "How long will that be? How many days, Alexander? How many months wasted because you took a vow in anger?"

"I was angry," he said. "I was hardly out of my wits. Tyre is strong enough to break me, unless I break it first. And Tyre serves the Persian king."

"Tyre refused to give you what you wanted."

"So it did," he said lightly enough. "It will pay for that. But even if it hadn't earned a drubbing, I wouldn't want it at my back. That's necessity, Mariamne, and soldier's sense. Even beyond a god's will."

"It holds you back from Egypt," she said.

"Not forever."

"Long enough."

He tossed his hair out of his face. He was a boy, after all, however brilliant, however much a king. "I'm going to take Tyre," he said.

"Or Tyre will take you."

"No one will ever conquer me," said Alexander.

"No man," Meriamon said, "maybe. There are still the gods. There is still, at the end of them, death."

No cloud shadowed the sun, but it dimmed for a moment, and the wind bit cold. Then Alexander laughed, sharp and short. "Death comes for every man. I'll live while I can, and hold my honor, and keep my word. When Tyre is mine, I'll follow you to Egypt."

• TWELVE •

The slow days turned from winter into spring. Alexander's causeway stretched toward Tyre. Meriamon was an emptied thing: a woman without a shadow, a priestess without her gods, a mage bereft of her magic. She was all winter, and no spring in her, though her body healed and grew strong again.

And yet, like winter in this stony country, she kept in her a memory of spring. Alexander would not speak to her, nor move, nor do anything but lay siege to an impregnable city. She would not pine for that. She was too stubborn. Since death did not want her, she would cling to life, and get back her strength, and wait.

Someone else was waiting, and in far less calmness than she. Meriamon could see that for herself, summoned to Barsine's tent and let in without even a judicious hour's delay. She had not gone willingly. Her memory of waking there, sick to death and wild beyond reason, could still trouble her in the dark before dawn. Trapped, suffocating, surrounded by enemies—no matter that they had meant her well. Her head knew that. Her heart knew only that they were Parsa, and they had taken her and held her.

Still, when the messenger came, the same young eunuch who had fetched her first from the surgeons' wagon, back before Sidon, Meriamon bent her head and followed him. Barsine was no enemy except by blood; and Alexander loved her in his fashion. No woman would ever be the other half of him. That was given long ago, and to Hephaistion. But she had known him since he was young, she pleased him, maybe he even reckoned her a friend.

Barsine's tent was as Meriamon remembered it: dim, shadowed, laden with the scent of Persian unguents. No light ever came there, unless it was lamplight. There was a new thing here and there, a box carved of cedar, a lamp bright with gilding, a vase with a frieze of women weaving and spinning. That was not a Persian thing; it came, maybe, from Athens. Thaïs had one like it, but on hers the women were dancing to the music of flute and tambour.

Barsine had been sitting in the shadows. As Meriamon paused, half-blinded, trying to breathe in the heavy air, Barsine rose and came to embrace her. She had not expected that. She stiffened; eased with an effort, returned the embrace.

Barsine stood back, hands still on Meriamon's shoulders. "You're well again," she said. "But thin. Are they feeding you enough?"

Meriamon laughed. "They all say that," she said. "Alexander, too. Yes, they're feeding me. Too much. You'd think they were fattening me for the pot."

Barsine smiled. She led Meriamon to a chair and saw to it that she had wine and sweets as was proper. Meriamon had to eat and drink a little under those grave dark eyes. She was hungry after all; she drank most of the cup of wine and ate a whole cake, and nibbled on another, for the taste.

As she nibbled, she considered Barsine. The lady was even more beautiful than Meriamon remembered, and yet it was a different beauty. Her face seemed fuller, her eyes gentler. Her body, that had been nigh as slender as a boy's, was richer, softer.

What had caused it, Meriamon knew very well. She had known it the moment Barsine embraced her. "I suppose," she said, "that I should offer felicitations."

Barsine lowered her eyes. Her hand went to the swell of her belly. "You miss very little," she said.

"I could hardly have failed to notice this," said Meriamon. She paused. There was no delicate way to say it. "It is his?"

Barsine did not look up, but her eyes glittered under the long lashes. "You doubt it?"

"I can count," said Meriamon. "You're slim and you carry small, but you've been carrying since summer, or I know nothing of childbearing. This one was conceived in Mytilene, if certainly no earlier. Does Alexander know?"

"Yes," Barsine said. "He has promised to take up the child, even if it is a boy."

"As his heir?"

Barsine looked up then. Her eyes made Meriamon think of, of all people, Thaïs. The same clarity of purpose; the same spirit, startling in the Persian face. "Parmenion has come back. He hounds my lord without mercy. If my lord can offer him a child of my body, then my lord may have a little peace. For awhile. Until he gets one of his own."

"If I can count," Meriamon said, "what makes you think that no one else can do as well?"

"You are a woman," said Barsine.

"And a man wouldn't notice?" Meriamon sat back. The second cake was gone; she had eaten it without noticing. She wiped her fingers with the cloth the servant offered, dipped in warm water scented with citron. "Maybe he wouldn't, at that. As close as you keep yourself, as quiet as you can be, you can conceal the child until the time is ripe, and bring it out, and let people decide whose it is."

"Precisely," Barsine said. "And my lord can let it be known that I am bearing. He can come more seldom for it, and stay more briefly."

She said it calmly, but Meriamon saw the pain behind it. And knew it for what it was. "He's known from the beginning."

"I told him."

"Then—he never really—"

"He did," said Barsine, soft and fierce. "That first time. He did. But I had to tell him. I had lied enough in keeping silent and letting him love me once."

"And a Hellene won't touch a bearing woman," said Meriamon.

"He was angry," Barsine said. "But he forgave me. He loves to forgive, as he loves to give. He saw wisdom in what I had done."

Meriamon had her doubts of that. No doubt Barsine needed to believe it. "So he keeps coming back to you, and keeps up the pretense. He won't need to do it much longer."

"Unless he wishes."

There was a silence. Meriamon let it stretch. After a while she said, "You wanted me to know. Why?"

"I used you," said Barsine. "I lied, a little. I let you think that I was free to accept him."

"You were talking yourself into it," Meriamon said.

Barsine smoothed her skirt along her thigh, long, slow, focused on it. She had done much the same when she played the bashful beloved.

Parsa, thought Meriamon. Parsa, always, no matter that all her men had been Hellenes.

Slowly Barsine said, "I wanted to see what you were."

"And what was that?"

"His friend."

"And now?"

"You are still. You could be more. If you would."

Meriamon was calm. She should not have been, maybe. But this was too fierce a battle to fight in anger. "Are you asking me to do that?"

"No," said Barsine. Still smoothing her gown with those long fingers; still centered on it, eyes lowered, profile cut as clean as a carving in ivory. "He may not go to Egypt now. Will you do anything to force him?"

"If I can," said Meriamon, "yes."

"I could help you," Barsine said.

"Why?"

Barsine could not have expected that, even from

Meriamon. For a moment she looked up; for a moment her eyes met Meriamon's. "I mean no treachery."

"No?"

"I love Alexander," Barsine said.

Truth. But what was truth to a Persian?

"He admires you greatly," said Barsine, "even when he curses you for a stubborn fool. He means to do what you ask, when his pride has salved itself in Tyre. But if he dies here—"

"If he dies here, Persia is safe."

"I am Alexander's now," Barsine said. "Persia is no part of me."

"Persia is all of you."

Barsine's breath caught. "How you hate us!"

"Yes, I hate you," said Meriamon. "I hate everything that you are. You marched out of Persis. You trampled my country under your feet. You murdered our kings; you mocked our gods, or strove to make them your own."

"You are as proud as Alexander," said Barsine. "And no more sensible in it."

"I am of Egypt. No foreigner has ever ruled my people in peace."

"Yet you would make Alexander your king?"

"Alexander, we choose. Alexander rules by our gods' will."

"We rule by the will of Ahuramazda."

"That is no god of Egypt."

"That is the Truth."

And there, in the ringing silence, was the heart of it. "Your Truth is one," Meriamon said, "and unyielding, and unforgiving. Ours is many; it shifts, it changes, it takes new shapes as the world grows."

"There can be but one Truth. All else is the Lie."

"No," said Meriamon.

"Yes," Barsine said.

"You are Persian," said Meriamon. "You will never be aught but that. As I will never be aught but Egyptian. Alexander . . . he is always Alexander, and only Alexander, but that is as endlessly varied as the faces of my gods. Cambyses, Darius, Artaxerxes the accursed, Ochos who drove my father to his death—they came in their Truth, and laid its yoke on us, and wondered that we hated it, and through it hated them. Alexander will be our king, our pharaoh, our Great House of Egypt."

"If he succeeds in taking Tyre."

"If he does that," said Meriamon.

"Can you protect him?"

There. At last. Meriamon swallowed a sigh, a curse on Persian indirection. She could barely protect herself. But she said, "The gods watch over him."

"You are a sorceress," said Barsine. "You are very powerful, they say. Will you guard him against harm?"

"He is guarded," Meriamon said. Not knowing if she spoke the truth. A good priestess, she told herself, should trust the gods to look after their own.

She rose. She needed the sun and the clean air. "Guard yourself," she said, "and the child you carry."

Kleomēnes was waiting outside of Barsine's tent, trying to look as if he had just happened by. Niko was glowering at him, as usual. Niko did not approve of her lapdog, as he called the boy.

Meriamon walked past them both. Niko fell in behind her. He had the sense not to say anything. Kleomenes, who was younger, stretched to keep up, for she was striding swiftly. "What happened?" he wanted to know. "You look furious. Has somebody been at you?"

She did not answer. There were too many words in her; they fell over one another.

"It was Barsine, wasn't it?" he said. "She's jealous of you, everybody knows it. The king thinks too much of you to suit her. What did she say? I'll give her what for."

Meriamon stopped short. Kleomenes went on past her, caught himself, scrambled back. "Kleomenes," she said.

She kept it gentle, but there was iron in it. "I know perfectly well that you're running out on Philippos. Even if there is nothing much to do in the hospital now."

He looked like a whipped pup, all droop and wounded eyes. "But there *isn't* anything to do," he said.

"You are still Philippos' apprentice. He won't love me for luring you away from your duty."

"But—" said Kleomenes.

"Go," said Meriamon.

He went. He dragged his feet, he looked back often, he even shed a tear. She hardened her heart and her eyes. He heaved a mighty sigh and turned his back on her.

She had no pity to spare. She turned from the way he had taken and went to the horselines.

Her mare was there, accepting a grooming with queenly condescension. The Thracian grinned at Meriamon and bobbed his untidy head. One way and another they had both acquired names. The groom was Lampas, which was not the name his father had given him, but he liked it, and answered to it. The mare was Phoenix. Meriamon said their names to herself, anchoring herself with them, inclining her head to the groom and laying a hand on the mare's neck. Lampas grinned even wider. Phoenix snorted and shook her head.

"You ride?" Lampas asked.

"I ride," said Meriamon.

It did not matter where. Phoenix wanted to run. Meriamon let her.

Niko caught them not far from the Leontes, and that because Meriamon had stopped to let the mare graze. He was riding the bow-nosed gelding, which had no speed, but was almost the mare's match for endurance. He had a pack with him, and a full wineskin, and Sekhmet riding in the fold of his cloak.

Meriamon eyed him askance. He did not say anything.

He was armed, she noticed, with sword and spears. He at least, it seemed, was prepared for a journey.

She shrugged. Why not? She twitched the mare's head up. The river ran loud and high, leaping down from the mountain. Snow lay thick on them amid and above the deep green of cedars. Alexander's men were up there, cutting down the great trees for his causeway. Meriamon touched the mare into a canter, toward the cedars and the snow.

The long ride and the clean air did much to restore Meriamon to herself. She was still a woman without a shadow, but there was no pain in it, or none that mattered. As the way grew steep, the river forged its path through thickening trees, outriders of the forests of the Lebanon. The ground was deep with their castings, the air dizzying with their scent, strong and pure and green. The trees were small here, but small in a cedar of the Lebanon was as high as a tower, and great branches spreading wide like outstretched arms.

"They pray to your Zeus," Meriamon said, halting under one of them.

"Maybe they have their own gods," said Niko. He tilted his head back, measuring the tree with his eye. "Titans, maybe. These are trees the way giants are men."

"We don't have anything like them in Egypt."

"No one has anything like them." Niko swung his leg over the gelding's neck and slid to the ground. He had taken to riding with a smooth bit as Meriamon did, kinder by far than the monstrosities that the warhorses endured. The gelding seemed to like it; he browsed happily enough around it while Niko unslung the wineskin and held it out to Meriamon.

She drank and handed it back, holding the wine in her mouth, letting it go down slowly. It was good wine, well watered: as good as the king had.

She dismounted, stretching stiffened muscles. She was

thinner still than she needed to be; her bones jutted in uncomfortable places. She rubbed one that ached particularly, trying to be discreet about it. Of course Niko saw. The corner of his mouth twitched. She set her jaw and rubbed harder. He shrugged out of his pack and squatted to rummage in it, with Sekhmet offering advice.

Meriamon wandered a little, leading Phoenix; or maybe the mare led her. And wisely: the hill moderated its slope, and the trees paused suddenly, opening on a broad cleared space that rolled down to the river. Cutters had been there, but not for a season or more. Grass had grown over the stumps; from one sprouted a young cedar, no taller than Meriamon's knee, no thicker than her finger.

The mare strained against the bridle. Meriamon slipped the bit from its mooring and hobbled her with a bit of old rein and let her go. She set promptly to grazing, like a sensible beast.

Niko's gelding followed her soon enough, hobbled likewise and freed of his bridle. Niko came up beside Meriamon where she sat on a stump, with bread and a bit of cheese and more of the wine.

They ate in companionable silence, listening to the calling of birds in the wood and the cropping of horses in the meadow. Meriamon was tired, but it was a good tiredness, with wind in it, and sun, and her troubles left far behind. The sun was still high, warm on her face, warm enough that she pulled off her cap and unbuttoned her coat and let the wind cool her skin.

Niko got up after a while and went down to the river. He stooped to drink from it, and stayed there, trailing his hand in the swift water. He would not be mad enough to swim in it, surely. It was snow-cold.

He stood straight and let his cloak fall. Meriamon opened her mouth to shout at him, but he stayed on the bank, clasping his right arm to him as he often did, staring down at the rushing water. Sekhmet wove about his ankles. He gathered her up. She was almost the same color as he was.

Meriamon dragged her eyes back to the horses. They grazed side by side, peacefully, tails switching, now one, now the other. It was not, Meriamon thought, as if she had never seen a man before. And yet there was something about him standing there, that made her insides clench.

He was not handsome. He was, in fact, rather unabashedly homely. He had a nose like a ship's prow and a jaw like an outcropping of granite. But he was well made, if one liked them long and lean, and he moved like a good horse. He was a pleasure to watch.

It was spring, and she was lately come back from a long sickness, and her body knew very well what it was for. Nor did it care that Niko was the last man in the world who would want the likes of Meriamon. He was male, was he not? And young and strong even with his scarred and twisted hand, and good to look at, there in the sun, with the cat on his shoulder.

He came up from the river and stood by her. His cloak was in his hand. He said something. "What?" she said.

"Nothing," said Niko maddeningly. He spread the cloak on the ground and sat on it. He hardly looked at her. He could stare at her till her skin crawled, when he decided to be obvious about being on guard. When she would have liked him to notice her, he was oblivious.

"Kleomenes notices me," she said.

He glanced at her then, sharp with ill temper. "What?"

"Nothing," she said.

He slapped at a fly. It had bitten him. He rubbed his shin, muttering.

It was not the fly he was muttering at. "That puppy. What finally inspired you to chase him off?"

"He's been shirking his work," said Meriamon. "Philippos is a hard man as it is; Kleomenes doesn't need to make him harder."

"He could use a good tanning."

"Oh, come," Meriamon said. "He's not as bad as that. I've been teaching him as much as I can. He's a good pupil. Just ... persistent."

"Pestiferous."

"I'd think you'd like him," she said. "He's clever enough, and he wants to do well."

"He moons after you like a lovesick calf."

His voice was venomous. Meriamon looked at him in surprise. He glared at his foot, which he had freed of its shoe. There was nothing at all wrong with it.

"I suppose," said Meriamon, "he is a little exasperating. Young things are. They do grow out of it."

"Not that one," Niko said.

"Why, what's he ever done to you?"

"Nothing." Niko pushed himself to his feet. Sekhmet chose that moment to leap down from his shoulder. He stumbled over her; his foot turned.

He did not fall on his bad arm. Not quite. But he fell hard; hard enough to knock the breath out of him.

Meriamon did not even remember getting up. She was on the ground beside him, reaching for him.

He had not harmed himself. The bone was all but mended; muscle had withered as muscle did round a broken bone. It was not a pretty thing, but it was beautiful to eyes that knew what it had been. She laid his arm in her lap, working her fingers into the bleached and whitened skin. He gasped. His hand twitched. Stiffly; barely to be seen. But it moved. She bent the wasted fingers one by one, carefully, easing when his breath caught.

He was staring at it. His lips were set tight; sweat ran down his face. Pain. And he had not made a sound. He never did.

"It's healing," she said.

He turned his face away, refusing what that healing meant. A withered arm. A twisted hand.

"No," she said, firm enough to bring his head about. "You've let it wither so that the bone can knit. Now you'll make it strong. It's going to hurt," she said. "I don't deny it. But you'll have two hands again."

"One and a half," he said.

"More than that," said Meriamon. "It will never be as strong as it was before, that's true enough. It won't be useless, either. How strong does it have to be to carry a shield?"

Hope leaped in his eyes, but he knocked it down and sat on it. "Philippos said I'd be invalided out."

Her breath hissed between her teeth. "He said *what?*"

"He said I'd heal enough for light work, if I didn't force it. But I won't do any more fighting."

"When did he say that?"

"Does it matter?"

"Yes!" she snapped.

"Somewhere back there," Niko said.

"Before Sidon?"

He shrugged. "I suppose."

"And he hasn't said a word since?"

"He hasn't needed to."

Meriamon wanted to spit. "That—maddening—man! You, too. Both of you. He's got eyes as good as mine. He can see what I see."

"Scars."

"Miracles!" She struck his shoulder with her fist. "Don't you remember Eshmun's temple?"

"That was nonsense. It didn't do a thing."

"It did," said Meriamon. "Look at this! This should have rotted and come off. It's healing. It's mending where only a god could cause it to mend."

"If a god did it," said Niko with a curl of the lip, "why didn't he do it all at once, instead of dragging it on and on?"

"Maybe he wanted to teach you patience."

He glared. She glared back.

Why she did what she did next, she would never in her life be able to explain. It was the sun in her, and the green smell, and the heat of temper sparking between them. She bent down. She kissed him hard.

He tasted of wine and cedar. He smelled of himself: horses, wool, clean sweat.

She straightened. Her cheeks were burning hot. His were scarlet. All the way down to the neck of his chiton.

His arm was still in her lap. He reclaimed it. Carefully.

He would not look at her. She could hardly look at him. He disliked her intensely; he had made that clear long since. Now he would hate her.

Her guardsman was supposed to fall in love with her. Not she with her guardsman.

He stood. He could not get into his cloak as easily as he had got out of it. She had to help him. The shame of it thinned his lips and pinched his nostrils tight.

She started to turn away, looking toward the horses. He caught her.

She stood stiff and still.

"Why?" he asked her.

Her throat had locked shut. She drove words through it. "I don't know."

His hand did not let go. She could break his grip easily enough if she tried. "That's not an answer," he said.

"It's all I have."

She waited for him to say something more. He did not. He let her go. She went to catch her mare.

• THIRTEEN •

As Alexander's causeway drew near the walls of Tyre, the Tyrians roused to defend their city. They had catapults on the walls, and armament in plenty for them, and galleys that could row to within bowshot of the mole and harry the men who labored there. Bolts and arrows were bitter.

Fire arrows were deadly, catching in the timbers, flaring into wildfire. Then in the balance of the equinox a storm blew out of Hades and gnawed great gaps in the mole, that needed long days to mend.

"At least," said Alexander, "we haven't got the towers up, to be blown down again."

Towers indeed. They were Alexander's inspiration—divine madness, people said, but he and his engineers built two of them out of wood from the forests and walled them with raw hides against fire. There had been siege-towers before, but never like this: as high as Tyre's walls, twenty fathoms and five, so high that men who climbed them came to the summit winded and reeling, and looking down felt as high as eagles.

If they had time to look down. Men who mounted the dizzy height went up to man the catapults against the engines in Tyre, and to shoot across the dwindling stretch of sea, every day a few lengths smaller, a few lengths closer to the frown of the walls. Men below manned catapults against the ships and held them off, while the workers on the mole widened and lengthened it and made it strong enough to last, Alexander said, until the world's end.

There had never been such siegecraft. But Tyre had its own arts in war. The Tyrians, seeing the towers rising level with their own, prepared a counterstroke.

They took a horse-transport, a wallowing big-bellied tub of a ship, and they fenced its decks with dry timber and filled it with tinder: broken branches, shaved wood, sulfur and pitch. They lashed yardarms to its masts and hung from them cauldrons filled with naphtha. Then they weighted the stern until it sank deep in the water and the bow lifted high, high enough to rise over the causeway.

Alexander's men saw it coming, towed by galleys. Catapult shot, bowshot, took a toll of the crews, but there were too many, too well protected. The ship's own crew grinned and jeered from the shielded decks. The galleys paused just within catapult-range, as if to gather their strength. Then, with a shout, the oars flew up; paused; swept down. The galleys leaped forward. The ship lurched in their wake. A torch flared high on the foredeck. Others kindled from it. The men on it scattered, dipping, darting. A handful shinned up the masts and out across the yard-arms, and dropped their torches into the cauldrons. One caught with a rush. The sailor above it dropped, plunging into the sea. The other cauldrons, slower, burned with a steadier fire, their kindlers diving as the first one had, but smoother, swimming hard for haven.

The crew below dropped over the sides one by one. One lingered longest: the captain, he would be, with his long plaited beard and his arms heavy with gold. The many scattered fires sputtered, wavered, seemed to ponder. All at once and all together, they leaped up.

The captain poised on the rail. It was smoldering; sparks sprang thick about him. He leaped, cutting a clean arc, sleek as a dolphin.

Even as he struck the water, the ship struck the cause-way at the foot of a tower. Men on the mole sprang forward with spears, timbers, anything that came to hand. Arrows rained about them. Tyre had unleashed a fleet, boats like cockleshells but full of armed men, running up the mole, springing into battle.

On board the fireship, one of the yardarms broke. The cauldron tumbled down, spraying fire. Then another; then another.

Someone had the sense to bolt for shore, to gather buckets and bails and cauldrons, to muster a rank of men to quench the fire. But the Tyrians had overrun the causeway. One of the towers was alight. As the line of Macedonians charged down the mole, the other sparked and smoldered and caught. Men boiled out of it, full into the army of Tyrians. They, massing, had fallen on the palisade that protected the towers, and torn it down.

Alexander's voice rose high above the uproar. Gathering his men, driving them forward, cursing the enemy with inventiveness that won grins even in the heat of the fight.

He drove the Tyrians back into the sea. But they had won their purpose. His towers burned like torches. All his engines, the timbers drawn up for the last stretch of the mole, the tools and the devices and far too many of the builders, smoldered into ashes.

"I'm not giving up now," said Alexander.

He was filthy, covered with soot, and smarting with burns, but that was nothing to the anger that burned in him. He would not have let himself be looked after at all, but he came to the hospital carrying one of the worst wounded, and Meriamon caught him before he could escape.

"I won't give up," he said. He was not talking to her at all. He was burning, and yet his fever was all of the spirit. Rage. Outrage. Mere men had dared to thwart Alexander.

"They burned my towers," he said. "They destroyed my engines. They killed my men. They dared. They *dared*—"

Meriamon got his chiton off. It was half burned to bits, and the other half was torn and tattered. He had not even had armor on. He had been on the shore when the attack began, contriving something intricate with his chief engineer. He had had his sword—no Macedonian would go anywhere without one. And, fortunately for his mobility, he had been wearing solid shoes, a bit of sense that he had learned from hard experience, taking splinters and worse from scrambling over rough-cut timbers. The soles were scorched almost through, but they had held.

The high color of his face was not all temper. He had burned it, more on one side than on the other, and singed his eyebrows. Blisters were rising along his neck and shoulder. His hands were burned, not badly, but when he came to himself he would hurt.

"I built those engines once," he said. "I'll build them again. I'll build them higher, harder, stronger. I'll show those sons of dogs what it is to make war against Alexander."

Meriamon set to work with cool cloths and salve. One of the wounded men was shrieking. He had come in among the first, a charred and writhing thing, faceless and handless but not, yet, voiceless. Naphtha had rained down on him and scoured his flesh away. The gods had not seen fit to take him.

"They shall pay," said Alexander. "They shall pay in blood."

She salved his hands and wrapped them in soft bandages. He did not see her. His anger was all that there was, a fire hotter than any that had burned on his causeway. Pride had driven him to build it, but wrath ruled him now, and would rule him after. If he could ever have withdrawn from this madness, that hope was gone. The Tyrians had burned it with his towers.

"Stubborn," said Meriamon. "Stubborn *fool*."

She waited to say it, though it rose up in her till she thought she would burst. She did all that she could for the wounded. She looked after the simply sick, and the odd mishap. She put Kleomenes to bed, doing it bodily, while he protested that he was perfectly able to keep on working—nodding even as he said it. Niko tripped the boy neatly and dropped him into his blankets, and sat on him until he fell asleep.

She exchanged bared-teeth grins with the one of the other boys whom Kleomenes' racket had managed to wake, and ducked through the tentflap. It was almost dawn. The camp was as quiet as it ever was, no hammering and singing from the causeway, no sounds of revelry from the tents. Somewhere over toward Old Tyre a cock crowed.

She was bone-tired, but there was no sleep in her. Sekhmet came, a shadow out of shadows, and wove about her ankles. She gathered the cat in her arms and turned to glare at the looming bulk that was the king's tent. "Stubborn, obstinate, pigheaded idiot."

"Who, Kleomenes?"

She directed her glare at Niko. "You know perfectly well who it is."

Niko shrugged. She heard it more than saw it: a rustle of cloth, a creaking of leather, a clinking of metal on metal. He was wearing his corselet, had put it on when word first came of the fight, and not taken it off again. They could do that, these Macedonians; live in armor, and never admit to noticing how it itched and chafed.

"Alexander is Alexander," Niko said.

"You're all as blind mad as he is."

"Probably."

She hissed, sharp and impatient. What had happened under the cedars had not changed anything. He was still Niko: stubborn, obstinate, pigheaded, and given to sulks. For all the difference it made, she might never have kissed him at all.

It was a mercy, she supposed. He could have fled from her, demanded another posting, gone back to Macedon, even. Instead he stayed, and was her guardsman, and was no different than he had ever been.

She walked. She did not much care where. Niko followed where her shadow had been. Before sickness took all the magic from her.

No. Not all of it. Only that part of it which made her more than a minor priestess of a foreign god. She was still a healer of sorts, still a companion to the Bastet-on-earth who purred in her arms, still a pharaoh's daughter.

Dawn lightened as she walked through the camp. It touched the edges of the mountains; it spread long across the sea. In a little while the king would come out to make the morning's sacrifice. Then the crews would go down to the causeway and set to work again, making nothing of fire and death and the enemy's assault. Alexander would have thought of something new to protect them, a new wall, a new shield, a strengthened guard. Alexander was always thinking of new ways to win a battle. He was like a god in that, or like a madman. Or was there any difference?

Meriamon paused on the eastern edge of the camp. The splendor of the morning was in her suddenly, filling her so full that she staggered. Strong arms caught her. One was stronger than the other, but not so much now, not so evident. She did not look at him, did not try to free herself. The boat of the sun lifted above the horizon, far and far behind the mountains' wall.

The shadows withered and fled. All but one. Running long and low out of the wake of the sun, sulfur-eyed, laughing with jackal-jaws agape, rising man-high, Macedonian-high, weaving and dancing about her, her shadow, her lost magic, coming with the sun to make her whole again.

As whole as she could be when she was not in Khemet.

The long light of morning spread about her. She stepped out of Niko's grasp. He did not try to hold her. Nor had he dropped her, or thrust her away. She could admire him for that.

"You're shining," he said. "Like a lamp in a dark room."

"Am I?" she asked him.

"Yes." His eyes drifted toward her shadow, danced warily back to her face. "Why?"

His favorite question. This time she could answer. "The gods willed it."

"Why now?"

"The gods know."

"You," he said, "can be infinitely exasperating."

She laughed. She had not done that in much too long. "Then I'm a match for the rest of you."

"*We* don't—" He did not finish it. Wise man. "It's easy to forget," he said. "What you are."

She did not say anything to that.

He shook himself, rattling his armor. "Well. You're still human enough. Are you hungry?"

Her stomach answered for her, loudly. That made him laugh. "Come on, then. Let's go badger the cooks."

Hellenes. She would never understand them. Stark awe one moment, laughing mockery the next, and an explanation for everything. Niko explained her to herself over bread sopped in honeyed wine, sitting in front of Thaïs' tent, with Sekhmet making her own breakfast of a fresh-caught mouse. "It's obvious what it is," he said. "You needed a sign that you haven't failed with Alexander. The gods want him here. So . . . that . . . came back to you." He paused. Even he was not ready to put a name to her shadow. "Shouldn't that make it easier to bear the waiting?"

"No," she said.

He was not listening. "I wonder what Aristotle would say? Not that I studied much with him, but Ptolemy used to tell me about their lessons, and the king is always talking about them. Reason and logic are everything to Aristotle. He'd even impute reason to the acts of the gods."

"Gods don't need to be reasonable," Meriamon said.

"But they are," said Niko. "We just don't see it, because our sight is too limited. If we could comprehend the mind of Zeus, we'd be Zeus ourselves."

"That's hubris."

He widened his eyes at her.

"I know what that means," she said. "Is your Aristotle that proud of his intelligence, that he'd claim to know the mind of a god?"

"Aristotle says that the world is a rational thing, and reason is the chief faculty of a man."

"Not of a woman?"

"Women," said Niko, "are the offspring of a flawed seed. Having no reason of their own, they submit to the rule and reason of the male."

Meriamon laughed aloud. "Aristotle says *that?*"

"Aristotle is the wisest philosopher in Greece."

"Ah," she said. "A philosopher. Wisdom's own sweet friend. I'm sure, if he used his eyes instead of his reason, he'd see what a fool he is."

Niko glared. "If Alexander heard you say that—"

"Alexander is a fool, too," said Meriamon. "All men are fools. The world is reasonable? The world is logical? Not that I've ever seen."

"You are a woman and a foreigner. How do you know what you can see?"

"I have eyes," she said.

"But do you understand what they tell you?"

She looked at him. Simply looked. His eyes shifted and wavered and dropped. But he said, "You're not a philosopher. You don't understand."

"And you are?"

"Well," he said. "No. But it's a Greek thing. We Macedonians are Greeks, when it comes down to it. That's why Alexander took so well to Aristotle's teaching. He's got the mind and the temperament for it."

"I haven't," said Meriamon. "I wouldn't want it."

"Why should you?"

She thought of throwing the dregs of her wine in his face. Arrogant, muleheaded Hellene. She set down her cup instead and said, "I want a bath. You might think about one yourself."

She did not wait to hear what he said to that. The servants were ready with the water and the basin, and Phylinna was waiting, as she was every morning, for Thaïs never rose earlier than midday if she could help it.

Meriamon was glad to wash off the dirt and the sweat and the stains of a long day and a longer night; and with them a little of her temper.

It was joy beyond expression to have her shadow back; to reach within and find its presence in place of echoing absence. But in the end it altered nothing. It brought her no closer to Khemet.

She was not surprised to find who waited for her when she came out, clean and combed and dressed and beginning to feel the tug of sleep. She had been expecting it; avoiding it.

Barsine's eunuch bowed low, with a slant of dark eyes toward her shadow. It lay quiescent. Where it had been, it was not telling. It would not be leaving again that it knew of.

Meriamon inclined her head and waited.

"Lady," the eunuch said. "My lady asks . . ."

Meriamon sighed. "I come," she said.

The tent was the same. It never changed. The air never stirred, the women never moved, except to go from bed to outer chamber and back. It was a matter of great moment to step outside and see the sun, a deed of high daring to wrap oneself in veils and go down to the market. Two of them would not be doing that again, Meriamon suspected. She was almost sorry for them, Parsa though they were.

She did not see them in the outer chamber, in which she waited for an interminable while. In the inner was only Barsine and, settling at her feet, the eunuch.

Barsine at least had changed. She was close to her time now, hugely swollen but serene. She looked like an image of a goddess, sitting in the carved and rug-swathed chair, wrapped in a great robe of purple thickly woven with gold.

Her eyes were clear still, regarding Meriamon with grave interest. "You look well," she said.

"I am well," said Meriamon.

"So his majesty tells me."

Jealousy? Meriamon wondered. But there was none that she could see. Only interest, and if not warmth, then something like concern.

"I hope," said Meriamon, "that my nurses haven't paid too high a price for letting me escape."

"The king dealt with them," Barsine said.

"Mercifully?"

"Very," said Barsine. "He sent them back with escort to their fathers. There was no place for fools in his army, he told them. Maybe the Great King would have better use for them."

Meriamon drew a slow breath. "That was no punishment."

"No? Their fathers might not choose to take them back. They had been captives, after all; and the world knows what barbarians do to the women they have taken."

"Not Alexander."

"The world knows him but little yet. They see the barbarian, no more. And he is so young."

"So is Horus young, and the Hellenes' Dionysos. They are no less gods."

"Were they known for gods when their years were few?"

Keen, that mind behind the quiet face. Meriamon acknowledged it with an inclination of the head, even a flicker of a smile. "You know what Alexander is."

"A blind man could see it," Barsine said.

"Even a Persian?"

"I am almost a Hellene."

"No," said Meriamon. "You are not that."

The fine brows drew together. "You hate us, then. You truly hate us."

"Not you," Meriamon said. "Not for yourself. But for what you are, yes."

"Why?"

"Need there be a reason?"

"I am Hellene enough for that," said Barsine.

Meriamon laughed. It was free enough, and the air seemed cleaner for it. "So you are. Well then. Would you love us if we had taken your empire, set it under our heel, given you leave to worship your gods—but worked our will with them first, so that you might know who was master?"

"But," said Barsine, "that is the way of the world, surely. For conqueror to become conquered, and for a new conqueror to rise up, and for him in turn to fall. Egypt has had its day. Persis, it may be, is passing as well, in the face of the king from Macedon."

"That doesn't trouble you?"

"It troubles me. I accept it. It is the will of heaven."

"There," said Meriamon. "There we differ. Egypt does not accept. Egypt rules, or it rebels."

"And yet its gods accept all who come, and make each their own."

"Except yours."

"We have no gods to give. We have the Truth."

"There is no one truth. Its faces are as many as there are gods in heaven."

"But—" said Barsine. And stopped. She sat back. She firmed her lips.

"You see," Meriamon said. "Your faith knows the way of adversaries, of two who can never be one, nor share what is theirs. Your king, your faith, your magic—there is nothing that ours can meet or match."

"We were never unjust to your people."

"No? Artaxerxes crushed us and slew our gods, slaughtered Apis' bull in his own temple. You call that justice?"

"That was long ago," said Barsine, "and richly earned. You had rebelled against him."

"We had taken back what was ours."

"You were conquered."

"We are never conquered."

The air rang like the clash of sword on sword. Barsine was taut, half on her feet.

Slowly she subsided. Meriamon, who had never sat at all, took the chair that waited for her, and willed herself to be calm. When she could trust her voice, she asked, "Now do you understand?"

"No," Barsine said.

"Then you never will."

"No."

There was a silence. It was oddly peaceful.

"I do," Barsine said after a while, "understand why you left us. You would have found us unbearable."

Meriamon did not feel that she needed to answer that.

The silence stretched again. Meriamon made no move to break it. Again it was Barsine who spoke. "Will you be with me when my child is born?"

That took Meriamon by surprise. "You want me there? Even knowing what you know?"

"You hate with a clean hate. And you are a healer."

"A poor one as my people reckon it."

"That is better than anything here."

"Not now. There are priests of Imhotep in the service of the king. He will see that they look after you."

"Priests," said Barsine. "Will they consent to be made eunuchs, then, to attend my presence?"

"You wouldn't," Meriamon said, shocked out of dignity.

Was that a glint of wickedness in the dark eyes? "I shall ask for you."

And Alexander would grant it. Meriamon knew that as well as Barsine did. He would say exactly what Barsine said, and be even less patient about it.

"I could strangle your child at birth," Meriamon said.

"You would not," said Barsine.

Clear, clear eyes. And a will as strong as any queen's. It was gentle, it seemed soft, but it would not yield for anything that Meriamon could do. She would have

Meriamon there, festering hate, feeble magic, and all; and that was that.

• FOURTEEN •

Meriamon frowned at Niko. "Close your fist," she said.

He did. It was not much of a fist, but it was more than he had had. "Open," she said. She set a ball in it: a small one such as children played with, tanned hide sewn over thick-wadded wool. "Now," she said. "Squeeze it."

He shook with effort. The muscles stood out in his jaw; sweat ran down his face.

His fingers sagged open. The ball dropped. Sekhmet bounded after it, batting it with a paw.

Meriamon smiled at them both. Niko glowered. "I'm as weak as a baby."

"Not quite," she said. She retrieved the ball. "Now. Again."

He set his teeth, but he obeyed her. She watched carefully. The bone was knit long since. His hand was twisted and shortened, ugly enough but far from what it could have been. He was, for all his doubts, getting his strength back, and regaining use of his hand. He would not get all of it. But neither would he be a one-handed man.

His fingers were stiffened and clawed. They would soften, she hoped, if he did as she told him. His thumb and forefinger could not meet, not yet, but she had hopes of it. He did not voice any objection to the game with the ball, which every other Macedonian she knew would have protested loudly and refused to have anything to do with. Niko gritted his teeth and knotted his brows and endured, till his face was wringing wet and his body trembling with exhaustion.

She caught the ball as it fell yet again, and tossed it toward Sekhmet. The cat pursued it joyously under Meriamon's bed.

Niko half-rose to go after it. Meriamon held him down. "Not now," she said. "Rest a bit. You're trying too hard."

"I want to be whole," he said.

She took his hand in hers, working her fingers into its knots and spasms. He jerked in sudden pain; she held him till he eased, and went on. "You'll be whole," she told him. "It takes time, that's all."

"I want it to be now."

He was as simple as a child. She had a sudden, powerful urge to kiss him. She did not. He had not welcomed it before, or ever said a word of it.

He was not aware of her at all, except as a source of pain and slow ease.

"You've been practicing with weapons," she said.

He started. She held his hand before it could pull away. "How did you know?"

"I've watched you. You're losing sleep on it. Why not do it in the day like everyone else?"

"I'm guarding you in the day."

"That's no excuse."

He shrugged one-sided. "I didn't think you would approve."

"Why not? It's making you stronger."

"Strong enough to go back to the cavalry?"

Her heart stuttered. She said steadily, "Strong enough for that. Since you're a left-handed man."

A long sigh escaped him. It did not look like relief. He was scowling at his hand, or at her fingers flexing his, making them bend and straighten. "I still can't hold Typhon's rein."

"You've tried."

It was not a question. His response was not an answer. "I was thinking. Did you see the horse that Peukestas brought in yesterday, that he said had come from Scythia? Did you see what it had for gear?"

"No," said Meriamon. "I was getting a catapult bolt out of some idiot's leg."

"It was something," Niko said. "It had a bit—not even like the thing you use on Phoenix, that wouldn't keep a stallion down for a heartbeat. It was just a broken link, nothing to hold the tongue, no bars to clamp the jaw, nothing. But the groom was riding as solid as you please. It's the saddle that did it. It's got padding, and arches that come up fore and aft, and hold you where you sit. You can't lose your seat for anything, unless you're hopeless to begin with."

"You rode Peukestas' horse," said Meriamon. She wished that she could doubt it.

"He's not much to look at—he's got a coat like a half-shorn sheep, and a head to match. But he's as tough as old leather. And his mouth: silk. I had him going from a gallop to a standstill and back, with hardly more than a finger on the rein."

"Did you buy him?"

"Peukestas wouldn't sell."

He did not, she noticed, sound unduly cast down. "So?"

"So I was thinking," he said. "If I could get one of the armorers to have a try at a saddle like that, and keep the bridle I've got—I wouldn't need so much strength to keep Typhon in hand. Even," he said with a curl of the lip, "this one."

"Why not trade Typhon for a quieter horse? Then you won't need to do anything at all."

"Typhon is mine," he said. "I bred him. I was the first man ever to sit on his back. And the last, too, if I hadn't let Amyntas look after him."

"Sell him to Amyntas."

"No," said Niko.

Meriamon shut her mouth with a click. She should have known better. She did; but she had to try.

"He's pure Nisaian, you know," said Niko. "I had his dam out of a Persian mare, and his sire was the king's own—Philip, that was, before he died. He's not the best-tempered of beasts, but he has heart, and brains . . . too much, if you ask some people. You've never really seen him, have you?"

"I've seen enough," Meriamon said.

"You haven't." He got up, freed from her grip at last, eager. "We've time before sundown. Maybe we can even talk to an armorer. The king might be interested, if we can make it work."

Meriamon could think of no good reason to refuse him. If she was there, she told herself, he would not try to ride the beast. Greek horses were flighty, and enough of them were wicked-tempered that she could almost forgive the ghastly bridles their masters hung on them, but Typhon had a name for viciousness. The grooms talked when she went to visit Phoenix, telling tales of men kicked and bitten, and Amyntas thrown and nearly trampled.

The beast was handsome enough. Not a delicate beauty like Phoenix, but big for a Greek horse—Nisaian certainly, a solid sixteen hands, deep-chested and proud-necked, with a fine straight head and a bright intelligent eye. Not, she admitted, a malicious one, but there was no kindness in it.

He greeted his master with upflung head and deafening whinny, half-rearing on his tether: they did not keep him hobbled, no hobble could hold him. Niko went in under the rope, catching it close to the halter, taking no notice of the pawing hoofs. The stallion bucked and plunged. For a moment Meriamon was sure that Niko would leap onto his back. Clearly he thought of it, but he had a little sense left. He soothed and gentled the stallion down, stroking the dampened neck, murmuring in the flattened ear. It quivered, flicked, rose.

Niko grinned at Meriamon. "He's a beauty, isn't he?"

He was that: gleaming copper, with a star on his forehead. Some brave soul—the groom, no doubt, with his bruises and his insouciant look, lounging out of reach—kept him spotless, his mane cropped and standing stiff, his tail brushed to silk.

"He'd fetch a kingly price," Meriamon said.

The grin vanished from Niko's face. "I'm not selling him."

"Pity."

"Well," said Niko. Clearly he felt that he could be forgiving, with his demon of a stallion eating sweets out of his hand—drawing back when the hand was empty, snaking toward it with teeth snapping, to be slapped smartly on the nose. "*There* now," said Niko to one or both of them. "He's testing, that's all. He has to know he can respect you."

"I'd rather be respected by a horse with more sense."

"Typhon has a lot of sense. He doesn't put up with idiots."

"You'd never know it."

Niko bared his teeth at her.

She exchanged look for look with the horse. There was a god in him, she thought. And not a gentle one. "Set," she said. "Your name is Set."

"His name is Typhon."

"It is the same."

"You call your cat Sekhmet."

"Sekhmet is her own cat. I don't ask her to carry my life in battle."

"Don't you?"

Meriamon's mouth was open. She closed it. He did not mean— No. He did not know what he was saying. He was being a Hellene, that was all: quick, and clever with his tongue, and no matter what it said.

"I'm going to get a saddle made," Niko said, more to the horse than to her. "And if it works well, who knows? I'll try the bridle, too. You'd welcome that. No more edges on your tongue. No more iron on your jaw. You'll learn what gentle is."

"Not that one," said Meriamon.

Niko ignored her. The horse's eye rolled, mocking her fears.

Alexander had had enough of idling outside of Tyre. What he called idling was the greatest siegecraft in the world, from dawn till long after dark and up again before the sun was up, building the bridge to the city. It was all but up to the gate now, the towers raised anew, and more of them, a wall of wood and reeking raw hides, flinging bolts over the walls and stones upon the ships that harried from the sea.

"There's nothing to do here," he said, "but hew wood and haul water. I'm for the mountains inland. They've been harrying our crews, keeping them from the timber-cutting. I'll settle them."

And gather a fleet. He did not talk in public about that, but Niko heard of it from Ptolemy, and went over it until Meriamon could recite the tale by heart. "The kings are coming back to Phoenicia out of the Great King's service, and bringing their fleets with them. Gerostratos is on his way to Tyre. Arados, Byblos, Sidon—their fleets are back, and their cities have surrendered to Alexander. He has ships now, if he'll only claim them. He can take Tyre by sea."

"How in the world—" Meriamon began, the first time or six. After that she did not need to.

"To begin with," Niko said, "he can drive off the boats that harry our crews. Then he'll find a way to break the walls."

"With ships?"

"There is a way," said Niko. "Alexander will see it, if he hasn't already. I'm just a soldier," he said, "and no general, but I see what's in front of my face. Ships are the key. Once he has ships, he has Tyre."

Meriamon was not at all sure of that. But Niko was off and running, and no word of hers could call him back.

Just a soldier, she thought. Oh, certainly. And Alexander was just a boy who happened to be a king. Niko had no such fire on him as Alexander had. No one did. But he had a power of his own, earth-deep, earth-strong, and he was full of it. He followed her dutifully as a guardsman should, but his mind was on the king, and his eyes whenever they were near where Alexander was.

He had the saddle he had been looking for. It was an

odd lumpy thing like a cushion gone bad, and Typhon regarded it in plunging, snapping, kicking mistrust, but Niko, with Amyntas and the groom and a sizable audience of hangers-on, got it on the horse's back. Then he let the beast get the feel of it, taking his time, losing idlers to livelier entertainment.

Meriamon had hoped—prayed—that he would let Amyntas do the testing. The boy was horseman enough, and the horse knew him and would accept him. But Niko was hardly one to watch when he could be up and doing. With no more warning than a word to the two who held the bridle, he sprang into the saddle.

Typhon stood rock-still. Meriamon remembered to breathe. The horse flung himself squealing skyward and came down plunging. Bucking, it would have been, but Niko had the beast's chin hauled against his chest. Using his good hand. The bad one gripped mane, then saddle. Holding. His legs clamped to the horse's sides; his body rode with the heaving, lunging, kicking motion, one with it, flowing into it.

The stallion was galloping, no longer plunging; slowing little by little, easing, smoothing, accepting this weight on his back: this and no other, that had been the first to tame him. His ears were up. Had been up, Meriamon realized, almost from the first.

It was play. For both of them. Niko grinned like a maniac, riding his maniac of a horse. Now his hand was on his thigh. His left hand. His right hand, twisted and clawed, held the reins in its weak grip.

Meriamon's hands went to her face. She wanted to close her eyes, but she dared not. That demon, that Set-in-flesh—it would kill him. It would break free and rear and twist and throw him, and trample him to bloody nothingness.

They danced up to her, snorting horse, grinning rider, and halted, breathing hard, both alike. "You!" she raged at them. "You idiots!"

Niko laughed. Typhon tossed his head. His mouth was

shut. She forgot his temper, forgot her caution, forgot everything in hauling his head about and prying his mouth open. He was wearing the Scythian bit.

Words forsook her. She let the bridle go. She got her hands on Niko and hauled him down, so hard, so sudden, that he could not even stop her. When she had his feet on the ground, she knocked them out from under him and sat on him, hands fisted in his chiton, screaming at him. "Have you gone mad?"

"Have you?"

That was not Niko. She got up slowly. Alexander was there. Ptolemy, too, and Peukestas holding Typhon's bridle, and Hephaistion. She was quite calm. A blank calm. She pointed toward the horse's head. "Look," she said. "Look at that."

They looked. Peukestas whistled between his teeth. "Herakles! I wouldn't have tried that."

"I'd like to," Alexander said, "on Boukephalas. Who," he said before Meriamon could say anything, "is a great deal more reliable than this spawn of Mother Night."

Niko got to his feet, a little stiffly. Meriamon spared no sympathy for him. He had not harmed his hand. She had made sure of that. "He likes it," Niko said. "He goes better with it."

"You caught him off guard," Ptolemy said.

Niko set his jaw and looked stubborn.

"You have to admit," said Alexander, "it wasn't the most intelligent thing you've ever tried. If not quite the least. There was a little matter of stopping a chariot with your bare hands."

Niko flushed. "Damn it, Alexander—"

"Damn it, Niko, is it your neck you'll break next?"

"No," Niko said. Fearless. Even with Alexander glaring down that royal nose at him, which was a feat: Niko was a good head taller than the king.

Suddenly Alexander laughed. "There never was any keeping you down, was there?"

"No," said Niko. "Alexander." He made a title of it, and of his stiff pride a grudging respect.

"Well," Alexander said. "I must admit it was impressive. But promise me you won't try that bit again till you've got it on a safer horse."

"Typhon is perfectly safe," said Niko.

"I wouldn't bet on it." Alexander exchanged glances with the stallion. His eyes narrowed. Meriamon moved to catch him before he tried the beast himself, but he stayed where he was. His glance shifted to Niko. "Tell me, Niko. If I asked you to ride with me, would you ride another horse?"

Niko stood frozen-still. His voice was almost too low to hear. "Ride where?"

"To the mountains," said Alexander. "To start with."

Niko drew a great sobbing breath, His whole heart was in his eyes. But he said, "You gave me another duty."

"So I did." Alexander looked at Meriamon. "Can you spare him, lady?"

"Do I need to?"

Alexander's head tilted.

"You have other Companions," Meriamon said. "Why do you need this one?"

"He seems to need me," said Alexander.

He did. But she said, "What if I need him?"

"That's for you to say."

Niko had not moved a muscle. What he wanted, she could see with her eyes shut. What she wanted . . .

"Take him," she said. "He belongs to you."

• FIFTEEN •

"I don't have to go," Nikolaos said. He had drunk enough at dinner to make him say it very carefully, but he was steady—mostly—on his feet. And he was not where

Meriamon would have expected him to be, with the King's Companions, making himself one of them again. He had been there for a while, but then he came to Thaïs' tent. The hetaira was gone, taking dinner with her lover and the rest of the king's friends. Meriamon was there alone as she liked to be, quiet with Sekhmet and her shadow, trying not to think of what the day had done.

Niko loomed over her as he had the first time she saw him, enormously tall and enormously foreign, in a cloud of wine and flower-scent. He had a garland on his head. He carried a jar of wine cradled in his weak arm, and a pair of cups. He looked down at her and said what he must have come to say. "I can stay," he said. "If you need me."

"I don't need you."

He sat down on the couch beside her. Sekhmet promptly established herself in his lap. She did not mind that he reached around her to fill a cup and hand it to Meriamon. He filled the other, set the jar on the table.

Neither of them drank. There was an ell-broad stretch of couch between them. It could have been as wide as Alexander's causeway.

"Why aren't you with your friends?" she asked him.

"Why weren't you having dinner with the king?"

"I wasn't hungry."

"You never are."

She frowned at the cup in his hands. There was a sphinx painted on the bottom, glimmering darkly through the wine. "I ate. Phylinna ate with me."

"Good."

She raised the cup to her lips. The wine was strong, the way the Macedonians liked it: dark and sweet and barely watered.

"The Persians have a saying," Niko said. "If you make a decision, first consider it sober. Then consider it drunk. If it's the same in both conditions, it's the right one."

"I thought it was the other way about. First drunk, then sober."

"As long as you do both, it doesn't matter."

"I have precious little head for wine," said Meriamon.

"I can drink for three of you."

He proceeded to do it. She caught his hand as he lowered the empty cup, and captured the cup. "I think you already have," she said.

"I'll stay if you need me," he said.

"I told you I didn't."

"Then who'll look after you?"

"Who looked after me before the king inflicted me on you?"

"He didn't—"

That was a lie, and he knew it. Meriamon laid aside both cups, the full and the empty. "Why don't you go? You have things to do, preparations to make. You're riding before sunup. You know how the king is. If you're late, he'll leave you behind."

"I won't be late."

"So go."

"No," said Niko.

She got a grip on him and pulled. He was set like a stone.

She stamped her foot. "Get out of my tent!"

"No," he said.

He was laughing at her. And Sekhmet in his lap, little whore, yawning in her face.

"I don't need you!" she shouted at him. "I've got Kleomenes."

That stopped him.

He was jealous.

She laughed.

He stood. Her head came to his breastbone. She sneered up at him. "What kind of Greek are you, turning down a fight to stay with a woman?"

That did it. His mouth opened, shut. There was everything to say, or nothing. In the end he said nothing. He took his wine with him. He left the cups.

Meriamon picked up the one that was full. The wine's fumes dizzied her. She drained the cup.

The king rode out before dawn. Meriamon did not see him go. She had given Niko back his pride. She did not need to watch him take it.

"He didn't take Typhon," said Kleomenes, who had been there, yearning after the king's cavalry as only a young thing could. "He had one of the king's mounts, the big grey."

Meriamon took a breath. She was seeing to the dressings of a man who had been burned when the fireship came. He was the last of the worst wounded, the only one who had not died. She mustered a smile for him. He had no smile to return. The bottom of his face was melted and seared, but his eyes were warm. "You're doing well," she told him, "with the gods' help." She patted his unburned shoulder and went on to the next man.

Kleomenes followed her, chattering happily. "Amyntas is in bliss. He gets to ride Typhon while Niko is away. Everybody was betting that Niko would take the horse and be damned. Except me."

"Why?" asked the man whom Meriamon tended. He had got a bolt in the thigh; for all that she could do, it had begun to fester.

"Alexander said he couldn't," Kleomenes said. "Even Niko listens to Alexander."

Meriamon snorted. Neither of them noticed. The wounded man yelped. "Hold still," she snapped at him. He held still, though his hands were knotted in the blanket.

Her temper cooled a little. "There," she said, lightening her hands. "There now. It's done."

She could as well have said it to Niko. He was gone. His own world had taken him, his war and his king. He would come back, if the gods were merciful, but not to Meriamon. What need? He had only been her guardsman because he could do nothing more deserving of his place. Now he was whole again.

As was she, with her shadow gliding in her wake, and her purpose undiminished though Alexander held to his lunacy of taking Tyre. There was no place in her fate for a great sullen oaf of a Macedonian.

Word came back quickly enough. Alexander had swept down on the Tyrian bandits like the wrath of heaven, broken their will and ended their raids and gone on to Sidon. There, the couriers said, he had found a fleet, and sworn it to his service. There were ships building, ships fitting, ships massing in the harbors from Arados to Cyprus.

Scores of galleys, the messenger said, gathered in Alexander's name. Meriamon was in the hospital when the man came. He had a festering sore in his foot, which troubled him little enough when he rode, or so he said, but Parmenion had sent him to the physicians once his message was delivered.

Even then he would not have said anything, but she gave him wine with poppy to keep him quiet while she lanced his foot, and after he had finished screaming he babbled out the whole of his message word for word. Not loudly, for a mercy. If Tyre had spies—and who knew but that one of the men in the hospital was in Tyrian pay?—it would give gold to know what force Alexander could muster against it.

If anyone could take the city, Alexander could. Even Meriamon had never doubted that.

Alexander's messenger did not know anything of a certain one of Alexander's Companions. There were so many to remember, after all, and Niko was hardly the greatest of them. Merely a rider in the cavalry, no officer nor prince, nor Personal Companion as his brother was and thus well known to anyone who knew Alexander.

Meriamon could not have expected otherwise. She left the hospital when it was time, went as she had taken to doing, to look in on Barsine. It never grew easier. It did become less unbearable the more often she did it.

Barsine was close to her time. She would be glad to be rid of the burden. Not that she said it; it was not her way to complain. No more would she dress other than in swathings of modest robes, although summer was well and fully come to Tyre, in heat that was almost enough to please Meriamon.

Meriamon left the stifling closeness of Barsine's tent, certain that it would be only a day or two longer. The women had gathered what was needful; they knew to summon Meriamon wherever she was, as soon as she was needed.

But not before morning. She went to the market in search of cooler clothing than she had, fine Egyptian linen, coarser weave from looms in Asia, a single mad extravagance: a bolt of Tyrian purple, deep-dyed, the merchant said, and fit for a royal lady. Gods knew, he wanted enough for it; but she bargained him down to a little less than a queen's ransom, and found a servant who would carry the whole of it for an obol and a flask of wine.

Thaïs was not in the tent. She seldom was. Not that she entertained other lovers than Ptolemy while he rode with the king, but she had friends among the hetairai, who liked to keep one another company.

Meriamon ate her solitary dinner. Even Sekhmet had left her to hunt in the shadows. Her own shadow was farther yet, prowling among the cedars. For a moment Meriamon caught the strong green scent, felt the softness of leafmold under her feet.

She did not miss Niko's presence. Of course not. His sulks and his tempers. His patent yearning to be elsewhere. What did she need a guard for? If she wanted someone to sleep across her door, Kleomenes would do it happily enough. He had offered more than once, but she had never needed him that badly.

It was quiet in the lamplight. The servants were all gone to sleep, except Phylinna, who was with her mistress.

The silence closed in. The noises of the camp came muted through the tent's walls. The flap was open, the veil down against the hordes of stinging and biting things, but no breeze blew. No air stirred at all.

Days were easy. Meriamon could fill them with light and occupation, could pretend that there was anything beneath but echoing emptiness.

It was not Niko's absence. Or not only that. Without her shadow to guard her, without Sekhmet to weave spells about her feet, she was naked to the night.

She rose from her couch. Her robe was thin, but in the still heat even it was more weight than her body needed. And yet she shivered.

There was another veil like the one that kept out the flies. Meriamon draped it over herself. She looked like a Persian lady, she thought somewhat wryly, or like a shrouded spirit.

She walked through the camp. What precisely she hunted, she did not know. An emptiness; an echo in the heart of things. Where people were, they almost filled it. But even they seemed thin somehow, stretched tight.

It was the siege, that was all. Five months of it, stretching toward half a year, and no end to it that any but Alexander could see. That had a price. Men's souls, men's courage, men's strength to face the enemy. Tyre suffered little enough, with its fleets to keep it fed. Alexander's army was nuisance only, a boy's bravado, brag and boast and nothing more.

Her hands were cold, but they were warmer than her heart.

What profit for her or for Khemet in this endless, bootless siege? Alexander would never have his way with Tyre. He would camp here until he died, and died mad, for a city he could not conquer.

Cold waves lapped her feet. She started back. Somehow, without knowing it, she had come to the sea. The causeway was a darkness across the starlit water. Torches flick-

ered along it; guards paced, now in shadow, now in light.
The towers at its end were dark. They had touched the
wall at last, only the day before, and Tyre had done nothing to stop it. Why trouble? Nothing in the towers or on
the mole was strong enough to break those walls.

The city was dark. Sometimes there were lights along
the wall or shining from towers. Buildings were tall in
Tyre: its people lived in towers, one atop another, like bees
in a great clustering hive.

Meriamon swayed on the sand. Here, between the water
and the sky, the emptiness was as vast as all heaven. Nothing below her feet but void. Nothing above her head but
sky. Nothing. Nothing. Nothing.

"Mother Isis!"

Her voice was thin in the immensity. And yet it anchored her. It, and the name that had flown out of her. She
was Amon's priestess; but it was the Mother whose presence came strongest to her, warm breast, soft voice, a wall
against the emptiness.

"Magic," Meriamon whispered.

Magi.

Yet . . .

She had quartered the camp. The Persians' tents were
quiet, no malice upon them, no hatred, not even enmity.
Alexander had won them with his mercy and his smile.
Their priests worshipped their Truth in peace. They
worked no magics against the king.

They were not, for once, the enemy. Bitter as that was,
as bitter as their own Truth.

Meriamon looked toward Tyre. Its enmity served Persia.
Its resistance served itself. It would accept an overlord; but
not within its walls.

"So," she said to the loom of it. "Your priests are
mages, too."

It was aware of her, dimly, as a beast is of a gnat upon
its hide. How long had it been adding this power to the
rest? Had it done so from the first, or had it waited until

Alexander was gone? Without the light and potency of his presence, his siege was a frailer thing. His will informed it still, his men went on unwearied with their labors, but the bright edge was gone.

This had taken the heart out of her. This had caught her when she was sick and driven her nigh down into death. For this her shadow had hunted, and gone so far that it could not find her again, until the sun and the king's presence and her own waxing strength had guided it back.

She staggered and almost fell, to know so much, so fully, to be so naked to it—no shadow, no Bastet-on-earth, no strength at all but what was in her body and her shrinking mind. She was no warrior. She was singer, seer, voice of the gods. She was eyes and a tongue, not a sword.

She was all that there was. Alexander's priests, his soothsayers, his wise men and his philosophers: they had no magic. They had talked it out of their world. It hid in their deep places among the women and the mysteries. Wine freed it. Alexander embodied it. But not here.

It had ridden in the fireship. It made itself one with every man and woman and child of Tyre, set the will of the city against the one who would conquer it. What bred it, what fed it . . .

Sight opened before her. The water at her feet stilled although the waves rolled elsewhere as before, stilled and smoothed and rounded as in a basin. Light welled within it, torchlight and firelight. Voices chanted in a tongue nigh as old as that of Khemet, so old that none now remembered the meanings of the words, but shaped them for sound alone. They were power purely, now the deep voices of priests, now the high voices of priestesses. Shadows moved: robed figures, cowled, their faces in darkness. Tall pillars rose about them. A curtain stirred in a wandering air. The lamps and the torches flickered. A shape loomed, a gleam of gold, a dark sheen of bronze, a glitter of carven eyes.

"Melqart," Meriamon breathed. Naming it. It was huge

and heavy, man-shaped, thrice man-high; like the Hellenes' Herakles it bore a club and wore for a cloak a lion's skin. But no god of the Hellenes had ever had such a face, broad and heavy, with a great braided beard and a nose like a ship's prow; nor squatted as this one did, half kneeling, half crouching, with its hands outstretched.

One of the priests stirred from among the rest, and moved toward the god's feet. His hands were lifted. Something wriggled in them: something small and pale, raising its voice in a sudden lusty cry. The priest paused, rocking and soothing it: eerie to hear a croon like a mother's from an old man's lips. The child quieted.

It was a boychild, well-formed, so plump that its limbs broke into rolls of fat. The priest smiled down at it, tenderly.

The god's hand was broad and curved like a bowl. Gently the priest laid the child in it. The chanting had ceased. In the silence, the sound of metal sliding on metal was startlingly loud. The child wriggled in its strange bed. Below it, the fire opened.

The chant began again, low and slow, but rising in long cadences like the sea, until it thundered to the roof. At the summit of it, the god's hand dropped. The child fell. The fire leaped to embrace it.

Meriamon knelt in the sand. Her throat was raw. Had she screamed? She could not remember. The scrying-basin was gone, the waves curling and falling, sighing as they withdrew.

She raised cold and shaking hands to her cheeks. They were wet, and not with spray. The power—the power that was in blood, human blood, blood of a child—

She dragged herself to her feet. Horror had sunk deep. Below it, beyond it, above it rose wrath. It was not the sunbright anger of the king. It was darker, deeper. It was as implacable as the Nile in its flood. "No," she said to the city and the night, and to the priests in their temple, in their reek of blood and burning, and their terrible gentleness. "No." She raised her fists and her voice, crying aloud. *"No!"*

In that word she set all her rage and her pity and her horror of any god who would demand not only blood but blood burned in fire. She made of it a spear. She thrust it with all her strength into the heart of the power.

It raised its force against her: arms as strong as iron, hands of bronze, buffeting her. She swayed under the force of them. Braced. Thrust deeper yet, though the power writhed like a live thing, battering her, rocking her on her feet. "Gods," she whispered. "O my gods. Amon, Osiris, Horus upon the throne of the horizon—Ra-Harakhte, O defend me. Isis— Mother Isis—if ever you loved your child—"

She was failing. She would crumple. She would fall. She would lie beneath the god's power, and for Alexander in his bright splendor—for Alexander, nothing. Defeat, death, the end of his empire; and Persia would rule as its Truth ordained.

That too was the power's doing. Alexander was never so weak as that, nor his defeat as certain. But if it came to the crux, and it was power against power, then truly he could fall.

She set her teeth, body and soul. She gathered every fading drop of strength. She shaped it into a word: *No.* She drove that word against the power out of Tyre.

It surged against her. She surged back. It held. She would fail, fall, crumble into dust.

For an endless while they hung in the balance. In the utmost instant, just as she knew that she could hold no longer, it fell.

It was broken. She knew that, there on the sea's edge, with the darkness stooping over her. Tyre stood, and maybe would stand for all that Alexander could do. But his enemies would be flesh and blood, stone and steel. Magic would play no part in it.

* * *

"Lady. Lady Mariamne."

Light stabbed her. She recoiled from it. Her head—gods, how much wine had she drunk?

Phylinna shook her none too gently. "Lady Mariamne. Will you wake up?"

Meriamon opened her aching eyes. Bed beneath her. Tent over her. Phylinna between, fairly dancing with impatience. "Lady! Lady Barsine is brought to bed. She's calling for you."

Phylinna would never understand why Meriamon laughed, or why she wept, sitting up and shaking sand out of her hair and groping for a robe that she did not remember taking off. The sand—she had not dreamed it, then. Nor the long stumble back to the tent, half blind, half mad, and worn to the bare bone, and her shadow, impossibly, holding her up.

Sekhmet, washing her paw with delicate strokes of a pink tongue, had a cat's disregard for mortal frettings. Meriamon had been there, and she had fought a battle. Now she was here. A child had died. Now one undertook to be born. That was balance, such as was in everything.

Balance. Surely. Barsine's child was a son, a handsome lusty man-child whose hair, when he shed the dark furze of birth, would perhaps be mouse-fair.

"His father cannot name him," his mother said. "Therefore I take it on myself." She looked down at the infant in her arms. Having shouted his presence in the world, he had subsided into a watchful calm. Almost Meriamon fancied that his newborn eyes could look into Barsine's own, meet them and understand the light that caught in them. "Herakles," Barsine said. "I name you Herakles."

• SIXTEEN •

Alexander was coming. Meriamon felt him in the earth. He came like the bark of Ra, the boat of a million years, that sails in the night in the land of the dead, and rises in the morning in the land of the living. A fleet came with him, but to the eyes of her power they were a host of candles about the fire of the sun.

Meriamon could hardly think for the power of it. It had brought her out of Amon's temple, drawn like a moth to a flame, but in Alexander's presence she had become inured to it. With Alexander's absence and now his return, she remembered what great light and fire had called her up from Khemet.

Philippos would get no use out of her. She sent a boy with word that she would not be coming to the hospital, and went down to the sea. The city was deceptively quiet. The siege-towers stood against the walls, but the catapults were motionless, the soldiers who manned them quiescent at their posts. No cloud of magic came out of Melqart's temple. That was hardly destroyed; she was never such a fool as to think so. Quelled, only. Dealt a brief defeat. But there would be no blood rite for yet a while. She had made sure of that.

Alexander would assure it. Or fall, and take his people with him. That was not prescience, not exactly. It was clear sight and long thought and the training given the royal stock of the Two Lands.

After a while Meriamon sat on the sand, clasping her knees. Her shadow stretched lazily ahead of her, half on the earth, half in the water. It bared its teeth at Tyre.

"A fine partisan you are," she said to it. It blinked lambent eyes at her and settled into a watchful doze.

As the sun rose higher, the day's heat rose with it. She dropped her mantle gladly. The dress she wore beneath it had made Phylinna catch her breath and wonder aloud if Lady Mariamne was turning hetaira. It was Egyptian, that was all, and modest enough for any decent sense, good white linen cut close from breast to ankle and leaving her arms bare. The air was delicious on skin that had been wrapped in wool too long, cool still for her taste, but pleasantly so. It played with the many braids of her hair, touched the sea in long light swaths, ran away toward the north. She fancied that she caught a breath of Khemet in it under the sea-smell.

Someone else came and sat beside her. She glanced without surprise at Thaïs. Phylinna was behind her, and a pair of the servants, carrying a Persian parasol.

"It is pleasant out here," said Thaïs. "And still cool. Are you happy now that it's become a furnace?"

"It's not as warm as Egypt," Meriamon said.

"No wonder you dress as you do."

Meriamon's cheeks were warm. She did not know why. Hellenes had no modesty at all.

Hellene men. Their women were as shamefast as Persians.

"I dress as all my people do," she said a little stiffly. "Is there something wrong with it?"

"No," said Thaïs. "It's very practical."

"And wanton."

"Well," the hetaira said. "Those straps over your shoulders—they'd drive a man wild, the way they slip and let your breast peep out. And the linen, as thin as it is . . ." Her eyes narrowed. She began to smile. "What a fashion you could set! It's better than nakedness. It hides so little, but just enough. Does our Niko know what a beauty you are under all the coats and trousers?"

Meriamon's face flamed. Had she been a man, sun-dyed red-dark all over, maybe it would not have been obvious. But she was decently pale, as a woman should be.

Thaïs forbore to laugh at her. "The Great King has sent another embassy. Did you know that?"

"Yes," said Meriamon, blessing Thaïs' mercy. She had felt the embassy's coming, too. Magi came with it with their sacred fire and their bone-deep certainty, carrying their mighty weight of Truth. They would be hoping to wield it against Alexander.

"He's coming," she said. "He's close. Can you feel him?"

Thaïs did not need to ask whom she meant. There was only one *He* in Alexander's camp. "Can you?" she asked.

"With all my souls."

Thaïs blinked at her.

Meriamon shook herself. Clear-eyed, hard-headed Athenian: no magic for that one, no mystery outside of her philosophy. Meriamon smiled, tricking a smile out of Thaïs. "I don't think I understand you," Thaïs said, but lightly.

"You aren't supposed to," said Meriamon.

"I'm Greek. I have to try."

Meriamon laughed. The sun on her back was hardly less potent than the sun of Alexander's coming on her face. "Look!" she said. "Ships." ·

Tenscore and onescore and three. Two hundred ships and more under Phoenician and Cyprian crews, sailing down out of Sidon, with Alexander on the deck of the flagship. Its sails were purple blazoned in gold with the emblem of his house, the sunburst with its many rays.

Tyre saw him coming. Whatever shock his numbers were, it hardly blunted their cunning. Ships of their own sailed swiftly out, some to close in battle, some to come about and wall the harbors against him. Outriders of his fleet lowered oars and drove straight for the narrow mouth of the northern harbor: iron-beaked war-galleys like great winged arrows. The beat of their drums echoed over the water, and the shouts of their masters, driving them to stroke swifter, swifter, swifter. No ship from Tyre was close enough, or fast enough, to catch them. Bolts and arrows failed and fell short.

The ship in the lead seemed to leap from the water full into the center of the ship-wall. Even from the shore, through the shouts and cries of men and the pounding of drums, Meriamon heard the clash of iron-shod ram on iron-shod prow, and the heavy thud of wood behind, and the rending, rushing sound of the ship's hull giving way, water pouring in, crew leaping into the sea.

But Tyre had not endured so long by giving way to a single assault. Alexander's ships sank three of those that walled the harbor, but behind those three were thrice and four and ten times the number, and more on the open sea, harrying the edges of the fleet.

It was victory enough for a beginning. The signal went out, calling the ships to moor along the strand.

Alexander leaped from deck to shallow water and waded to the sand, first of all his men. Meriamon had not gone as far down as he was, or tried, with the whole army streaming from camp and mole and half-ruined town, shouting his name. It was a force, that passion of love, strong enough to shatter stone. But Alexander was stronger. He drank it in; he turned it all to light.

She could not see him, slender youthful figure that he was, even in a scarlet chiton; he was engulfed in taller, broader men. And yet he towered over them. Not one of them but knew where he was, and who he was, and what he was to them.

"Alexander." She said it to herself, softly. Thaïs had not moved from beside her, but even that uncompromising face was rapt, seeing nothing but the king.

Meriamon stood, shaking sand from her dress. She held out her hand.

Thaïs took it, let it draw her to her feet. A little of the blind enchantment left her eyes. "Well," she said. "Now we'll see what Tyre says to that." Her glance took in the fleet drawn up along the strand, the men swarming from the ships, horses rearing and calling as grooms led them from the holds.

Chaos; but chaos with a heart of law, and a smallish man in scarlet whose presence filled it everywhere.

Alexander went up from the shore to the camp, walking briskly. That was as much of a miracle as anything Meriamon had seen: going as he chose to go in so thick a crowd. Where he went, a path opened. He paused often to clasp a hand, to grip a shoulder, to exchange a word, but his progress was swift, and no one hindered him.

He took the throng with him, all but those who had to stay with the ships. Meriamon picked her way on the trampled sand, aware that she had left Thaïs behind. Her heart tugged her toward the king. *Later,* she told it.

She realized that she was cool, as if in shade, but neither mantle nor parasol covered her. She had left them both behind. Her shadow served for both. What men saw as she passed them, she did not know. Nothing, maybe. A cloud across the sun. A woman wrapped in a dark veil, walking slowly toward the mole. No one spoke to her or ventured to touch her.

Many of the ships had not come in with the others, but sailed around behind the bulk of Tyre. Now one by one they appeared on the southern tip of the isle, oars out, rowing toward the strand. The city made no move to stop them.

They backed oars a shiplength from the shore, men springing down, wading or swimming, or lowering boats from the larger galleys. The smaller ships ran full to land and beached there. They were in a fine high humor, all of them, Phoenicians here as those to the north had been of Cyprus. If it troubled them to be assaulting a city of their own nation, they showed no sign of it.

Sekhmet appeared from wherever a sensible cat went to escape sun and trampling feet, and padded at Meriamon's heel. People saw no more of her than of Meriamon. There was quiet where they were, however sudden, and a path to walk in.

It was not the power Alexander had; people knew him and gave way before him. They did not know Meriamon or the power that was on her. It was a shadow-thing, a thing of art and stillness.

There were Macedonians among the Phoenicians, big fair-haired smooth-shaven men rising like trees above the little dark bearded sailors. They lent a hand with the hawsers as all the rest did, or stood in colloquy with the captains. One had charge of the horse-transports, seeming to be everywhere at once, now on deck, now in the hold, now on the ramp with one of the horses. New ones, Meriamon saw, and Nisaian from the look of them, fine blooded stock. The one on the ramp must have been a full seventeen hands: the man at its head was no great deal taller.

The horse was giving him no trouble. It paused as it came into the light, raised its head and drank deep of the air. He murmured in its ear. The ear flicked back, pricked forward again. Delicately for all its size, it picked its way down the ramp.

Nikolaos looked well. Wind and sun had darkened his skin to bronze and turned his hair flax-fair. His eyes were more startling than ever before, like raw silver. He hardly favored his weak hand at all.

He handed the horse to one of those who waited on the sand, and turned to call out to someone. As he turned, his eyes' path crossed Meriamon. He checked for an instant. Perhaps perceiving a shadow where none should be. Perhaps . . .

He did not see her. His eyes did not return to her, nor did he approach. He went back to the ship and vanished below.

She left before he came out again. The touch of his eyes, however unwary, had shaken her to the root. To him she was nothing but aggravation. To her he was much too much.

He had his place now, a command under the king, in the fleet he had wanted, with the horses he loved. He would not want to be reminded of a hated duty, an even more hated incapacity.

The gods knew, she had troubles enough without adding this one to it. The Great Wife of Amon should be a maiden, but his singers could live the life of the body if they chose; but Meriamon had never so chosen. The gods took too much of her.

Now, when they should have all of her that was or could be, she skittered and scattered over this impossible foreigner. It was a test, surely. A judgment. A proving of her fitness.

Her heart, fickle thing, yearned now toward the man on the ship. She forced it toward the king, and her body after it.

Sekhmet suffered no such agonies. She streaked toward the ship and vanished in Niko's wake.

Meriamon wished heavy hoofs on her; then hated herself for it. Sekhmet did as she pleased. If that was to play the harlot with an oaf of a Macedonian, then Meriamon could hardly stop her.

Alexander received the Persian embassy almost as soon as he came to his tent. Proper royalty would have kept them waiting for days upon his leisure, but Alexander had never been one to be proper when he could be unpredictable. Certainly, Meriamon thought as she fitted herself into an accommodating shadow, the Persians were caught off balance. They should have expected something of the sort; but no Great King would ever have summoned them and then received them at once, as he was, with his chiton damp and stiff with sea-salt, and a cup of mountain water in his hand.

It was the same emissary as before, and the same white-robed priest-princes with him, father and sons. The hot dry fire-scent was strong on them, the wall of righteousness as broad and high as Tyre. There was an air of desperation in it as in the manner of the ambassador, for all his haughty dignity. He had come to beg on behalf of his king; and that sat ill with him, so ill that it was a sickness in Meriamon's belly.

Blessed sickness, that it came from a Parsa nobleman in front of the Macedonian king. She drew herself up.

As she stood straight, the ambassador went down, prostrating himself before Alexander. Alexander's body tensed as if to step forward, but he stood where he was, still holding his cup. The Persian rose. Alexander handed the cup to him and said, "Drink. You look as if you need it."

The Great King's ambassador looked nonplussed. He took the cup; it would have fallen else. He touched it to his lips. It rattled against his teeth. He lowered it, not hastily, but not slowly either.

"Well?" said Alexander.

"It is . . . very good water, your majesty," the Persian said.

"It ought to be. It comes from springs in the Lebanon." Alexander went to a camp stool and sat on it. There were chairs; some of them had been the Persian king's. He took no notice of them. He looked up at the tall Persian, and it was the Persian who, all at once, seemed the smaller. "What does Darius want?"

"His family."

The Persian's directness made even Alexander blink. Then he smiled. "So. Even a Persian can come to the point if he has to. What will he give me if I let him have his family back?"

The back of his hand, the ambassador's glance said. But his voice was level. "The Great King, the King of Kings, offers the King of Macedon ten thousand talents for the return of his mother and his wife and his children."

"Ten thousand talents?" Alexander tilted his head. "That's a fair handful of coppers."

The ambassador drew a long breath. "In addition," he said; pausing as if he expected Alexander to interrupt. Alexander simply sat and waited, limpid-eyed, half-smiling. "In addition, the Great King, the King of Kings, offers the King of Macedon the half of his kingdom, from the Euphrates to the sea, to be held by him in bond of friendship. In earnest of which, the Great King, the King of Kings, offers the hand of his daughter in marriage, to seal the alliance and to firm the bond of peace between king and king."

Alexander's smile was gone. Something else had taken its place; something to which Meriamon could put no name. Glee, she might have thought, except that there was anger in it too, and startlement, and a tinge of disbelief.

Focused, intent on the ambassador and the king, she had not noticed who else was there. There were always people; Alexander was never alone even in sleep. But she saw the one who came forward. He had not been there when she came, nor did she remember when he had come in. For all she knew, he had slipped in through the back of the tent.

Once she had seen him, she could hardly forget him. Parmenion was out of his armor for once, in a chiton that surprised her: it was rich enough for a prince's. She would hardly have expected it of him.

His words were exactly what she had thought they would be. "Now there's a fine end to the war," he said. His voice would never be less than harsh, but he was clearly delighted. "If I were you I'd take it, money, kingdom, girl, and all."

"If you were I . . ." Alexander looked from him to the Persians. They stood with eyes cast down, jaws set hard against humiliation.

Alexander looked again at his general. There was a faint line between his brows. "Yes," he said, "that's what I'd do if I were Parmenion. I'd take the lot."

Parmenion smiled.

Alexander smiled more sweetly than the old soldier ever could. "But I am not Parmenion," he said. "I am Alexander. And Alexander says to Darius: No."

The Persians stiffened. No more so, for all of that, than Parmenion.

"Why should I take half a kingdom?" Alexander said. "Asia is mine already, and its treasure with it, and Darius' daughter, too. If I want to marry her, then I will; I don't have to ask her father's leave." Alexander stood. He plucked the cup from the ambassador's slack fingers and handed it to a page. "Does Darius want kindness from me? Tell him to come himself, and ask for himself. He'll get nothing from me otherwise."

The Persian stared at Alexander. He was tall even for one of his people, head and shoulders above the king, his fluted hat raising him higher still; robed like a king himself, with his great curled beard and his air of invincible dignity. Alexander beside him was an upstart boy, a little cock-a-whoop, an urchin playing at being king.

Alexander met the Persian's eyes. The man did not flinch. He was too much the nobleman for that. But he caught his breath. He bowed again, down to the carpet. Then, with ceremony, he retreated.

His retinue followed him in haste that bordered on unseemly. All but the Magi. They waited for the rest to withdraw, making no move.

They were aware of Meriamon. It was nothing so obvious as a turn of glance upon her, but her presence was marked, her essence known and named. Her shadow raised itself above her head, cobra-slender, cobra-deadly. She felt its swaying in her bones.

The Great King's sorcerers neither attacked nor fled. There was no enmity in them. No warning. Simply acknowledgment, as of power to power.

The embassy was all but gone. The Magi stirred. They did not bow, did not look at the king at all, but neither did they turn their backs on him. Gliding in their robes, as smooth as if they walked so every day, they backed out of his presence.

· SEVENTEEN ·

With Alexander back and the fleet on guard, the siege leaped from long waiting to labor that was more like war. His causeway was built, his towers raised, but he had another inspiration for breaking down the wall.

He dreamed it, maybe, or a god taught him. He listened to everyone who had an opinion, and studied the city, and went hunting in the hills for a whole long careless day, and came back shouting for his engineers.

Rams. Of course. But rams mounted on ships below the wall, shielded as the towers were against the Tyrians' fire. They could move where they needed to go, testing the walls, and stop where they chose to stop, drop anchor and batten hatches and hammer at the huge impervious stones. Nor only were there stones in the wall; stones lay deep-sunken in the water, barring the ships' approach. Under a hail of bolts and fire arrows, divers bound ropes round the stones, and men on shipboard drew them up with cranes and made channels for the ramships.

It was the maddest thing Alexander had done yet, and it seemed the most useless. People looked at him and muttered about gods and insanity.

Nor had Tyre been idle. Its catapults shot missiles from above. Its galleys, sailing close, cut the cables of the ramships. Alexander armed galleys against them. Tyre withdrew its ships and sent divers with knives. Alexander anchored his ships with chains.

Tyre gave him a day's grace. Then it caught him napping. Quite literally: he liked to sleep for an hour in the noon's heat, lying under a canopy to the south of his causeway, while the Cyprians in the north and the Phoenicians in the south moored or beached their ships and took their daymeal. Tyre raised a screen of sails across its northern harbor, gathered its ships, and readied an attack.

Meriamon had seen the sail-wall in the morning when she came to the hospital, and wondered what it was. Something new for the war, she supposed. She came out of the tent into the blazing heat of noon, and the wall was still up, the wind making it belly and flap.

There was no wind, no breath of air. There were men atop the towers that warded the harbor, tiny at that distance, moving quickly.

Niko was standing near the tent, peering toward the city. Meriamon did not pause to wonder at that, or to reflect that he was often about, doing one thing or another. "What are they doing?" she asked him.

"I don't know." He shaded his eyes with his hand. "They're up to something."

Without thinking about it, she started toward the shore. Niko walked with her, his long strides keeping pace with her shorter, quicker ones. Her eyes swept the water. There was the causeway, looking as if it had been there since the world was made. There was the fleet, moored or beached, one desultory galley stroking landward. The ramships lay at anchor, their scrabbling and thudding stilled for once. Even the sea was still.

She began to run.

Alexander was under his canopy, eating and talking to a handful of people. When he was done, his guards would hurry them out and he would sleep.

The man on guard today was Ptolemy. He saw who she was, and his brother behind her, sweat-streaming both, and both a little wild. He got out of her way. She pushed a great hulk of a Macedonian from her path, slid round another, came face to face with the king.

"Mariamne," he said, glad as always to see her, raising his brows at the figure she cut. She had forgotten to bring a mantle. Her dress was wet, and it clung; and Egyptian linen, when it was wet and clinging, might have been no garment at all.

"Alexander," she said, taking too many breaths to say it. Even in Khemet one knew better than to run in the full glare of noon. "Why are all your ships on shore?"

"We always stop at midday," someone said.

"Tyre knows that," said Meriamon.

Alexander had turned to say something to the man who spoke. He spun back to face her. He understood. It appalled him. "Zeus Pater!" He was running even before the words were out.

The Tyrians dropped their wall of sails and loosed their ships and fell on the Cyprian fleet. But even as they closed for the kill, Alexander came, driving hard under sail and oar, circling the city from the south and falling on the Tyrian ships; and none too soon. Moored or beached and empty of crews, the ships were sitting prey for the Tyrian war-galleys. Even with warning from the city, so swiftly did Alexander come that he caught the enemy's fleet before it could come about, and drubbed it soundly. He drove its remnants back into the harbor and bottled them there, while his Phoenicians barred the southern haven. Tyre's fleet was broken; it would be land-battle now, and shipless siege, until one or the other yielded.

Alexander was in no mood to celebrate his victory. "I made a mistake," he said. "I slacked off. I could have lost the war for it."

Meriamon did not argue with him. Other people tried; but he snarled at them until they stopped. He was rising to a rage. Not the anger that had begun the siege; that was mere pricked pride. This was a more terrible thing. Fury at himself. He had erred. He had almost failed. Because he had not planned for everything. Because he had let himself become predictable.

There was predictability, and then there was predictability. Slackness, complacence—those he would destroy wherever he found them, and in himself most of all. Hot temper and swift movement—those he was known for, and those he would wield, and no matter the cost.

He flung his rams against unyielding walls. He smote again and again, his men catching the fury that drove him, hurling it into stones that chipped and crumbled but would not shatter. Tyre, trapped in its defenses, dropped stones and cauldrons of fire. The stones tumbled wide. The fire sizzled and went out as it struck the shields of wetted hides. Here a man fell, crushed by a stone; there one died when, looking up from pouring water on the hides, he breathed a sheet of flame. They mattered nothing. Alexander was in a rage. Alexander would conquer or die.

Even stone must yield at last, and even Herakles' walls could not stand forever against Alexander's wrath. One of his ships found a flawed stone and hammered at it until it gave way, loosening the one beside it, and the one above it, and the rubble within: breaching the wall. Alexander himself was at the ram, his voice a whipcrack, lashing his men, cajoling them, urging them on. The wall shook with the force of the attack.

Someone shouted. The men at the ram scrambled back. A whole length of wall buckled and crumbled and fell, some within, some into the sea. A cheer went up. Alexander's voice snapped over it. A ramp slid from the ship's side and crashed down inside the walls of Tyre. Alexander was on it almost before it fell, running mad-alone against the Tyrian army.

His men barely paused. They thundered after him, chanting their paean, which for many was simply his name.

There were too few of them, and too many Tyrians. They fell back. But the wall was breached. Alexander had set foot in Tyre.

And, having done it, he drew back. He left the city with its broken wall, called all but the guards from the ships and the causeway, and went back to camp. Tyre, expecting renewed assault, received nothing. No move. No word.

The first day after the wall was breached, Alexander whiled the time with his poets and his friends, being Greek. The second day after the breach, he went hunting in what cool the morning had and idled the rest of the day, except for an hour with his generals. He talked particularly to Admetos, who led a company of the Royal Hypaspists, the Shieldbearing Guard, and to Koinos who commanded a battalion of the phalanx. He dined in company that night, awash in wine.

Meriamon was there because he asked, and because the air was so full of power. Her skin rippled with it, the small hairs quivering and rising erect. Her shadow was almost solid. It would not go hunting when she would have let it go. The hunting was better where she went.

She went as what she was: royal Egyptian. She wore her gown of sheerest linen folded into myriad pleats and cut as close as her skin, and over it a broad pectoral of lapis and gold that the king had sent her, knowing that she would wear it; and golden armlets, and rings of gold and lapis on her fingers and in her ears, and a fillet about the many plaits of her hair. She would have given much for a wig, but there was none that would do; and both Thaïs and Phylinna averred that her own hair was wonderful enough, as black and thick and waving as it was. Phylinna oiled and plaited it and bound the end of each plait with a bead of gold or lapis or carnelian. Meriamon painted her eyes herself with kohl and lapis and malachite, drawing the long lines longer, firming the arch of her brows. Thaïs anointed her with scent that could only have come from Khemet, rich as it was, with a hint of spices, a hint of musk, a suggestion of flowers.

She did not know what she was making herself beautiful for. The king would approve; he liked his friends to look their best. But she would have been happy to be simply Meriamon, and not this princess, this royal lady in her jewels and her unguents, with a lotus flower in her hand. How that had come there . . .

Her shadow smiled a fanged smile. She raised the bloom to her face. Its sweetness dizzied her. It smelled of the Nile; it smelled of Khemet. There was power on it, in it.

Tomorrow Alexander would finish what he had begun. He would end the siege. He would take the city, or he would fall. Tonight might be his last upon the earth, his last as the madman who fancied that he could conquer an unconquerable city.

What she could give him, she would give, and be living reminder of what he must fight for. Khemet's waiting was ended, for better or for ill.

She remembered little of the king's banquet. She had a couch to herself near Alexander's own. She ate, perhaps. She drank. She did not say anything that she recalled. People stared at first, Hellenes astonished or disgusted by her foreignness, hetairai narrow-eyed, measuring the familiar stranger, reckoning her potential as a rival. Phoenicians, of whom there were a few, offered her reverence. They knew what she was.

She was too busy being it to remember what she did. Alexander was her opposite. He did not need to be anything but Alexander. Sometimes he was everywhere, drawing every eye. Sometimes he was nowhere at all, effacing himself, letting the revel go on without him. He rested in that, talking softly with Hephaistion who had come to share his couch. No one took much notice. The king lay back against his friend's breast, half-drowsing, toying with a cup of wine. Hephaistion smoothed his hair. The Companion's face was still as it often was, like an image carved in ivory, beautiful almost to insipidity, but for the eyes. They held a calm that Alexander had never known, but in which he rested; a peace that was not placidity, a focus and a center, and far down in it a spark of youthful mirth.

Hephaistion was water, deep and seeming quiet. Alexander was fire. Even at rest he could not be still. He turned the cup in his hands, quick eyes darting round the room, catching now and then. More than once he smiled or said a word, bringing its object into his orbit, holding the man or woman there, letting go. His lover was his lover here, and that entirely. So might Alexander be, maybe, in the inner room, when the lamp was lit and there were but the two alone. But here he was multifold, now king, now friend, now lover, now simple joiner in the feast.

Meriamon's inward eye saw the woman who sat veiled within a Persian tent, watching as another woman nursed a swaddled child. Barsine was his lover, too, but she would never have what this one had. No woman could. No man either, perhaps, nor boy. Achilles had but the one Patroklos. There could never be another.

Alexander rose. Hephaistion drew up his knee and sipped from his cup and looked not at all abandoned. The king came to sit on Meriamon's couch, smiling at her. His garland had wilted in the heat; he looked, not ridiculous, but young and rather rakish. She could hardly help but smile back.

"Give me your blessing?" he asked her.

She raised her brows. "Do I have a blessing to give?"

"I think you do."

"And it matters to you?"

"It matters," he said.

She thought about it. "There's a god in you, you know. Nothing else could have brought you to this."

His eyes narrowed as if against the sun. He was not looking at her now; he saw beyond her, beyond any horizon that she knew.

He blinked, shook himself. He saw her again. His flesh was mortal flesh, his mind a mortal mind, if not quite like any other. He said, "You, too. You even more than I are a god's child. Why don't you take the power that's in your hand, and rule Egypt?"

"That is not given to me," she said.

"I could die tomorrow."

She inclined her head.

"You're calm about it," he said.

"Would it stop you if I wailed and gnashed my teeth?"

"No," said Alexander.

"So then," Meriamon said. "You will do what you will do. May the gods protect you."

He bowed to that. Not afraid, no, not Alexander. But that bright surety was won at a cost. No peace for him, no moment's stillness; and the god's fire in him wherever he was. What he needed of her—she had no worship for him. But she had the gods' voices in her, clearer maybe than he had ever heard them. She was their instrument. He was one of them. Or would be. If he lived past the morrow.

The third day after the sortie dawned with a sea like glass, no whisper of wind, no breath of air to stir the water, or lift the pennants, or cool a body risen from a hot and sleepless bed. Alexander's men were up before the first light, the Shieldbearers and Koinos' phalanx armed and ready. Their fellows looked on them in varying degrees of envy, even the veterans for whom war held no mysteries. Alexander changed it. He made it shine, because he was part of it.

He came out just as the light began to rise, splendid in his scarlet cloak, with his golden lion helmet in his hand. He gave it to a page as he advanced to perform the morning's sacrifice—a bull for Zeus this day, and another for Herakles, whose city the king meant to take. As the bull's blood streamed upon the altar, the sun leaped into the sky, turning his hair bright gold. The thighbone of Father Zeus' bull, wrapped in the fat and laid in the fire, sent its smoke up to heaven; that of Herakles' bull mingled with it, half savory, half terrible. The king's men shared the meat of the sacrifice, partaking of its strength. They seemed to finish all in the same instant, springing up with a shout and running to the sea.

Tyre was waiting for them. The ramships had gone out in the dawn; the booming and battering mounted with the light, carried on the still air, until surely the dead could hear and wake. As the king's men readied to board a pair of ships, Koinos' company on one, Admetos' Shieldbearers on the other with the king leaping ahead of them to mount the bow, metal glinted on the city's wall, and figures moved, gathering. Men ran out on the causeway, reckless of bolts or arrows, but none fell. Tyre had easier prey. A ship or two of Alexander's had faltered on the voyage from Sidon, run afoul of Tyrian galleys, and fallen to the enemy. Their crews were up on the walls. There could be no doubt of that. Heralds' voices rang over the water, proclaiming it. Even as the echoes died, figures as small as dolls, as effigies, as amulets, spun and wheeled down from the wall. They made no sound. They fell without grace or wit, dead before they left the wall, slaughtered like the bulls upon the altar. One fell full upon the deck of a ramship. The outcry of its crew reached even to the camp, a raw howl of rage and loss.

Trapped, the Tyrians, and desperate to folly, with their walls falling about their ears, and Alexander's army struck not to terror but to rage by the death of their fellows. The ramships backed oars from the great ragged gap in the wall and made way for their king. His two ships ran up to the rock. Each bore a bridge, lowering even as it approached, crashing down amid the rubble.

Admetos the commander hardly waited for the ramp to fall before he was on it, up the crumbling treacherous slope into Tyre, full into a Tyrian spear. The men behind him, his men even before they were Alexander's, saw him fall. They had seen the murder on the walls. Blood for blood and life for life, and sweet revenge for the long siege.

Alexander came behind with the second wave of men.

That was never his place, but for once he had yielded to honor and sense, and seen a good man die for it. He thrust through the ranks and seized the lead. The Tyrian line stood firm before him. His eye swept along it. He raised his sword. He charged, and all his men charged with him, bright shields, long spears, implacable will.

The Tyrians stood while they could. But they had no spear to match the sarissa of Macedon, three manlengths long and wielded from behind a wall of shields. They wavered and broke and ran.

A cry went up from the walls. The harbors were breached, Phoenicians pouring in from the south, Cyprians from the north, and Alexander himself in the center with the pick of his army. Tyre, beset from three sides, broken and battered and breached, fought as it could. Street by street, alley by alley, its fighting men fell back. They held for a while in one of their shrines, that of Agenor near the city's center, but Alexander broke their line again with his Shieldbearers and drove them out.

Melqart's temple rose at the summit of the city, its walls of cedar from the Lebanon, its roof sheathed in gold, and before its gate two tall pillars, one of ivory, one of beryl the color of grass. There Alexander halted. There the princes had taken refuge, and the King of Tyre himself, barricaded behind doors of bronze.

Alexander's men were sacking the city. The fighting had turned to butchery. Blood ran in the streets. Life paid for life, and for resistance that should never have been. Tyre had defied the gods. It paid in all that it was.

Meriamon was there. Her body lay in its tent in the camp with Sekhmet mounting guard over it. Her soul rode in a soldier's cloak, a wisp of shadow with ember-eyes. Niko had come in with the Phoenicians, but he had taken a company ahead of the rest and gone straight for the temple, knowing where Alexander would inevitably be. He was close by the king now. There was blood on his sword.

As if he had only now noticed it, he moved to wipe the blade on his cloak.

The king stood in front of the temple's gate, between the pillars. For all the press of men about him, he was alone. He could not fail to know that his men were slaughtering children, or that they were destroying the city in their anger. Here was the center of it, the heart of the resistance.

To Meriamon's sight, freed of the body's constraints, Melqart's temple was a shape of shadow and light, washed in the blood of sacrifice. The princes huddled in the outer courts and prayed to all their gods and to their king, who had no more courage to face Alexander than they. The priests held the sanctuary, and their strength was the strength of despair. They called on the god. They wove a mingled magic of will and chant and blood—blood of their own children, that the Macedonians loosed in their fury. The power grew like a cloud, waxing and pulsing, spitting lightnings. A moment more, a bending of will, and there would be no end to it. Tyre would fall, and Tyre's conquerors with it, and the sea would devour them.

Meriamon spread her soul's wings and rose from Niko's shoulder. He could not have been aware of her presence, but her absence touched him: he glanced about, eyes rolling a little, like a startled horse. She paused in the air above him, hawk-bodied, woman-headed, beating her wings against the force that came out of the temple. Alexander felt it. He swayed, braced. She struggled toward him. Each wingbeat battled the weight of a world. Each handbreadth was bought in the soul's strength.

Within arm's reach of Alexander, her wings failed. She dropped. A soul could not die, nor could the earth break it, but such power as the priests raised could trap and bind her, and swallow her with the rest in the city's fall. The bonds closed in about her, the power's weight heavy upon her, crushing her shadow-body.

She gathered every scrap of strength, every flicker of

will. It made a pitifully small spark. She opened her heart
to it. She beat her wings with all her strength. The tips
brushed the stone of the paving. But she was rising, driving upward, flinging herself at the king. Just as her
strength died, just as she plummeted, her talons seized his
cloak.

He saw her. She looked up into a face grown vast to
hawk-size, soul-sight. She saw the eyes wide and silver-
pale, terrible as the lightning's fall. "Do you feel it?" she
asked him. "Do you see it? What the old sorcerers did to
Mu, to Atlantis, they would do to Tyre. To you, Alexander.
To all that you would do and be."

He reached down. To his hands she had substance, if no
weight. Gently he freed her claws from his cloak, cradling
her in his palms, raising her to meet eye with eye. What
the men with him thought he was doing, she could not
imagine. Maybe they saw a bird tangled in his mantle.
"What can I do?" he asked her.

"Defeat them," she answered.

"How?"

She tucked her feet under her, folded her wings. His
hands enclosed her, warm and solid, ward and wall against
the power that rose in the temple. "Will it," she said.

"Will it? Want it? That's all?"

"For you," she said, "yes."

"But—" He stopped. "Aristotle would howl."

She laughed. She sounded to herself like a bird twitter-
ing.

Alexander looked a little disconcerted. But then he
grinned. "This is impossible, you know."

"Only to a rational Greek."

He laughed at that. His eyes lifted from her to the gate.
They saw what she could see. The cloud of power. The
lightnings growing more frequent, joining, one to one, two
to two. When they were all one, then Tyre would fall.

"No," he said. His voice was quiet. It had no particular
force in it, no power but what was in him from his birth.

He walked forward. One hand still cradled Meriamon's soul-self. The other reached to set palm against the door. As flesh touched bronze, the city rocked.

"No," Alexander said again. And pushed.

The gates were bolted and barred. Even as strong as he was for his size, even trained from youth in the arts of war, Alexander was neither a big man nor a weighty one. He could not open gates of bronze, bolted with bronze.

"Yes," he said. "I can."

The gate moved. The power behind it rocked and swayed. His brows drew together. He was not straining, not yet. He shifted his feet, bracing them. He set Meriamon in the fold of his cloak and brought to bear both hands and all of his weight.

"Your will," she said in his ear. "Your will is all that you need."

"It's all one," he said, a little breathless. He relaxed suddenly, as if to retreat. But he was only gathering his forces. With suddenness that nearly cost her her perch, he flung the whole of him, hands, weight, will, the god that was in him, all, into one single concerted thrust.

Gate and power held. The earth was uneasy, swaying harder now, hard enough for simple men to sense. Someone cursed, caught off balance, knocked from his feet.

"Be still!" Alexander's voice, sharp, no smoothness in it.

The earth was still. The power reared up. The gate burst open.

Light flooded through the temple. Alexander rode on it, his men behind him. Priests and power broke and scattered and fled.

But the princes held. Here at the end of things, they found their courage. They made a living wall about their king.

Alexander's Shieldbearers would joyfully have slaughtered them all. But he said, "No."

They stopped. They did not lower swords or spears, but neither did they strike.

The line of Tyrians opened. King Azemilk came forward. He was not as tall as Alexander, nor even as broad: little long-bearded hawk-faced man like all his people. But proud, even defeated. He went down on his knees, stiffly; then on his face. "Tyre is fallen," said the King of Tyre, and each word was bitter, bitter. "Alexander is victorious. All hail Alexander, lord of Asia."

One by one, raggedly, but clear enough, the princes echoed him. "Hail Alexander. Hail the lord of Asia!"

• EIGHTEEN •

Tyre was fallen. Its king had made his submission to Alexander, and received pardon. But his people, for their resistance, paid in lives and wealth and freedom. Alexander, thwarted, was no merciful creature, and he had been thwarted to the edge of defeat. He took the city and all that was in it. He sold its men into slavery. He made his sacrifice to Herakles in the temple that had refused him, before the priests who had defied him, and he held games of victory on the shore where he had camped so long.

On the last night of the games, while Alexander's army in city and camp alike completed their triumph in wine and song, Meriamon walked on the sand by the quiet sea. There was a moon; it gave her shadow substance, and gleamed coldly on the ring in Sekhmet's ear. Tyre was a darkness against the stars, sparked here and there with light. The long sad train of its people had gone in the morning, some inland to Damascus, some in ships to Hellas and the isles. New citizens would come after Alexander was gone, people from the villages of the mainland who would fill the city again and make it strong under

Alexander's rule, at the bidding of a Macedonian commander.

That was war. To the victor, everything. To the vanquished, if he was fortunate, his life.

Someone came toward her over the sand. She was not surprised to know that gait, that angle of the shoulders, that lift of the head against the stars.

"Do you know what troubles me most?" she said to him. "I think I like war. Even the grief that comes after it."

Niko stopped a little distance from her. "I think I hate it," he said.

It was the dark and the solitude, and neither able to read the other's face. It opened the gates between them. It turned the walls to air.

"Blood," she said, "I hate. And slaughter of children. But strong man against strong man, city against invader, king against king—so must the world be."

"I won't kill children," he said. "Or women, unless they're trying to kill me first."

"I know. I saw."

He moved closer, standing over her. She could see his face now, the gleam of his eyes. "That was you. The—thing—that was with me."

"What did you see?" she asked.

"Something," he said. "Like a bird, but not. It was you. I thought it might be."

"It was easier," she explained. Or tried to. "Knowing you, and knowing you knew me. But you couldn't see me. The king would have sent me back if I'd gone with him. He could see, you see."

"I see." His voice was perfectly flat.

She bit her lip. She wanted to laugh aloud; but that would not have been wise at all. "Do you mind? Terribly?"

"Well," he said. "No. Not terribly. You could have told me."

"And been forbidden?"

"Do I have a right to forbid you?"

"Would it have mattered if you did?"

"Probably not," he said after a while. His hands settled themselves on her shoulders, starting as they touched bare skin under the almost-nothingness of veil. Coming back carefully, as if they could not help themselves. The one that was whole and supple. The one that was remembering, slowly, to be strong.

She did not flinch or move away. Her heart was beating hard. He would shake her now, call her witch and deceiver of men, pay her as she deserved for making such use of him.

He said, "You are more than anyone knows. Even the king."

"He knows," she said faintly.

He heard her. "Not all of it."

"Enough."

"You seem like such a little thing," he said. "With those long eyes and that husky voice, and a way about you— now creeping like a brown mouse, now holding your head up like a queen. And showing yourself in clothes that would incite an army to riot, but no army would ever dare, unless you wanted it."

"You don't like my dress?"

He opened his mouth. Shut it. Said, "I like it too much."

"It's cool," she said. "And sensible. Thaïs had one made for herself. When winter comes, she says, she might try Persian trousers."

"Gods!" said Niko. "My poor brother."

"Why? Because his woman wants to be warm in winter and cool in summer? You Hellenes—you go naked all year round. What can you say of what a woman should wear?"

"Nothing," he said. He let her go, half-turning from her. "I forget myself. I'm sorry. Lady."

She pulled him about. Temper burned the silliness out of her; she could see straight enough, and her heart was exactly where it belonged, and not in her throat, or fluttering somewhere about his head. "Oh, come!" she said. "We know each other well enough to be honest, surely. And none of this 'my lady' nonsense. I'm no queen or goddess. And you're not my guardsman. You're a captain now, with men of your own. I saw you win a footrace today, and a mounted race. What did the king say when he saw you back on Typhon?"

"About what you would have said," said Niko. "I won, didn't I? And stayed on, too."

"And kept him from making a meal of the horse that came up behind him on the final turn. Idiot horse. He could have won by a furlong instead of a length, if he'd kept his mind on what he was doing."

"I suppose you could have done better," he said acidly.

"Not at all," she said. "I yelled myself hoarse. So did everybody else. You're a favorite in the army. And you think you can play the servant with me?"

"I am nothing," he said, "and no one, beside you. You could be Alexander's equal if it suited you to try. You do your gods' will instead. You bully and cajole and trick him into doing it with you. When are the two of you going to see what a match you make?"

"Not we," said Meriamon. "He wants no wife."

"He would if you wanted him to."

"I don't." She was holding his hand, the right, the one that was hurt. She brought it to her cheek. "I don't want him."

The stiffened fingers twitched. Straightened: he caught his breath with the effort and the pain of it. Curved to fit her cheek.

He snatched his hand back. "Of course you want the king! He's the only man who's fit for you. He's brilliant, he's splendid, the god is in him. He finds you fascinating. More than that, he likes you. Trusts you. Loves you, maybe. If either of you could admit it."

"No," said Meriamon.

He clasped his crippled arm with his good one, tightly, shaking just hard enough to see. "Then you are both fools."

"No doubt," she said.

"If I were Alexander," he said. "If I were the king, you would know that I wanted you. And so would I."

"If you were Alexander," she said, "then I would want him."

"You should not."

He said it so firmly that she laughed. She knew better. She had no mirth in her. It was all anger and incredulity and a white mad joy. He wanted—*he* wanted—

He did shake her then, until she stopped giggling. "I thought," she said, gasping. "I thought—you—couldn't stand—"

"I can't. What does that have to do with it?"

His sharpness brought her to herself a little. Familiar; bracing. Finding its match in her temper. "Sometimes I wish I did want the king," she said. "He's a simpler thing. Fire and willfulness, and a genius for commanding armies. You . . . I never know what you will do or say."

"I'm just a trooper in the cavalry. I'm not even anything particular to the king."

"He knows who you are," said Meriamon. "And what you are. You weren't brought up with him as Ptolemy was. But you're not his father's son, either."

Niko started. His hands tightened to pain. "What do you—"

"They're brothers. I can see that. Did Lagos ever know?"

Niko let her go. He drew away. This time she did not try to stop him. When he wandered down the strand, she followed. "He knew," Niko said. "From the beginning. He married her knowing that she had Philip's baby in her belly. Philip wasn't king, and wasn't likely to be either, with his brother the king young enough yet and likely to live for a while, and capable enough of siring sons. So she went with Lagos, and when her son was born Lagos took him up and called him his own. By the time Perdikkas died and left a baby to inherit, and Philip got himself named king, Ptolemy was Lagos' son and that was the whole of it. Except that Philip had a long memory for women—he always kept track of them, the way he kept track of everything else that ever concerned him—and our mother didn't forget, either. So everybody knows, but nobody talks about it."

And no wonder. Ptolemy was the elder. He could lay claim to Alexander's throne.

Niko saw well enough what she was thinking. "He wouldn't. He's not that much of a fool."

"No," said Meriamon. "Ptolemy has more sense than most. He knows what's best for himself and for his people."

"And he loves Alexander." Niko stopped walking. "We all do. Even the ones who started by wanting someone else to be king—they came round, one way and another. It takes a rare man to resist him."

"Or woman?" Meriamon waded out into the water. It was neither warm nor cool, lapping gently against her knees, tugging at her skirt. If she opened her senses wide enough, she could find a glimmer in it that had been the Nile, a memory of the greatest river in the world, river of power as of water, rising unknown and unseen in the deeps of Africa and pouring its gathered waters into the sea. In that gathering it gave and it took, gave the Two Lands their riches and their power, and took them back, and carried them to the Great Green, the sea at the bottom of the world.

She turned. Niko stood on the water's edge, dark shape of head and shoulders, white glimmer of chiton. "Your mother refused a king," she said.

"He wasn't king yet."

"But he would be. And when he was, when she had his son to wield as a weapon, she said no word. She kept the life she had chosen. She gave her husband another son who was all his own."

"That was plain good sense. Alexander was born by then. Everyone knew what he had for a mother."

"A woman with a mind of her own."

"A harpy." Niko shook himself. "Well, no. Maybe she's not as bad as that. They had a love match, those two, even when he went a-roving. He always came back, or she did, or both at once. It's not true what they say, that Alexander and Olympias paid off the assassin who killed Philip."

"I know," said Meriamon.

"You saw it, I suppose."

Meriamon did not answer. She did not need to.

"She was wild when he died," Niko said. "Wild with joy one moment, because he'd got his comeuppance. Wild with grief the next. But cold all through it, and making sure her son got what was his. She's a terrible woman. There's a goddess in her, I think; or a Fury."

"Intelligence, maybe," said Meriamon, "and impatience with men's follies. That sours fast, if one isn't careful."

"How do you stand us?"

She laughed. "Come here," she said.

For a wonder he obeyed her. She took his hands in hers. "Don't ask why," she said, "or doubt. Just accept."

"But you are—I'm not—"

She stopped his lips with her hand, reaching high. "I didn't see, either. Till now. You so tall and so strong, and I so little, and no beauty—"

He lifted her suddenly as if she had been a child, setting her level with him, face to face. "You are beautiful." He said it as he would command a trooper in parade.

"I am not," she said. "Pretty, sometimes, when I work at it. For the rest of it—"

"And what do you see in me? I'm a cripple. I've got a face like an old sandal. If I had any rank to add to it, or power in myself, or any touch of godhood—"

"You are yourself," she said. She set her hand against

his cheek. It was rough with stubble. The long jaw, the long mouth, the uncompromising nose, would never delight a sculptor; but they were his own. "I would have you exactly as you are. Even when you sulk."

He glowered. "You have a tongue like an adder."

"Surely," she said. "We match, you see."

"I have no magic."

"You have eyes."

They looked hard at her. She curved her arms about his neck. He held her easily. She did not weigh a great deal more than his armor, which she had discovered for herself when she tried to lift the lot of it. She played with the hair that curled on his neck. "And you have very handsome hair," she said. "Almost as bright as the king's. Did you get it from your mother?"

"Yes." It was hard to tell in the dark, but she thought he might be blushing. She laid her cheek against his. Oh, indeed: it was burning hot.

"Poor boy," she said. "I embarrass you."

"You can't be any older than I am," he snapped.

"Oh, but I am. I was born a good half-year before the king."

"That makes you ancient," he said, dripping irony. "Three whole years' worth."

"All women are as old as time; and I am a woman of Egypt. I was ancient when the world was made. To us all you Hellenes are children."

"So," he said, "I've heard."

She laughed. She was aware, not at all unpleasantly, that her body pressed close against his, and that he was warm; warmer than the night.

"My smallest sister is bigger than you," he said.

"You are enormous," she agreed.

The heat that rose in him was fierce enough to burn. He set her down abruptly and splashed back to shore.

There he stopped. "Niko," she said. He did not turn, but

neither did he run away. "Niko, do you want me as much as I want you?"

His voice was very much itself, for all the rigidity that it came out of. "Are all Egyptians that blunt about it?"

"I don't know," she said. "I never wanted anyone before."

His shoulders shook. She wondered if she had driven him to tears. "You never—" His voice caught. Laughter. It was laughter. It stopped abruptly. "You aren't . . . sworn, are you? To take no man?"

"Of course not," she said.

"But the gods—"

"The gods celebrate life as we do. They would hardly forbid me."

"I don't understand you."

"Nor do I," she said, "often."

He turned. She could not see his face. He was a shadow, tall against the stars. "It's not right, of course," he said in careful, flawless Greek. No soft Macedonian burr. "You are royal and I am not."

"Your mother is royal kin."

"I am not a king," he said, "nor a king's son. And I have nothing to give you but a valley in Macedonia, with a hill fort above it, and good grazing for horses. It's much too cold for you there."

She stared at him. "Are you offering me marriage?"

"I am telling you why I cannot."

"That," she said, "is the most presumptuous thing I have ever heard."

"Yes," he said tightly.

She wanted to shake him. She often did. It was becoming a habit. "That's not what I meant! How dare you presume what is and is not suitable for me? I am my own woman. You are your king's man. If I ask him, he will do no more and no less than give you to me."

"No!" He was shouting. He lowered his voice. "Mariamne. Mari—Meriamon. Don't ask him."

"You don't want me."

"I do want you!" He forced calm again, forced softness. "It's that ... you keep him safe. In a way. While you're here, and Egypt is there, the ones who want him married off are less likely to press him."

"There's Barsine," said Meriamon.

"What, and Memnon's brat? Even Arrhidaios can count on his fingers, and anyone who knows babies can tell you that's no newborn. Two months, is he? Three?"

"Two," she said. She drew a slow breath. "Yes," she said. "I suppose it's true. Egypt needs me; Alexander needs me. I can't bind myself to anything until that is done."

"You can't," he said.

"But," said Meriamon, "outside of binding, where the heart is, there I am free." She came out of the water, advancing on him. He stood his ground. She set her palms flat on his breast over his heart. "Not now," she said, "but soon, I shall claim you. Will you let me?"

His chest heaved. He was trembling. But then, in a breath's pause, he steadied. That was the splendor of him: that courage to face what he was most afraid of, and overcome it. "Maybe," he said.

She hit him. He caught her. She hooked his knee and spilled him into the sand. He had let her, knowing she would do it. That was answer enough. She dusted her hands and gathered her skirts and went back to the camp. Whether he followed, or when, she did not need to know. He had her mark on him. The gods would look to the rest.

·PART THREE· .

EGYPT

• NINETEEN •

Alexander's army marched from Tyre in the full heat of summer, traveling in the cool of the morning and in the cool of the night, and resting in the day's heat. The mountains of the Lebanon fell away with their snows that cooled the eye even as the sun battered it blind. The green uplands, the little rivers, faded and shrank. Dun earth, dust and flies, and heat that would not relent for any wishing, and no blessed green: harvest was over where any water was, the fields stripped bare, and only here and there the relief of an oasis. This was desert, the Red Land indeed though far from Khemet, and it had no mercy on any who would invade it, whatever his right to it.

They marched beside the sea, cool glorious blue that no man could drink; its salt was cruel to fair Macedonian skin seared raw by the sun. The fleet sailed in it, keeping close to shore and putting in with water, wine, bread and meat and daintier things. Hephaistion had command of it, received as calmly as he did everything that mattered, and managed with admirable competence.

Nikolaos sailed with him. It was a sore choice between the ships and the horses, but the ships won the toss. Meriamon, for her part, would not leave the land. Not for fear of the great water or of the ships that sailed on it; but Alexander marched with the army, and she wanted to be with Alexander. If Niko was fleeing her by taking to the sea, then so be it. He still came in every night, beached his ship and slept on the sand with his men. She sat with them sometimes near the fire that kept the flies at bay, and heard their songs and stories, and told her own, as much as she could with no song in her. That had not come back, not even yet, though Khemet's nearness rose in her like a tide.

There were cities along the coast, and villages in the green places, huddled about a spring or a river now thinned to a trickle or gone dry. The people there worshipped a god who was one alone, and owed their allegiance to a city of priests in the inland hills. The temple there, people said, was like the temple of Melqart in Tyre, and built by the same hands, but the god in it wore no earthly form, nor allowed one to be ascribed to him. The Macedonians thought it very strange. Meriamon thought it rather like Amon, who in his chief semblance was hidden and had no face that mortal eyes could see.

The cities received Alexander with welcome or at the least without resistance. He bought what he needed from them, of water little for they had none to spare and he had ships conveying it from the rivers of Syria, but of their harvest whatever they would offer. That grew less as he marched southward, and his ships supplied more, sailing by night as well as by day to meet the army's need.

At last they came to Gaza. They had had warning as far north as Tyre that the commander of Gaza, Batis the Babylonian, was not minded to surrender to Alexander. They found the city locked and barred and its people as defiant as if they had never known the lesson of Tyre. "I'll break you," Alexander said to their envoys. "Gaza is no Tyre. It can't stand against me."

"We can try," said Batis' men. The chief of them, squat heavy-bodied Babylonian like his commander, looked Alexander up and down and said, "You've never lost a battle, have you? Maybe it's time you learned."

Alexander's face was burned scarlet by the sun; it could hardly have reddened more. His eyes in it were almost white, like the sun in the merciless sky. "Do you dare delay me?"

"We'll stop you if we can."

"Then try," said Alexander. "Try and be damned."

* * *

Tyre had been pure frustration. This was maddening: the city squatting in its sandpit, the army drying to leather outside of it, and no hope of moving while Batis was there to raise the country against them. Behind was retreat more bitter than Alexander ever meant to endure. Beyond was desert as bitter as any in the world. Seven days—seven marches through the furnace of the gods to the gateway of Egypt.

Batis was as stubborn as his enemy, and as deaf to reason. He would hold or he would die. What had befallen Tyre cost him not a moment's hesitation.

There was malice here. Not in Batis, perhaps; Meriamon saw him on the walls, and he was as any other man, light and darkness mingled, and a black root of obstinacy informing all that he did. The seed from which it sprouted, the source which gave it its strength, was no part of him at all.

And yet there was no temple here, no circle of priests working power out of sacrifice. There was nothing that she could see. Only the dark thing, the quiver in the senses, the pervading, numbing hostility. The land itself might have spawned it, or the air, or a god whose name she did not know. Melqart, no; he had never wished ill to Alexander, whatever his priests might have done. She had not seen him at all in his city, as if he had withdrawn from it, left his priests and his descendant to settle their quarrel as they would.

This was different. This was both more real and less, more solid and less certain. A will set against him. A mind, or minds, that would destroy him if it could.

Arrhidaios knew about it. In Tyre his keepers had kept him close, and he had gone with Alexander to Sidon. On the march they had relaxed their vigilance, perhaps because he could hardly go far in that country, or want to. In Gaza he took to following Meriamon about, helping her as he could, fetching and carrying when she was in the hospital, or making a looming second to her shadow when she

walked abroad in the camp. Her shadow rather liked him.
He could see it; he talked to it, easily, a child's prattle in
his deep rumble of a voice.

Even before she was fully aware of what was beneath
the earth, she heard him say to her shadow, "Do you feel
it, too? It's all dark underneath. It doesn't like us at all."

" 'It'?" she asked, pausing in her stride.

Arrhidaios shrugged and looked guilty. "Nothing," he
said. Nor could she coax any more out of him, though she
cursed the Greeks who had taught him. "It's bad," was all
he would say.

She let it go. He stopped telling her shadow about it, almost stopped talking at all, walking hunched and low, like
a dog with its tail between its legs.

She found herself walking the same way, and shooting
glances over her shoulder. The shadow behind her was always her own, sulfur-eyed, jackal-grin, but more and more
it was no grin but a snarl. Its ears lay flat against its head;
its hands, human-fingered but tipped with claws, flexed
and eased, flexed and eased.

Even a fool could see sense if she had her nose rubbed
in it. Meriamon rose up on a day out of count, brazen sky,
hammer of sun, and Alexander's army burrowing like desert rats; and Gaza on its rock, a ship in a sea of sand.

He was in the front as he always was, as filthy and sun-
scorched and water-starved as they, and in a towering rage.
That he had been in it for the greater part of a month, and
no end to it that anyone could see, had done nothing to
lessen it. Quite the contrary. The glare he turned on
Meriamon was actual white pain, so sudden and so fierce
that she gasped. Her shadow glided forward against all
logic of sun or shade, ears flat, teeth bared, the ghost of a
growl in its throat.

Alexander regarded it as he would have done Peritas,
who, being a sensible creature, had taken refuge in the
shade of the engineers' tent. Meriamon's shadow was nei-

ther sensible nor an earthly creature. It barred the way between Meriamon and the king.

"Down," he said to it. "Peace. I won't harm her."

It subsided slowly. He looked from it to Meriamon, then about him to the struggle of the siege.

Abruptly he signaled his trumpeter. "Call a rest," he said, "and water—double ration. You," he said to Meriamon, "come with me."

She went with him. It was hardly cooler under the canopy, but one of the king's pages was there with a jar of water, and wine to mix in it, and a soldier's ration of bread and fruit. Peritas' tail thumped the ground, raising a puff of dust. Alexander knelt to ruffle his ears.

Meriamon waited. Urgency was fierce in her, but patience nested in it, allowing him this moment's indulgence. She gained time to measure his mood.

The bright power that had sailed out of Sidon was darkened now. Wrath stained it, and the long rankling of siege piled upon siege. What was in the earth here was little enough in itself—a small malice, a feeble resentment, a touch of the old dark that had been before the gods. But his souls were open to it, ripe for its taking. It was soft, supple, creeping round the walls of his spirit, pouring cold over the fire that was his strength. It would not break him but subvert him. Not lightning out of heaven but a serpent in the heel, subtle and deadly.

She sat down abruptly. Her knees had given way. Arrhidaios squatted by her, brown eyes worried. "What is it, Meri? Are you sick?"

"No," she managed to say. "It's the heat, that's all. May I have a cup of water, please?"

He went eagerly as she had hoped, to fetch a cup and fill it. She tucked her feet under her. She was no woman of the desert, to scorn the weakness of chair or stool, but the chair that was closest was too great a height to scale. In a moment she would try it. She leaned against its leg.

The carved and gilded wood was cool, cooler than her cheek. She closed her eyes.

She knew when Alexander came to stand by her. She would always know where he was, however far he went, however feeble her strength. He crouched as his brother had, but lightly, without the audible grunt and creak of bones. "Something's wrong," he said.

She opened her eyes. His face filled her vision. His nose was peeling. She said so.

He rubbed it. His eyes were clear grey, the color of flint; one was perceptibly darker, odd to meet from so close. The white light seemed to have gone from them, but she could feel it beneath.

Tyre had done that. Gaza had deepened it. Where great light was, was greatest dark. Where the highest god walked, the god of the netherworld paced after. And Alexander would not be thwarted. His spirit would not endure it.

She shivered, though the air was as hot as she could ever have wished. She who was a king's daughter knew what a king was. This one knew gentleness, knew mercy. But that was the work of his will, of long teaching at strong hands. If he loosed the bonds that constrained him, if he opened himself to the fullness of his power, to the dark as well as the light, then all that he had wrought, he could destroy. And Khemet would know a tyrant worse than any out of Persis.

Her heart hardened. It would not happen. The gods would not let it. But what was here, what he tried to do— that was deadly dangerous.

"Alexander," she said, "do you feel the ill-will that is here?"

"I could hardly miss it," he said.

"No," she said. "Not Gaza. Not Batis and his soldiers, though they share a part of it. They've called up something else. Waked it, brought it with them—it doesn't matter which. It means you no good."

"No more did Melqart's priests," Alexander said. "They

gave way easily enough, and there was more to them than I'll ever see here." He smiled and helped her up. "There now. You're heatstruck, that's all, and half mad as we all are with another siege so hard on the heels of the other. It will be over soon; we'll bring you home to Egypt. Did you know I've had embassies from Mazaces the satrap? He's minded to let me in without a fight. Wise man, Mazaces."

"The Parsa are not always fools," she said. "Or cowards, either."

Alexander set her in the chair, as solicitous as if she had been a queen, and smiled down at her. It was a bright boy-smile, with no shadow in it. "They aren't, are they? I've liked the ones I've met. Very much, some of them. Queen Sisygambis is more of a man than most of the men I've seen; and Artabazos is a philosopher. It used to drive Aristotle wild when I said as much, but I meant it. I still do."

Meriamon heard him out. He was talking around her, and he knew it as well as she. When he finished she said, "I think you should forget this siege and go on. It's ill for you. It turns your mind on itself and gnaws it to pieces. Better to leave it behind, and find your strength in Egypt."

"I can't do that," he said much too reasonably. He should have been furious that she should see a weakness in him, and speak of it so clearly. "With Persia rising like a wave in the east, and the sea-cities barely subdued, I can't leave one to think it's thwarted me. Others will follow once they see what one can do, and I'll have the whole war to fight again."

"Not if you die here."

There. She had said it. It was cold and hard in her heart, and true, a seer's truth.

He laughed. "Oh, come! You've been listening to my soothsayers. Mutter, mutter, mumble, mumble, and dark days lie ahead, and things worse than dark, but they know and I know what they mean. *There's* the danger. If I'm made to think I'll die, so I will, and the enemy will have his way."

"I haven't listened to anyone," she said, "but the gods who are in me. I see death for you here. What is the word the Greeks use? Hubris. I see it in you."

His eyes went wide and pale. "Lady," he said with careful control. "Mariamne. You are what you are, and I grant you fair indulgence. But you are not Alexander."

"Nor are you," she said, "when you speak so. There is a god in you, I have no doubt of it. But even gods must acknowledge their limits."

"I'm not a god," he said. Quickly. Fiercely. "I am a king. I do as a king must. Hellas calls me to this war, Egypt waits for me, Asia cries out to me. Tyche—Tyche who is Fate—commands all that I do."

"Even your Tyche, who is like and unlike our Ma'at, allows a choice. If you leave now, you can come back with all Egypt behind you and scatter this city to the winds."

"If Persia will let me, or Phoenicia stay subdued." Alexander's face was firm, set against her. "I thank you for your trouble. You mean well, I know. But I won't change my mind."

She stood. He had to retreat quickly or be overset. Arrhidaios stood behind him with a cup in his hand, staring at them both. She took the cup with as much of a smile as she could muster, and drank it down. "Thank you," she said.

Arrhidaios' eyes shifted away from her. "You should listen to her, Alexander," he said. "She sees the bad thing, too."

Alexander did not turn on his brother. The softening of his face was never for Meriamon, and his words though gentle had no yielding in them. "So do I. It doesn't scare me."

"It should," said Arrhidaios. "It's bad."

"Why, what does it look like to you?"

Arrhidaios knit his heavy brows and pulled at his beard. For a moment he might have been right in the head: a man of the king's council called on to settle a difficult dispute.

Then he covered his eyes with his hands and shrank down shivering. "It's bad," he said, sobbing it. "It's bad!"

"Hush," said Alexander, kneeling beside him and holding him tightly. "It can't hurt you."

"It doesn't want to. It wants you."

"It won't get me."

Arrhidaios clutched his brother's arm, pulling him about, face to face. "It bites you," he said. "Like a snake. Niko caught a snake. It bit a dog. The dog swelled up and died. Niko killed it, and a dog ate it, and it died too."

"I'm not a dog. I won't die."

"It's bad," said Arrhidaios. "It's *bad!*"

Alexander's lips were tight. Meriamon could see the flesh reddening and swelling where Arrhidaios gripped him. How strong the man was, she well knew. But Alexander voiced no protest. "Hush," he said. "Hush."

Soon enough Arrhidaios hushed. He let Alexander go, only to bury his head in his brother's shoulder. Alexander rocked him, murmuring in Macedonian, brother-words, mother-words, comfort-words.

Over the rough dark head he met Meriamon's stare. He did not speak. Nor did she. She left them there, the king and the one who could have been king if he had grown as a man should. Simple earthly sickness, it might have been, that addled his wits in youth. Or mischance: a nurse's carelessness, a guardsman's failure to watch over him. Or poison sent awry. Or an ill working, a spell sung in the dark of the moon.

The darkness was fouling all that she thought of. She fled it as best she could, seeking the nearest refuge.

Thaïs was just out of bed—was it still only midmorning?—and retching into a basin. That was a common enough sight after a Macedonian drinking-bout, but Thaïs did not often succumb to it. Meriamon would have gone by; Phylinna had matters well in hand. But she paused. She was counting, reckoning mornings and frequencies.

Yesterday, yes. And the day before. Not the day before that, but Meriamon had gone early to the hospital and stayed late, and she had not seen Thaïs at all.

It was admirable distraction from what beset her. She went to kneel by Thaïs, taking the basin from the servant. The girl was delighted to be relieved of such duty; she backed away.

Thaïs lay back at last, exhausted. Phylinna wiped her brow with a dampened cloth, clucking to herself. Meriamon leveled an eye at the servant, who retrieved the basin and took it elsewhere. To the privies, Meriamon hoped, and not simply to the back of the tent.

Thaïs sighed. It caught. Meriamon looked about swiftly for another basin, but Thaïs said, "It's over. Just . . . a last remembrance."

"Does Ptolemy know?" asked Meriamon.

"Not yet." Thaïs seemed not at all surprised that Meriamon had guessed. Meriamon was Egyptian after all, and a physician. She could hardly fail to know what these morning indispositions meant.

"Will you keep it?"

The hetaira closed her eyes. After a moment she opened them. They were as old as Khemet. "I don't know," she said.

"Do you want to?"

"I don't know that, either."

"Maybe you should ask its father."

Thaïs stiffened at the word. Offended? Startled? "No," she said. "This child is mine. I'll do the choosing for it."

Meriamon did not say anything. Fathers chose in Hellas, she knew that: to take up the child and rear it, or to expose it on the hillside. But that was a living child. Whether its mother would bear it at all—that was another matter.

Her hand went to her own middle. No life kindled in it. None would. She had bought power and purpose, and a destiny, and paid in the children she would have borne. Yet she could feel—could imagine—the spark caught, swelling, waxing into humanity. It hurt. She had not expected that.

Thaïs sat up. She wobbled; Phylinna steadied her. She waved the maid away. Color came back to her cheeks. She looked like herself again. The little page whom Ptolemy had given her after Tyre, eunuch already and reared for Tanit's temple, stood with cup and bowl. Thaïs smiled at him. He blushed and ducked his head. He was a pretty thing, less oily-sleek than most of his kind, and endearingly shy.

"Do you know what I discovered last night?" asked Thaïs in her bright brittle day-voice. "Thettalos is back."

"The Thessalian?" Meriamon had heard the name, but at the moment she could not remember where. "One of the cavalry?"

Thaïs laughed. "Oh! I forget. You came after Issus. He was gone by then—he wintered in Hellas, and summered there, too, till he decided to come back to Alexander. They're dear friends. He's the best tragic actor in Hellás. He has a troupe that he takes everywhere, and they do the plays at festivals. Have you ever seen the tragedy?"

"Once," said Meriamon, "or twice, when I was small. We have part-rites of our own. Osiris' are famous, that are sung in Abydos."

"Then you know what it's like, though no one does it as well as Thettalos. He's going to do scenes tonight, just for the king's friends. Will you come? Niko will be there," said Thaïs, wicked. "He never misses a performance."

That decided it. Meriamon would not go. She did not need to contend with the disturbance that he was, with all the rest that beset her. She heard herself say, "I'll go."

Thaïs clapped her hands. "Oh, good! I'll wear my Egyptian gown. I have a new collar. It's not as handsome as yours, but I look very well in it. Almost a proper Egyptian."

* * *

Meriamon, improper Egyptian, regarded Thaïs in her finery and smiled. The hetaira would never look anything but Greek, but the sheer linen and the golden pectoral set off her body's richness admirably. She preened in it, shaking her head to make the plaits dance. Her hair did not take well to the hundred tiny braids that Meriamon wore, but she professed herself well content with a simpler fashion, narrow plaits about the face, the rest caught up in a fillet: more Greek than Egyptian, but very becoming. Meriamon said so.

"You of course are exquisite," said Thaïs. "What I would give for bones that fine . . . and those eyes! If you ever tire of being a priestess, you'd make a splendid courtesan."

"I'll remember that," said Meriamon, trying not to blush.

The king's friends were gathered in his tent, in the central hall made larger by the removal of the inner walls. A half-circle of couches faced another of the walls, and emptiness in front of it, an absence waiting to be filled. There was wine and a flute player, and a blind man plucking sweet random notes on a lyre.

Thaïs went at once as she always did, to Ptolemy's couch. Meriamon could not see one that was empty. Most had two already, man and woman or man and youth. There were a few on which men reclined alone.

One was Niko's. Meriamon sat in the woman's place and took the cup that the servant filled for her. He was massively silent. She slanted a glance over her shoulder. "Good evening," she said.

"Good evening," he replied civilly. "You're looking very pretty."

"And you," she said.

His brows flew up. She laughed at his expression. Pretty, no; that was not the word. But his chiton looked new, and seemed—was—heavy raw silk. Its hem was embroidered with gold. He had his good cloak draped over the couch, the one he had taken as booty in Tyre, the beautiful amethyst purple of a lighter dyeing. It was not so highly prized as the deep-dyed royal vermilion, but she loved the color of it. A fillet bound his hair, raw silk again, and a thin strand of gold. She smoothed a lock that was minded to stray. "You're very pleasant to look at," she said.

"I'd rather look at you."

"Then we're both content," said Meriamon. She considered briefly. No one was looking, nor, on reflection, would she care if anyone did. She stretched out, leaning on her elbow, her back against his front. He hardly flinched. Brave man. She sipped her wine and nibbled the dainties that came her way and decided that she liked to have him so close. As close as her shadow, but warmer.

The king made an entrance as he liked to do, with Peritas on a lead and, somewhat surprisingly, Arrhidaios walking behind. The king's brother had a clean chiton and an eager expression. He greeted Meriamon with delight. "Meri! You'll see Thettalos too."

"I will," she said.

"Sit with me?" he asked.

Meriamon did not know what to say.

"Niko won't mind," said Arrhidaios. "Will you, Niko? You can sit with Alexander."

People were grinning. Niko, for a marvel, did not even frown. "You can sit with the lady," he said, almost managing not to sound relieved.

A little man tugged at Arrhidaios' arm: the chief of his guardians, speaking softly. "Come, my lord. Here is a couch for you, right in front, and a pretty lady to wait on you."

"I want Meriamon," said Arrhidaios.

She started to rise. Alexander's voice stilled them all, even the watchers who had begun to laugh. "Go on, brother. Thettalos is coming out soon. Don't you want to hear him?"

Arrhidaios' face clouded. "I want Meriamon," he said.

"You may help Meriamon in the hospital in the morning," said Alexander firmly.

"Promise?"

"I promise," Meriamon said.

Arrhidaios did not like it at all. His brows knit, stubborn. The servant tugged at him.

Slowly Arrhidaios yielded. Meriamon sank back to the couch. Alexander's eyes flashed over her and her companion. His smile was sudden and quite dazzling. When she had blinked the brilliance away, the king was at ease on his couch and the servants had dimmed the lamps, all but those which illuminated the space near the wall. They made a half-circle within the half-circle, a house of light amid the crowding shadows.

The notes of the lyre, present but forgotten through the rest of it, gathered and came together. The flute wove among them. A drum began to beat, blood-beat, pulse-beat.

He came out of the dark: a slender youth in a purple robe, dancing, swaying, with a golden branch in his hand. His face was white as marble, white as death, the eyes as deep as the darkness behind the stars. The skin of a spotted panther was his girdle and his cloak. His hair streamed down his back, tawny gold, loose long locks like a lion's mane.

He sang as he came. His voice was neither deep nor light, neither man's nor woman's. Youth's, maybe, just broken and finding its depth. The purity of it walked cold down Meriamon's spine. Zeus' son, he, child of the gods, god become man beside the stream of Theban Dirce: Dionysos in the madness of wine.

"From Lydia come I," he sang, "from fields of gold, from Phrygia, from Persia's sunstruck plains, from strong-walled towns of Bactria, cold-bitter Media and blessed Araby. All Asia have I conquered, and all the salt sea coast, all the fair cities, Hellene, barbarian, all: all mine, all worship me, all know that I am god."

Meriamon struggled to breathe, to see what eyes could see. A man in a Tyrian robe, in a worn and tattered panther-skin, his wig a lion's mane, his mask—his mask—

She tore her eyes from it. They fell on Alexander's face. Half was in shadow, half in reflected light. The same face, ruddy to the pallor of the mask, and yet inescapably the same. The same expression, even, half mad, half exalted. He knew. He saw the god and the tribute. He took it as his due.

She must have said something, made some move. Niko's arm settled over her. His voice murmured in her ear. "Hush. Watch."

She watched. There were other people, other singers; or maybe it was only the actor's skill, evoking them as surely as if they had been living flesh. There was a war of sorts. Women serving the god in a madness of ecstasy. The young king refusing him, denying his divinity—that too a madness, implacable, inescapable. He took arms against a god. His own mother slew him, rent him asunder, and the god, dancing, laughed. "Too late," he sang, "too late you knew me; too late you spoke my name."

Alexander never moved, hardly seemed to breathe. The mask's strange smile was his own. The mask's eyes, lightless dark, bore deep within a gleam of fire.

"Thus," sang the god, "my father Zeus ordained. So let it ever be."

• TWENTY •

"Hubris," said Meriamon. She had been saying it too often. She knew that. People had stopped listening. Alexander was the young god, Herakles incarnate, Achilles come again, undefeated and undefeatable. That Gaza resisted him so well and so long—that was outrage, and the town would suffer for it.

Having made an isthmus of Tyre and bound it irrevocably to the land, he made nothing of raising a hill in front of the mount of Gaza, to set his siege engines level with the walls. But Gaza was not Tyre. Its people knew what they had to hope for if their resistance failed. They had reason to fight, and fight they did.

On the morning when Alexander's hill drew level with that of Gaza, the king had his engines ready to begin the ascent, the crews waiting in the cool of the dawn, the priests around him at the altar as he blessed his work with sacrifice. It was the king's duty to take the first victim. The wreath was on his head—odd to Meriamon's eye as she watched, to see the green leaves brought from far away, and the king's hair fallow gold under them, for it was near sunrise, the light of the torches gone pale. A little wind played with the garland, plucked a leaf and sent it spinning. The sacrifice, a fine fat ram, baaed inquiringly. Alexander smoothed its head before he raised its chin, the knife in his hand. As the knife touched the woolly throat, he started and staggered.

A bird. Desert falcon, Meriamon thought, seeing the flash of wings against the sunrise. It had had something in its claws—a stone: someone held it up in a trembling hand. People stirred and muttered. Voices cried out against the omen.

"Quiet!" Alexander's voice cut across the growing roar. The ram blatted and lunged. Two of the priests flung themselves on it. They went down in a flurry of hoofs and robes and tattered garlands.

One way and another the king made his sacrifice. But the omen was given. Aristandros the seer spoke it as the ram's flesh roasted on the altar. "You will take the town, my king," he said, "but look to yourself. This day for you is perilous."

Meriamon was close enough by then to see Alexander's face. It was as pale as the mask of the god, and as still. He moved abruptly, took off his garland and laid it on the altar. "I'll remember," he said.

He passed her as if she had not been there. She almost reached, almost stayed him. But something held her back.

Her eyes met Aristandros'. The seer's were as dark almost as an Egyptian's, and wise. "He listens to you," she said.

The seer shrugged slightly. "As much as he listens to anyone."

They watched him go, walking steadily as he always did, and yet managing to touch and be touched, speak and be spoken to, win his army all over again as if he were its lover and it his beloved. "He is mortal," Meriamon said. "Pray the gods he remembers it."

Foot by straining foot the engines mounted Alexander's hill to the southern wall of Gaza. Bolts and arrows and stones rained down on them from the city. Some of the arrows were fire arrows, but the engines had known such at Tyre, and overcome them. Alexander's archers did what they might, but it was ill shooting from below, and the catapults no use until they should rise to the summit. First one, then another wavered and slowed and halted as its crews fell or scrambled for cover.

Batis, seeing them so beset, loosed his sortie. A stream of howling Arabs poured out of the southern gate, swarming over the hill, attacking the siege engines with fire.

Alexander had been holding back. He stayed out of range of bolt and arrow, and therefore of the fight, though he paced and fretted and made his pages miserable. When Batis' sortie overran his engines and bade fair to drive his men down off the hill, he could bear it no longer. He shouted for his Shieldbearers.

They looked at one another, and at Hephaistion. He

looked into Alexander's eyes and saw nothing there to touch.

Fate, he thought. Gods. Madness. His belly clenched. "Alexander—" he began.

Alexander was past hearing him, or any voice but the one in his own soul. Hephaistion breathed a word—prayer, curse, he did not know which—and braced to leap into the fight. The others fell into ranks behind. Alexander bolted ahead of them, into the thick of the battle.

There was no mistaking him, however fierce the press. He was all blood and gold and fiery temper, hewing a path through the enemy. He had no fear at all. The god was in him.

The Arabs had their own gods, and their own madnesses. He hewed one down and leaped over the body, springing at another.

Hephaistion saw the flash of a blade. " *'Ware behind!*" he shouted. Alexander half-spun. A knife plunged toward his corselet, bent and slipped and snapped, the man who wielded it sinking down dead with Alexander's blade in his vitals. Alexander laughed, sharp and short, and swung his shield edge-on. A swath opened before him. For a moment they stood alone, he and Hephaistion, an island in a sea of shouting, screaming, struggling men. Alexander did not speak, or glance at his friend. He was oblivious to anything outside of himself.

Hephaistion knew better than to grieve for what he could not change. He took the time to breathe, to wipe the sweat from his forehead, to take in what he could see of the fight. It was going well. Even as he watched, a clump of men—some in Arab dress, some in Persian—broke and ran for the gate. A company of Shieldbearers sprinted to catch them.

Alexander stirred, looking about for an enemy to fight. It was raining missiles still—a stone larger than Hephaistion's head thudded to earth within his arm's reach, bounced and struck another and shattered. A shard stung his thigh between tunic and greave. He raised his shield, firmed his grip on his sword. Two robed Arabs with knives had brought down a Macedonian. Alexander sprang to even the odds, too quick for Hephaistion to follow. There were men in his way, swords, spears, bodies innumerable. Hephaistion struggled, fighting blindly like a stag caught in a thicket, antlers snared, hounds snapping at his belly.

He saw it beyond him, out of reach or help or hope. A god helped it, maybe, or the dark thing that was in the earth of Gaza. As Alexander leaped, danger from the sky forgotten, eyes only for the man who had fallen, a bolt fell from the walls. In the last instant he saw it. His shield flew up. The bolt pierced it. Pierced his corselet; pierced his shoulder.

He stopped, swayed. His face wore no expression but surprise.

He firmed his feet, gathered himself, went on. Hephaistion, trapped still, hacking at a man without a face, cursing endlessly and helplessly, saw the blood trickling down, scarlet on gold.

The faceless one fell. The way was clear.

Alexander was no longer in it. His sword rose and fell, cutting through the thicket of the enemy, pressing toward the walls. Hephaistion knew as clearly as if a god had spoken, what was in that mad brilliant mind. He had an army to lead, a battle to win. Pain was nothing, a wound—however deep—an irrelevance. It was a price. He had paid it. Now he would take Gaza.

He was conscious when they brought him out of the fight. Bled out, white with shock, and cursing them for taking him from the battle. "I've paid the price," he said. "The city's mine for the taking. Aristandros said it. Let me up. Let me get back. Didn't you hear? Batis thinks I'm dead. Let me go back before my men think the same!"

Meriamon's hands stopped him. She had no strength to

match his, but her touch brought him up short. Philippos had come in with the others, having followed the battle as he always did, as mad in his way as his madman of a king. He had got the corselet off on the field and cut the bolt out, but the bleeding that came after, once begun, would not stop. Nor would Alexander. He had lost an ungodly lot of blood. It weakened him enough to slow him down; when he collapsed, they carried him to safety.

Meriamon had needle and thread to hand, and an iron will to go with it. She set to work sewing him up.

He fought her. Her shadow laid itself on him and held him still, and opened the gates of sleep. He struggled, but the pain was beyond even his endurance. It overcame him, and darkness with it, and blessed relief for the surgeons.

It was a bad wound, and it did not want to heal. As quickly as it closed, he opened it again, insisting on being taken in a litter to the siege, and then refusing to stay put, getting up to point out a new angle for the sappers or to order the shift of a catapult. Even wine with poppy could not keep him down. He refused to drink it, or he drank too little to matter. He had them mining the walls, and he had to be there, he said. "You know what they did when I went down," he said to Meriamon, not for the first time. "They won the skirmish for me, but they didn't storm the walls. They thought I'd been killed. They have to see that I'm alive and fighting, or the whole siege will collapse."

"That might not be a bad thing," she said.

He struggled up on his couch. She had got him to allow that much: a couch under a canopy, well out of range of the enemy's fire, and runners to carry his orders to the sappers and the crews on the siege engines. She propped him with cushions, though he gave her no thanks for it. He was going to get up and prowl again. She knew the signs.

"There are drugs," she said, "that can keep a man down for as long as they must. I am not above using them. The wound is festering now—it could kill you."

"It won't," he said.

She would not hit him. It was not fear of striking a king. It was fear of her own temper; that she would not be able to stop. She stood over him, looming as much as woman could: a small woman in a great towering mantle of shadow. "I see now," she said, "what a mistake I made, letting you think that you might be the son of a god. You are still mortal flesh. You can still die."

He looked at her with clear pale eyes, seeing shape and shadow both, and showing no fear of either. "I know," he said. "I know that I am mortal."

"You do not."

He touched the bandages that bound his shoulder. There was pain: his lips were tight, his face waxen under the flush of temper. "This tells me so."

"You don't listen."

"Am I supposed to turn coward, then," he snapped, "and slink out of Gaza with my tail between my legs?"

"Gaza hates you. The stones themselves are turned against you."

He struck the couch with his fist. It shook him: he gasped. He would not let her touch him. "That is nonsense!"

"It is not."

He pushed himself to his feet. He stayed by the couch, face to face, fury to fury. "Listen to me," he said. "Yonder is Egypt's gate. This is its gatehouse. If we leave the enemy in it, we trap ourselves beyond. We must have Gaza. We must not allow it to hold against us."

"Then take it," she said, "and have done."

She had caught him off balance. "You won't let me—"

"You can stay where you are. Your generals can do the fighting. Take it and put an end to it."

"I have to be out there," he said. "They need me."

"Why?"

"I'm the king."

"They need you alive and whole and able to rule them."

"A king rules from the front."

"So can he die in the front."

Alexander sat down rather abruptly. It was not weakness, not all of it. His eyes were almost black. The mood that hung on him was blacker yet.

Meriamon drew back softly. She had said all that it was wise to say. He was what he was: king, and Alexander. He was also, for all his brilliance, no more than a boy. One tended to forget it. He was adept at looking younger and smaller than he was, and seeming harmless, but that was his own deception, for his own ends.

She thought of the god in the terrible, beautiful play. It had been strange afterward to meet and speak to the man who wore his mask, and find him neither young nor mad: a soft-spoken aging man with a shy smile. He was like herself, she had thought then. The gods spoke through him. He had no part of them.

Alexander was more than a voice. The god who had wielded Thettalos, Dionysos lord of Asia, was in the king: in his way was the king. But even Dionysos had worn mortal form, was bred of mortal woman. The madness that was in him was divine madness, but it took shape in mortal flesh, and suffered mortal frailty.

Alexander had never had to think of it before. He knew battles, and death's bloody face. He had shed blood enough of his own. But that he was mortal, that he could die: that had not come home to him. It did not, often, when one was male, and young, and king, and beloved of the gods. This pain that was in him, this wound that festered and would not heal, edged everything he did with a new intensity.

He spoke suddenly, startling her. " 'Better, say I, to delve the earth as a peasant's slave, than be king of the weary dead.' "

"And yet," he said, "when the gods gave Achilles to choose, whether long life without glory or glory beyond all others and death before his time, he chose glory. He chose death. He died young."

Meriamon shivered.

"I am of Achilles' line," said Alexander, "as I am of Herakles'. If I choose to live all my life in a moment, who are you to allow or forbid?"

"Nothing," she said. "No one. But my gods have need of you."

"Your gods," he said. "Not mine."

"They are all one."

He fell silent again. That was Greek, to talk in poetry and name old names and look for excuses. So did children do, dreaming children's dreams. But this man-child dreamed like a god, with the world for his plaything.

"Aristandros said that I would take Gaza," he said.

"Then you shall," said Meriamon. "Through your generals."

"I can fight. A lighter corselet—a horse under me—Boukephalas knows not to toss his head—"

"Boukephalas will toss you if you insist on being an idiot."

He glared. "You wouldn't."

"We get along, he and I. He has a liking for Phoenix. If you come out of this alive, I may be inclined to consider a breeding. He sires good foals, Niko says."

"Bribery."

"Certainly," she said. "Your men are going sour here. Water is increasingly hard to come by. And there is still the desert to pass before we come to Egypt."

"You don't call this desert?"

"This is green and fertile country in any but the driest season. Desert is the Red Land. Desert is the road to Egypt."

"You're trying to talk me out of it."

"No," she said. "Send for your generals. Tell them what you want done. You can trust them to do it. Or can't you?"

"I have the best army in the world," he said hotly, "and the best generals anywhere."

"So use them," said Meriamon.

He held her glare for a long moment. Then he spun away from her. Shouting for Nikanor, for Philotas, for Krateros, for the rest of his generals and his council of war.

Alexander had heard her. Heeded her. He wielded his army from a judicious distance, commanded from Boukephalas' back. He resisted the lure of the fighting.

But it was too much for him. The harder his engines labored, the more the walls trembled, the closer he came.

The walls crumbled and fell, eaten away below by the sappers, above by rams and hurled stones. When they went down, Alexander went over them. He left his horse with the pages, safe as he was not. He was on his feet, running as lightly as any of them, leading his troops from the front as a madman must. His high voice rang above them, urging them on.

Once it broke. He rocked and nearly fell. A stone had struck him in the thigh. He steadied. His voice went up again. He went on, limping, leaning on his spear, but fiercely, determinedly afoot. His wrath was the color of blood.

He took Gaza. The city that had defied him, that had wounded him twice and all but killed him, suffered more terribly than Tyre ever had. Its defenders died to the last man, valiant in despair. Its women and children fell prey to the victors, who killed them or kept them, raped them and sold them, and knew no mercy.

And he did not stop them. They brought Batis to him, bound and naked and bloodied and yet alive. Alexander looked at the man who had come closest of any to defeating him; at whose command he had been wounded, in whose cause he now could barely stand, with a great throbbing bruise on his thigh and only the gods to thank that the bone had not broken: a little thick hairy man with a big belly, who reeked like a goat. Alexander said to him, "Do you regret what you have done?"

Batis spat in his face.

Alexander stood with the spittle running down his cheek. His men leaped with swords drawn. He stopped them. His eyes were wide and fixed, the color of water, which was no color at all. Meriamon, watching, staggered. It was as if the earth heaved; as if the darkness rose, enveloping him.

"Take him," said Alexander softly. "He would be Hektor to my Achilles. Let him be so. Do to him as Achilles did to Hektor."

Some of those near him gasped. Most grinned wide and white and vicious.

"What will he do?" Meriamon asked the man next to her, one who looked horrified. "What is he saying?"

The man would not answer. There was no one else to ask: the rest who could hear her were cheering the king, a sound like lions' roaring, deep and deadly.

Batis did not begin to scream until they drove the spike through his heels and threaded the ropes on it. He did not stop when they bound the rope to a chariot and whipped up the horses, and drove horses and chariot and screaming, tumbling, writhing man round the walls of Gaza. He screamed for an appallingly long time. Even after he stopped, the sound went on, as if the earth had taken it up and the wind become a part of it.

"Hektor was dead," said Niko. "Achilles killed him before he dragged him."

He sounded quite calm about it. Not appalled; not revolted. But he said it, and in Meriamon's hearing.

She had seen worse under the Parsa. They were as cruel as cats; lives mattered little to them, particularly the lives of foreigners.

"There has to be a lesson," Niko said. "Tyre was not

enough. Gaza has to be the end of it—defiance, resistance. They have to know better than to stop Alexander."

She walked away from him. He followed. She was aware of him like a hand on her back. She ignored him. Alexander had gone away when Batis stopped screaming. His charioteer dragged the body for a while, making sure that it was dead. She did not see that there was any doubt. What tumbled behind the chariot and sent the dust up in clouds, no longer looked anything like a man.

She was not thinking of Batis. Appalled—she was that, but distantly. Surprise had no part of it. Alexander was Philip's son, and Philip had been no weakling. Myrtale was his mother, Myrtale who had been given the name Olympias. The ram and the serpent. Deep earth and red fire. The warrior and the sorceress. She wielded the wild magic that roiled on the edges of things, far from the stately power of Khemet. Chaos was her realm, and blood her mystery.

Alexander who dreamed of Herakles, who mounted sieges that no sane man would have ventured, who took cities that could never be taken—Alexander was no tame thing. He had the lion in him: Sekhmet, goddess and destroyer.

Meriamon walked softly on the torn and bloodied earth. It was quiet now. Truly; wholly. The darkness was gone out of it. Alexander had taken it into himself, and transformed it into fire.

She found him deep in the city, sitting on a fallen column. He had a child on his knee. It was filthy, it was bone-thin, but it smiled at the man with the bright hair, and played with something that shone: the brooch of his cloak. "Clear the city," he said to the man who waited by him, "and round up the prisoners. We'll ship them off to Tyre."

"And that one?" somebody asked, cocking his chin at the child.

"I'll keep him," the king said. "Queen Sisygambis lost

a page to fever, just a little while ago. I'll clean this young one up and give her a present. Maybe a girl, too, to go with him. See if you can find one who matches him."

"But—" said someone else.

Alexander took no notice. He patted the child and smiled at it, and said, "You'll belong to a queen. She's a great queen, the greatest there is. You're very fortunate."

Maybe he was, Meriamon thought. Maybe he would not mind that a male entire could not serve a Parsa lady. He would be alive at least, and given to a just mistress. No one else in Gaza had that surety.

She had not come to say anything to the king, though his glance invited her to speak. She needed to be near him. To see him inside and out. The dark was gone, the malice burned away. Sekhmet the goddess, Sekhmet of the lion's head, knew calm as well as wrath. Dionysos was god of wine and laughter. Yet, for that, a god.

Alexander went to his tent long after the sun had set, when the city was settled and the dead attended to, the wounded and the dying entrusted to the surgeons and the rest of the army fed, warmed with wine, and sent victorious to bed. He went alone as few others did.

Someone was waiting. Not one of the pages, but adept enough in a page's work, having done his share of it in his time, and not so long ago, either. He did not say anything. He never needed to. He filled a cup and held it out.

Alexander dropped into the chair that waited for him, took the cup and drank deep of well-watered wine. The restless energy quivered and sparked in him still, like summer lightnings in the sky over Pella. But there was an edge to it, a quiver of exhaustion.

Hephaistion got the chiton off him. The bandage on his shoulder was filthy, stiff with more than sweat. He frowned at it. "Shall I call Philippos?" he asked. "Or the Egyptian woman?"

"No." Alexander's voice was quiet, no sharpness in it, but it suffered no argument.

Hephaistion would have argued regardless, if it had mattered enough. He shrugged and set to work peeling the bandage from bruised and tender flesh. The wound, that he could see, was no worse than it had been before. It was healing. Maybe. At last. As for the thigh, with its great swollen bruise . . .

"The things you do to yourself," he said.

Alexander did not reply to that. His lips were set tight. He would never give in to pain, no more than he gave in to anything else, man, god, or force of nature.

"Someday your muleheadedness is going to get you killed," Hephaistion said. Not looking at him while he said it; getting fresh bandages from the box by the bed, bringing the padding and the jar of salve that the Egyptian had made: odd little woman, but clever with her arts and her potions. He set to work with them.

"So," said Alexander when he was almost done. "You think I'm a fool, too."

"Not a fool," said Hephaistion.

"Mad, then."

"Not that, either."

Alexander shifted. Hephaistion frowned. Alexander stilled, but only for as long as it took to finish off the bandage. Then he was up and prowling.

Hephaistion sat on his heels and watched. There was an odd comfort in it, in doing what he had done for—what, ten years now? Being still while Alexander fidgeted. Being quiet, simply being there.

Alexander stopped and turned on his heel. It caught at the heart, that movement: the grace of it, swift and entirely unconscious, even with the stiffness of bandaged shoulder, bound and bandaged thigh. "I had to do it," he said.

Hephaistion waited.

Alexander's voice came quicker, harder. "I had to make an example. That kind of defiance—that kind of resistance—I had to break it. They're saying I lost my temper; I went too far."

"Did you?"

Alexander laughed: a strangled sound. "Do you know, I knew you'd say that? After Thebes, you didn't say anything."

"There was nothing to say."

"Thebes was worse. This was a Persian rebellion. A necessity of war. That was Greece, and I destroyed it."

"I was angry enough myself, then," said Hephaistion.

"And now?"

"You did what you had to do."

"What would you have done?"

"Killed him."

Simple, that. Absolute. Alexander came in a long stride, standing over him; wound fingers in his hair. It was not a gentle grip, but neither was it cruel. Hephaistion let it pull his head back, met the fierce colorless eyes. "Killed him first?" demanded Alexander.

"Killed him," said Hephaistion, "slowly."

"That wasn't slow enough?"

Hephaistion paused, for tact. "It was . . . convincing."

"It went too far." Alexander let him go, went to the bed, sank down onto it. "Gods," he said. "How he screamed."

Hephaistion rose. Alexander lay on his back, open-eyed. His face was stark.

There was something to be said for Persian beds. They were wide enough for a troop. Hephaistion lay beside Alexander, not touching him.

"Do you remember what Aristotle used to say," said Alexander, "of what is right, and what is proper, and what is just? And what he said of kings? That a king must be stronger than other men. That he should be master of himself."

"A king must also do what is necessary," said Hephaistion. He set no particular emphasis in the words.

He did not need to. Alexander's glance marked everything that Hephaistion wanted to say.

Alexander said it aloud, himself, as he had to. "Achilles was not a king," he said. "He was a haughty boy. He did no more and no less than it pleased him to do. And when it came to the end—he died like a fool, from a coward's arrow. So, almost, did I." He drew a sharp breath. It hurt, maybe: his body stiffened, then slowly eased. "The gods were testing me. I failed."

Hephaistion opened his mouth to speak, but closed it again. He opened his arms instead. Alexander seemed not to see; then suddenly he was there, holding hard, with strength that was always astonishing. He wept as hard as he clung, though he did not weep long. He never did. The fire in him burned away tears.

In a little while it had burned away the rest of it as well. He lay in his friend's arms, quiet as he was after love; sad, one might almost have said, if one had not known him so well. He was never so still as he was now, never so close to peace.

And yet, when Hephaistion yielded at last to sleep, Alexander was still awake. For all Hephaistion knew, he lay awake nightlong, wrapped in his friend's arms, his mind gone away where none but a god could follow.

• TWENTY-ONE •

The road from Gaza was a testing of fire. But for the ships that followed faithfully along the sea-tracks, the army would have died for lack of water. Even with them, with the sun beating down and the flies devouring the sweat as it streamed from men and beasts alike, and for each man but a sip at morning and a sip at midday and a bare cupful at evening, it was a bitter march.

The king had no more to drink than the least of his men, nor would he ride, or take his ease on shipboard. What his men endured, he too would suffer; and no matter that he was wounded, limping, unwontedly silent since the fall of Gaza.

It was not a black silence. Grey, rather. Still. A gathering of strength, for what end none knew, perhaps not even himself.

He was still Alexander. In front of his army he had not changed. He marched with them, jested with them, shared the heat and the flies and the choking, clinging dust.

His shoulder healed. Whether the heat did it, or the rigors of the march, or simply the strength that was in him, the wound ceased to fester, began to close.

Or perhaps it was Egypt, reaching out to him across the sand.

Meriamon marched as they all did, foot by foot, parched and sunstruck and caring not at all. Niko tried to drag her on board his ship. She stared him down. "The earth," she said, "under my feet. I need it." She knelt on it, set palms to it. "Here, Niko. Feel."

He eyed her as if she had gone mad; transparently chose to humor her. "So?"

"So!" She set her hands on top of his, pressed them down into the sand. "Do you feel it?"

"I feel sand," he said. "And a stone. It's cutting me. Do you mind . . . ?"

It was indeed: the earth drank his blood. She wrapped the cut, regretting the pain; but she smiled at him. "Now your blood is Egypt's."

"This isn't—"

"Soon," she said. "It surges under us like the sea. My land. My gods. My magic. Soon we'll pass the gate. Soon I'll be whole again."

He understood more than he knew. Poor Hellene: it baffled him. He fled back to his ship.

* * *

Seven days, they marched. Seven days in the forge. Seven days to the gate in the desert, the city on the easternmost mouth of the Nile, the strong fortress called Pelusium. There, if there should be resistance, Alexander would find it: in walls as strong as those of Gaza, as those of Tyre.

Fleet and land force came in battle order. Mazaces the satrap had promised submission, but Parsa faith was never absolute except among their own. On the last day before the approach to Pelusium, Alexander called for an early halt and doubled rations for his troops. Their spirits were high, for all that they had suffered. They were Alexander's men. They had never lost a battle.

Meriamon was dizzy with the nearness of her country. She could have taken her water bottle and her bag of belongings and gone on alone. Would have, if it had not been for Alexander. He was her purpose. She could not be aught but where he was.

She found him with the horses, alone but for a pair of pages: so rare a thing that she stopped and wondered for a moment what was lacking.

Only the flock of his friends. She came forward in the long light. Boukephalas saw her: he raised his head and neighed. She greeted him gravely and offered him the bit of bread that she had brought.

Alexander looked up from examining the horse's hoof. "Did you know, he's twenty-four years old? And still going strong. You'd think he'd been romping through a pasture instead of this forge of the gods."

"He's good stock," said Meriamon. "Tough. Like his master."

Alexander set down the hoof and slapped the stallion's neck. "He's got more sense than I have. Always did."

She did not contest that.

He noticed. He draped his arm over Boukephalas' back and leaned in seeming ease, but his body was taut. "Tomorrow we'll be in Egypt."

"Yes," said Meriamon.

"You say it will welcome me."

"As a bride," she said, "and her beloved."

"Are you going to bet on that?"

"Certainly," she said. "I wager the Two Lands."

He laughed. "Now there's a stake for a king!"

"It was yours from the womb."

The mirth went out of his face. He ran a hand down the stallion's neck. Not uncertain; Alexander was never that. But his mood had gone dark. "Was it?" he asked. "Is it mine without question? Or must I be tested? After Tyre, after Gaza—will your country refuse me because I wouldn't set it first?"

"Tomorrow," she said, "you will see."

His brows lowered. "Is that in the bet, too?"

"Yes."

"But," he said. "Can it be so easy?"

"Was Tyre easy? Was Gaza? Have you paid no prices, Alexander?"

"There are always prices," he said.

"None that you cannot pay."

"Ah, but will I?" He straightened. "No. Don't answer that. I've been no good to anyone since I left Gaza. That was a comeuppance. You were right in that. Are you pleased to hear it?"

"No," said Meriamon.

"Then what will please you?"

"The sight of you," she said, "in the Great House of Egypt."

"And very odd I'll look there," he said.

"It is where you belong."

"So you say," said Alexander. Then he raised his head, shifting as he of all men could, catching fire again, finding the god where he had retreated from the testing. "So I'll see for myself. Will you be with me?"

"It's for that I came."

He smiled his sudden smile. "And now you'll have it. I hope it brings you joy."

* * *

She went to her bed with a light heart, even though there might be dreams. Tonight she would open her heart to them. If there was darkness, if there was fear—she would face it, and strike it down. Khemet's power was in the earth beneath her feet. Khemet's gladness sang in her blood.

Too much, maybe. She was not afraid to admit it. They were not in Khemet yet. But there was no quelling the singing that was in her.

The camp had no water to spare for a bath. She cleansed herself as best she could with sand—a desert expedient, and better than one might have expected, if one did not mind sand in one's hair. Better certainly than the Hellenes' rancid oil scraped off with a strigil, that made the camp smell like a kitchen gone bad. As clean as she could be, and shivering, for night in the desert was cold, she sought her bed.

Her shadow stretched out over her. She would have released it to hunt, but it would not go. No more would Sekhmet who came to curl purring at her side. So guarded, with a prayer against ill dreams, she gave herself up to sleep.

It was the same dream. She had known that it would be. Edjo and Nekhbet loomed over her smallness, serpent and vulture vaster than she had ever seen them. She had come to the gate of their power. It thrummed in the dry earth. It rang in the sky. The stroke of it could kill.

Tonight she had no fear. As when first she dreamed this dream, she found comfort even in its terrors. It was Khemet. It was the Two Lands. She came of the gods' will, guiding the gods' instrument.

"Instrument enough," said a voice above and behind her. A voice she knew: a woman's voice, soft and heart-stoppingly sweet; but huge as no mortal voice could ever be. "Instrument, and more than instrument. His will is as much his own as any god's."

"Yet," said Meriamon though she could not turn, not yet, not unbidden, "he is a man, and mortal."

"So even was I," said the voice with a flicker of laughter. "Mortal flesh, mortal woman. Even as are you."

"I am no goddess!"

Meriamon's voice echoed in the dark country. A terrible silence met it.

Even now she was not afraid. She was beyond fear. Much more softly she said, "I am no goddess. That burden is not given me."

"Is it so you reckon it?"

"I will be Osiris when I am dead, as all the dead are, female and male alike. In this life I am only Meriamon."

"So," said the voice. The goddess. Meriamon sensed no anger in her.

"You spoke to me," said Meriamon when the other did not go on. "Over and over, night after night. I never understood you. You were too far away."

"Not that," said the goddess. "It was not time for you to hear."

"And yet you spoke."

"Even the gods have their fates and their destinies."

Meriamon stood quiet in the grasp of the night. It felt like her shadow, narrow god-strong hands, blunt clawnails; unmoving, but gentle enough. She was aware all at once of Sekhmet's presence, a warmth spread over her feet, a rumble of purr. The cat was not forbidden to look on the face of the one behind Meriamon, nor was she blinded by it, or struck with terror. She was a goddess herself, a goddess' image.

"So she is," said the great one behind. "So is the one you bring to us. He bears a great burden of pride. But he learns. He begins to understand."

"He could die for it."

"If such is his choice."

Meriamon pressed her hand to the coldness in her middle. She knew what the gods were. She had belonged to them for all the days of her life. Still, to speak so, to hear in such a voice what she most feared . . .

"Child," said the goddess, and her voice was the gentlest in the world. "Child, look at me."

The hands on Meriamon eased. She did not turn at once. She needed a moment to draw breath, to firm her will.

It was only a woman. A little long-eyed Egyptian woman in a linen gown, with a wig over her hair. She was beautiful as queens could be, or great ladies, or simple farmers' wives in the fields by the Nile: elegant oval face, delicate nose, mouth full yet finely molded.

"Nefertiti," said Meriamon. Not to name her. Simply to name what she was: *The beautiful one is come*.

The beautiful one smiled. "That is a name of mine, and of many of my daughters. And you, beloved of Amon: would you have another name of me?"

"I need none," said Meriamon. She should have bent down in homage, but it was late for that—even knowing what she knew, now, looking at that lovely mortal face, those dark mirthful eyes. "Mother," she said, and put it all in her voice. "Mother Isis."

"Now you know me," the goddess said.

"But," said Meriamon. "It should be—it ought to have been—"

"It ought to have been Amon?" The goddess' brows arched. "Ah, but he has done his duty, and now that it is done . . ."

"Not all of it," said Meriamon.

"All of it that matters in this place." The goddess seemed not at all perturbed. But she had been a woman once, as she herself had said, and a queen; and Meriamon was royal enough when she chose to remember it. It was not as strange as that, to speak blunt words to the queen of earth and heaven.

Mother Isis laughed. "Oh, indeed, we are kin; and it is joy to see a child so fearless."

"I was always yours," said Meriamon.

"You are," the goddess said. "And your king, and all that is."

"Then ... the rest?"

"They, too," said the goddess. "I am their mother and their queen. My king who died and lives again—his realm is death, and life that comes out of death. Mine is all that is. This that you do, in Amon's name as you did it, was done for me."

"And he? The king whom you made?"

"He above all," the goddess said.

"Then," said Meriamon, "it was not the others at all. It was you."

"I, and they by my will. Do you see, child? Do you understand?"

"No," said Meriamon. "But I will. I'm Amon's singer. I did as he bade me. This shadow that walks with me—"

"Ah," said the goddess. Her smile warmed. Meriamon's shadow grinned with jackal-jaws and bowed to the ground. "Friend," the goddess said. "Brother. Anubis my beloved, it is well?"

"It is well," said the shadow. Its voice was deep, with a growl in it, and a touch of laughter. It turned from the goddess to Meriamon, and she knew. It would leave her. Now that she was returned to her own country. Now that she had no more need of it.

It shocked her, how much it hurt. She had accepted the guardian for need and for obedience, when she took the burden on her of departing from Amon's temple, of bringing the king to his throne. Its loss in Tyre had been bitter, but her strength had gone with it, and what power she had outside of Khemet. To lose it now would matter nothing. She had come home.

It had become a part of her, living in her shadow, guarding her body and her souls.

It had turned from the goddess to face her. It—he. She would think of him as he was, here where he was more whole than she, more truly real. His ears flattened, then pricked. His eyes were keen.

"You have served well," said Meriamon steadily, "in stooping so to serve a mortal woman, you who are more by far than mortal creature."

The jackal-head dipped, assenting. The bright eyes never wavered. There was no resentment in them. Had never been, even at the beginning, when she was new to the power that he lent her, and high-handed with it, because she was afraid.

She drew herself up. Serpent-shadow, vulture-shadow, loomed above her and filled the sky. They were great, but greater still was the woman before her. Who was no image of divinity. Who was goddess wholly.

Meriamon bowed then at last. Bowed to the ground. Stood straight then and faced the goddess and said, "I have done all that was required of me. What little remains I shall do: open the gate of the Two Lands, set the crown upon his head. Then am I freed to go?"

"Do you wish to be?"

The question was not entirely unexpected. It was Meriamon's dream, after all, and Meriamon's goddess. Of course she would ask the difficult thing, the one that most needed answer.

"Yes," said Meriamon. And, "No. I was a guide and a goad. Once that's done, he'll need little enough from me."

"Except your friendship."

"He has friends in scores."

"Not as you are."

"And how is that?"

The goddess did not answer. Not directly. She said, "Look before you."

Meriamon looked. She saw darkness, and the dry country, and the shadowed sky. But as she looked at it, it shimmered. She held her eyes steady. Like water in a basin, like wine in a cup, it steadied. She looked in it as in a mirror.

She did not remember all of what she saw. It poured into her, filled her, overflowed. Later, when she needed it, it would come back. But even what she remembered was enough.

"This," she said as the vision faded and the darkness came back. "This—it's but a beginning. And what it is— what you are, and will, and will be—"

"—will be," said Mother Isis. She held out her hands. "Come, daughter. Kiss me as a child ought, and go. What you must do, you will know. What you must choose, you will choose."

"And if I fail?"

"Even gods can fail," the goddess said, "if they set out to do it." That was stern, and Meriamon's eyes dropped.

Warm fingers touched her chin, lifting it. They were human fingers; no power in them, no awe. They needed none. They simply were. "Child," said the goddess. "Meriamon. I am with you. Remember that. I was with you from your beginning. I will never leave you."

Meriamon bit her tongue. She would not say what a child would have said.

But the Mother heard it. She smiled. "I promise," she said lightly, but with all heaven in it. "Now, child, go. Be strong. And remember."

"—Remember."

Meriamon started awake. Sekhmet glowered from the hollow of her side, and expressed her opinion of fools who talked in their sleep.

Meriamon soothed her with a long rub under the chin. The dream was fading, but its essence was burned deep. What it had taught her . . .

Not Amon. Not the gods of Memphis or of Thebes, though they had had a part in it. Not simple kingly necessity had brought her out of Egypt and led her to Alexander. That was but a beginning. This that she did was more and greater than she had ever known; and she had thought it the greatest matter in the world.

"It still is," she said to Sekhmet. "But now I know the size of it. Or I begin to." She sat up. She knew the feel of dawn, the taste of the air at night's ending.

As she rose, something stirred in her shadow. She whirled. Sulfur-eyes laughed at her. Jackal-jaws gaped in mockery of her astonishment.

She could not embrace a shadow. But she could grin until her jaws ached, and say in a voice that caught, "You came back. You stayed with me."

Her shadow showed teeth. Of course it had stayed. It was hers.

"But—"

She broke off. She knew better than to argue with air. Even air in Anubis-shape, daring her to try. She looked at it long, sidelong for it was nothing to stare at direct, and let it know how glad she was. It was not displeased, either. Heart-whole and shadow-whole and full of the dream's remembrance, she went out into the rising day.

• TWENTY-TWO •

Pelusium gave itself wholly to Alexander, the strong gates flung wide, its people streaming from it in their hundreds and thousands to meet him as he came. Nor were they the folk of the city alone; they had come from every town and city within a day's ride or Nile-sail, thronging to look on the king who would set them free.

The Persians made no move to stop him. Mazaces the satrap received him at the gates of Pelusium, graceful in surrender as Persians could be.

"Doesn't it trouble you?" Alexander demanded of him in Meriamon's hearing.

"What, lord king?" the satrap inquired with lifted brow and air of innocence.

"This," Alexander said. "Bowing to me. Calling me king. Knowing that your king is still alive and still king, and could come back to claim you."

"He could," the satrap conceded. "I doubt that he will. This province is my trust. I give it over to the one who best can rule it."

Alexander could hardly argue with that, and Mazaces would not. He had done what he had done. He would live or die by it.

From Pelusium by ship up the Nile and by land on its banks, Alexander's army advanced toward Memphis. It was a march of triumph. He had fought no battle, shed no blood. Not in Egypt. The Persians were gone or had surrendered, the weight of them raised from the land, their presence blotted out in sun and sand and black Nile mud.

Meriamon rode in the throng at Alexander's back, quiet, effacing herself among them. He knew who had brought him here; and she. It was enough.

That Mazaces held the place of honor at his right hand, where by most rights she should have been, and that the crowd of soldiers and servants and hangers-on contained a sufficiency of Persian faces, troubled her less than she might have expected. They were defeated. They had to see Alexander where he was, and the people where they were, shouting Alexander's name. It was a bitter blow to their pride. They bore it well, that much she would give them. Better than she could have begun to.

The Nile was quiescent, months yet from the flood, a broad dreaming river flowing from the world's heart. They marched through the marshes and fens of the Delta, the green thickets loud with birds, tall fans of papyrus and bulrush-spears, the arrow-dart of a crocodile, the roaring of the river-horses in their deep wallows, and round the fleet as it rowed beside them, flocks of the little boats of Egypt. Every village and town turned itself out to see the king; every city opened its gates. They sang as he came, and sang as he went, songs of the coming of the king.

He drank it like wine. But no less than she.

Her music had come back. It was in her the morning after she came to Pelusium, washed in seawater and water of the Nile, red earth and black earth under her feet and the sun's boat sailing up over the eastern desert. She stood outside the walls and opened her heart, and the song came to fill it. If there were words in it, she did not remember them. They would be a hymn, the waking of Ra, of Amon, of Khnum the Creator, ram-god, sun-god, lord in the Two Lands.

Her voice was raw, too long unused, but in a little while it remembered its power. She had forgotten what it was to be voice and voice alone, a body of pure song. What had filled the high temple in Thebes and soared over the chants of the priests, now rang through earth and heaven. It raised the sun from the horizon. It brought the day into Khemet.

"Such a big voice for such a little woman."

Tomorrow they would be in Memphis. Tonight they were in Heliopolis, the city of the Sun, Alexander within in the royal house, the bulk of his army camped in the broad fields to the east of the river. The Red Land stretched wide and far; the Black Land lay about them in the long light of evening, under the blue vault of heaven.

Meriamon had been singing to herself as Phylinna plaited her hair. There was an Egyptian maid now, and a plenitude of wigs if she wanted any, but tonight she was content with what she had had since Asia. She smiled at Thaïs, who had decided to be Hellene from the modest coil of her hair to the elegant turn of her sandal. "Am I too loud for you?"

"Of course not." Thaïs cooled herself with a palmleaf fan. "And this is winter," she said. "Gods forbid I ever see this country in summer."

"It's very cool," said Meriamon, "for Egypt." Still, she did not reach for the cloak draped over the back of her chair. Even the chill was blessed, because it was Khemet.

"You haven't stopped singing since we came to this country," Thaïs said.

"I'm home," said Meriamon.

"In every bone and sinew of you." Thaïs sighed, not for sadness, not for impatience; if anything, for envy. "If I saw Athens again, I would be happy. But not like this. Are you all so much in love with Egypt?"

"It's ours," Meriamon said. She held still while Phylinna, frowning, held the mirror, and the new maid painted her eyes. Phylinna did not like to see her place so usurped, but Ashait was more than her match for strength of will.

They were not enemies for all of that, or even for that Ashait was a free woman and drew wages, while Phylinna was a slave. That was a feat of diplomacy which neither went so far as to acknowledge. It was admirable, thought Meriamon, and much more amusing than not.

Ashait smoothed the last stroke of kohl, paused, frowned slightly; added a touch more of lapis. "Now you are beautiful," she said.

Meriamon rather thought that she was. It was the being in her own country, and the gladness that blazed out of her, even more than gold and paint and royal linen. Tomorrow she would bring Alexander to Memphis—and let Mazaces think that he had done it; she and her gods knew better. He would take the crowns of the Two Lands, the crook and the flail, the rule of the Great House. No power would stop him, no force stand against him. She had sung the wards about him, and the land had welcomed him. He was its renewer, its healer and restorer.

She saw visions in the darkness of her closed eyes. They made her smile. She looked again at the light of eve-

ning in this room of a palace in which she had been as a
child, at the painted walls and the bright-gilded pillars and
the windows looking down into the garden; and, still smiling, at Thaïs making herself beautiful to dine with the
king.

Under the full folds of her gown Thaïs was beginning to
round with the child. Her morning sicknesses were over;
she was thriving, for all that Meriamon could see. But she
had not yet told Ptolemy. It never seemed to be time. If he
noticed, he said nothing, or perhaps simply thought she
grew plump with the largesse of Egypt. Men could be
blind to anything that had to do with women's matters—
and Hellene men worse than most.

Meriamon's forehead was stiff. She was frowning. She
smoothed it away. She had no time now for Niko. She had
a king to crown, and gods—a goddess—to serve. If he
should find another Egyptian woman, or a hetaira in the
king's following, one of the many who had come upriver
from the cities of the Delta—

She would kill him. She would quite simply kill him.

Colors in Egypt were brighter than they were anywhere
else in the world. By day, in the sun, they blinded: red and
green and blue and white and gold. By night they glowed
in the light of lamps, bright clean colors, sunlight colors,
shining joyous against the dark. Hellenes rolled their eyes
at them, not for any lack in their own artistry, but for that
every wall was covered with them. A palace could hardly
be a palace unless it teemed with painted people, animals,
birds and fishes, flowers and trees, gods and demons and
beings of the spirit world; and everywhere the march and
dance of the scribe's art, each symbol an image in itself.
To Meriamon whose father had commanded that she be
taught to read the old holy writing, every wall and lintel
spoke in its own voice. To the Macedonians it meant nothing, but it made them uneasy.

She read a little for Alexander when dinner was done

and the wine was going round. It was nothing so wonderful, only the names and titles of the king for whom the
hall was made. He had a great many of those.

"He was a braggart," Alexander said.

Meriamon forbore to bristle. "He said what he had
done, and who he was. Would you do any less?"

"I'd give it fewer words," said Alexander, "and more
action."

She smiled in spite of herself. "Ah, but you are a barbarian from the bottom of the world."

He laughed, but then he sobered. "I am that." He rose
abruptly from his couch. People stared. Some—Persians,
an Egyptian or two—began to rise. He waved them down.
"Come with me," he said to Meriamon.

No one followed but the guard, and the dog Peritas
heaving himself up from the foot of the couch. Meriamon
went in silence. So, for once, did Alexander. He took her
through passages that she might have known, and across
courts that she remembered from long ago. The memory
was bittersweet: the scent of her mother's perfume, the
sound of her father's voice.

Whether this to which he brought her had been the rob-
ing room before, she did not recall. Its walls were painted
with forests of palm and papyrus, and hunters moving
through it armed with bow and lance, and a flock of geese
startled into flight. Laid out in it were garments so familiar
that she stopped, and for a moment could not go on.

Alexander caught her arm. She had not been aware that
she swayed. "Are you ill?" he asked in sudden concern.

"No," she managed to say. Then, more strongly: "No.
It's only . . . I'm remembering too much."

"So you are," he said. "I didn't think. If you'd rather
not—"

She shook herself. "I'm well enough. What did you
want to show me?"

He did not take offense at her tone, though it was
sharper than she would have liked. He went to the table on

which lay the regalia of the Great House, and took up the false beard. "Can you see me wearing this thing?"

She looked at it. It was absurd, she could not deny that, like a blue braided phallus on a string. "You wear garlands in your festivals," she said. "They're hardly more prepossessing."

"They're Greek."

"And this is not." Meriamon touched the robe of linen with its stiff pleats, its armor-thickness of embroidery. She would not venture to lay hand on the two crowns: the White with its lofty peak, the Red like a helmet encasing it, low before, high and narrow behind.

He had no such scruples. He held them up in front of his face, turning them, tracing with a finger the curve of the golden tongue that bound them together. "I know what you want me to be," he said. "You want me to be Egyptian. But I'm not. I was born and bred in Macedon. What this is, what it means—that's not the kind of king I am. We're easier about it where I come from. We don't keep the kind of ceremony your priests are willing on me."

"Do you refuse it?"

She did not mean the ceremony. Nor, in his answer, did he. He said it slowly. "No," he said. "No. But . . . it has to be different. Do you see?"

"It has been the same for a thousand and a thousand years."

"And a thousand before that." He was not smiling. "I know how old this country is. But I am a new thing. If your gods mean me to rule, they must mean that I rule in my way, or they would never have bred me in Macedon."

"You will have your Greek games still," she said, "and your festival in the manner of your people. Is it so terrible that you should be crowned in the Egyptian way, in the Great House of Egypt?"

He took time to think about that. While he did it, Peritas came back from sniffing about corners and leaned against him. He set the crown in its place and rubbed the dog's ears absently, frowning at the table and its burden.'"There is courtesy," he said at length, "and policy. I like your people. They're odd, I don't deny that, and as old as their places are, sometimes I wonder if there is anything like a young thing here. But they know how to laugh."

"Laughter is all that makes the world bearable, sometimes."

He glanced at her. His frown had not lightened. But there was more in it of reflection than of distaste. He lifted the crook and the flail, shook out the gilded lashes of the latter. They clicked on one another, soft but distinct.

"That is for the master of men," she said, "and that for the shepherd. To guard and to guide; for justice and for mercy."

"So the priests told me," Alexander said. "They also said that I could be crowned with the war-helmet if I wanted it: the Khes—Khep—"

"Kheperesh."

"Keperos."

"Kheperesh."

He could not say it. "It sounds Persian," he said, "and a fine jaw-cracker that is."

"It is not Persian," she said stiffly. "It does not even begin to be Persian."

He smiled his sweetest smile. "You know I never meant to insult you. But how you can say *s*—*st*—" He shook his head, as if with the movement he could shake the stumble from his tongue. "But then the Persians can't say my name."

"What, Alexander?" She said it easily enough. "So. Would you wear the Kheperesh, if the two crowns suit you so ill?"

"I thought about it," he said. "I am a soldier, after all; and I come with an army. But it doesn't feel right. This is an oddity, and this"—his finger brushed the false beard—"is ludicrous, but it's not war I'd make in Egypt, nor war that Egypt has given me. It's had enough of that. Peace is what I would wage here."

"Egyptian peace? Or Macedonian?"

He paused, frowning again. She could almost see the turning of his mind. "My generals would say that there is no difference. That the peace should be my peace, and therefore Macedonian. So would Aristotle say. Only Greeks are made to be free, he taught me. Barbarians are by nature slaves. But as I come to know those barbarians—even Persians—I wonder. Aristotle is wise, but he hasn't seen what I've seen."

"We have never been slaves," said Meriamon, "save under the Parsa. And that, we fought with all that was in us."

"So," said Alexander. He faced her fully now, crook and flail held lightly in his hands. There was a new light in his face. "There is the heart of it. That they took away your freedom. That they made you slaves."

"It took you so long to understand?"

"I had to see. To be told—it's not enough. You lost a war. More than one. The price was, is, high; but it's the same price wherever war is. It's justice, of its kind. But that you bore so deep a rancor for so long, against a race who ruled you well enough by any lights . . ."

"They ruled us."

"Will you hate us, too? We'll rule you."

"You, we chose."

"Yes." He raised the crook. "Macedon is a land of shepherds. We understand this, I think."

She inclined her head.

He looked at her. His eyes were steady. "Why do you allow it? Why don't you simply set up your own king, and bid me go back where I came from?"

"You are the king who was given us."

"That's no reason."

"It's all you'll have."

His temper sparked. She waited for the flare; but he was

master of himself. "Very well," he said abruptly. "I'll be crowned as an Egyptian, though I'll look like twenty kinds of fool for doing it. I'll do it for you, and for no one else. Because it will please you."

If he had hoped to discomfit her, he was disappointed. She shrugged. "You do it for the gods, whether you admit it or no. If you please to serve them in my name, then who am I to quibble?"

"I'm still what I am," he said. "I'm still Alexander of Macedon. Nothing that I do here will change it."

"You were always what you are," she said, "and always will be."

Meriamon was very tired, walking back alone to her chambers. There should have been a guard, she supposed, or a servant. But someone had forgotten; or she had slipped away before anyone could see. She had not been taking notice.

There was someone waiting for her. A lamp was lit and set on the table. A figure sat in the best chair, the one with the carved and gilded back. It was a small figure, and thin, and for a moment she knew that it was dead: a tiny wizened mummy of a man. Then his eyes glittered, and she saw the life burning strong in them.

His robe was simple to starkness, the robe of a priest; the light gleamed on his shaven skull. He wore no ornament, carried no mark of honor. Of rank he had little, nor wanted any, nor needed it. What he was, was clear for any eye to see, if that eye was gifted with magic.

Her breath caught. Her heart stopped, then leaped. She bowed down to the floor. "Mage," she said, all reverence. "Great priest. Lord Ay: I marvel to see you here."

"Come," he said. His voice was like his eyes, rich and vibrant. Was that laughter in it? Or impatience? "Up. It's I who should be bowing to you, and these bones are too stiff for that."

She rose to her knees. "You? Bow to me? What in the world for?"

He laughed. It caught on a cough. The shadow behind him stirred, became a young priest with the skin and the face of Nubia, as black almost as Meriamon's own shadow. Lord Ay waved the boy away, never taking his eyes from Meriamon. Or from what stood behind her, as solid almost as the young priest, resting an air-light hand on her shoulder. "Every living thing has a shadow," the old man said. "None but you, in all the world that I know of, has such a shadow as this."

"You were one of those who gave it to me," she said.

"Not I," he said, "nor any human creature. This is of the gods' bestowing. We asked them to protect you. They answered in their own fashion."

She sat on her heels. It was comfortable enough, and Ay did not seem to mind it. Now that she had time to think, she wondered to see him here, whom she had thought safe in Amon's temple, far up the Nile in Thebes. "You've come a long way," she said, "to see the king."

"I came to see you."

She frowned.

He smiled. "Come here, child."

After a moment she obeyed. The young priest set a stool beside the chair. She thanked him gravely. He was a stranger: new since she left. He trembled when he looked at her, and shied from her shadow. She wanted to tell him not to be ridiculous, but she would not shame him so in front of the mage. She sat on the stool and waited for Ay to speak.

"Well then," he said, "I came to see the king; but first I came for you."

"To take me back to Thebes?" She did not know what she felt. Joy? Relief? Reluctance so deep that it shook her body?

"That is with the gods," he said. "Though some in the temple would be glad to have you back among them. No one has quite so pure a voice for the morning hymn, and the workings in the inner temple lack somewhat of savor without your presence. There may even be a broken heart or two among the younger priests—it seems that I heard word of such."

That was mischief, and too much like him. She meant to fix him with a stern stare; but that lacked force, with her cheeks as hot as they were, and her mind darting not to a certain few young idiots, but to one whom Ay had never seen. Whom, gods grant, he would never see.

His smile was as innocent as a child's. "No, I didn't come to fetch you, though I would have been happy to do it. I came to talk to you."

She breathed a sigh. Regret, maybe. Relief. "About Alexander?"

"About the Great House."

"Alexander is pharaoh. In Memphis he will be so for the world to see."

"Will he?"

Ay's voice was soft, his face serene, but she stilled, within and without. "The gods have ordained it," she said.

"Have they?"

"They have told me," said Meriamon.

"Tell me."

She took his hands. They were stick-thin, dry and withered, but there was strength in them. She gave him all that she had, not in empty rattling words but in the voice of the heart, tale and vision both: the king, his wars, her dreams from beginning to end. It was a world's worth, passed between breath and breath, a single endless moment.

She let him go. If she had been tired before, she was exhausted now. Ay seemed more than ever a dead thing. His eyes were closed; his face was still. He hardly seemed to breathe.

He stirred. He opened his eyes. She met them, then looked away.

"So," he said. It was a sigh. "That is how it is. We

guessed. We never would have dared to believe the whole of it."

Meriamon knotted her fingers in her lap. Her gown was as tired as she was, the stiff linen softening, falling out of its pleats. The servants would have to wash it again, and stiffen it, and set the folds with stones, and spread it in the sun. So much labor for a few hours' display.

She was avoiding what she should be thinking of. That Ay—Lord Ay who had taught her father what he knew of magic, who was a mage to match any that there was—was in awe of her. Of Meriamon. She had power enough, she could hardly deny that, but she was never as great as he. She was a child still, an infant in the ways of magic. She would never have his brilliance or his artistry, or his strength of will.

"The gods speak to you," he said, following her thought as he could, for he was a master of mages. "And you answer them, and give them respect but no fear. Do you even know how rare that is?"

"Would fear be any use," she asked, "except to make them impatient?"

"Who but you would think of that?" He sighed, and shook himself. "There. You are tired, and the hour grows late. Tell me why we should accept this king of yours."

"The gods chose him."

"That was hardly answer enough for Alexander. It is never enough for me."

She frowned at him. The awe was gone, at least. He was pricking her with impossible questions, knowing full well what he did. It was almost comforting. "Isn't it a little late to talk of rejecting him?"

"Maybe," said Ay. "Tell me why we should not."

"He has an army, thousands strong and devoted to him. The Parsa have surrendered to him. If we refuse him now, he can destroy us all."

The old man seemed a little surprised to hear her speak so bluntly. "Would he destroy us?"

"Yes," she said, not hesitating. "He can't bear to be crossed. And he has never lost a battle."

"Then he may indeed be worse than the Parsa. Worse even than the ones whose name is effaced from the earth."

She shivered. They were the Hyksos, those nameless ones, the Shepherd Kings, and no more than that, no face, no shape, no memory, and any name that they had given themselves was lost for all of time. It was a sensation like pain, that namelessness, a void in the heart of her magic. But she said, "He is the gods' chosen. I know that for a certainty. As do you, or you would never have come here."

"So well you know me," said Ay. He was not smiling, though his words were light. "What if the gods have chosen that we suffer?"

"They haven't," said Meriamon. Too quickly; but she did not try to take it back.

"He is a foreigner," said Ay. "A barbarian even to the Hellenes whom he rules. Once we have accepted him, there will never be another of our blood on the throne of the Two Lands. Is that what you wish?"

"Am I given a choice?"

"He calls you friend," Ay said. "He trusts you. If you went to him tonight, with the arts which you command—"

"I am not an assassin!"

"Did I say that you should kill him? Dissuade him. Convince him to depart from Khemet. How you do it, and how thoroughly . . . that is for you to determine. Only be certain that he neither takes the throne of the Two Lands, nor seizes it, nor ever destroys it."

Meriamon sat stiff on the stool. She would have risen, but her knees would not bear her. She searched the old man's face, looking for a sign that he jested; that he did not mean what he was saying.

"I am not joking," he said. "I am asking whether you would do this. For Khemet. For our freedom down all the long years."

She could not breathe. She had forgotten how. This man

had sent her out—had sung the words that made her more than simple woman, gave her a god-born shadow, weighed her down with the burden of the gods' will. Now he bade her cast it all away. Because he saw what she saw. Alien blood in the Great House of Khemet. And no hope, no dream of restoration.

"Without Alexander," she said, "we have nothing."

"We have you."

She closed her eyes. It was dark, dark as the land of the dead, and cold. And she was tired, so tired. To take the crowns, the crook and the flail, even the beard—other women had done it, other women ruled, through the long years—to be lord in the Great House—

She could do it. Her hands were small, but strong enough. Her will was firm to command, if command she must.

Her shadow stirred at her back. Her hackles rose. It was the gods' creature, yet it was also hers. If she defied them, even Mother Isis, took what Ay bade her take, ruled as her blood was meant to rule—it would stay. Would protect her.

And the Parsa would come. Or Alexander, disenchanted, with the world at his back. And she would resist them. And fall as her father had; but fall free.

She drew a shuddering breath. It stabbed her. She drew another, bitter-edged. "We have failed," she said, "we of the Black Land, to rule ourselves and our kingdom. So in the end would I. What we do now . . . it saves us. Not as we were before, we can never be that, in so much you see true; but we shall endure and be strong—and more than we, our gods. That, I was shown. If Alexander takes the throne as pharaoh in Memphis, all the world shall know our gods, and Mother Isis shall be worshipped wherever men are. If he does not, we dwindle and fail, and our gods sink with us, down into the long night."

There was a silence. Meriamon opened her eyes, but kept them downcast, fixed on her knotted fingers. She was aware of Ay's presence, the rattle and catch of his breathing, the quick nervous breaths of the young priest behind him, the murmur of wind about the walls. She had not known what she would say until she said it. Now that it was done she was emptied, lightened. That she could have been what her father was, done what he did, and died as he died—that was almost joy. So likewise that she would not do it.

"I love him, I think," she said. "Not as a woman loves a man—that's no part of it. But as a soldier loves a general; as a priest can love a king. There's a light in him, even when he's being mad, or maddening. He's full of the god."

"Ah, but which god?" asked Ay. "If it is Set, and not Horus, or Amon who begot him . . ."

"It can be all three. And Dionysos, too—and that is Osiris, who is lord of all that lives or is dead."

Ay pondered that, sitting as still as Osiris himself, only the glitter of his eyes betraying that he lived. Not much longer, Meriamon knew, and that was grief. The rattle in his lungs was stronger by far than it had been when she left Thebes, and there was little of him left but will and magic. But he would see the end of this, for good or for ill: Alexander crowned and taken into the Great House, and Khemet made greater by it or diminished to nothing, a nation of slaves under a tyrant's heel.

"This is the gamble," she said. "The great throw. We began it long ago. Should we shrink from it now, when the end is so near?"

"That part is yours," he said, "to accept or to cast away. I only tell you what can be."

"You test me," she said. She did not ask why, as perhaps she was meant to. She knew. Because the power was in her, here at the crux, to let it go on, or to stop it before it was unstoppable. And, more than that, because Ay was never one to go blindly where anyone led, even a god. He wanted her to think. To choose. To decide for herself.

It was terrifying, that freedom. Knowing that her

shadow waited as Ay waited, and would not move to compel her. The gods in their majesty, the Mother herself who was queen of them all, would speak no word. What Meriamon said, what she did, were hers and hers alone.

"No," she said. "I will not stop him. If that makes me a coward, then so be it. At least I am an honest coward."

"Or as brave as any in the world," said Ay. "To refuse power when it is offered, when you have blood-right to it—that's no common cowardice."

"No; it's noble. Royal, for a fact." She rose. Her knees wobbled. She stiffened them. "This is only a beginning. That's what you're telling me. Making me see."

The bright eyes hooded. The old man smiled. "Now you begin to understand."

She almost hit him. She glared instead; then, all unwillingly, laughed. She embraced him, careful of his fragility, and set a kiss on his brow. "I'd forgotten how exasperating you can be. And—for all of that—how necessary."

"What, like one of the priests' purges?"

"Very like," said Meriamon, shocking the poor young priest into immobility, and making Ay laugh. That too she had forgotten: what it was to share laughter with a kinsman. By that more than anything, she knew that she had come home.

• TWENTY-THREE •

Meriamon rose long before dawn on the morning of Alexander's crowning in Memphis. Even at that, he would be up before her: the priests and the servants would have seen to it. They had been instructing him for much of the day before, and finding him, they said, a quick pupil. "If not," Lord Ay had said, "precisely tractable." He had been amused.

Meriamon smiled, thinking of Alexander and Ay together. Ay would not have compelled the king to do anything against his grain, but there was a strong magic of persuasion in the old priest's presence.

She prepared herself carefully. It had been a long while since she walked as a priestess of Amon. The gown, the wig, the paint went on like armor, heavy, stiff with disuse. She was to be nothing in this rite except eyes and a voice; she held no rank and accepted no honor but that of a singer of the god. On that she had been adamant. Ay, wise man, had not pressed her. Alexander might have, but she had hardly seen him since they came to Memphis. He needed for this brief time to be in Khemet wholly, without her to stand between, distracting him with familiarity.

With dawn as yet the faintest glimmer on the horizon, she left the Great House and walked down to the temple of Min—Min and not Ptah of Memphis, because Min oversaw the fruits of the land, and hence the reign of the king. The streets were full of people, but they were quiet, their ebullience muted by the cool and the dimness. She slipped through them like a shadow. She felt light, empty, neither joyful nor afraid. Eyes, no more, and when the time came, a voice.

She knew that there was more to her than that. But the solid center, the knot of fears and joys and confusions, was in part buried deep, in part left behind in the Great House, in the keeping of a certain Macedonian guardsman. Now she must be all Khemet, all priestess. This had walked up out of Thebes. This had come to the field of Issus, and found the king whom the gods had chosen.

Such a little thing, she had been. So pure in her emptiness. So unformed, like clay before the potter shapes it.

Her journey had been the shaping. Alexander—king, god's chosen, but man and friend besides—was the fire that had made her strong.

Alexander, and his friends who had become hers. And Nikolaos.

She stood on the terrace between the Great House and the temple of Min, no longer a shape of air and darkness, but earth and flesh, with life burning in it. The sun was coming. And with it, the king.

He left the palace as the sky flushed bright with dawn. He came as Lord of the Two Lands: no Hellene king mounted on a horse, but pharaoh borne high on the shoulders of princes, under a canopy of gold, and before him the princes of Khemet, and behind him the lords of the Two Lands, and behind those the foot and the chariotry, to the sound of drums and trumpets. Two priests walked ahead of them all in a cloud of frankincense, and between them a lone priest chanting the processional.

As the king left the Great House, the procession of Min left the god's dwelling, the god borne as the king was borne, on the shoulders of a score of priests. The god's white bull walked before, and the long line of priests behind, carrying the panoply of the king and the images of the gods. They for this day suffered Min to stand preeminent, but their presence was strong, blessing the rite with their mingled power: Amon and Mut and Khonsu, Ptah and Sekhmet and Nefertem, Horus and Osiris and Mother Isis, Khnum, Sobek, Set, Hathor, Thoth and Bastet, and all the gods who were in Khemet.

They met upon the terraced square, wide it seemed as a city, just as the sun rose. A shout went up from the priests and the people. In its aftermath, the air still throbbing from the force of it, Min's priest stepped out into the center of the square, looking small and yet strangely potent in the empty space. Priests followed him bearing cages. One by one he opened them, brought forth a flapping, protesting goose, and flung it into the sky. The birds floundered, steadied, beat their way upward. "Bear word," the priest cried to them in a voice as thin and clear itself as a bird's, "to the four realms of heaven, that Horus the son of Isis and Osiris takes the two crowns, that the son of the living gods receives the White Crown and the Red Crown over the land of Khemet."

Meriamon, on the edge of the square, lowered her eyes from the birds to the glitter that was the king. Her souls knew him, always. Her sight saw a stranger.

He had put on the kilt. He looked well in it, was built for it with his wide shoulders and his graceful compact body, though his fair skin was odd, given as it was to going red and peeling when sensible skin went bronze-dark. He wore the headdress with its lappets over the shoulders and its twisted tail behind, striped blue and gold. They had not succeeded in painting his eyes—no Hellene would suffer that, reckoning it a thing for barbarians and women—but the face under the headdress, at this distance, was a royal mask. What he was thinking, only the gods knew.

When the priests took off the headdress, there was no mistaking the bright-gold mane, or the way, perhaps forgetting himself, he shook it out and back. A murmur ran through the gathered people. Wonder, surprise. A full mane on a king, and yellow at that: astonishing. Min's priest frowned slightly. The murmur died.

Alexander's face did not change at all. His eyes were lifted, fixed on the horizon. They remained so as the priests vested him with the regalia of the Great House: crook, flail, even the false beard. As the priests approached with the crowns, his gaze focused.

Meriamon felt it in her bones. A gathering. A swelling of power. An awareness in the earth, that here at last, after far too long, a true king stood again in the heart of the Two Lands. She sank to her knees, unmindful of anything but the earth beneath. She laid her hands flat on the stones. Men had quarried them, shaped them, set them here, but they were Khemet too, under the sky of Khemet, before Khemet's king.

He was as still as ever, but his feet were braced a little apart, as if against the rocking of a ship. As the joined crowns touched his brow, he stiffened. His eyes were wide.

He felt it at least as strongly as she. White heat. Pure raw power, centering in him. For this moment, from this moment, he was Khemet. His heart was her heart, his life her life. As he prospered, so must she. If he failed, so would she fail, unless an heir be found to restore the power.

Across the sun-shot stretch of paving, his eyes met Meriamon's. The light in them was terrible, and yet it did not blind her. Had it been so, she asked him with the voice of the soul made strong by the power that was here, when he was made king in Macedon?

He answered her, soul to soul. Alike, he said, yet different. A darker earth, a younger power, milder, weaker, less fiercely potent. He showed it to her. It made her think of water from a rock, and of a ram upon the altar, offering its throat for the sacrifice.

This was nothing so gentle. It was the eye of the sun, ancient and terrible. And yet he was master of it. As willingly as the ram, it offered itself to him.

He took it. He held it as he held the crook and the flail: shepherd's rod, master's whip, persuasion and force matched and balanced.

"For you," he said in the voice of the heart. "For you I do this. Because you want it so badly."

"I?" she asked him silently. "Not you?"

He was motionless in the center of the square, an image of a king. But inside her he laughed, and that was all Alexander. "Well. I too. But I'd have done it Greek-fashion, and never mind the rest of it."

"Then you would have been a foreign king," she said, "no better than Cyrus or Cambyses, and no more truly king in Egypt. This makes us yours. And you, ours."

"For a while," he said.

"For always," said Meriamon.

* * *

Alexander gave himself to Khemet and accepted Khemet in return, and the Two Lands were glad of him. An hour after, he put on a chiton and bound his brows with a garland of Nile lilies and went to his Greek games; and that was all for his Hellenes.

Meriamon could not have gone to the games in any event, since she was a foreigner, and worse than that, a woman; but she did not miss them. She could never understand what pleasure these people found in hour after hour of watching naked men running and leaping and fighting. The horse-games might have been a little more interesting, and the contests of music and dance, though she would rather not have had the judges giving prizes. Were they not all showing the best that they had?

She said as much to Niko. She was sitting with Thaïs in one of the courts of the Great House, listening to a flute player who had taken a second in the competition—an Egyptian, and he should have been more sensible, but he had imbibed enough of the Hellenes' silliness to be dismayed that he had not won. Niko, who had come looking for his brother, accepted a cup of wine from the servant's hand and seemed inclined to linger.

"What is this about choosing the best?" she asked him. "Can't anyone be happy to be what he is?"

"No," said Niko. Then, before she could snap at him: "The best is what every man should strive to be, or what's the worth in anything?"

"And if he can't be? What then? He gnaws himself in silence, and wishes he were dead?"

"He tries harder," Niko said.

She frowned at him. "You won the races again. Ptolemy told us. Don't you get tired of winning?"

He laughed, which made her frown the more blackly. "Never! I love to win. Typhon lives for it. Aren't you proud of us?"

"I don't understand you," she said.

"What, are we a mystery? And you an Egyptian."

"We're not mysterious at all."

"No?" His hand took in the whole of it: the court with its trees and fountains, the walls that the Hellenes called the work of gods or giants, the sky the pure deep blue of lapis; and beyond, to the mind if not the eye, Black Land and Red Land and the inscrutable tombs of the old kings. "This country is like nothing else that ever was. The size of it—vaster than anything in the world, and older, and stranger, with its myriad gods. And you can't understand why we look for the best, and reward it when we find it?"

"We don't need to look. We are."

Ptolemy came back then, and none too soon in Meriamon's mind. Niko was grinning. Incorrigible.

She left soon after that. Her temper had cooled somewhat. She could—should—have been in Amon's temple with her own people. Lord Ay was there. But she was not minded to face them. She was the one who had gone away. She had spoken with the gods; she had become a stranger.

"I am home," she said to herself. "I *am*."

And so she had been till she saw the awe in Ay's face. Till she knew that she had changed.

The land was still her own. The people had gone strange. Narrow dark faces, long black eyes; light and small and quick, their language like the rattle of the sistrum.

She could walk among them, and no one stared, or reckoned her a foreigner. It was the other whom they gaped at, striding to catch her, big fair Macedonian with his improbable eyes.

She was not as alien as he was. Neither was she one of them. She walked between the worlds.

She always had. That was what it was to be born royal and gifted with magic.

The streets were thronged. They could not have walked side by side if Niko had not been so much larger than anyone near, and so determined to breast the flood. She walked in the lee of him, and no one jostled her.

A suspicious bulge in his mantle wriggled and became Sekhmet, treading the breadth of his shoulders to spring lightly down into Meriamon's arms. The cat looked highly pleased with herself. As well she might, who had escaped from standing guard over Meriamon's chambers.

Beyond the Great House, past the avenues of the temples, vast sky-roofed halls with their ranks of sphinxes, the city of giants became a smaller thing. The streets narrowed to human-width. The houses shrank and dwindled until they were no more than huts of mud and palm-trunks, with dogs and big-bellied children playing in the dust in front of them, and women chattering as they fetched water from the cistern. Someone was baking bread, someone else was brewing beer. Children's voices rang in unison from a little temple, reciting a lesson. Under an awning a potter plied his trade.

From here one could not see the temples or the palace, or the White Wall that had been raised about it when the world was young. This was another Egypt, less wonderful to see, but more truly itself.

"Now this I could learn to like," said Niko, stepping over a dog that had lain down in the street and had no mind to move. He grinned at a child who stared at him from a doorway, thumb in mouth, eyes black and round and shiny as olives. "Temples and palaces—they're pleasant to look at, but they aren't much good for living in."

"I've never lived anywhere else," said Meriamon. "Except in tents, following the king."

"Could you learn?"

It was such an odd question, and asked so simply, that she stopped. He went on a stride or two, halted, turned on his heel. She was aware of him, but her eyes were on the rest, the small mean houses with their bright paint on doorpost and rafter, the dog and the child and the gaggle of women at the cistern, whispering and giggling and darting glances at the foreigner.

"I don't know," she said. "I never thought of it."

"No," said Niko, and all the brightness had gone out of him. "You couldn't. You belong in the temples and the palaces. I belong here."

"You are a nobleman," she said.

"I am a shepherd's son, a breaker of horses. My feet knew the feel of earth before they ever walked on marble."

"Carpets," she said. "We walk on carpets."

"The only carpet I ever knew was grass where the sheep had grazed it."

"I've walked on grass," said Meriamon. "It's very strange. Here it's sand, and mud in season."

His expression was odd. After a while, and not happily, she recognized it. Pity. "They never let you set foot in it, did they? You were always in a litter, or on a horse."

"I used to play in the garden," she said. She was not going to be angry, or to defend herself. To him least of all. "There was a pool, with lilies. I was always falling into it."

"Or jumping in?"

A smile tugged at the corner of her mouth, for all that she could do. "I wasn't supposed to. But if I went too close to the edge, and once I had got wet . . . what use to come out until I'd had my fill of it?"

"We had a pool," said Niko, "out by the mares' pasture, where the river cut through a bank. We all swam in it. It was ghastly cold, and there were fish that liked to bite at dangling toes and fingers. We thought it was the best thing in the world."

Meriamon's smile broke free. She began to walk again. He walked with her past the women with their laughing, knowing eyes. One of them said something that brought the blood rushing to her cheeks.

He did not see it. Maybe. And he knew no Egyptian. She walked faster. He lengthened his stride, easily, humming to himself. Blessed innocent. If he lived here, he would have them all falling in love with him.

She was long lost. She could not even stay angry with him for being Nikolaos.

When the games were over, Alexander took a company of friends and Companions and, escorted by a small army of priests, rode out of the living city into the city of the dead.

This was the Red Land, the dry land, and yet it was not lifeless. The city of tombs was full of shrines, and each shrine had its priests, greater and lesser in the degree which the dead had endowed. Roads ran through it, wide and level and smoothly paved, scoured clean by wind and sand and sun.

There was no grief here. Only awe, and the fields of monuments to the immortal dead. On the far edge of it down an aisle of sphinxes, huge man-headed lions crouching forever on guard, lay Apis' temple and tomb.

The king had seen Apis-on-earth in the city of the living: the black bull with the star on his brow and the image of an eagle astride his back. He had his temple and his harem, his priests who served him and offered him sacrifice. Alexander had paid him reverence, and he had accepted it, bowing his great horned head and suffering the king to touch him.

Here was the tomb of the bulls who had been Apis, dug deep and walled strong amid a cluster of shrines and temples. There, wrapped like a king and laid to rest, was that Apis whom Cambyses had killed.

"He took the city," said Apis' priest, standing in the dim echoing chamber under the weight of stone and years, "and woke in the morning to hear, not wails and lamentation, but laughter and rejoicing. A god was born, his captives told him. A child of heaven had come to earth and blessed his city.

" 'And does it matter nothing that his city has fallen?' the king demanded of them. They only laughed and sang with all the rest, even when he tormented them. Then he was struck with wonder, and although he was a Persian and his Truth was inviolate, he yearned to see for himself what face a living god would wear.

" 'Bring the god to me,' he bade his servants. And they obeyed, and brought him the god. Damp yet from its birth, wobble-legged, bawling for its mother: a black bull-calf with a white forehead.

"Cambyses laughed aloud. 'This is your god? *This* you worship? See how I give it reverence!'

"He swept out his sword, and before any could stay him, thrust it into the rump of the calf.

"It died of the wound, and the Great King gave it to his cooks, and that night he feasted on it, he and his princes. Such," said the priest, "was Cambyses' reverence for the gods of Egypt."

"And Ochos," said Meriamon. "He too, when he had slain my father: he slew the Apis and dined on its flesh, for he was not to be outdone."

"No wonder you hate them," said Ptolemy. The others, even Alexander, had looked at the dead thing in its wrappings and its reek of grave-spices, and retreated rapidly. Ptolemy regarded it with something very like reverence. "Poor thing, to die so young. Was it born again quickly?"

"Soon enough," said the priest. "Apis is always reborn; always to a cow who conceives of fire from heaven, who bears no young after. We reverence the Mother of the Apis as we do her son."

"I saw her in the temple," Ptolemy said. "A fine creature, that. I can see that a god would favor her."

Meriamon watched him after that. He was no different than he ever was, and yet something about him had changed. It was she—she was seeing him anew. He was interested in what was here. He wanted to know. He walked with the priest, and asked questions, and listened to the answers. The echoing gloom, the dry scent of death, seemed not to trouble him. He seemed almost to be at home here.

More than she. She was glad to leave the tombs, to walk in the sun again. Time enough and more when she was dead, to walk these passages. Now she would live, and breathe the clean air, and turn her face to the fire of Ra.

• TWENTY-FOUR •

Arrhidaios loved Egypt. "Colors," he said. "And all the warm. And people laughing."

Thaïs grimaced. No one, it was clear, had warned her that beauty lingered longest in a serene face. Hers was mobile always, and more of late, as her belly swelled with the child.

She caught her breath now. Arrhidaios stopped talking and stared at her. Meriamon poised, alert.

"It moved," said Thaïs. "It kicked me."

Her surprise was pure. No joy in it, but no anger either, simply astonishment.

"Babies do that," said Arrhidaios. "Myrrhine let me feel when the baby kicked. It kicked hard. She said it hurt. Does it hurt, Thaïs?"

"No," Thaïs said.

Meriamon did not ask who Myrrhine was. Someone in Macedon, no doubt. She kept her eyes on Thaïs. The hetaira let her hand fall from her middle, where it had flown when the child moved, and shook herself, and went on with what she had been saying. "So I told him," she said. "Finally."

"Had he guessed?" asked Meriamon.

"He said not." Thaïs filled her cup with wine. The bright brittle look was on her as it sometimes was, but rarely now when there was only Meriamon there, and

Arrhidaios who had wandered in a little while ago and settled contentedly at Meriamon's feet. "I am clever," Thaïs said, "after all. And men never look, once they're sure one has the proper count of breasts and thighs, in suitable proportions."

"Ptolemy is hardly as blind as that."

"Maybe he wanted to be."

Meriamon narrowed her eyes. "What did he say?"

"What would you expect him to say?"

Arrhidaios said suddenly, " 'If it is a boy you may keep it. If it is a girl, see that you expose it, and that all is done duly and properly, before I return.' "

The women stared at Arrhidaios. He smiled, pleased with himself.

"Where on earth did you hear that?" Meriamon asked him.

His smile wavered. He shrugged, with a touch of sullenness. "I don't remember."

"It's a play," said Thaïs.

"Yes!" cried Arrhidaios. "Thettalos was in it. He said the baby had to be a boy. It wasn't. So they put it out on the hill. But somebody came and found it. Somebody will find your baby, too."

"I hope not," Thaïs said.

"You won't keep it, then?" asked Meriamon.

"I didn't say that!" Thaïs' voice was sharp. She drank deep from her cup, and drew a long breath after, as if to summon patience. "I didn't say that at all. Nor did he. He wants me to keep the child. Even"—her voice wavered a fraction—"if it is a girl."

"Do *you* want to keep it?"

"Does it matter what I want?"

"To Ptolemy," Meriamon said, "I think it does."

Thaïs held her stare for a long moment. Then the bold eyes lowered. She sighed. "He would have shouted for a festival, if I hadn't forced him to be reasonable. As it was, he drank much too much, and told far too many people, and made a perfect fool of himself. You'd think," she said, "that he'd never sired a cub before."

"Hasn't he?"

"Not that he'll admit to." Thaïs set the cup on the table with a small, definite click. "And when are you going to admit that Nikolaos is in love with you?"

The shift left Meriamon mute. It was evasion, of course. Thaïs hated to speak of things that came too close to her heart. It was like her to cut to the quick of Meriamon's.

Arrhidaios spoke in the pause. "Meri, are you going to have a baby for Niko?"

Meriamon rose from her chair. What she said, if she said anything, she did not afterward remember. She hoped that she left in something resembling dignity.

She came to a halt in a passageway that looked only vaguely familiar. Her eyes were burning dry. One learned to do that in Khemet: tears made the kohl run.

A child for Nikolaos. A child for any man. A child to fill this womb of hers that the gods had made barren, to mark her as their chosen—the price she paid, to be their slave and servant.

She shut away the thought, with its grief and—yes, its anger. It had never hurt so much before. It had never mattered.

She looked about. One way seemed as good as another. She went on as she had begun, through the painted corridors. People passed her. One was agitated. He was looking for Arrhidaios. She would have told him where the king's brother was, but he was past before she could speak, looking as distracted as she felt.

The next runner was looking for her. He was one of the king's pages, a boy so fair that he looked unnatural, like a bleached bone. He had been in the sun again without a hat: his face was crimson, and it had begun to swell. "I have a salve for that," she said.

"The king said you did, lady," said the boy, "and I'm to fetch it later. But first he wants to see you."

She thought of not wanting to see him. But the boy would be upset, and she had nowhere to go that was not painful. She shrugged. "Why not?" she said.

She had shocked the poor child. His back was rigid with disapproval as he led her through the corridors. He bowed her through every door, so scrupulously, exaggeratedly correct that she almost laughed.

A man caught them as they turned to go to the king's chambers. He was one of the Old Macedonians as the younger ones had taken to calling them, a man who kept his beard and dressed in the rough wool of the uplands, even in Egypt. He looked at the page with no pleasure at all, and at Meriamon with barely restrained disgust. "My commander wants to see you," he said to Meriamon.

She could understand his accent. Just. She would not have stopped, but he was barring her way. "And who is your commander?" she asked.

She had offended him. But then her simple presence did that; this merely added to it. "Parmenion," he said, "will see you now."

"I am going to see the king," she said.

"You can see the king after you see Parmenion."

Alexander's page was no help at all. He shifted from foot to foot, but he said nothing. For once Meriamon would have been glad of one of the older boys, one who could be as arrogant as this great bristling scowling man.

So could she be. "Very well," she said. "I'll spare your general a moment. Tell him he may find me in the chamber of the birds."

She was gone before the man could muster wits to speak. The room she had spoken of was close, and small as rooms went in this palace, with a wall that was open on one of the gardens. The others were painted with birds of every kind that was in Khemet, from the fowl of reed and sedge to the falcon of the desert, swimming and feeding and flying in a long band above painted ranks of pillars. There was a couch to sit on, carved with birds, painted and gilded, and a stool, and a table, and little else but light and air.

Meriamon settled herself on the couch. Alexander's page, finding his courage at last, said, "Lady, the king—"

"The king will wait a little longer," she said.

"But—"

"He will wait," she said. There was iron in her tone. A flush could not show on his face, as scarlet as the sun had seared it, but he looked down quickly and was silent. He had taken a guard's place, she noticed, beside and behind her. She thought of sending him back to his master. But there was comfort in his presence, and he was a witness, if Parmenion ventured to harm her.

They waited in silence. Meriamon began to wonder if there was any use in it: if Parmenion would come at all. As she considered rising, stretching the knots out of back and arms, going to find the king, she heard the sound of feet. Soldier's boots; the clanking of armor. She willed herself to remain as she was, half-reclining on the couch.

It was only one man, pausing at the door, then opening it.

Meriamon hoped that she was not gaping like an idiot. Niko looked ready to stand guard on the king. His armor was polished till it shone, his cloak hung in impeccable folds. He had his best sword, and his helmet had a new plume.

He hardly looked at her at all, which was as well: it gave her time to recover herself. "Go on, Leukippos," he said. "Tell the king we'll be along as soon as we're done here. I'll look after the lady."

Leukippos grinned, sudden and startling, and set off at a run. Niko took his place.

Meriamon found her tongue at last. "What in the gods' name—"

"Some people need to remember that you're a king's daughter," Niko said.

She could hardly argue with that. "But," she said, "where did you come from?"

"Thaïs told me you'd run off. I ran into Marsyas in the hall; he told me where you were."

"How hard did you hit him?"

"Wouldn't you like to know?" said Niko. Then, before she could hit him herself: "I didn't need to. I'm a King's Companion, and I outrank him. Maybe I rattled my sword a bit. For appearances. After all."

"After all," said Meriamon, dry as sand in a tomb. She had not expected to find him comforting. His solidity was an anchor. His levity lightened her heart, even now. There was no nursing ancient grievances under that bright pale stare.

But they did matter. He did not know, could not.

He would learn.

Parmenion came at long last, with a pair of guards who established themselves at the door, and a glare for Niko. Niko stood at parade rest, wearing no expression at all: the perfect guardsman. Parmenion's glare slid from him to Meriamon.

"Well," the commander said. "Have you something to say?"

His insolence was breathtaking. Niko stiffened perceptibly. Meriamon allowed herself a slow smile. It was sweet; it was puzzled. "I? But, commander, it was you who expressed a desire to speak with me."

"I am not accustomed to running at a woman's bidding," Parmenion said.

"No," said Meriamon. "I can see that you would not be. Except, of course," she said, "if that woman is a queen."

"You are not that," said Parmenion.

"True," said Meriamon. "Will you speak now? The king is waiting."

Parmenion paused. She watched his face suffuse with anger; she watched it smooth itself clean. No rough soldier, this one, for all his rudeness. He knew courts and kings. She could hardly blame him, she supposed, for trying to cow her or prick her to temper, and so gain the advantage.

He gave no signal that she could see, but one of his guards fetched the stool. He lowered himself into it, stiffly, and set his hands on his knees. "Very well," he said. "You're no fool; I shouldn't have treated you like one. Can we be honest with one another?"

"Have we ever been anything else?"

"On my side of it," he said, "no. You have name enough for truthfulness, whether you speak for your gods or yourself. Suppose you tell me, then. If Alexander agreed to it, would you marry him?"

She opened her mouth, closed it. "He never would."

"He well could," said Parmenion. "He should. You're a king's daughter. You know what a king's first duty is. To give sons to the line."

"He knows that," she said. "There's Barsine's Herakles. A fine child, growing well and quickly."

"Too quickly," said Parmenion, "for one as young as he's supposed to be." She was silent. His mouth twisted: perhaps a smile, perhaps not. "Don't take me for an idiot, lady. That's Memnon's brat, and you know it as well as I do. So, I'll wager, does Alexander. He visits them both as seldom as he possibly can, and stays hardly long enough to exchange a word or two. No, Mariamne. That was a weak deception, and it gets weaker the longer it goes on. Alexander has no son alive, and no chance of getting one. Unless," he said, "you see to it."

Meriamon's lips set tight.

"You know he has to have a Macedonian queen," Parmenion said, oblivious to her silence, or not caring to notice it. "But Macedon is on the other side of the earth, and time runs on. While he plays king in Egypt, he can take an Egyptian wife. He's thought of you, don't think he hasn't. He likes the look of you."

"Not as a woman," she said more faintly than she would have liked.

"That's for you to teach him, then, isn't it?"

Meriamon wanted to close her eyes and breathe deep, but that would be a betrayal. She said as calmly as she could, "Have you considered sending for a properly Macedonian bride? Once she was here, he could hardly pack her off again without insulting her mortally; or more to the point, her family."

"Macedonian women do not tramp about with the troops."

"Not even briefly, to give your king an heir?"

"It's not done."

His face was a shut door. Meriamon could find no chink in it. "Why, then? Why choose me?"

"Who else is there?"

"Half the nobility of Egypt have daughters of appropriate age," said Meriamon.

"Is any of royal blood?"

"Several," she said.

"None is a king's daughter," said Parmenion. "Or the king's friend. Or as likely to win him over."

That, unfortunately, was true. Alexander had said it once where Meriamon could hear. He did not like to bed strangers. Friends were the best lovers. Dear friends were best of all. He had been looking at Hephaistion when he said it, and Hephaistion had laughed and made a jest of it, but it was true. She knew it as well as they.

Her throat was trying to shut tight. She willed it open.

Parmenion spoke again before she could begin. "You have to marry. Every woman does. Why not marry a king? You can't be queen in Macedon, but if they call you queen in Egypt, who's to gainsay them? Isn't this what you've been aiming for since you tracked us down in Issus?"

"No," she was going to say. Did say, but no one heard it. Someone was at the door: a high sharp voice raised, the guards' deeper tones, a sudden flurry.

The door was open, and Alexander was in it, in a fine hot temper, but smiling. "Parmenion! So that's where you've got to. And Mariamne. Am I interrupting something? Should I come back?"

Meriamon wondered distantly what he would have done if she had taken him at his word. She did not; and Parmenion seemed to have lost his voice.

She started to rise. Alexander waved her down again, looked about, found the other stool, pulled it up beside her. His eyes were bright as he looked from one to another of them. Bitter-bright. "Let me guess. You're talking about marrying me off again."

"How can you tell?" asked Meriamon. She did not mean it for coyness. She honestly wanted to know.

"Parmenion," said Alexander. "You. In the same room. And there's a look you both get . . . Have you settled the contract yet?"

"We could hardly do that without your knowledge and consent," Parmenion said.

"No," said the king. "But you might get the haggling over before you started on me. It's logical, I suppose. As long as you're looking to drag me to my duty. And now we're here, with all the priests and the princes, and enough Persians to be properly horrified when the new pharaoh marries the old pharaoh's daughter. It would be a very economical wedding."

"Then you'll assent to it?" Parmenion asked. His voice was as level as ever, no quickening of eagerness in it, but he had eased visibly. He was poised still, for all of that; knowing his king, and wary of this new complaisance and its attendant, unwonted stillness.

Alexander paused as if in thought. "I made a joke of it once, or a challenge. That didn't make it less sensible. Not that I need anyone to give me Egypt. That's done, and well done. But establishing my rule here, giving what I can to a woman of this country . . . that's tempting."

"This woman will have you," Parmenion said. "There's

none better suited. She's not as much for looks as some, but she'll do. Her family, if she has any— Do you have family, lady?"

"None alive," Alexander answered for her. And when Parmenion raised a brow: "I asked. She has cousins, maybe, in Ethiopia. There's only Amon's temple and the priests, and they won't give trouble."

"Good," said Parmenion, still warily, but playing the game, if game it was. Netting his prey. "The sooner you get her bedded and bearing, the happier we'll be."

Meriamon rose very slowly. Neither seemed to see her. Niko did. She was aware of him, a shiver on her skin. What he was thinking, she could not begin to guess.

The voice that came out of her was her own. No god wielded it. And yet it seemed hardly to be part of her. " 'We'?" she said. " 'We', Parmenion?"

He looked at her then. "Of course, we. The king will take you. You can hardly refuse him."

"Oh," she said. "But I can."

He did not seem to understand. Even Alexander looked blank.

She faced the king. She spoke as gently as she could. "You are my king," she said. "I would follow you to the ends of the earth. But I do not want to marry you."

That was shock, that wide pale stare. Fury. And maybe, under all the rest, relief.

"I do not want to marry you," she said again. "Nor you, me. We are not for one another."

"That is nonsense," said Parmenion.

She paid no heed to him. "Alexander, look at me. Do I look like anything you would want to call wife?"

The king's head tilted. He was angry. Dangerously so. "Do I look like anything you would want to call husband?"

"No," said Meriamon. "But king, yes. And pharaoh. And friend, if you will still have that."

"No one has ever refused me before," Alexander said. He sounded almost calm about it.

"As one suffers, so one learns."

The old gnomic words made Alexander laugh, but it was fanged laughter. "Why?"

It was hard, but not as hard as it had been, even a moment before. The worst was knowing that Niko was there and listening, and saying nothing. "It's not that I have any distaste for you, or any fear of what you are, or, Mother Isis knows, any vow or bond that keeps me unmarried. Nor would it go so ill if I accepted. There have been worse matches made, and they prospered well enough.

"But," she said, "what you would want out of this union—what your counselors have been urging you to do—that would fail."

"What?" asked Alexander. "Egypt? It's mine already; I've no fear of losing it, unless I lose everything."

"No," said Meriamon. Trying not to shout it. Trying to speak calmly. "Egypt has nothing to do with it. You need—your counselors want—heirs. I cannot give them to you."

The silence was abrupt, and to Meriamon, terrible.

Parmenion broke it, roughshod. "Of course you can give them. There's not much to you, but what there is is sound, and young enough to bear a whole troop of sons."

"No," Meriamon said again. "There will be no sons for me. Nor daughters. No children at all. This that I am"— her hand gestured to her shadow where it lay watchful— "and this that I do, in speaking for my gods—it has a price. That price is my hope of children."

"For always?" Alexander asked. His voice was soft, almost gentle. "For ever?"

"For always," said Meriamon. Her eyes were burning with unshed tears. "It never mattered. Much. I had so much to learn; so much to do. Then there was the shock of leaving Egypt, and the shock, almost greater, of coming back. It seemed little enough price to pay for Egypt. Others have paid more. Others have died."

"Was I worth so much?" asked Alexander. Soft still. But no pity. If she had not loved him before, she would have loved him then, and known him for her king.

Her answer did not come at once. She said slowly, "I had thought so. It was only a dream that I was losing: a hope of children who might never be born, even if I hadn't given them in sacrifice. And in return, all of Egypt was gaining its king. But what I did for it—am I any better, after all, than the priests in Tyre, giving their firstborn children to the gods?"

"They gave living children," Alexander said. "You gave children who had never been conceived."

"That is so," she said. "And it is better to be doomed to barrenness than to be condemned to virginity. But I am not the woman to give you the sons you need."

They stared at her, all of them. She drew herself up. "The grief is old," she said, "almost as old as I. I am sorry that I cannot be what you need me to be. There will be a queen for you, Alexander. And sons. My gods have promised me that."

• TWENTY-FIVE •

Meriamon felt swept clean. She had left the three of them in the chamber of the birds, speechless all, and even Niko had not tried to follow her.

There was pain in that, but no surprise. She should have told him the truth from the beginning. If he hated her now, she had only herself to blame for it.

She went down to Amon's temple. It was smaller by far than the great temple in Thebes, but great enough for a stranger to marvel at. She hardly saw its splendors. They welcomed her there, glad enough that she knew a pang of guilt: she had been neglecting them shamefully. When she put on the vestments and bound her hair beneath the heavy wig and sang the god's office, she made herself pure prayer.

Or as pure as she could be with a small cold knot of pain in her heart. And all for a pack of Hellenes. What were they to her? This was her place and this was her world. She had left it for a while. She would never leave it again.

The old ways closed in about her, and the old, close-walled existence. If she was restless, if she remembered too much and too often, if her dreams were strange again, as if she had not done all that she was sent to do, then that was only to be expected. The tamed cat of the temple had been loosed for a time to be a hunter. Now she must be the god's again, and live within his walls, and bind her days with the cords of his worship.

Sekhmet was not with her. The cat had let herself be taken to the temple in Meriamon's cloak, but the next morning when Meriamon woke she was gone. A hunt through the temple yielded nothing. There was no use in hunting through the city, not as large as it was and full of cats, though Meriamon did enough of that. Sekhmet belonged to no one but herself. She would come back, or she would not.

It was much the same with Meriamon's shadow. It had not abandoned her: it came and it went. But it hunted every night, and Meriamon had no will to restrain it. It was not hunting in the city. It had promised her that. In the days it slept, waking only to startle a novice with keener eyes than most, who happened to be staring at it when it opened lambent eyes and yawned.

"I'm a fallow field," Meriamon said to Lord Ay. She had been in the temple for a hand of days. She was settling, she thought, not badly. All things considered. "I'll never bear fruit in children. I've done what I was born to do. What's left for me now but a round of empty days?"

Ay regarded her gravely enough, though there was a glint in his eye. "Those are grim words for one so young," he said.

"Not as young as that," said Meriamon.

"Oh, you are ancient," he said, "and weary and wise. You brought us a king. Do you think there is nothing greater that you can do?"

"Isn't there?"

He shrugged, coughed. His young priest tensed, clean cloths in hand. Ay waved him away. "Nothing greater in the world's eye," he said, "maybe. But small things have their own splendor. Now that the gods have freed you, you can be simply Meriamon, as you have never allowed yourself to be."

"But what is Meriamon?"

He looked at her. His eyes were dark, but there was a brightness in them. "What would you like to be?"

"Happy."

When he smiled, all the lines of his face seemed to curve upward. "Surely that is simple enough."

"It's the most complicated thing in the world." Meriamon was sitting on a stool at his feet. She clasped her hands between her knees, frowning ahead of her. "I thought I knew what I was going to do. Go out of Khemet, however terrifying a thing that was, and bring back its king. And I did it. It took longer than I'd ever expected, and cost me both more and less: more in time and comfort, less in courage. Then, I thought, I would come back to Amon, and be what I was before. Nothing would have changed."

"Except that the Parsa were conquered."

"But that was simply part of it. The world would be all different, and I would be exactly as I was before—except that the old hate was gone."

"Old hates leave great gaping holes in one's heart," said Ay, "when they are gone."

Meriamon sat very still. "Yes," she said slowly. "Yes. But it's not gone. It's simply . . . vindicated. There are still Parsa faces in Khemet. They still weigh down the world with their Truth. Now it's simply another truth, and our gods are come into their own again."

"Would you wish them to be destroyed?"

"No," she said, surprising herself a little. "They have their place, and their purpose in the gods' eyes. But not in Khemet."

Ay inclined his head. "Wise indeed."

"I still hate them," said Meriamon, "for what they did to us. That won't change. What has . . . I thought I could be happy if I came back to my own kind. They—you—are still that. And I've done everything that I was sent out to do. But it's not enough."

"Maybe you have not done all that the gods intended."

Meriamon sat upright. "But I have! Alexander is king in the Great House."

"Will he stay there?"

"Khemet has had warrior pharaohs before. Even foreign pharaohs."

"None like this," said Ay. "He is as restless as a fire, and as little inclined to linger."

"It doesn't matter," Meriamon said. "He has done what needed to be done. If he goes away, if he makes war against the Parsa in their own country, Khemet is still free."

"But are you?"

She met his eyes. Something in her was quivering, coming awake. Something that she had not known was there, or had not wanted to know. "What more is there for me to do?"

"The gods know," said Ay.

"I don't want to do any more. I want to go home. I want to be myself."

"Maybe your self is in what more you must do."

She shied at that, like the mare she had left behind with the rest of her life among the Hellenes. She was not wearing a wig. Her many plaits slipped out of the ring that caught them at her nape, and slithered down her back. "What if my self is the wife of a Macedonian soldier? What then, Father Ay?"

He barely blinked. "Why then, I would wish you happy, daughter."

She crumpled slowly. "No. You wouldn't. He wouldn't have me. I can give him no sons."

"Did he tell you so?"

Much too shrewd, that one, and much too keen of eye. "He didn't need to," she said. "I know what men are, in Hellas as in Khemet. And I won't be his whore."

"I doubt that he would ask it of you."

"How do you know?"

Her tone was unspeakably rude. Ay only smiled. "If he is the one I think he is, I know that he would have you however you are, and whatever you may do."

"I wasn't running away from him," said Meriamon. "Or even from Alexander."

"You were not," Ay said. "You were running away from Meriamon."

"I can't run back," she said.

"Why not?"

"I left," said Meriamon. "I never said a word."

"Then you have no words to unsay."

Except what she had said to Ay. She got up. She meant to stand over Ay, to say something irrevocable. Instead she found herself walking away, back to the duties she had chosen.

They were empty, that once had been all the world. They rang hollow. The singers with whom she sang were not those among whom she had been raised and trained. They were strangers, and they watched her sidelong, curious and even hostile. They knew what she was. Not all of them forgave her for it. The young priests doing their season's service in the temple, with the lives of merchants or nobles or even princes behind and before them, had other thoughts than jealousy.

One of them spoke to her, a day or two after her colloquy with Ay. He was a quite presentable young man, well-spoken and not too bold, but not shy, either. She did not recall what he said, or what she replied. She was too busy realizing that she could like him: he was in awe of her, but overcoming it, and he looked as if he knew how to laugh.

He was slender, and tall for a man in Khemet. His body was shaved smooth as all the priests' were, but he did not look as if he would be a hairy man: smooth brown limbs and quick grace, the beauties of her people. His dark eyes smiled at her. He ventured a touch, a brush of fingers along the line of her shoulder, ostensibly to smooth her plaits.

Her throat closed. He was quite beautiful and quite charming, and quite suitable for a princess of Khemet. And when he looked at her, she could not see him at all. Long lanky sandy-furred body, face as nearly ugly as made no matter, sulks and scowls and sharp-edged words, and strength that was earth to her air and emptiness.

He did not want her. She did not want him to want her, and so be robbed of sons.

And if he were left out of it, then what of Alexander?

Ay asked her that. She had no memory of seeking him out. She was simply there, in the room in which she had left him. "What of Alexander?" he asked again. "Will you leave him to find his fate alone?"

"We are not mated," Meriamon said tightly.

"Not in the flesh," he agreed, serene.

"Nor in the heart, either. I was a messenger, that was all. My message is delivered. My task is done."

"So you say," said Ay.

She walked to the wall and back. She was pacing the

way Alexander did. It helped him think, he said. It did nothing for her.

She stood over the priest. Her shadow was awake: she felt it behind her. "If I go to Alexander now," she said, "I may never come back."

"That is in the gods' hands," said Ay.

She would never be as serene as he was, though she lived the count of his years thrice over.

"How will you know until you have done it?"

She laughed painfully. "You were never such a tangle of fears and follies as I am."

"Certainly not. I was worse."

She embraced him suddenly, careful of his fragile bones. He was stronger than he looked, for a moment, holding her almost painfully hard.

She drew back. Her eyes were pricking with tears. "I don't want to go."

"And yet you do."

"I shouldn't."

"You think so?" There was sharpness in his voice now; a touch of impatience. It stung her, as it was meant to. "I think that you have done quite enough brooding over 'should' and 'shouldn't.' Go now and do what your heart tells you."

"The gods—"

"Some of us," said Ay, "are not privileged to speak with the gods face to face. To us they speak through the heart. You asked to be simply Meriamon. Maybe that is the beginning of it."

She ducked her head. Her cheeks were hot.

"There," he said more gently. "You've won yourself a little indulgence. Now it's time to be up and doing again."

"Past time," she said. Accepting it—and well past time, he would have told her.

She bent again and set a kiss on his brow. It was all the thanks he needed, and all the promise.

* * *

Alexander was getting ready to leave Memphis. Meriamon had had rumors of that even in the temple. She should have known how close he would be to doing it, once he had decided on it.

"Tomorrow," said the guard at the inner gate. He was not happy about it. "Just the king and the King's Squadron and a handful of servants. The rest of us are staying here, with Parmenion to look after us."

Meriamon's stomach clenched at the name, though she chided it for a fool. Parmenion was neither enemy nor friend. She was nothing to him, since she could not give Alexander sons.

But he was staying here, and Alexander was going away. "Where?" she demanded, a little fiercely perhaps: the guard looked alarmed.

"Maybe you should ask him," he said.

She could have pressed. But he was only a guard, after all, and Alexander was within. Her heart knew it, and her skin, sensing the force of his presence.

He had found the wrestling-court in the princes' palace, and made good use of it. Meriamon heard it long before she came there: shouts and laughter, a sudden hush, a whoop and the sound of hands slapping thighs in approval.

The court was full of men, and not a chiton among them. They wrestled and tumbled in pairs, or stood about, free of themselves as young animals, and cheered the combatants on. The center of their attention was a tangle of oiled limbs, sun-brown but fair beneath. Some of them belonged to Ptolemy. The rest, leaner and longer and yet astonishingly like Ptolemy's, almost put Meriamon to flight.

Niko was getting the worst of it. He was fast and he was strong, but his brother had the greater weight; and his crippled hand failed him in the holds. That made him angry; she saw the glitter of his eyes. But he was grinning, a predator's baring of teeth. Even when he broke under his brother's assault and crashed to the mat, the breath that broke out of him was a laugh. Ptolemy set a knee on his chest and straightened to claim the victory.

Niko twisted. Ptolemy's knee slipped on sweat and oil. Niko pulled him down.

They lay side by side, knotted like lovers, in a roar of laughter.

Niko was up first, pulling Ptolemy with him. They leaned on one another and panted, wringing wet and gloriously content.

Neither of them saw Meriamon. She had shrunk back among the Macedonians—Egyptians too, now that she noticed, red-dark and small as children in this company, regarding her in curiosity. But then they were properly kilted, and they did not mind that she was a woman. In much too brief a while, the stillness had spread.

She could not be invisible with so many eyes on her, even in her shadow's shadow. She straightened her shoulders and lifted her chin and put on her most royal aspect. "Has any of you seen the king?"

Throats cleared. Eyes slid sidewise. Bodies shifted, hands rose, chitons appeared as if from air. One splendid young thing blushed scarlet all the way down to the hand over his privates.

"He's in the baths," said a voice she knew much too well for comfort. "Shall I take you to him?"

"I can find him," she began to say. But Niko was in front of her with his chiton in his hand, covering as much of him as it needed to. Someone tossed him a cloth. He pulled the garment over his head and belted it, and used the cloth to wipe the sweat from his face. He was already walking, not even a glance to see if she would follow.

She would happily have refused. But a woman in the court was more than Alexander's men had bargained for. They were going to cramp, some of them, trying to cover themselves without being obvious about it. She took pity on them.

The baths were not far away: through a passage, down

a stair. Niko was standing in the passage. It was cool there, and dark after the bright sun of the courtyard. For a moment he seemed as dark as her shadow and no more solid: shape without definition, and a gleam of eyes. Then slowly he came clear.

She stopped. What she wanted to do was perfectly mad. Well then, so was she. She held out her hands.

He looked at them. Her heart chilled. Her hands began to fall.

He caught them. His grip was warm and much too strong to break. "You didn't need to run away," he said.

"Yes, I did."

"Not from me."

"It wasn't you," she said.

"I'm glad of that."

There was a silence. Her eyes were on their clasped hands. Hers were so small, and his so big. And yet they fit.

"I was false to you," she said. "I let you think that there was more of me than there was. That . . . I could give you what a wife gives her husband."

"Can a woman be a eunuch, then?"

"You'll have no sons of me."

He regarded her steadily. His eyes were clear. No shrinking. Regret, maybe, for what could not be; but none for what he was choosing. "I'm not a king, that I need them."

"Every man wants them."

"Not every man gets them."

"But if you can—"

"There are concubines," he said. "If it comes to that."

The purity of her rage astonished her. She pulled him hard, nearly oversetting him. Her arms locked about his middle. His heart beat under her ear. It was not beating nearly hard enough to please her. "If you take me—if you look at another woman—I swear to you—"

"You would," he said. Not even a flicker of fear. "You could do it, too."

She bent her head back to glare at him. "How can you be so calm?"

"I talked to the old priest," he said. "The Lord Ay. He told me what I was bargaining for."

"Obviously you didn't believe it."

"I believe it," he said. "I know you. You're not like our Macedonian witches. Your power is real."

"So is theirs."

"Not like yours. Theirs is wild magic—it comes and goes; more often than not it fails them. You have all the magic of Egypt in you."

"A few tricks. A shadow with eyes."

He laid his finger on her lips. "Stop it. You said you were going to claim me. I'm ready to be claimed."

"Even by the likes of me?"

"You should have thought of that when you put your mark on me."

She hid her face in his chiton. It was not a logical thing to do, not in the least. The wool pricked her cheek, washed to softness in Nile water and dried in the sun. It smelled of that, and of clean sharp sweat, and a suggestion of leather and horses.

His heart beat no faster than it had from the first. His breaths came deep and even. Her ears, trained to catch every nuance of a body's working, found in it no flaw or frailty.

Damnable arrogant Hellene. She pulled away from him. "I don't want to be protected. Or sheltered. Or watched and guarded like a child that can't leave its mother."

"A queen should have a guard," he said. "Kings do. Even Alexander."

"A guard," she said. "Not a nursemaid." She pulled free, though he did nothing to hold her. "I have to see the king."

He stepped aside. The corner of his mouth was—almost—turned up. Laughing at her.

"You are horrible," she said.

He grinned and sketched a bow. "At my lady's pleasure."

She swept past him. He fell in behind.

There was a war on in the baths: a party of Companions, with Hephaistion for commander, behind an earthwork of benches and towels, and the king mounting a siege with half a dozen pages and a troop of bemused Egyptian servants. Not that bemusement kept them from the game. They had amassed an armory of sponges, and somewhere they had got hold of a basket of onions, with which they kept up a steady barrage. The price of death or captivity was to be hurled into the bathing-pool, which was already full of grinning, yelling bodies.

Alexander raised a shout and flung his army on the barricades. They poured over it, toppling the whole length of it, and swept it all into the water.

The king emerged dripping and triumphant, ducking a last fusillade of onions. Meriamon held out a towel that was almost dry. He shook the water out of his eyes and started. "Mariamne!"

He looked so much like a boy caught with his hand in the honeypot that she laughed. "Meriamon," she said, "yes, and that was a noble victory."

"Wasn't it?" He took the towel and wrapped it very deliberately about his middle. Gravely she handed him another. Just as gravely he dried himself with it, eyes sliding toward the melee in the pool. "I think your countrymen are shocked."

"No Persian satrap would ever do such a thing," she agreed.

He laughed aloud. "Oh, Herakles, no! Can you see Mazaces getting his beard wet?"

"Mazaces has a beautiful beard," she said.

Alexander rubbed his chin. She knew why he made his Companions go shaven: one less handhold for an enemy in a fight. But she doubted that Alexander could have raised much beard in any event. He grinned at her as if he could read her thought, and said, "I'm a wretched excuse for a Persian."

"I should hope so," said Meriamon.

He went in search of his chiton. By the time he found it the battle had splashed and tumbled to a halt, and the combatants were climbing out of the pool. Most of them avoided Meriamon's eye as the young men had in the court. Hephaistion smiled at her, so perfectly at ease with himself and her presence and so unconscious of his own beauty that she forgot to breathe. He said something; she mumbled something in reply.

Niko shifted his feet. The hot blood flooded Meriamon's cheeks. "Like a bitch in a pack of hounds," she muttered under her breath.

Niko arched a brow. Devils take him: he had heard her.

Alexander spared her the humiliation of Niko's reply. He strode up to her, shining clean in a fresh chiton, combing his hair back with his fingers. He shook his head; the bright mane fell into its lion-sweep. He smiled at her. "I've missed you," he said.

She almost broke down at that. By the time she found her tongue, Alexander had taken her hand and led her out of the bath. His pace was quick as it always was, but not too quick for her to follow. "I'm going out of Memphis," he said. "But I suppose you know that. Did you come to talk me out of it?"

"That depends on where you're going," she said.

"Siwah," he said.

The word rang empty in her brain.

"The oracle," he said, "of Zeus Amon. Your god and mine both."

Her wits scrambled themselves together. She was in worse case than she had thought, if she did not know that of all names he could have spoken. "You're going all the way to Siwah?"

"From Dodona to Siwah, you said to me. Did you think I'd forgotten? I have dreams, too, Mariamne. This one bade me seek out the voice in the sands."

"And then?"

"And then the god will speak. Or he will not. That's in his hands."

"What will you ask him?"

"Come with me and see."

She stopped so suddenly that Niko nearly collided with her. Alexander, still holding her hand, was brought up short. "You want me to go to Siwah?"

"I can hardly command you, can I?"

"You are king in the Great House."

"You are a king's daughter," he said, "and the gods' own." He paused. His eyes searched her face. One was dark and one was light, as if he could not decide what he felt. "Do you want to go?"

"Yes," she said. She had not known it until she said it. "I want to go to Siwah."

Light flooded his face. "Now I know my dream was true."

"You doubted it?"

"No," said Alexander. "But two certainties are better than one. Especially when the other is yours."

She let him draw her onward. "Parmenion will be disgusted," she said.

"What? That I'd take a woman on a pilgrimage?"

"That it's such a perfect trap for his hope of your dynasty, and I'm such hopeless bait."

"Poor Parmenion," said Alexander. There was something like compassion in his voice. "Someday I'll do my duty. But not here, and not yet."

Her tongue quivered. Words had come to it, from the gods perhaps. Or perhaps not. A page was running toward them from the baths, and an older man from the palace,

and someone was calling down the well of a stair, hunting
for the king. What Meriamon would have said was lost in
babble and confusion; nor could she get it back.

•TWENTY-SIX•

Alexander sailed out of Memphis in much less state than
he had sailed in, with but the Royal Squadron and his personal Companions and their beasts and their servants
crowded into a handful of ships, and a few others who
would come with him as far as the Nile's mouth. One of
those was Thaïs, in spite of her swelling belly. She did not
say why she came. Meriamon did not need to ask. A hetaira, Thaïs had said often enough, was not well advised to
fall in love with her patron. It was bad for business. But
Ptolemy, like his brother, was a very difficult man to resist, once he had got under one's skin.

Another of the followers was Mazaces who had been
the satrap. He sailed with remarkably little escort for a
Persian, no more than a handful of guards, a troop of servants, and the one of all his women who, having been born
a Scythian, had no objection to travel. She went swathed
to the eyes in veils and surrounded by wary eunuchs, but
she seemed to thrive on the journey. Probably she had not
known such pleasure since she was taken captive.

Meriamon might have liked to talk to her, and the eunuchs could hardly have prevented it; but the woman knew
little Persian and no Greek at all, and Meriamon knew not
a word of Scythian. The best that they could do, the first
evening when the fleet had moored and the company made
camp, was a civil greeting and an exchange of glances in
what might, in other circumstances, have become friendship. When Meriamon would have tried for more, Mazaces
came down from the low eminence on which he had

pitched his tent, haughty as all the Parsa were even under
a barbarian master, and put an end to it with his presence.

Meriamon turned her back on him. That was rude, she
knew it perfectly well, but she could not help herself.

"Wait," the Persian said.

She might not have obeyed him. But the woman was
watching, and something in her eyes made Meriamon
pause. There was no hate in them, and no fear. Only pride
when she looked on the man who owned her.

He was not ill to look at. Persian noblemen seldom
were. They bred themselves like their horses, for size and
for beauty, and he had a sufficiency of both. Meriamon
would have liked to see what his face was like under the
beard that hid it from just below the eyes to just above the
breastbone. What she could see of it was cleanly carved,
with a nose like the arc of the new moon.

What he saw when he looked at her, she could imagine.
Too small, too plain, and much too shameless in Egyptian
linen, with the shape of her body clear to see. She met his
eyes boldly. They lowered. Persian courtesy, never to meet
one's stare direct: shiftiness, one might think it. "Does it
trouble you," she asked, "that if your king catches you,
you will die a traitor's death?"

"My king is Alexander," Mazaces said.

His Greek was accented, but fluent enough. Better than
hers had been when she came to Alexander's camp. "You
are Persian," she said.

"You are Egyptian," said Mazaces.

"He is the king we chose," she said.

"So was he mine," he said, "when I came to know
him."

"And what of your Great King?"

"My Great King," he said, and his voice though soft
was deeply bitter, "left me to make what peace I could in
a province rent with war and rebellion. There was even a
fleet of Macedonian pirates looking to carve a kingdom
outside of their king's reach. Did you know that?"

"It came to nothing," she said.

"Because I fought it," Mazaces said. "If the king goes on as he has begun, he will take Persis as he took Asia and Egypt. Then he will be Great King. What will you do then? Will you rebel against him?"

"He will be our Great King," said Meriamon.

"Just so," Mazaces said.

Meriamon frowned at the blaze of the sunset.

"Surely," said Mazaces, "you who can comprehend many truths, can foresee an empire in which both Persis and Egypt dwell at peace."

He was smiling. Mocking her, a little, but gently. And not as an enemy will.

She must have said it aloud. He said, "I am not your enemy. Nor is any who calls Alexander king."

That was more than she could contemplate in comfort. She turned away again. This time he did not try to call her back.

She wandered slowly to her tent. It was the same one in which she had lived for so long with Thaïs, more honestly home than anywhere she had been since she left Thebes. Thaïs was out, no doubt with Ptolemy.

Niko was in, coaxing a smile and a plate of sweets out of Phylinna. A sleek tawny shape uncoiled in his lap and greeted Meriamon in tones redolent of impatience.

"Where was I?" Meriamon demanded of the cat. "And where, pray, were you?"

Sekhmet yawned, baring each pearl-bright tooth. She left Niko's lap to coil about Meriamon's ankles, marking her. Meriamon swept her up. She was purring thunderously.

"She moved in with me," Niko said, licking honey from his fingers. "And a fine companion she's been, too. She nags like a wife."

"I don't nag," said Meriamon.

"You don't," Niko agreed sweetly. "You let your eyes do it for you."

"When have I ever—"

He laughed. "Sit down," he said, "and have a honey-cake. They're good."

Meriamon sat, but she was not hungry. "You've had Sekhmet all this time and you never said a word? I was half frantic."

"Well," he said, "and so was I, when you went away and never said a word. Fair's fair, Mariamne."

"Meriamon."

"Mariamne."

She sighed, sharp with temper, and gave it up.

He divided the last cake in half. "Here, eat. You never do eat enough to keep a bird happy."

"Have you ever seen a bird eat? Pigs are ascetics beside them."

"You are quite impossible," he said, grinning and feeding her the cake, till she must eat or have her face smeared with honey. It was good, she granted him that. He downed the other half all at once, and sat smiling at her.

"Why do you look so smug?" she demanded.

"Wouldn't you, if you were going to marry a princess?"

"Who said that I would marry you?"

"You did," said Niko. "I told Ptolemy. He was enormously pleased."

"And Alexander? Did you tell him?"

"Well," Niko said, "no. Not yet. We thought it might be politic to wait a bit. Seeing that you wouldn't have him, and it pricked his pride. I'd hardly want to flaunt my good fortune in his face."

She sucked in a breath. She would never have believed his impudence—except that he was Nikolaos. "So I'm bought and paid for, am I?"

"You have a dowry. Lord Ay assured me of that. He'll be talking with Ptolemy when we get back from Siwah. Do you want to be married in Memphis or in Thebes?"

She opened her mouth. Closed it. Realized that she was not breathing.

"Memphis might be better," said Niko. Cheerful; infuriating. "Then Alexander can be sure to come. He isn't going to Thebes, I don't think. Once he's been to Siwah, if the god favors him, he'll be turning back toward Asia. Darius is still alive, and he's still Great King. It's time he had his comeuppance."

"He hasn't already?" Meriamon asked faintly.

"This is only a beginning. Of course," Niko said, "for you it's all there needs to be. Egypt is free. What's the rest of the world to that?"

"Nothing," she said. "Everything."

"Exactly." He leaped up, pulling her with him. Sekhmet had just time to spring to his shoulder before she was spilled on the carpet. "Come to dinner now, and stop scowling. It won't be so terribly long till the wedding. Unless . . ." He paused. "If you'd rather . . ."

"Not till the king knows," she said.

"Then we'll wait." He sounded perfectly happy about it. Mad, she decided. And maddening. And irresistible.

They followed the westernmost arm of the river, bearing west as it divided in the mists and marshes of the Delta. This was the broad lotus-blossom of which Upper Egypt was the stem, rich land and fertile, spreading wide on the shores of the sea. At the mouth that was called Canopus they left the ships and mounted their restive horses and turned west, away from the Nile. The land narrowed to a long spit of sand: the sea on the right, Lake Mareotis on the left, blue water and blue water, and the sky more blue than they.

On the point of land between the lake and the sea was a traders' town. Rhakotis, its people called it, good Egyptian name though they were more Greek than not, merchants and travelers who moored their ships in the broad sweep of the harbor with its wall of island. If Pelusium was the easternmost gate of the Two Lands, then this was the gate of the west: much lesser and weaker, but lovely in its setting, and the land about it, though narrow, was rich.

Alexander took a boat on the lake with a handful of friends, and Meriamon because she had been in sight when he came down to the water. He was in high good humor, dressed in an old rag of a chiton that must have driven his bodyservants to distraction, and a broad-brimmed hat with a purple ribbon tied about it. Sekhmet batted at a dangling end.

"She doesn't mind boats at all," Hephaistion said, offering to scratch her under the chin. She thought about it for a while, then regally deigned to allow it.

"That's an Egyptian cat for you," said Alexander. He leaned on the rail. A gust of wind tugged at his hat; he caught it before it could take flight, and let it drop to hang by its cord about his neck. His eyes were on the ragged line that was the town, and the shape of the island beyond it.

"Look at that," he said.

Everybody was looking who was not needed to sail the boat. "It's pretty," someone said.

"Good land, too," said someone else. "And very good climate. Not too warm as Egypt goes, with wind off the sea. Less fever than you'd expect—no marshes on the lake's rim to breed sickness in summer. The river drowns them before they can begin."

"Good harbor up yonder," said Niko, down the rail with Nearchos. "Did you see how the island makes a wall against the open sea, and the harbor inside it, with reefs to break the waves? I'm surprised the Phoenicians didn't grab it ages ago and make one of their sea-cities out of it."

"Greeks kept them out," Nearchos said. "We're sea-people too, don't forget."

"Egypt had somewhat to say in it besides," said Meriamon.

"I could build a city here," Alexander said.

His voice was quiet. People kept talking up and down the boat, taking no notice of him. But for Meriamon the world had gone suddenly still. Niko was listening too, she noticed, and the black-curled Cretan, and Ptolemy who had come up beside Niko.

"I could build a city," Alexander said again. "Here, in this place, between the lake and the sea. A gate for all of Africa; a gate to the riches of Egypt. Egypt has always looked inward from Memphis and Thebes. Now I say it should look outward to the world."

Meriamon clung to the rail. The ship rocked gently on the waves; but she felt as if it rode in a storm. Her shadow was wide awake. Sekhmet crouched on her shoulder. The gods were listening: a tautening of awareness in water and sky.

This alone was not what she had come for. And yet it was part of it. This place, this time, this new voice speaking softly, shaping a city that would be.

It was not Alexander's voice. Ptolemy, solid imperturbable Ptolemy with his feet on the earth and his mind on practicalities, was dreaming aloud. "And a wall there, and of course we'd have to build a bridge between the island and the mainland, and if ships are to find their way in, we'll have to put something, some marker, on the rock at the island's head. A tower, maybe. White. You can see a white tower a long way away. And on top of it, all night long, a light . . ."

"A city," said Alexander, sharp and painfully clear, "to rule the world."

"We can do it," Ptolemy said. "That's one thing a king does, after all, to make his mark on the world: a mark that lasts longer than most. A city founded in his name."

"Alexandria," said Alexander. "I like the sound of that."

"Alexandria," said Meriamon. Naming it. Making it true.

•TWENTY-SEVEN•

Once Alexander had decided on something, he swept everyone else with him. In an entourage of engineers who had come up with him from Memphis, he paced the boundaries of the town and marked each point for the workmen who would come. He could have done it with pen and papyrus in decent privacy, and he had drafters there to do just that; but he had an audience to play to.

They were marking out the limits with powdered chalk, for the surveyors to follow with lines and stakes. As they came round to the midpoint of the western side, they wavered and halted.

"More chalk!" Alexander called out.

There was a pause. It stretched.

"Well?" said Alexander.

One of the engineers cleared his throat. "There isn't any more," he said.

"And why not?" the king demanded.

There was another pause. Feet shuffled. The spokesman said, "It didn't get packed when it should have."

"Oh?" said Alexander. Soft. Gentle.

"Well then," said Ptolemy, brisk and practical. "We'll have to make do, won't we? What have we got?"

"There's this," Hephaistion said, shrugging out of the pack that he seemed to wear as easily as his chiton, and rummaging in it. He brought out a bag and untied it and poured its contents into his hand: the meal-ration of the Macedonian soldier. He looked about at the men who crowded in, curious. "Well? Can you help?"

They traded glances. One grinned, then another. Packs dropped; sacks came out. In a moment the captains had their men in ranks, piling up sacks and keeping tally; and Hephaistion stood watchful, but smiling.

Alexander's high light mood was back. He grinned at his friend. Hephaistion let his smile widen.

The small mound of grain grew. The engineers eyed it dubiously, but Diades the Thessalian laughed and dipped out a handful and began again where he had left off.

"That was an omen," Meriamon said. "That Alexander's city was marked out in barley meal."

"A good omen," said Niko.

They sat in the door of Thaïs' tent. The sun had set a little while since, but the sky was full of light. The surveyors were out still, following the line Alexander had walked.

"Did you notice," said Meriamon, "the birds only come down to feed where the line is marked already? They don't touch the new line at all."

"Aristandros says the city will be fruitful, and people will come to it from all over the world."

"He sees with a clear eye."

"As clear as yours?"

He was only half laughing at her. She watched the line of men as it moved slowly down to the lake's edge, pacing and pausing, dipping and rising. Ptolemy was with them. He had come to dinner, eaten a mouthful, gone away again. Alexander had laughed and called after him, "You're even madder about this than I am. Will you be asking for the city when it's built?"

Ptolemy had grinned over his shoulder. "Not as long as you're using it," he said. "If you get tired of it, now . . ."

"If I get tired of it," Alexander said, "which the gods forbid, it's yours."

"Your brother has changed," Meriamon said now.

Niko glanced sharply at her. "Why? Because he likes this place?"

"Yes. And not just this one town that will be a city. All of Egypt. As if . . . he was meant to be here."

"Are you prophesying?"

"I hope not," she said. And when he stared at her: "Alexander is enough. I don't need to see signs and omens for every man in his army."

"I didn't think you had a choice."

She rose with enormous dignity. "I am tired," she said. "I am going to sleep."

He let her go without protest. That was surprising. Until she heard him behind her. He was going to corner her, then. She swallowed a sigh.

He did not say anything as she lit the lamps, only stood by the door. He had Sekhmet in his arms, purring as she always did for him. If she could be anyone's cat, Meriamon thought, she would be Niko's.

The bed was made up long since, with a sprinkling of herbs to make it sweet. Phylinna's hand, that. There was water for washing, and a jar of ointment for cleansing the paint from her face.

It would not be the first time she had done it under Niko's eyes. She almost ordered him out. But she did not. She opened the jar, began carefully to wipe away the kohl and the malachite and the dusting of lapis. She did not always use the bronze mirror. Tonight she did. It was a shield of sorts.

He took it from her hand and held it for her. She would not look at him over it. She fixed her eyes on her reflection, though she hardly saw it. Paint, here. Kohl, there. Gone, effaced, vanished.

If she could efface herself, make herself nothing, no gods, no fates, no prophecies . . .

"Meriamon!"

Her name. Her self. Grey eyes on her, and in them something like fear.

"Don't go away like that," he said.

The mirror was gone. She was holding his hands. Or he hers. "You have not a grain of magic in you," she said.

"I think you have enough for both of us."

"Too much," she said. "It's only going to get worse, the closer we come to Siwah."

"Then you're going to need me, aren't you? To keep you from flying to pieces."

"I'm not that fragile!"

He smiled his slow smile, the one that warmed his whole long homely face and made it beautiful. "Certainly you're not fragile. That's why you need me. The bow can't be strung every moment of every day."

"I'll rest after Siwah."

"So you will." He let go her hands and touched a forefinger to her cheek, tracing the curve of it as if it were a lesson he would remember. "You can rest now. I'm here."

"You are not restful," she said.

His hand found its way to her shoulder. "Such a little woman," he said, "to stand so high."

"Such a great gawk of a man," she said, "to fit me so well." She stood as high as she could, and set her hands on his shoulders. She was dizzy, looking up at him. "Do you know how impossible we are?"

"What's impossible? This is Alexander's army. We're what his empire will be. Not Macedonian or Egyptian or Greek or Persian, or anything but man and woman under the one king."

"And I said you had no magic," she said.

"I don't." He was sad, a little, but philosophical. "It's logic, that's all. And hope."

"Hope and logic are very great magics."

"Love, too?"

"Is that what this is?"

"You didn't know?"

She narrowed her eyes to see him better. "I don't suppose it can be anything else. Unless there's another word for what makes you follow me about like a dog after a bone."

"That's habit. I can't get out of the way of looking after you. Since no one else seems inclined to do it."

"So," she said much too lightly. "I'm a habit, am I?"

"A welcome one," he said. "One I want to keep."

He stooped. His face filled her vision. Not ugly, not beautiful. Not any longer. Itself purely.

She could stop him now. She knew it as she knew what the gods wanted. She could hold him back, push him off, win herself free of him. He would go; he would sulk for a while; he would come again, but later. After Siwah.

Her heart was cold. None of them knew what that road was. Oh, they thought they did, those soldiers and scouts, talking to travelers and desert tribesmen. They knew that it was desert, days without water, bitter marches in a season of wind and storm. They did not know what it would be with Alexander at the head of them, and the god waiting.

She wound her fists in Niko's chiton. The wool was rough, reassuringly solid, and he beneath it, warm breathing man with no taint of magic. Only trust in her, and eyes to see the shadow that walked with her.

She pulled. He followed unresisting, only raising a brow when she halted by the bed. "Are you sure?" he asked her.

"No," she said. "Yes." She pushed him down. The bed creaked. She was going to laugh; and that would be fatal.

He wrapped long arms around her and pulled her into his lap. He was grinning like an idiot.

She began to laugh. No; that was too dignified a word. She began to giggle. There was nothing to laugh at, and everything. The two of them. This world they were in. This city that would be, a stretch of grass and sand between a lake and the sea.

He tumbled backward, and she on top of him. The bed rocked but held. Built for the trade, that. She sat on him, grinning as foolishly as he.

The plaits of her hair hung down. He caught a pair of them. "Now I have you," he said.

"Not yet," she said. Her gown had ridden up shockingly. One of her breasts had escaped the top of it. She felt his eyes on it; and the stillness.

Time yet, and still, to escape. If she would. He was trembling.

Poor boy, she thought. And almost laughed. Certainly he was a boy. Just as certainly he knew what a woman was for; had proven it often and gladly. He should be teaching her, not waiting for her to give him leave.

Her gown galled her. She rid herself of it. His eyes were enormous. "What," she asked him, "you haven't seen a woman before?"

"Not a woman who was you," he said. His voice was faint, but his wits were keen enough, considering.

"Hellene," she said, but tenderly. "You'll talk your way through anything."

"Not anything," he said. He sat up, and she knew that he was going to leave her; then he had tossed aside his chiton.

She had seen it before. Been close to it, even. And yet this was not the same. Not in the least. This was frightening. Exhilarating. Like being a hawk, and taking wing, and soaring into the sun.

"Meriamon," he said. Calling her back.

"That's twice," she said.

His brows went up.

"You used my right name," she said. "Twice. If you say it a third time, you will have claimed me."

"So I shall," he said. He touched the tip of her breast. It quivered and tautened. "Meriamon," said Nikolaos.

It was not like flying. More like learning to fly. Awkward; laughable, sometimes. It hurt. Very much, at first. She set her teeth and endured it, but he knew. He started to draw back. She locked arms about him, holding him.

"I'm too big for you," he said miserably.

She bit her tongue. She must not laugh. "Bigger than a baby's head?"

He went scarlet.

Her tongue was starting to ache where she had bitten it. "Be brave," she said. "Try."

Blessed courage: he tried. It did not hurt so much. After a while it did not hurt at all. A while after that, and even the memory of hurt was gone; then was only pleasure.

·PART FOUR·

SIWAH

•TWENTY-EIGHT•

Alexander left the engineers behind in Rhakotis, and the Persians with them, sharing the townsfolk's bemusement with the city that was taking shape already in stakes and string between the lake and sea. Maybe he would have liked to stay with them and watch the city grow, but the god was calling him. He took the Companions and the few pages and servants whom they needed to look after them and their horses, and turned his back resolutely on the newborn Alexandria.

One who was neither servant nor Companion nor voice of the gods, made it abundantly clear that he was coming to Siwah. "I can ride," said Arrhidaios. "I ride as well as anybody. I walk, too. I want to see the god in the sand."

"I know you can ride," Alexander said with remarkable patience; but he was always patient with Arrhidaios. "I want you to stay here and help with my city, and take care of Peritas. Mazaces is staying. He's the best rider in the army."

"Except you," said Arrhidaios. His brows knotted. "Mazaces can take care of Peritas. I want to come to Siwah."

"And what will you do when you get there?" his brother asked.

"See the god," said Arrhidaios. "You said I didn't have to stay with Parmenion. I don't want to stay with Mazaces, either. I want to stay with you."

Alexander sighed. "You always get your own way in the end. Maybe you should be king instead of me."

Arrhidaios made a sign against evil. "Don't talk like that, Alexander. You know it's bad luck."

"I know you're not going to like this road we take. If

you complain, even once, you have to come straight back. Promise?"

"Promise," Arrhidaios said solemnly. Then he grinned and whooped and ran to fetch his horse.

"I hope I don't live to regret that," Alexander said.

"You haven't yet," said Hephaistion. "There now, it's only his wits that are addled. He sticks like a burr to anything on four legs, and he's as tough as an old soldier."

"He sticks like a burr to me, too," Alexander said. "Gods help me, I couldn't leave him with Parmenion when he was so insistent that he wanted to come with me, and Mazaces is no kind of guardian for him. If I could have left him in Macedon . . ."

Hephaistion carefully did not say anything.

Alexander's glance was wry. "No, he wouldn't have lasted long there. Not Philip's elder son, addled or no."

"He won't be any trouble. He never is."

"No," said Alexander. "One can almost forget him, can't one?"

One could not. But Hephaistion did not say it. Alexander went like his brother to see to the horses. Hephaistion had duties of his own, but he lingered in the empty field that had been a camp, brushing sand over the embers of a fire.

When he looked up, the Egyptian woman was there, and Lagos' son behind her. There was a sheen on them that he well knew. He smiled to himself. They had taken their time about it; well past any decent wager.

Whatever she had done to make herself and her guardsman glad, she was somber now. Her eyes were dark behind their mask of paint. "It's going to be a harder road than even Alexander knows," she said.

"A death-road?" asked Hephaistion.

When she was intent, her long eyes seemed to grow even longer, and to slant like a cat's. She looked, in fact, very like the cat that rode on Niko's shoulder, with her high-cheeked face and her slender supple body. "We will

walk the road of coming forth by day. Whether we will
walk out of it—that is with the gods."

Hephaistion glanced at Nikolaos. Niko shrugged. He did
not stand in her shadow, Hephaistion noticed. Few people
did. Rumor had it that the thing had eyes, and that it freed
itself from her at night and hunted in the dark.

She was only a small woman in Persian trousers—
because, she had been heard to say, nothing else made
sense for hard traveling—talking in that husky voice of
hers, and staring straight through Hephaistion. Seeing
gods, no doubt, and prophecies.

She blinked. Not a cat after all but a desert falcon,
fierce and focused. "Stay with Alexander. Don't leave him
for anything, day or night."

"Not even to make water?"

A line appeared between the painted brows. "Not even
then."

"He's going to hate the sight of me," said Hephaistion.

"Let him. He'll be alive and sane to do the hating."

Hephaistion thought about that. She waited. That was a
virtue of hers. She never pressed for answers that needed
thinking on.

Finally he said, "Is it going to be as bad as that?"

"I don't know," she said. "I only know that I could very
easily be afraid."

There were some who would have scoffed at her.
Hephaistion was not one of them. She spoke for her gods.
He knew that in his bones, as surely as he knew that
Aristandros spoke for the gods of Hellas. If she could be
afraid, then he could be cautious.

It was not so grim a prospect to be at Alexander's side,
night as well as day. So had they been when they were
younger, eating from the same bowl, drinking from the
same cup, sleeping on one cloak and wrapped in another.
There had been plenty in the world besides them; Alexander could never forget that he was Alexander, and He-

phaistion had pride of his own. But in the middle of it, always, then as now, were they two.

The Egyptian knew. Neither she nor her guardsman had moved, but they were two, and together.

A woman and a man. He did not know if he liked that, or approved of it. It was not Greek, or properly philosophical. A woman could not be a true soul. That was for men.

This was not as other women. Nothing that she had ever done showed the least concern for propriety, or for anything but her gods and her lover and—yes—her king. He bent his head to her. She bent her own in return. "I'll look after my king," he said.

Alexander's company rode out of Rhakotis in a prancing, jingling procession, with the king at their head in his bright armor. But once they had left the town behind, they dismounted and freed the horses from their bits and sent all but a few of the beasts back to Rhakotis, packed away their gauds and put on marching gear and marched. The Companions were inured to it: they shouldered their packs, pulled their hats down over their eyes, and fell into a long, swinging stride that made nothing of sand or stones. The handful of horses kept pace in a herd, some on leads, most sensible enough to follow their fellows. The servants held their own ranks just ahead of the rearguard, none loaded down more than the Companions themselves, carrying the pots and kettles, the extra foodstuffs, and the tents and poles.

They went light and they went fast. Meriamon felt the eyes on her—and not only Niko's. They were waiting for her to give up, she was sure, and mount Phoenix and ride. The mare would not have minded; she was desert-bred and she did not have to suffer the war-bridle. But Meriamon had her pride. She had softened somewhat in Memphis; still, she was no weakling. She could keep pace.

They followed the coast for a long while, keeping to the road that led to a town called Paraetonium, and thence to the village of Apis. The green and wet of the Delta sank away behind them; the Red Land claimed them. There was water in plenty, and provender: ships from Alexander's fleet paced them, putting in in the evenings as they had on the road from Tyre.

It was not ill marching. The sea cooled them with its breezes, though it brought no rain. The road was broad and smooth, a traders' road, with people on it now and then. Those looked with curiosity on the armed company, and told tales of raiders inland. "You'll want your spears then," they said, "and camels if you can get them—horses and mules aren't much good for the deep desert."

"Even horses that are desert-bred?" Alexander wanted to know.

"Horses can't carry as much," said the traveler, himself on a camel and speaking barbarous Greek, "or go as long. There will be camels in Paraetonium. If you have sense you'll buy them."

"We might, at that," Hephaistion said. He eyed the man's mount, somewhat dubiously to be sure, but with interest enough. "Would this one be for sale, by any chance?"

The man's eyes narrowed. "She is a racing camel of a line of champions."

"So are they all," said Hephaistion sweetly. "We'll buy our camels in Paraetonium, then. I don't suppose you have cousins with camels to sell?"

"My uncle bred this beauty," the man said. "Her sisters are almost as good as she. Her mother is better. But you won't be wanting racing camels; you'll be wanting good beasts of burden. Ask for the house of the rock. Anyone can tell you where that is."

"The house of the rock," said Alexander. "We'll remember."

The traveler went on his way, loping eastward. He vanished amazingly quickly. They continued on the westward road.

Meriamon set one foot in front of the other. And then again. And again. She had found the rhythm of it. She could leave her body to its walking and let her mind and her souls wander as they would, seeking out the powers in earth and air. Often at first her shadow left her to hunt, but as the days stretched, it clung closer.

This no longer was Khemet, though the power of the Nile was a memory in the earth, a quiver in the air. Stronger by far was the Great Green, the sea that surged and breathed beside them. Poseidon, the Hellenes called it, Poseidon Earthshaker, lord of horses. It was no enemy to Alexander. It suffered his ships to ride on it, and murmured beside his camp in the nights, and held back the fierce heat of the desert.

That at night was no earthly heat: on the contrary, the nights could be cold, even bitter. But to Meriamon's senses the Red Land was a flame in the dark. Old things were rising, strong things, enemies for long and long of the Black Land and the people who dwelt in it: devourers of flesh, drinkers of blood, eaters of souls.

No Parsa magic, this, feeble matter of fire and dogma that that was. This was sunk deep in the earth, woven with it, old and strong and black. The gods of the Two Lands had overcome it long ago. Now a king out of the Two Lands trespassed in its domain, and would lay claim to the oracle in the heart of it.

While they kept to the sea it had no power to do more than trouble their dreams. When they turned inland, then it would rise up against them.

Alexander had his guardsman as Meriamon had hers. Neither he nor she was about to turn back. Meriamon doubted that they could. This road was ordained for them. Each step had the inevitability of a prophecy.

That too was dangerous. It lulled the mind; it weakened the wits. She made herself ride, sometimes, and so separate herself from the earth. In camp she kept to the light and the company of men, and when she slept, she did not sleep alone. Everyone knew who kept her company—as far as she could see, the greatest scandal was that it had not happened sooner.

She found herself missing Thaïs, even with Niko to share her tent. The hetaira would have come, but Ptolemy would not let her. Even that would hardly have stopped her, if Meriamon had not bidden her remember the baby. "This is not a road for an unborn child," Meriamon had said. Thaïs had not been happy at all, but in the end she yielded. Ptolemy had given her a host of errands to run and matters to see to, which she took on happily enough, once she had resigned herself to staying behind.

She had the Persian tent still, pitched in a field outside of Rhakotis. Meriamon had a smaller one for the march, and Phylinna to look after it. Phylinna was a gift. She had given herself, nor would she be refused. For all her citified elegance, she had proven herself an able trooper. She marched without complaining, she kept up handily, and still she managed to look as if she had just come in from a morning in the agora.

She approved of Niko, though she would never be so crass as to admit it. She also approved of Arrhidaios, who spent most of his evenings near Meriamon, and most of the marches beside or behind her. Addled he might be, but he was large and he was strong, and he doted on Meriamon. "You're well guarded," Phylinna said, "and thank the gods for it. This is no journey for a woman."

"So?" Meriamon asked. "Then why did you make it?"

"Because you insist on doing it, and someone should be here to look after you."

Meriamon could hardly argue with logic. They were a wall, all of them, and a shield, as the whole company was for Alexander.

She said so to Niko, the night before they came to Paraetonium, while the wind chittered and flapped in the tentwall, and Phylinna snored on her mat. It had been disconcerting at first, having the servant next to them, and not even a blanket between for decency; but the woman could hardly sleep outside in the chill. Niko was in comfort. He ignored her. Meriamon was learning to.

"I'm glad we're good for something," he said now.

They were nested in the bed, she in the warm middle, he curved around her. He ran his hand over her breast and belly and let it come to rest between her thighs. She laid her own over it. "I know it's not your custom to share a bed all night long. You're guarding me. Losing sleep for it, too."

"Less than I was losing in my bed alone, wishing I were here," he said.

She smiled, though he could not see it. "Did you really?"

"You doubt it?"

"I thought Macedonians were made of sterner stuff than that."

"We are. Except when it comes to wicked-tongued Egyptian witches."

"Wicked, am I?"

"Terribly."

She turned in his arms. He was ready for her. She grinned at him. "Then let's be wicked, and put the night to flight."

They did their best to do just that. Her shadow came back in the middle of it, and laughed soundlessly at the spectacle they made. Niko laughed back. Bold child. If he did not learn prudence . . .

In a little while she stopped worrying. A little longer, and she stopped thinking at all.

There were indeed camels in Paraetonium. Every camel trader in that part of the world must have had word that a fool with an army needed transport to Siwah. The town reeked of camels. The air was full of their roaring and their flatulence. The herds had stripped every bit of green from the town, and given a day or two longer would strip it from every town within a day's march.

"When they don't have anything to eat," the traveler's uncle explained, "they don't eat, or drink either. When there's food and water to be had, they make up for lost time."

Alexander's face was expressionless. Meriamon suspected that he was trying not to laugh. The house of the rock had turned out to be not quite impossible to find, and its tenant to be a reasonably honest man, as camel dealers went. He was no more disposed to sell Alexander his fine racing beauties than his nephew had been, but he had lesser beasts enough. One of which was doing its best to take Seleukos' head off.

"Bulls," said the dealer. "Not the best choice for the use you're going to put them to. You'll take she-camels. They're gentler, and you get milk from the ones in calf. You'll be glad of that if your water runs out."

"It won't," Alexander said. "Siwah is five days' march from Apis, no? We'll take water in plenty, if we have camels to carry it."

"Five days with good luck and fair weather," said the dealer, "and supposing you don't meet raiders. Not that they'll bother you, I don't think, unless the young ones have a mind for a little sport."

"Five days," said Alexander. "There are three hundred of us, with servants, and a score of horses."

The dealer frowned. "Horses? Hadn't you better leave them here? I can see that they're well taken care of, and at a fair price, too."

"I think not," said Alexander with perfect courtesy.

The man opened his mouth. Alexander smiled. He shut it again. He had just discovered, thought Meriamon, that Alexander was Alexander. He blinked, shrugged. "You'll do what you'll do. Now, about those camels . . ."

They had their camels, and drovers for them, and saddles, and grain in addition to what the ships brought in, and waterskins now lightly filled. They would see to those more properly in Apis. Alexander was not displeased with the price he paid for the whole. Nor, much more to the point, was Hephaistion, who did the paying. He was quarter-master here as he had been on the road from Tyre, and he was good at it. He had everything in order and the price haggled down almost within the limits of reason, and the whole caravan on the march by sunup.

They looked like a proper caravan now, men in the fore, camels behind except for the rearguard, and horses in the center, away from the camels. Phoenix did not mind them; she had been foaled among them. The Macedonian horses loathed everything about the great stinking beasts. Boukephalas would have entered into battle with one of them, had not Alexander hauled him off. He was still prancing on his lead, throwing up his head and snorting in disgust.

"I don't think he'll ever forgive me," Alexander said.

Meriamon slanted a glance at him. He looked like any other man in the company in hat and chiton, cloak and sandals, and a short spear for a walking stick. He carried his own pack though the pages had most of his gear, and swung out as cheerfully as the lowliest trooper. If he sensed what waited in the desert, he showed no sign of it.

"He'd forgive you less," she said, "if you left him behind."

"I know," said Alexander. Boukephalas thrust his nose into the king's shoulder; he sighed, but he laughed. "I never did have much luck with traveling light."

"I call this light enough," she said, "for an army."

"This is the lap of luxury," said Alexander. "Light is a knife in your belt and air in your wallet, and one cloak for two of you. Light is hunting down your supper with the knife, and sharing the cloak, and knowing yourself for a rich man."

"Do you wish it could be that simple?" she asked him.

He did not answer at once. They measured a dozen strides of the road. Then two dozen. Halfway through the third, he said, "Sometimes. This is close, when you come down to it. Even with camels."

She smiled. He grinned back. "It's going to get interesting, isn't it?" he said.

He knew. Better than she, maybe. And he was always one to laugh at fear.

He did not say that she could go back and be safe. For that, more than anything else he had done or not done, she knew that she loved him. Not as she loved Nikolaos, no; of course not. But as a woman could love the man who was her king.

• TWENTY-NINE •

From Apis that was a fleck of green in the Red Land, a huddle of houses against the Great Green, the road bent south and turned its back on the sea. This was the pilgrims' road to Siwah, a thread strung between the sea and the oracle. It made its way through a land both bleak and unforgiving, red sand and barren rock and the bitter vault of the sky. No rain fell here. No river ran. No Black Land sprouted green to gentle the earth.

The power in this place was alien and enemy. It knew Meriamon for what she was. And more than her, it knew Alexander.

Set was a god, as often ally as enemy. Typhon was far away in windy Hellas. This was Enemy pure, earth that would not be conquered, sky that would not be ruled, even by gods. Khemet's power had driven it back beyond the mountains of the sunset, and walled itself against it with the tombs of its kings. But here it was whole and it was strong, and it had Alexander's army in its hand.

On the first day it did nothing. The sky was clear of aught but birds: the desert falcon, the vulture that was holy in Khemet. The way stretched before them. Often there was nothing to mark it among the sand and the stones, but they had taken guides in Apis, men who swore by their names that they knew the way to Siwah. Alexander would have had them swear on images of their gods, but Meriamon stopped him. "Their names will be enough," she said. He found that very odd, but he did not quarrel with her.

Trust, she thought. He trusted her to know what men in this land would do. She trusted the land not at all. It was quiescent. Biding its time.

The second day passed. The birds wheeled. Alexander sent scouts to see what interested the vultures. A lion's kill: a gazelle scoured to bones, and jackals feeding on it. Aristandros saw no omen in that. Meriamon wondered if she was a fool for thinking it a message.

That night they made a waterless camp. There was an oasis, the guides promised, within the next day's march. The water in the skins was sweet enough, if redolent of leather. They had provisions in plenty, and the last of the fodder for the horses and the camels. They were comfortable, as travelers in the desert went.

Meriamon sat on the camp's edge and watched the sun go down. The sounds of the camp went on peacefully in back of her: men talking, horses snorting, camels chewing their cuds. The guides had shown them how to build fires out of camel dung, hardly a necessity now as the day's heat radiated out of the sand, but later they would be glad of it.

She felt rather than saw Niko squat on his heels beside her. Sekhmet walked from his shoulder to Meriamon's. Meriamon reached up to smooth the cat's fur, and started. "Sparks," she said.

"Air's dry," said Niko.

"It's always dry in the—" She stopped. He was grinning. She had no laughter in her.

There was a wind blowing. Not much of one, but persistent. It picked up a handful of sand and cast it across the top of a rock, and rested; then amused itself in sculpting a dune. It blew from the left hand. South.

The horizon was the color of blood. The zenith was the color of lapis, deep pure blue. She turned her eyes southward. Blood-red, blood-crimson. Sparks leaped in it. Flickers of lightning.

She drew herself up. Her trousers were full of sand. She shook them out, taking great care. Not that it would matter. But she preferred to be clean while she had the choice.

The guides were already with the king. "You're sure?" Alexander asked them as Meriamon came up.

The oldest of them did his best not to look offended. "We know the signs, lord king. There will be storms within a day, maybe two. That is the khamsin blowing, the dry wind."

"It blows out of Siwah," Alexander said, "and to Siwah I will go. Can we make the oasis if we march through the night?"

"Night is not safe," the man said, "lord king."

"Is day any safer?"

The man rubbed at his beard. "Demons walk the night, lord king."

"The dry wind walks the day, if what you say is true. Should I fear a demon that may growl at me, over a sandstorm that can scour the flesh from my bones?"

"You should not speak lightly of these things," said the guide. "Lord king."

Alexander's blood was up, but his mind was cool enough. He scanned the camp with a swift eye; met Meriamon's stare. "Well?" he asked her.

"I don't like the look of the sky," she said. "If we had water enough I'd say stay, and wait it out."

"But we don't," said Hephaistion. "We have enough for

one more round for the men. Barely enough for the horses. Precious little for the camels, even if the men and the horses go thirsty. Camels," he said, "need a great deal of water, when they need it."

"They can go longer than you think," the guide said.

"Horses can't," said Hephaistion. "Men shouldn't. If this storm is bad and we're held up, we won't be in good case."

Alexander paced along the line of them, turned sharply. "We'll rest half the night. After that, we march."

The wind died down near middle night. Meriamon did not ease for that. Alexander, unfortunately, did. By the time the trumpet sounded the Wake and Arm, it was nearly dawn. They had drunk their ration of water and eaten their bit of bread, struck camp and turned their faces toward the southward road, when the sky began to lighten in the east.

It was cold, frost-cold. Meriamon huddled in the soldier's cloak that Niko had got for her before they left Rhakotis. Sekhmet was a warm weight in a fold of it. Fortunate cat: she could ride when humans had to walk.

Meriamon's shadow strained at its bindings. She loosed them. It wandered a little distance but came back, bristling, teeth bared in a soundless snarl. It was almost solid, she noticed. It dropped to all fours and paced behind her. A Companion who wandered sleepily out of his place in the line shied away from it, muttering something about "bloody great dogs."

The stars faded. The wind was blowing in their faces: brief hard gusts, a sting of sand. The sun rose as it had set, in blood. The light it cast was strangely dim, and dimming.

"We're going to get it," Ptolemy said. He was walking with his brother, just behind Meriamon.

Word came back down the line. "Push on as far as you can before it hits. Then barricade yourselves—behind a camel, if you can. Watch the camels! They know what to do."

A march of Hellenes was never a silent march unless they were mounting an ambush. Even in dry desert someone was always singing, and everyone was talking. Now the sound of voices sank away. The wind was growing stronger, the sting of sand fiercer.

The camels walked on, each beast seeming made up of half a dozen disparate parts, and every one moving in a different direction. For once no one commented on it. While the camels walked, they were safe. Some of them made a litany of it and marched to its rhythm.

All at once the camels stopped. The beast in the lead raised her head on its improbable neck and turned it from side to side. The drover shouted and struck her with his goad. She took no more notice of him than of the flies that swarmed on her hide. With great and deliberate care she folded her legs beneath her, joint by joint. First one, then another of the caravan followed her.

Their backs were to the south, Meriamon noticed, and their faces to the north.

The horses were shifting about uneasily. Phoenix, wise to the desert, was sweating. Her eyes rolled white as Meriamon approached, and she shied from the hand on her bridle. "Go on," Meriamon said to the groom. "I'll look after her."

The Thracian set his jaw. "No," he said. "You go."

Meriamon got a firmer grip on the bridle and half dragged, half coaxed the mare toward the nearest of the camels. The company had gone to ground already, except for those with the horses. Boukephalas was quiet, almost alarmingly so. Alexander had his bridle, was stroking his neck, talking to him. Meriamon cried out. The king threw up his head, remarkably like a horse himself. "Here!" she cried.

After a moment he moved toward her. She forgot him and set to work persuading Phoenix to lie in the lee of the camel. The mare knew what she was supposed to do; was glad to do it. But the air was full of thunder. The earth was throbbing like a heart. It was more than a horse could reasonably be expected to endure.

The sun was a feeble flicker. The sand was thickening. A shape loomed out of it—two shapes. Alexander; Boukephalas. The stallion lay down willingly beside Phoenix, and greeted her with a flutter of the nostrils. She flattened her ears and snaked her head. He offered no presumption. Her trembling quieted.

"Where's Niko?" Meriamon asked. Shouted. The wind was rising.

She tried to get up. Alexander pulled her down. "Not now, idiot! He was back there the last time I looked—with Ptolemy. Hephaistion, too."

There was nothing of mind in what she wanted. To go, to find him. But Alexander was in her way, and he would not move. She subsided slowly. "Mother," she prayed. "Mother Isis, look after him."

If the goddess heard, she had keener ears than anything living. They were in the mouth of the furnace. One moment there was wind and sand and a crackle of lighting. The next, a lake of fire, a blast of heat, sand to scour the flesh from bones even through a soldier's cloak. Every drop of moisture sucked from skin and mouth and eyes. And howling like every voice of every torment that had ever beset man or beast or demon below.

It was a paean. A song of triumph. That they were taken. That they would be destroyed.

"No," said Meriamon.

Not precisely said. She had no voice to say it. It was burned out of her. But she willed it. There was more than earthly malice in that wind, and more than earthly destruction in the storm. Her souls were flayed raw. What it had done to the simple magicless Macedonians, she could not think; dared not, or she would despair.

She could not move. There was a weight on her. It was alive; it breathed. It was shielding her.

Alexander. She knew the bright heat of him. A different heat: welcome. It was barely touched at all.

It offered itself for what she must do. She shaped the words with her souls' tongue. She made the wall, stone by stone, word by word of shaped and focused power. Half of them the storm scoured away. Half it battered against, blow on blow.

But they held. Patiently she heaped them one on the other, making a ward against the storm, raising it over the small trapped souls, men, beasts, even a desert mouse cowering under a stone. The flesh that housed them could perish even yet, drowned in sand. But they would escape uneaten.

There was little of her left when the wall was made. She had just strength enough to set the last stone and curl up behind it, and wait.

Silence.

She had gone deaf. Or dead.

Something moved. A voice spoke in her ear. "Herakles!"

Sand sifted down, hissing. The weight scrambled off her. She got an elbow in the ribs.

She was definitely not dead, unless the dead could hurt.

A hand got a grip on her, heaved her up. Light blinded her.

Alexander looked like nothing human, covered in sand from head to foot, and his eyes staring out of it, blazing pale. He shook like a dog. Sand flew.

The world had changed. What had been a bare stony valley with a bit of scrub for the camels to graze on, was a sea of sand, great undulating dunes stretching to the horizon. North was a haze of storm, shot with lightnings. South was a still clear blue.

One of the smaller dunes heaved. A camel rose out of

it, shook itself as Alexander had, looked about with an air of vast disgust.

"My sentiments exactly," said Alexander. He sounded a great deal calmer than he looked. He eyed the hillock nearest him, and began to dig. Meriamon burrowed already where her bones told her to burrow, no mind in her at all, only a madness of fear.

Niko was coiled in a knot, death-still. She gasped. Her mouth was full of sand. She dragged him out bodily.

He struggled, unknotting, coughing hard enough to knock him flat, and Meriamon with him. Her hands were locked on his arms. He tore free, rolling to all fours, and coughed himself into shaking silence. He was ghastly to look at, sand caked in his hair and brows and clinging to his skin, and sweat plowing furrows in it. He was quite the most beautiful thing Meriamon had ever seen.

He tasted of salt and of sand, and of himself. His shaking stopped. She stumbled to her feet, drawing him with her. Other mounds sprouted their crop of men and beasts, snorting and blowing and shaking off clouds of sand.

They had lost no one, and every one of the animals was safe. One or two of the camels had strayed, but those came back on their own as the company took count of itself. The worst casualty was a man who had got a stone in his eye. He would keep the eye, Meriamon judged. She did what she could to stitch and bind the cut above it. No one else had more than a bruise or two, and a few unfortunates had had the skin scoured from exposed portions of their anatomy.

"That will teach you to stick your arse out in a sandstorm," Alexander said to the worst wounded of them; but he had a smile for the man after, and that was as good an anodyne as anything Meriamon could muster.

They had a sip of water each—not quite all of it, but there was a fair distance to go yet, the guides said. Once they had shaken the worst of the sand out of clothes and hair and seen to their packs and their animals, they took the road again. Even as parched as they were, their spirits were high. The storm was gone. The sky was serene. By night they would have water enough for all of them, man and beast.

It was hard going. The sand was deep, and could be treacherous. The curve of the dunes lured them away from the straight path. The sun sank, slowly at first, then with breathtaking swiftness.

"Soon," the guides said. "The oasis is close. Soon we come to it."

Each rise of sand invited the certainty that water lay on the other side of it. Each downward slope looked only to another dune. Red sand, dun sand, blue sky. No green at all. Not a bush, not a leaf, not a blade of grass. And of water, nothing. Not even the shadow of it.

The guides were moving more slowly now, pausing more often to confer with one another. Most of the Companions were too tired to care about anything but putting one foot in front of the other. So should Meriamon have been—she perhaps more than any, for the wall that she had built of magic and her souls' substance, to guard them all in the midst of the storm. But she was past exhaustion in a white fierce clarity. She knew in her skin that Niko was beside her. She was aware of Sekhmet riding on his shoulder, of Phoenix stepping delicately behind, of Alexander working his way up from the rear, a flare like a torch in a dark night.

When he passed, she fell in beside him. His glance acknowledged but did not forbid her.

The guides had stopped again. The chief of Alexander's scouts was with them, addressing them in a fierce low voice. "You *what?*"

"We know which way is south," one of the guides said, just as low and just as fierce. "It's only—"

"Only what?"

They whipped about. Even the scout looked suddenly, horribly guilty.

"What don't you know?" Alexander asked again.

None of them would answer.

"It is only," Meriamon said, "that there is a whole world to the south of this place, and Siwah is a very small portion of it." She fixed the chief of the guides with her stare. "How long have you been lost?"

"We are not lost," the man said, "lady. We know where we must be."

"Are we anywhere near water?" Alexander demanded.

There was another silence.

The scout could not spit: he was too dry. He managed to look as if he had done it. "They're lost, Alexander. Don't you doubt it. They've been lost since we dug ourselves out of that sandpit."

"The storm changed everything!" cried the youngest of the guides. "How were we to know that it would make a new world?"

"Sandstorms do," Alexander said mildly. He looked about. There was nothing to see but sand. "I don't suppose it will be any better at night? Navigating by the stars, or however you do it?"

"We go by the land," the chief of the guides said, "lord king. There is always something that never changes: a shape under the sand, or a turning of the hills."

"How much time do you need to find it?"

"We have been looking," the man said. "Nothing is as we remember." He threw up his hands. "Nothing! Never in all my years have I seen it so. The very earth has shifted, I swear by the gods."

Meriamon shivered.

Alexander did not hear the truth that she heard, or did not care. "In a word," he said, "you're lost. And so, therefore, are we."

"We are not—" The guide snatched off his headcloth and scratched fiercely at his swarm of lice. "Lord king, we are not lost. We are here, and Siwah is there, to the south. We have only to walk until we come to it."

"Or," said Alexander, "until we die of thirst."

"The gods will provide," said the guide.

"Then you had better pray," said Alexander. "Or better yet, find a landmark that you recognize. We'll camp here while you go about it."

The guides stared at him. He smiled his sweet terrible smile, and went back down the line.

• THIRTY •

By morning the water was gone. The wine without it was deadly stuff, nor could the beasts drink it even if there had been enough. The guides had not found the oasis. They knew where Siwah was, they insisted on that. Their insistence had an air of desperation.

Alexander shrugged. He was as dry as anyone else. Someone had tried to save out a flask of water for him. He had smiled, thanked the man, and passed it round the man's company. Now he said, "We'll go on. What's a dry march or two to the likes of us?"

His men cheered. He flashed them his brightest smile and took his place at the head of the line, and led them out of the camp.

He was carrying them with his strength. And yet they were tough, these Macedonians. They marched behind their king, erect under the weight of packs and armor, and their eyes were bright and their faces were firm and they knew nothing of defeat or despair.

They did not feel what Meriamon felt: the malice under their feet, the ill-will in the sky. It had them, and it would kill them. And they laughed at it.

She walked as straight as she could, slipping and scrambling in sand. She kept her head as high as it would go. She worried about Phoenix, but the mare was lively enough. They all were.

And for how long? Four days at least to Siwah, the guides said. The camels were irritable already, trying to wander off, biting their handlers when they were dragged back. They wanted water. In four days they would do worse than want it. They would be dead for lack of it.

She stumbled and went down. She stayed there on hands and knees, shaking her head. There was a darkness in it. Trap. Trapped. Thirsty—thirsty—

"Meriamon!"

Niko. Always Niko.

Her head spun. He lifted her, shook her. She tried to push him away. It was like pushing at a wall.

He slapped her. She gasped. She could see again. He looked furious.

Not as furious as she. "Put me down," she said through gritted teeth.

He kept on holding her, and he kept on walking. She struggled. He did not even trouble to tighten his grip. She lay in his arms, glaring.

Anger was a power. It cleared her mind. It named what had felled her. Enemy.

The sky was still dark. Grey. She tried to banish it, to bring back the blue. A wind brushed her cheek. She shivered. It was cold.

The marchers halted. They were all staring upward.

Alexander's voice rang out, seeming to echo in the empty spaces. "By the dog! It's going to rain."

"In the desert?" someone said.

"Taste the wind," said Ptolemy. "That's rain." He paused. His voice sharpened. "Quick, everybody. Get out your tents, your waterskins—anything you've got. If the gods are with us at all—if they've ever listened to a prayer we've said—"

"Zeus!" cried Alexander. "Skyfather! Did you hear that?

You'll have a hecatomb of fine bulls when I get back to Memphis, if you give us rain now."

There was no sudden stillness. No listening pause; no silence of awe. The men ran to do as Ptolemy bade them, some muttering, some speaking aloud of madmen and desperation. But they ran. They unfolded tents, skins, cloaks, hauled out pots and jars.

The wind blew harder. It was a water-wind as the khamsin had been a fire-wind. It massed clouds above them. It gave them nothing that they could drink, not a drop. Already there was light on the far side of it, dry naked sky, pitiless sun.

"Zeus!" cried Alexander, high and peremptory. "Father Zeus! Can you hear us?"

He was standing on the summit of a dune. A long shaft of sun caught him, striking fire in his hair. He spread his arms wide.

Meriamon's feet were on the ground again. She almost leaped back into Niko's arms. The earth was humming. It was Alexander—not working power, but being power; drawing it up from the deep places and down from the sky.

He did not know what he was doing. He would call it prayer, if he called it anything. Making the gods listen. Taking no notice at all of the Enmity that beat upon him.

The sky shattered.

Meriamon raised herself on her hands. Whether she had flung herself flat, or been flung, she would never be sure. She drew a breath, and choked. It was like breathing a river.

Rain. Hard, driving, relentless, miraculous rain. Alexander's madmen were whooping and dancing in it, trying to drink it as it fell, gagging and half drowning themselves, and laughing all the while. But they were gathering it in everything they had. Alexander egged them on. He was whole, grinning, sopping wet. Not even a scorched eyelash after the bolt that surely had struck through him into the earth.

The rain stopped as suddenly as it had begun. The silence was enormous. The clouds thinned and paled and scattered, blowing away southward. The thirsty sand drank the last of the wet, glistening in the new-washed sun.

They were all wet to the skin, men, horses, camels. They looked at one another. Then at the full waterskins; the jars brimming over; the pools made of tents, with camels drinking from them in long noisy draughts.

No one said the word that they were all thinking. Miracle. Gods' gift. Four days' worth, by the quartermaster's measure.

They took time to make sure their armor and weapons were dry. By the time they marched, they were only a little damp around the edges. There was water in them, pure sweet rainwater, and they went the swifter for it.

The desert was coming to life about them. Dried branches put forth leaves. Flowers seemed to spring beneath their feet. Small creatures came out of hiding to feed on the new bounty, or simply to revel in it.

"Water is life," said Niko. "I never knew it before as I know it here."

"Desert is very close to the truth of things." Meriamon was weak still, and sometimes she was dizzy. Her eyes did not seem to want to see very far, but what was close was bitterly, painfully clear. Niko's face, now. Peeling where the sun had burned it. Raw on one cheekbone from the scouring of sand. Rough with fair stubble. His hat shaded it, cutting a sharp line across it, part in sun, part in shadow.

They had stopped ahead. Some of them had spears. None of them moved; they seemed hardly to breathe.

Meriamon made her way to them. Alexander was lost amid the taller men, until one of them shifted. She saw what had stopped them.

Two of them, eye to eye with Alexander. His eyes were wide. One was almost black, and the other was almost silver. Theirs could not be anything but wide, cold and yellow and slit-pupiled. Their hoods were spread. Their forked tongues tasted the air. Tails coiled, long bodies raised and swaying gently, they were as tall as the king.

One of the Bodyguard jerked forward, spear up, face a rictus of disgust. Ptolemy caught him and hurled him back bodily. "You fool! Do you want to kill the king?"

"I'm not going to die." Alexander's voice was soft, a little blurred, as if he spoke from a dream. He did not glance at Meriamon, could not have seen her coming, but he said, "Meriamne. Did you ask your gods for guides?"

"I don't think I needed to," she said. The serpents swayed toward her. They were beautiful, all supple length and glistening scales. Their hoods were like the headdress of Pharaoh in his great house. Very, very carefully she bowed to them. She went low and low, but with an eye always upon them. "Great ones," she said to them in the oldest of tongues, the language of priests from the dawn of the Two Lands. "Handmaidens of Edjo in the house of the horizon. I bring to you the lord of Upper and Lower Egypt, king from across the sea, son of that one whom you know."

The nearer serpent hissed. The other dipped its head and flowed along the sand southward and westward. At the length of a furrow in Thebes it stopped, curved round, raised its head again.

"It says," said Meriamon, "follow."

Alexander shook himself. For a moment she thought that he would laugh, or say something unfortunate. The serpent that had not moved could strike in an eyeblink. Would. She knew that as she knew the feel of the earth beneath her feet.

But he only tilted his head, looking from her to the serpents. Maybe at last he understood what this was that he did. "Go on," he said. "I'll be behind you."

* * *

Meriamon did not want to lead, but Alexander was adamant. She was a shield of sorts. And an interpreter, though surely it was obvious what their guides wanted of them. They were allowed to rest at night. The serpents left them then, and they breathed a little easier, all of them, until the fear struck. If they were being led into perdition—if their guides did not come back—

The serpents came back the first morning, and again the second. By the third the travelers were something like comfortable, even the horses, who the first day had been unmanageable until their grooms took them to the rear and kept them there. Horses were on speaking terms with divinity, and often foaled of the wind; but snakes were the Enemy, even snakes who belonged to the gods.

Meriamon spent most of the first day upbraiding herself for doubting that the gods were looking after their chosen king. She had been perilously close to despair, even after the rain. That was the malice in the earth, working on her weaknesses. It had little enough to do, when it came to that. She had never been perfect in her faith.

This was hardly a sign for her. The gods knew the Enemy—they could hardly escape it. They wanted Alexander in their oracle. Meriamon was but a means to their end.

It was a comfort of sorts, to be insignificant. She walked behind the serpents, keeping the pace they set. Alexander walked behind her. His Companions walked behind him. The camels kept the outer line, with guards to watch for raiders, and the horses held the rear, just ahead of the rearguard. The land did not change from day to day. It was the same barren undulation of rock and sand. The same blue infinity of sky. Even the same vulture hovering against it, wide wings, blood-speck of head peering down. Nekhbet's eyes, Meriamon thought. As the hawk that flew over them was Horus, winging into the sun. And when night fell, the sky would be the arch of a goddess' body, the stars the garment that clothed her, and the moon the jewel on her neck.

They were not in the world any longer. That the guides, born and bred to this country, had not known the shape of it after the storm, nor had they known it since—Meriamon had known in her heart, even then, what that meant. Now she let herself acknowledge it.

Where they were . . .

They taught in Thebes, and likewise in Memphis, that the gods dwelt beyond the horizon. That the horizon of the west, the Red Land between the river and the sunset, was both living earth and land of the dead. That one could walk through a door, or through the words of a spell, or even through the wall of a storm, and come to that earth on which no living creature walked.

It was exactly like the land of the living. The sun rode there, the priests taught, when it was night for living men; and who was to say that Alexander's company had not somehow turned itself about and entered day-in-night?

She stooped, the morning of that third day, and took up a handful of sand. It was simply sand. Dry, whispering as it trickled from her palm. She had eaten bread before dawn, fresh from baking in a fire of camel-dung, and drunk wine thinned with water from the rain. She knew what she had been doing before she had to rise and eat: her belly was warm with it still, and Niko kept smiling to himself in odd moments. Ptolemy was chaffing him for it; he snapped back, stung. Their voices were living voices, rough-sweet and pleasant to hear at her back as Edjo's servants slithered in front of her, leading her to the oracle.

And yet there was her shadow. It walked beside her, and it was a man with a jackal's head, its body as solid as her own. No one looked at it askance, or said anything of the stranger in the mask.

Its name touched the edge of her tongue. She almost said it. *Anubis*. Guide and guardian. Though for her it had always been more the latter; and here their guides were Edjo's serpents.

She was not afraid. That surprised her. There were two

of her. Flesh walking in the land of flesh. Ka-spirit walking in this land, the dry land, the land of coming forth by day.

She glanced back. The company held their ranks, marching as they had marched since Rhakotis. They sensed nothing amiss. Now and then one fell out to relieve himself or to shake a stone out of his boot. Someone was singing about a boy with cheeks like a peach.

Her shadow left her side to walk ahead. Edjo's serpents slowed for it. It came up between them; they went on. Its ears tilted back at her, then flicked forward. Guarding her still.

Someone else took her shadow's place. It was not Niko, though he was close enough. Arrhidaios watched her shadow with wide interested eyes, and said, "We're somewhere else. Aren't we?"

That was one way to put it. Meriamon said, "We'll be safe." Or so, at least, she hoped.

"There are things back there," Arrhidaios said. "Watching. The horses don't like them."

Meriamon kept her eyes sternly to the front. "What sort of things?"

"Things," said Arrhidaios, shrugging. "Like him"—he tilted his chin at her shadow—"but ugly. They just watch. They have knives."

She stumbled and almost fell. Arrhidaios caught her hand to steady her. "Are you all right, Meri?"

"Yes." She said it through stiff lips. "They cannot touch us. I know their names."

If names were enough. If the scribes and the priests had known truly, and not through a veil of lies and guesses.

She was marching through simple desert to an oasis and a temple. There were no demons behind the company.

"I can count them," said Arrhidaios proudly. "Seven and seven and seven, and three more sevens. Six sevens."

"Six sevens," she said. "Yes. That is their number."

She would not look back. If she looked back, her bowels would melt.

Words came to her. She spoke them, slowly at first, faintly, then louder and stronger. "In truth I walk. In the Hall of the Two Truths I walk. In Osiris' name, in Horus' name, in the name of Isis, Mother, goddess, lady of the living and the dead, I defend me. From the bearers of knives, from the eaters of souls, from the Powers that wait upon the day of judgment, deliver me."

Silence. Her shadow paced without pausing. Edjo's serpents slithered on either side.

She looked over her shoulder. Her eye caught Niko's. He smiled, sudden warmth, a surge of pure strength.

Alexander was beyond him. He had been down the line, keeping company with the singers. Once away from them, he lost his air of lightness.

He knew.

She waited for him to come level with her. As she waited she sang softly, little more than a croon. "I am the hawk of the desert. I am the cat soft-footed in shadow. I am the sand across the empty track. I walk unseen. I walk defended. No demon touches me."

She stopped. Alexander was beside her.

"You see them, too," said Arrhidaios before Meriamon could begin. "You do, don't you, Alexander?"

Alexander patted him on the shoulder. When he spoke, it was to Meriamon. "What are they?"

"Watchers," she said.

"Armed?"

"It's their way," she said.

He frowned at the three who led them. "Tell me," he said. "Tell me that that is a Nubian in a mask. And that those, back there, are more men who like, for reasons best known to themselves, to wear the heads of animals and carry naked knives and follow strangers through the dry land."

"They're not men," she said. "But the rest is true enough."

She saw him shiver. "What . . . do they do?"

"They watch." That did not satisfy him. She said after a moment, "They judge. But that is in the hall. This is the open land."

"Is it?"

She glanced upward in spite of herself. If that vault was the vault of a ceiling, and about her walls as vast as a world, and under her feet not sand but smoothed stone . . .

Stone of every kind that was in the world, laid in patterns that lured the eye, and having won it, netted it and drew it down and down. Pillars like tall fans of papyrus or like the trees of the Lebanon, inlaid with gold and precious things, lapis and carnelian and malachite. Vault the color of the sky at night, or perhaps the sky on the verge of morning, when all was darkest, and day a dream to which there was no waking.

"No," she said. "It is the desert of Libya, and tomorrow we will come to Siwah."

"What do they judge?" Alexander asked her, pitiless as a child, and as innocently persistent.

"Souls," she answered him.

"We're alive, I think," he said.

"We are," she said. "This is the land of the living. This is the sun that rises in the morning and sets at evening. Those are the stars that rise and set."

Each word came with the weight of a world. Here the worlds met. Here, if she slackened, or if she failed to name each name as it was given in the morning of the worlds, the world she built would crumble and fade.

"This is sky," she said. "This is the sun, that is the boat of Ra, that sails on the sea of the million years. This is sand, Red Land of the west, desert beyond the green fields of Egypt. This is life."

Her foot turned a stone. She picked it up. It was sharp-edged; it tried to bite her hand as it had bitten her foot.

She smiled at it. Pain was life. Pain was real. Pain was power in this shifting, wavering place.

The desert melted into mist. The hall stretched before her. She knew its name. The Hall of Twofold Truth. And in it, moving from behind her to take their ancient places, six sevens of Watchers. Man-formed, now man-high, now as vast as giants, with the faces of hungry beasts. Their knives glittered in the pitiless light. Their teeth gleamed. One that wore a jackal's smile met her eyes with eyes the color of blood, and sketched what might have been a bow.

She shot a glance over her shoulder. Her shadow kept its place as it always did, and its eyes were as clear as the living sky of Khemet. And yet it too was of this place.

The Watchers closed in slowly. Beyond them swayed a balance. Her shadow's image stood beside it, ears pricked, alert. In his clawed hand, stirring with the airs that moved in the hall, lay a feather. Its name was Justice. Below the balance crouched a beast. Its jaws gaped. Its eyes gleamed. Hungry.

Meriamon's souls quailed. They knew its name; none better than they. Eater of Souls.

Something—someone—wavered before the balance. Dead soul, woman's it might have been, slender and afraid. Behind her rose a throne, and on the throne the lord of this place, dead god wrapped in cerements and crowned with the Two Crowns. The crowned head bent. Its face was a mask, the mask of the dead. In the pits of its eyes was the darkness between stars.

The Guide laid the feather in one arm of the balance. In the other he laid a beating, crimson thing: a heart, and in its essence a name, the name of the soul that waited upon the judgment. The balance quivered. If the heart proved the weightier, the stronger in truth, then the soul was free, and freed to enter the lands of ever-living. If the heart were the lighter, the feebler in justice, it would fail, and the soul would fall, and be devoured. The soul stretched out her hand, as if she could sway the balance, send her heart swinging down under the weight of her will.

The feather dropped. The heart flew up. The soul wailed. Watchers caught her before she could flee, bound her with cords of night and sorrow. They took no heed of her struggles, or of her keening that was like the cry of a bird. They cast her into the waiting maw.

"Zeus Pater!" Alexander's oath rang among the pillars. No god came to it, no flare of levin-light in the dimness of ages. Nothing of Hellas had power in this place.

Alexander sprang past Meriamon. His hand was on his swordhilt, the blade half-drawn. She seized his wrist with both hands and held, though he dragged her nearly off her feet.

He halted. His eyes were wild. "That thing," he said. "Those things—"

They circled. Eyes, fangs, ill-will so strong that it choked like a stench. Living flesh, living blood, cold steel in this place of all places in all the worlds—

Death was the penalty for walking living here. Cold blades would pierce their flesh that was so warm and solid, cut out their hearts that dared beat where all hearts were stilled, sunder their souls and cast them into the maw of the Devourer.

Alexander had never been afraid of anything, in the world or out of it. He laughed in their faces.

"Walk," Meriamon said. Her voice was thin with strain. "For the love of life, walk!"

He walked. He left a trail of light. The hall trembled in it like an image caught in water.

Meriamon's magic, quelled and cowed as it had been, found strength it had not known it had. It willed another image, another world, a world of light and the living. She built it of the light that was her king. She made it grow about her. She made it strong, she made it real, she fixed it with the power of the word and the will and the name.

The hall of the dead was gone. They walked in the

world of the living. Living sand under their feet. Living sky over their heads. The sun was westering, but it was high still. And the night ahead of it; and morning that would bring them to their end. Siwah. Or, if they failed the test, the Hall of Twofold Truth, and six sevens of Watchers, and the Eater of Souls with jaws opened wide to devour all that they were.

"Sun," she said. "Sky. Earth. Sand. Stone." Over and over. No elegance in it after a while. No fine turn of phrase. It was not the elegance that imparted power; it was the name, and the will behind the name. To make the world real. To hold the Watchers at bay. To bring night and not everlasting day; stars that changed and set, and not stars that could not die.

Her body, or her ka's body, walked in the wake of the shadow and the serpents. A white light walked with it. In the sun, a second sun. In the night, a beacon.

"Alexander," she said. The name resounded through all the levels of the worlds. The name that his father had given; that, nonetheless, the gods had willed. *Alexander*.

• THIRTY-ONE •

Sometimes Meriamon's soul was her body's image, walking as her body walked, with a stone clutched in its palm. Sometimes it was a bird with a woman's head, fluttering through a changeless sky, under stars that did not move. Whatever it was, it knew what it followed, the serpents and the Guide; and what it followed them to, the presence beyond the horizon. A place of living green, a forest in the heart of the desert, and the temple in the midst of it, the halls and the courts, and the fountain of the Sun from which the rest of it sprang.

There were others who followed her. Shadows, but

shadows with faces, and about them, in some greater, in some less, a shimmer of light. Deep earth and green silences and a tang of iron: Nikolaos her guardsman and her beloved, guarding her without fear in this most fearsome of places. Earth too but with a sharpness that was fire, a suggestion of brimstone: Ptolemy, clear kin to Niko, and kin likewise to the rioting fire that was Alexander, less than he by far but potent enough in his souls' center. And with them one who was all earth shot through with light, now blurred and dimmed and muddied, now shining forth as clear and pure as a star out of clouds in Hellas. Arrhidaios in the souls' shape, bred of Alexander's blood and kin, with a beauty and a strength in him that caught her unawares. It did not weaken her spell, but made it stronger, broadened and deepened it and held the world to its solidity.

Greater than any of them, so bright that he cast shadows in the shadowless land, was the one who walked closest behind her. He was coming to a destiny. Whether it was the one he wanted, or whether he would be given another altogether, the gods were not telling.

"If I am," she heard him say to the shadow beside him. "If I really am—but if I'm not—"

"The god will tell you," the shadow said. Cool softness like water, a chill that was iron, a glint of sudden brilliance: Hephaistion walking close behind his king, guarding him as Nikolaos guarded Meriamon.

"But if I'm not the god's son," said Alexander, "if I've let myself believe it because I want to, and claimed all the rest in the name of a lie, then how will I live with myself after?"

"I don't think it is a lie," said Hephaistion. "You have to live inside yourself. The rest of us can see what you are. You're blazing like a torch in the dark, did you know that?"

There was a pause, as if Alexander looked down at himself. "I look just the same as I always have."

"Exactly," said Hephaistion.

"But," said Alexander all over again. "If I'm not—"

She did not see what Hephaistion did to silence him. It was something subtle, she supposed. The others would have laughed and cheered them on, else.

Doubt was the Enemy. She had suffered from it once, when her souls and she were one creature. She would again, very likely, when they were reunited. If they were. Her bird-soul liked the freedom of the sky, even under stars that did not change. Her ka was comfortable walking the track behind its guides. Her body did what it did. The place it was going to was close now. It could see the shimmer on the world's edge, the blessed, impossible green. Some of the trees were in flower, sweet scent, fragile blossom; others in fruit, green or glowing ripe. After so long in the red land and the dun land, the sight almost broke its heart.

Not it alone. The shadows of men came up behind it and streamed past it. Whether it had slowed or they had begun to run, she did not know. The guides were ahead of them still. She had no need of them. That was neither trick nor deceit, the place that opened before them. It was real in every world. The god's house, the place of his prophecy. Siwah.

"Meriamon."

The name spun a cord, thin as spidersilk and as strong. It netted the bird-soul in its wandering. It looped round her ka. It wound them together so quickly that even the winged thing had barely moved before it was done.

Flesh was leaden heavy after so long in the spirit. The sun was brazenly bright. She blinked in it.

"Meriamon," said the taller of the two shapes in front of her.

"Meri," said the other. "Meri, look. You almost got lost."

In more ways than one. She stared stupidly at the track she had been on. It led past the oasis and out into the desert. Her body would have followed it, blind and unguided, until sun and thirst struck it down. Her souls would have gone past the Lake of Fire and the Lake of Flowers, and entered the high hall, and seen the Watchers with their knives and their hungry eyes, and the Eater of Souls under the golden scale, and the dead king upon his throne.

A thought, a word, a turning of the will, and she could go. They would weigh her heart against the feather of Justice, and find it sufficient or find it wanting, and grant her dissolution or life everlasting. She need only speak. Or not speak. For one of her blood and her power, it was as simple as that.

"Meriamon!"

Real fear, that. And temper. "You're always calling me back from edges," said Meriamon.

"And I'm tired of it, too," Niko said. "When are you going to stop mooning and dreaming and act like a sensible woman?"

"I can't," she said. "It isn't in me."

"You can try."

He was perfectly unreasonable. He had also brought her fully to herself. She had expected to be much more tired than she was. Her feet were sore, which was hardly surprising: she had walked an ungodly way. She was thirsty. And hungry. She was very much in the flesh.

"I could have been comfortably dead," she said.

"Not while I have anything to say about it."

"You think you do?"

"I know I do."

She glared. He glared back. Suddenly she began to laugh. So, after a moment, did he. And Arrhidaios, making no effort to understand them, simply being glad that they were glad.

For all the eternities that she had been soul-lost, the world of the living had advanced no more than a drip of the water-clock. Alexander's Companions were only now come through the wood—a forest of tangled branches, a track dim to darkness after the glare of sun on sand, then sudden sun and open space and the temple's gate. The priests came forth in a wailing of pipes and a rattling of sistra, the high voices of women and the deep voices of men, and a whirl and sway of dancers. "Welcome," they sang. "Welcome, lord of the Two Lands!"

The serpent-guides were gone. Meriamon's shadow was in back of her again, a shape without substance. Alexander stood in front of his Companions, dusty and wayworn: disheveled boyish man in a purple cloak much stained with travel, no height to boast of, too much brow and nose and cheek for proper beauty, his face red and his nose peeling and precious little dignity about him. Then he moved, and one forgot everything but that he was Alexander.

The eyes. They ruled the rest of him, and the world with it.

Meriamon was beside him. Someone had moved to give her room. Ptolemy. She bent her head to him. He dipped his own in acknowledgment.

The crowd of welcomers had halted and spread in ranks along the wall. A man came down the aisle which they had made. He was neither old nor young, neither large nor small, neither beautiful nor ugly: a brown shaven man in a robe of white linen. He wore no ornament but one, but that was enough, a heavy collar of gold and lapis and carnelian. He carried a staff of dark wood, very old, and its head was a carven serpent. Meriamon felt the stir behind her as the Macedonians saw what it was.

The high priest of Amon's temple at Siwah advanced toward Alexander. Alexander waited, standing lightly, no sign of the tension that was in him; unless one knew him, and saw the way his hand clenched and unclenched in a fold of his cloak. He looked, Meriamon thought, like a warhorse on the edge of a battlefield. Alert, upheaded, not quite quivering.

The priest paused at several paces' remove. He was of

a height with Alexander. His dark eyes met Alexander's light ones. They were keen, measuring. Alexander lifted his chin a fraction. It was not for him to speak, the gesture said. He was the guest. Let the master of the place give him greeting, or refuse it.

The high priest smiled very slightly. He bent his knee; slowly, with the grace of one who surely had been a dancer, he went down in obeisance. His voice went up in clear if accented Greek. "I give you welcome," he said, "son of Amon."

Alexander's body snapped erect.

The priest went on. "Protected of Horus, face of Ra in the world of the living, child of the god who dwells in the wood and the spring, Great House of the Two Lands: welcome, welcome, welcome!"

The last he sang in the tongue of Khemet, and the choir of women echoed him, sweet eerie voices ringing from wall of stone to wall of trees and up into the sky. Amid the torrent of sound, he took Alexander's hand. Alexander made no effort to resist him. "Come with me," he said, soft and breathtakingly ordinary after the priestesses' chant.

His Bodyguard stirred uneasily. He was rapt; enspelled, one might have said. But he mastered enough of himself to turn. "I'll go," he said. "I'm safe. No one will harm me here."

They did not like that, but his eyes were on them. Nor could any meet them.

Except Hephaistion. As the priest led Alexander away, he moved to follow.

Alexander paused again. "No," he said. Hephaistion stopped. His face was perfectly still.

Alexander smiled. There was all the love in the world in that smile, and all the regret. "If I could share," he said, "I would. Only this, sweet friend. Only this of all that we've ever done or had or been . . ."

"I can never be king," Hephaistion said, soft and calm. "Nor would I want to be."

Alexander touched his shoulder. Hephaistion stood stiff. Alexander seized him suddenly in a strong embrace and held him till his arms came up, a fierce, hard grip more like war than love. As abruptly as it had begun, it ended. They stepped apart. Alexander's face now was as still as Hephaistion's, as whitely, blankly rapt.

The high priest was waiting. Alexander turned to follow him.

Meriamon went in behind them. She did not ask. She was not invited. No more than Hephaistion did she want to be a king, but she was royal born, and the voice of the gods. They were in her again.

That, maybe, was what it was to be pregnant: that swelling fullness, that sense of a life inside one's body, part of yet apart from one's own. Pregnancy filled the belly. This filled the heart and the head.

They took Alexander to the inner temple. She went where her feet led her, past the door through which he had gone, into a broad pillared hall open to the sky. There the choir of priestesses had come. There were the strongest of the priests, a full fourscore of them, ranged for all the world like the Macedonians' phalanx, and in the center of the square a great gilded thing like a ship yet on shafts like a litter. On its deck rode the image of the god. In Thebes he was most like a man, but ram-horned. Here he wore no human shape at all. He was a strange squat thing, a dark stone studded with brighter stones, and brightest of them all a great emerald.

The power in the stone rocked Meriamon to her foundations. Every god gave a part of himself to his image, and his worshippers gave what they had, the force of their worship. This was old, old and strong, its green stone like an eye, transfixing her, stripping her soul bare.

She had nothing to fear from it. Doubt was a failing

even of gods; or why had Osiris died and been brought to life again? She had seen his realm, its beauties and its terrors. Dissolution she did not fear while her name endured. Nikolaos remembered it. Alexander knew it. Mother Isis herself had spoken it in the deeps of Meriamon's dream.

Here in Amon's temple, it seemed not at all amiss that her heart should go out to the Lady of earth and heaven. Or that she took her place in the ranks of priestesses among those whose voices were deeper yet purer, and sang as they sang, the hymn of praise to the god.

The high priest came out of the inner shrine. Alexander was not with him. The king would be sitting in the small dark room, alone with his thoughts and his god. His father, he would be thinking. Hoping. Dreading.

The hymn reached the highest of its high notes. The priests bent, all eighty as one, and set their shoulders beneath the shafts of the Sun-boat. As the hymn spiraled down into a deep clear note like the song of bronze on bronze, the boat rose up. It was a mighty weight even for fourscore priests. As they stood erect its power focused. The priestesses' voices wove about it. The priests' strength bore it up. It rode upon them both as on a sea of sound and light. The god within it came awake.

The high priest spoke no word. The hymn itself shifted, changed; became a croon, a shape of pure sound. What it asked, what it wished, Meriamon knew in her bones.

The boat began to sway. The priests swayed with it, not as men who moved it, but as men moved by it. Holding to it for all the world like sailors in a swell, bracing against the oars, struggling to hold their boat steady.

The high priest watched. His eyes were intent, glittering. Reading each movement as a captain reads the shifting of wind and sea.

Who am I? Alexander asked. *What am I? What is meant for me?* And more perhaps that she could not see; the wishes of his heart, beyond her perceiving.

The god answered. Answered gladly. Answered long and clear, and never a word in it.

Then he was still. The priestesses' song died away. The litter bore down on the men who carried it. They bowed beneath it, lowering it to the ground.

The high priest bowed low, and kissed the stone of the paving.

As he rose, his eye caught Meriamon's. She started, stiffened. In that glance was everything she would have asked, and everything she might have answered. Doubts faced and stared down. Dreams understood. Purpose, choices—decisions she had never known she would make, until she had made them.

And under it she thought, how strange. He was a man and no eunuch, and yet in that moment his face seemed to her to be a woman's face, his body a woman's body, his hands a woman's hands, giving her greeting, blessing her with a goddess' graciousness. And he—the goddess— smiled. Meriamon could not help herself. It was presumptuous, no doubt, and yet she did it. She smiled back.

But then, before she was a goddess, Mother Isis was a woman. A woman could understand what even a goddess could not, and share the joy that was in it.

•THIRTY-TWO•

Alexander came out of the temple silent and exalted. Hephaistion was waiting for him, not in the front of those who waited, or even in the front ranks, but a little apart. Those who wanted an oracle had had one. Hephaistion had not asked. He would not judge it mummery—he had seen enough on the march to Siwah, and he had seen what the Egyptian woman did. Her magic was a quiet thing, no

wands or spells, no smokes or stenches or sleights of char-
latanry. It was all words, and indomitable will.

He did not want to hear a prophecy. Of those who had,
he noticed, few were minded to tell anyone what they had
heard. Something about this place discouraged babbling.

Alexander's coming was as quiet, and yet as potent, as
the Egyptian woman's magic. One moment he was still
within. The next, he stood outside the gate, and his men
were running toward him. Moths to the flame, Hephaistion
thought. His own heart yearned forward, but he quelled it.
It was pride, he knew that very well. Let the little men
flock and bleat. He would go to his lord in his own time.

His eyes had no pride. They fixed on the king in something like hunger.

Alexander was taken purely out of himself. He looked
like a man who has seen a god; or who has discovered that
he is one. The light that had always been on him, bright
as a beacon, seemed both dim and scattered to what was
on him now. That had been like sun behind a cloud. This
was the sun laid bare.

"He knows what he is now," Ptolemy said, standing beside Hephaistion.

Hephaistion laughed. It cut his belly like pain. "Was
there ever any doubt of it?"

Ptolemy looked at him oddly, but said nothing.

Alexander would not speak of what the god had said. Not
even to Hephaistion.

"I suppose you told the Egyptian woman," Hephaistion
said in the quiet of the night. He had not been asked into
Alexander's tent, but he had gone in spite of it. Alexander
did not cast him out. His welcome was as warm as always,
his smile the one he kept for his friend.

It did not waver in the face of Hephaistion's bitterness.
No, Hephaistion thought. Let it bear its proper name. Jealousy. "No," said Alexander. "I didn't tell Meriamon."

"She knows," Hephaistion said. "I'd wager gold on it."

"Maybe," said Alexander. He had been reading by the light of the lamp. Hephaistion knew the book: his *Iliad* that he had had since he was a boy.

Alexander had risen to embrace his friend. He sat again in the chair, rolling the book and binding it, still smiling faintly. The light of the oracle lingered in his face.

Hephaistion stayed where he was, erect and stiff. Something in him wanted to throw itself down and weep, and flay them both with words. *I am your friend, your Patroklos. Everything that you have, you give to me. Everything that is mine, I share with you.*

Everything but the kingship. And this.

He turned blindly.

"Phai."

The old name, the love-name. It had been a mock for boys once, because it sounded like the name of Socrates' boy-courtesan: Phai, Phaidon. But Alexander had taken the shame out of it.

It stopped him now. It did not bring him about.

"Hephaistion," said Alexander. "Everything I can share with you, I do. But some things—"

It was like him to know the precise turning of Hephaistion's mind. "Some things," Hephaistion said, "are yours alone." His voice was flat.

"If I could," Alexander said, "I would."

He meant it. Hephaistion, turning, saw it in his face. But there was a limit to his yielding, and they had come to it.

It would be very easy to quarrel. A glorious, rancorous fight, with every grief and transgression of years raked up and flung in each other's face. There was a black pleasure in the prospect of it.

And what would be the use of it? It would not break down the wall of silence. It would not make Alexander any less Alexander, or Hephaistion any less himself.

"It always amazes me," Alexander said, "how you think yourself out of your tempers—and nothing to be seen of it but a muscle-twitch here, an eyeblink there."

"Am I as transparent as that?" Hephaistion asked.

"Clear as granite," Alexander said.

Hephaistion's teeth ached with clenching. He unlocked his jaw, willed his body to unknot. "I thought I had more pride than this," he said. "Or more sense."

"You needed to be sure," said Alexander. He did not look as if it angered him. "People need that. Even you."

"Damn you for knowing that," Hephaistion said, but calmly.

Alexander smiled. It was still his smile. The brightness in it was knowledge, that was all. The god had always been there.

Hephaistion bent his head to the god. He smiled at the king who was his friend: a smile with edges, but real enough when all was considered.

The king and his Companions lingered a while in Siwah. Alexander was eager to be gone, but his men needed a day or two to rest. They camped in a broad cleared space among the trees, and were given whatever they asked for by way of food and drink and even company. Some of the women and boys of Siwah were intensely curious about these big fair strangers; and the strangers were pleased to assuage that curiosity.

Alexander's curiosity was of another order. The sheen of the god lingered on him after a night's sleep, but it was dimming, becoming part of him. He wanted to see the spring that was famous even in Hellas, that was bitter cold at noon, and at midnight hot to boiling.

Or so the tales said. It was cool enough when they went, he and a friend or two and Meriamon, though not exactly icy. The sun was directly overhead. The tangled branches of trees kept off most of its heat, but where the spring was, was an open space, much trampled by pilgrims' feet. The water bubbled out of a rock into a little mossy basin, and overflowed into a trickle of a stream that wandered away into a thicket.

There was a flock of crows in the trees, flapping and quarrelling and making a dreadful racket. The priest who guided them made a move to chase the birds away.

Alexander stopped him. "Let them be," he said. "They belong here rather more than we."

The man looked as if he would have argued, but after a moment he shrugged. "As you will, lord," he said.

Alexander smiled at him, melting him where he stood. Someday, thought Meriamon, he would meet a human creature who was immune to his smile. She doubted that it would be soon.

He knelt by the pool's edge and dipped in his hand. "Cool," he said. He sipped. "Sweet, too. Pure water from the rock."

"It is the god's gift," said the priest.

"So is all that is," said Alexander. He straightened, restless already. As the others came to taste the water and remark at its cool purity, he wandered back to the trees. They were olive trees. He reached to touch a branch, ruffling the grey-green leaves. "Strange to find olives here in the middle of the desert."

Meriamon had not gone to the spring with the rest. It was cool in the shade of the trees, and the crows' clamor was surprisingly pleasant. They were laughing, she thought, taking joy in being alive.

Alexander sat on the ground beside her. Sekhmet, after a moment's thought, left her lap to occupy his. "I miss Peritas," he said.

"You'll see him soon enough," said Meriamon.

"A week, probably," he said. "If there are no more arguments from the desert."

"There won't be," she said. "It wanted to keep you from coming here. Now that it's failed, it will be only too glad to be rid of you."

He raised a brow at her. "You felt it, too? That the land didn't want us to be in it?"

"It never did love us of the Black Land. We're noisy;

we're many. We infest the clean desert, we poison it with water, we make green things grow like a blight across it."

"I'd think that would be the Nile's fault," he said. "Seeing that its floods are what make your land rich."

"That too," she said. And after a pause: "You're going back to Rhakotis, then."

"And Memphis. And after that, Asia."

A chill ran through her. It was not entirely unpleasant. "You won't stay in Egypt?"

"I can't." He had said it maybe too quickly. He softened it with a smile, though that did not last long. "I'd like to stay. But there's Darius and a whole empire on my eastern flank, and a small matter of unfinished business for the League of Hellas. I came out here, after all, to fight Persia."

"You've done that."

"I've begun it. That's all it is: a beginning. If I'm to make it last, I have to go through with the rest of it."

"And what is that?" she asked him.

"All of it." He grinned at her expression. "Hubris again, maybe. And maybe not. There's a whole world out there. Did you ever think of that? Persia first—Persia is dangerous as long as I let it resist me. Then, who knows? There are lands to the east beyond Persia. There are lands to the west, Italy and Sicily where Greeks already are, and wild places beyond them, and finally the sunset gates, the Pillars of Herakles. He set them up, my ancestor did, or so they say. I'd like to see them for myself."

"You'd like to do everything a mortal man can do."

"And a little of what a god can." He met her stare. Lightning, she thought. Striking at the heart. "Don't tell me you didn't know it. You're the one who led me here."

"Not I," said Meriamon, "but the gods who speak through me."

"It's all one," he said.

"Is that what you learned in the god's chamber?"

He lowered his eyes. She blinked, dazzled. The world

seemed very dark here at high noon in the grove of the
Sun. He stroked Sekhmet from head to twitching tail, over
and over, to the rhythm of her purring.

"I learned . . ." he said. Stopped. Frowned. "I learned
. . . too much, maybe. It was comfort of a sort, not to
know. To wonder if I was mad, or my mother was lying,
or everything I did was foolishness. I was never ordinary.
I never could be. But when I knew . . . that changed
things. It wasn't myself, you see. It was always the god."

"The god begot you," said Meriamon, "through his chosen instrument. That doesn't mean he is you, or you are
he, any more than any son can become his father."

"Philip wasn't ordinary, either," Alexander said, sharp,
almost angry. "Not in the least. They say I get my gift of
warfare from him. He was more solid; saner. But he was
a brilliant general."

"Every man is what his life has made him."

Alexander was not listening. "I'm better in the tight
spots. I think faster. I always did. That's my mother—she's
lethally quick. If she'd been a man, Macedon would have
been hard put to seize as much power as it did. It's as well
she was born a woman. Then she could marry Macedon
instead of conquering it."

"Or destroying it in a war."

"So they would have, both of them. Gods know, they
tried hard enough as they were; and she trapped in a woman's body, and he trapped by every woman's body he set
eyes on. There's irony for you. Brats by the cartload, and
his heir, his king who would be, bastard-bred of a god."

"Through Philip's body," said Meriamon.

"That wouldn't matter to him," said Alexander. He
parted Sekhmet's toes to make the claws come out, white
and gleaming sharp. "I think I'm happy to know what I
am. I know I'm terrified."

"Of course you are. You're only half mad."

He laughed. "And which half would you say that is?"

"The half that makes you do what no one else would

do, and do it brilliantly. I'll never forgive you for Tyre, you know. Even if you did come to Egypt in the end."

"I had to do it," he said. "And I came, as you say, where you wanted me to come. Did what you wanted, too. I'm surprised you aren't trying to make me stay and be a proper pharaoh."

"Would I tell you if I were?"

His head tilted. He thought about it. "Probably," he said. "Or I'd know."

"I'm that transparent?"

"You're that honest."

"So," she said, "are you."

"Then it's as well I was born in Macedon, where people aren't subtle, even when they're killing one another. I'd not have lasted a week in Persia."

"In Egypt," she said, "you might have managed a month."

"And what of you?"

"I'm god-touched," she said. "No one else would try."

He sprang up, light and smooth, hardly jarring the cat on his arm; drawing Meriamon with him, holding her face to face. "I'm almost sorry you don't want to marry me."

"There's plenty of almost for both of us," said Meriamon.

"Poor Niko," Alexander said. "I hope you were planning to invite me to the wedding."

She blushed, so sudden and so fierce that it burned away every scrap of wit. "We were going to tell you."

"Not ask?"

She stared at him blankly.

"I am, after all, his king. I have some say in whom he marries. Particularly if the lady is a foreigner."

At least the heat was gone. The cold, perhaps, was worse. "You are my king also," she said.

"So I am." His eyes narrowed. "If I forbade you, would you still do it?"

She could not keep her gaze on him. In part because it

would have been a glare. In part—in great part—because he was her king.

"Mariamne," he said.

That was not her name.

"Meriamon," said Alexander.

Her eyes rose. Glaring.

"Come now," he said. "You know I wouldn't stop you from doing what you've got your heart set on. Though what you see in him, out of all the men in my army—"

"If you can't see it, I can hardly explain it to you."

That gave him pause. Then he laughed. Delighted with her. Damn him. He knew perfectly well what she spoke of. He had Hephaistion.

She should have been appalled. That she could think such things of him. That he could see it.

And if she could not think so, and he could not see, then he would not have been her king. Kings, gods—they thought too much of themselves, too often.

Alexander had a very high opinion of himself, no doubt of that. But he knew it. He could even laugh at it. Sometimes.

He all but dragged her back to the spring, the men waiting there, the eyes and the smiles—greeting, not mockery; little good as that did. She was blushing again. So, she noticed, was Niko. There was something about secrets badly kept; they had a way of mortifying.

In the end she would shrug and live with it. And no thanks to his majesty the king, who was getting up a water-fight, and shocking the poor priest into speechlessness. It could hardly be blasphemy, since it was the god's son who did it; but kings were more staid in this part of the world.

• THIRTY-THREE •

The desert let them pass unmolested out of Siwah. Its power was quiescent; if not conquered, then certainly subdued. No gate opened on the other side of a storm. No guide came for them, nor did the way lose itself in front of them. It was quiet, all of it. Quiet to rest in.

At Rhakotis the city was shaping itself. Deinokrates the architect had sent to Memphis for rolls of papyrus and boxes of chalk and crews of men to begin the marking and digging of foundations. It was like old days in the valleys of the kings, but these labored to build not a tomb but a living city.

For far too long the Two Lands had looked backward to a splendor that was gone. Now it would look forward again under a king whose face was toward living glory and not the splendor of the dead.

Their passage to Memphis, rowing up the slow strong stream of the Nile, was a triumphal procession. The army was waiting for them. Like, Meriamon thought, a lover for his beloved. They were that, with Alexander.

She had the same rooms she had had before in the Great House behind its white walls. She went to the temple to sing the offices, but she did not sleep there, and no one asked it. Amon's priests from Thebes had gone, and Lord Ay with them. He had left a message for her. It was written in the most ancient of the tongues the priests knew, drawn and painted as meticulously as the writings on the temple's walls.

When she held it in her hands, it seemed to stir gently. The eyes of the beasts and birds, the men and women and gods, looked for a moment like the eyes of living things.

Words were power. Words written were the strongest of strong magics.

These were, in the end and after the invocations of the gods and the full forms of his name and hers and the wardings against ill use or misuse, supremely simple. "Do as your heart bids you. May Mother Isis guide your steps."

She took the message back with her to her rooms. There was dinner to go to: Alexander's last in Memphis before he took the road to Asia. People were coming who had had far to go, as far as Elephantine in the uppermost of Upper Egypt. All the Companions of Siwah were invited to it, and for the rest of the army there was a banquet laid on in the soldiers' messes.

It was, in short, an obligation. She was still in the robe of a singer in the temple. She took off the heavy braided wig, running fingers through her hair. Phylinna had the bath things ready, and the other wig, the state wig that was suitable for a royal lady.

Tonight she would be that, every inch of her, even to the scent she wore. She had walked in the land of coming forth by day. She had spoken with the Lady of the living and the dead. She was the daughter of the Great House of the Two Lands, and this was the feast of her victory.

And yet she lingered. She put down the message from Lord Ay, and took it up again. She was following her heart. She had been doing it, truly and wholly, since Siwah. And yet . . .

Sekhmet came mincing from wherever she had been. She was getting thick about the middle. The gods knew how she had managed that, with all the wandering and hunting she had been doing. She sprang as lightly as ever to Meriamon's bed and curled in the center of it, and went calmly to sleep.

Meriamon sat on the coverlet beside her, smoothing her fur. She began to purr.

Phylinna was waiting. Meriamon stood. She was mooning like a girl on the eve of her wedding. Which this almost was; but not for a while. She shook herself and went to the cooling bath.

The banquet was as splendid as she could have imagined. Alexander looked magnificent in a gold-embroidered chiton and a new purple cloak, with a crown of golden oak leaves hardly brighter than his hair. Meriamon might have liked to see him robed and crowned as pharaoh, but his face was turned already toward the east; and he had his army to think of. They wanted to see their own proper king. The princes of Egypt, maybe, needed to see him as he was. They did not look displeased.

The feast itself was as Egyptian as anyone could wish. The Macedonians bore it bravely. They were not compelled to drink beer, which they were glad of. Their opinion of Egyptian beer was, to put it mildly, jaundiced. "Cat piss," Niko had pronounced it, magisterially, after a good two jugs of it.

There was wine, and it was quite acceptable. There was goose prepared in a dozen ways, and duck, and dove and quail, and lamb and goat and beef, and oryx and gazelle, and great platters of green stuff, and fruit, and cheeses, and more manners of bread than a Hellene could have dreamed of, with a dizzying array of sauces. All eaten in music and in song, with dancers and players and a whole troupe of acrobats leaping and tumbling among the couches.

Nikolaos was not there. Meriamon had the couch to the right of the king's, high honor and quite scandalous for a woman, even a royal Egyptian; and two servants to wait on her, and people staring at her. She smiled, and spoke when spoken to, and ate as much as she could stand. That was not very much. It never was. She drank more than she usually did. The wine was rather more than acceptable. In fact it was good. Very good. Excellent.

Niko was busy. Some people had to get ready for the march in the morning, after all. He would come in before the night was over, if not to the hall then to her rooms. He had said he would, that morning when he left her, getting up even earlier than she and running off to do something unintelligible. There had been an air about him of suppressed excitement. Of surprises, and of great secrets.

Whatever he was up to, she would know soon enough. What niggled at her was no more than uneasiness on the edge of changes.

He was not waiting for her when she came back to her rooms. Sekhmet was on the bed again, or still. She grumbled about moving to make room for Meriamon, but she was much too lazy to leave the bed. She settled for walking deliberately down the length of Meriamon's body and then halfway back up again, and coiling herself against Meriamon's hip.

Meriamon's body was full of wine. It had been almost too much to sit up while Phylinna washed her, cleansed the paint from her face, plaited her hair down her back. But her mind was sharply, almost painfully alert. It counted each breath as she drew it. It marked the slow turning of the stars, and the first faint glimmer of dawn upon the horizon. It knew the touch of each hair of Sekhmet's coat as she stroked the sleeping cat.

And made a discovery that shocked laughter out of her. "Sekhmet! You didn't!"

The cat yawned and stopped her ears with an upcurved paw. She did not want to hear about it.

"I hope it was one of the temple cats," Meriamon said.

"I think it was the king of the stevedores' quarter," said Nikolaos.

Meriamon started. She had not heard him at all.

He was barefoot, with his sandals in his hand. He looked extraordinarily pleased with himself.

"Where have you been?" she demanded of him. Not furiously, no. Of course not. Merely vehemently.

"I do think it was the big he-cat from down by the

docks," Niko said. "He courted her for days. I'd hardly blame her if she gave in simply to shut him up."

"Maybe she likes great grinning louts," said Meriamon.

"You'll never get her to admit it." He set his sandals in their usual place next to the clothing chest, and unfastened his belt. His chiton was plain and somewhat workworn.

The lamplight did wonderful things to the planes and angles of his body. He paused with his chiton in his hand, frowning at the other, the twisted one, and flexing the stiffened fingers. They were moving more easily now. He hardly seemed to notice any longer that there was anything amiss. He could ride, he could hold a shield. He could not play the double pipes, but then he had never been much good with them.

"Does it hurt you?" she asked him.

"No." His voice was abstracted, but peaceful enough. "Sometimes a twinge or two . . . no. I had Typhon on the Scythian bit again. He likes it. I'm thinking of keeping him on it."

"What does Alexander say to that?"

"Alexander thinks I'm starting to make sense. Ptolemy says I never did, why should I start now?"

She smiled. He grinned back. Yes, definitely he was keeping secrets.

He had had a bath. He smelled of clean skin and sweet oil. His hair was damp, curling as it dried.

Her body woke for him. But he was not ready, not quite yet. He stretched out beside her. Whatever he was thinking of, he was bursting with it.

"Tell me," she said.

His eyes were wide. He played a very poor innocent. "What's to tell?"

"You know better than I."

He bit his lip. He was trying not to grin.

She measured him with a surgeon's eye. "I happen to know," she said, "that when I touch you there"—and she did—"and there"—and she did that—"you howl."

He did. He bolted halfway out of bed. She wrapped arms and legs about him and trapped him. "Tell," she said.

"Under torture?" he asked, affronted.

She straightened her best finger. She threatened his most sensitive rib.

"I'll tell!" he cried. He was laughing like an idiot. She had to wait for him to stop.

"I've been talking," he said at long last. "To the king. And to Ptolemy. And Mazaces—did you know he's going to stay in Egypt? Alexander is keeping him on. He knows the place, after all. And he's not too badly hated, for a Persian."

"He won't be satrap again, surely," said Meriamon. Her lips were tight.

"Not likely," said Niko. "No; Peukestas will be governor here, and Aischylos of Rhodes. A Macedonian and a Greek. And Egyptians to stand behind them."

"That's well," Meriamon said. She had known about Peukestas, of course. But one never knew. Kings could change their minds.

"I've been talking to Deinokrates, too," Niko said. "He's down from Rhakotis, getting more men and having a last word with Alexander. They're calling the place Alexandria already. It looks as if it's going to stick."

"Of course it will," said Meriamon. "The gods have said it."

"I'm going up there," he said. "I'm going to help build it."

"We're going straight to Tyre," she said. "There won't be time to stop by Rhakotis again."

"I'm not going to Tyre," said Nikolaos. "I'm going to Alexandria."

"But—"

And he said. " 'We'?"

There was a pause.

"I'm going to Tyre," Meriamon said very carefully. "I'm going with Alexander."

"Of course you aren't," said Niko. "You hated it there. You spent every moment wanting to be in Egypt."

"I was supposed to be in Egypt. He was dallying, building that mole of his."

"And making the greatest siege in the world," Niko said.

"It kept him out of Egypt." She shook herself. She was letting him lure her from the straight track. "He's king in Egypt now. He has to go and conquer Persia."

"Of course he does. I'm not going with him. I'm going to help Deinokrates build his city. It's going to be splendid, Meriamon. All the best of Egypt, and all the best of Hellas. We'll build temples to our gods, and temples to yours: Amon, of course—"

"Isis," she said. "Build a temple to Isis."

"Isis," he said, obliging. "And a market, Meriamon. A market for everything in the world, and ships to bring it, and a harbor for the ships to anchor in. And a place for philosophers. Alexander was particular about that. Somewhere for them to do their thinking, and somewhere for their teaching, and scribes to copy their books, and a library to keep them in. We'll have a theater, and festivals to match the ones in Athens. We'll have a gymnasium. We'll have the greatest city that ever was."

"And places for ordinary people?" Meriamon asked. "Will you make room for those?"

"Everywhere," he said. "Cities aren't made, you know. Mostly they just grow. Here we'll learn from their mistakes."

"So we shall," she said.

He did not hear the echoes in her voice. His smile dazzled her. He kissed her thoroughly, drew back still grinning, said, "I knew you'd see it. We can be married there. Or if you'd rather, we can go with Alexander as far as Pelusium. It won't be much of a wedding for a king's daughter, but he'll be there, at least, to bless it."

"I'm going with him," she said. "To Tyre. And wherever he goes after that."

The brightness faded from his face. He frowned. "But why?"

"Because he is my king."

"He's your king in Egypt. He's not staying here."

"It doesn't matter," she said.

"But," said Niko. "You wither and fade outside of your Black Land. Your magic is weak. The air is too cold or too wet. The sun is wrong. The sky is too narrow."

"All of that is true," she said. "It makes no difference. Alexander is my king. Where he is, my power lies."

"Does he know that?"

Bless the boy. He was jealous.

Her heart was cold and small and hard. She understood now. What Ay had meant; what he had bidden her to do.

There were gods in it somewhere. They felt very far away and supremely indifferent. Even the Mother of them all. She had seen her beloved slain and rent in pieces, and gone up and down the Two Lands in search of them. She would hardly have pity on a woman whose lover was simply determined to stay in Khemet. Fine good sense, she would reckon that.

"Alexander knows," Meriamon said. "He's not displeased. I'll go back to working with Philippos, and Aristandros might decide to make use of me. There will be other Egyptians with us. And Thaïs, of course. And Phylinna. It's not as if I'll be all alone."

Niko looked blank. Stunned. "But *why?*"

She drew a deep breath. She prayed for patience. "I have to. The same way I had to leave Egypt in the beginning. Because it's where I must be. And—" She stopped. Very well: let him know the truth. "I want to. Yes, this is my country. Yes, there is no place like it. But I want to see other places; other skies. There are whole worlds that I've never seen. He said that to me, did you know? When we were in Siwah. I know what he meant. I want to see them with him."

"You should have married him after all," said Niko, hard and flat.

"No," she said. "It's not that kind of wanting. It's what you want in his city."

He did not want to understand that. His face was set against her. He was growing angry: his scowl was as black as she had ever seen it.

Her hand tried to creep out, to smooth the scowl away. She clenched it at her side. But never as tight as she clenched her heart, lest she break down and cry. "I love you," she said. "Don't doubt it for a moment. When I can come back, I will. I promise you."

"Will you come back? Will you ever?"

She looked into the grey glass of his eyes. There were visions there. "Yes," she said. "I will come back. I will die in Khemet, in the Black Land where I was born."

He shivered so hard that the bed shook. But his temper was stronger than his awe. "Maybe I'll find another woman. Maybe I won't care if I ever see you again."

"Maybe," she said. The word was soft and cold.

He rolled to his feet. "By the dog!" he cried. "Don't you even care?"

She looked up at him. Remembering how she had first seen him: a shadow against uncertain light, towering, swaying just visibly. It had been pain then, of his wounds and his exhaustion. It was pain now; and if the wounds were of the heart, they were all the deeper for that.

No deeper than her own. "Your brother will be king in Egypt," she said. "Did you know that?"

"What?" She had caught him off balance.

"I saw it," she said. "Your eyes are like a scrying glass."

He squeezed them shut. "Oh, gods. I wish I could hate you. It would be so much simpler."

"You're not even afraid of me."

His eyes flew open. "Why should I be?"

She crooked a finger. Her shadow reared up. It grinned in Niko's face.

He grinned back nastily. It shut its mouth, nonplussed. "Is that your real shape," he asked it, "or do you have one you were born with?"

It looked at Meriamon. Its eyes were, of all things, laughing.

She did not see what there was to laugh at. Her heart was going to Asia with Alexander. Her body wanted to cling to this beautiful fearless idiot and never let him go.

She went still. She could hardly—he would never—

And why not?

She stood. They towered over her, both of them, shadow and man. She stretched out her hand. She laid it flat over Niko's heart. She looked him in the eye—eye to eye, and that was a feat. She hoped that he was properly in awe of it. "I am going with Alexander," she said. "You are coming with me."

His brows went up. "What if I won't?"

"You will."

"How? By sorcery?"

"Because you love me."

"If you love me, you'll stay in Egypt."

"No," she said.

If he was a fool, he would decide that she did not love him. He would break away, and rage at her, and fling himself out.

He raised his hand. Her shadow tensed. He laid it over hers, closed his fingers, turned her hand palm up. It was scarred still from the stone that had pierced it on the march to Siwah. The mark would not fade, she suspected. It was a reminder, and a remembrance.

"You have will enough to rule a world," he said.

"That's Alexander," she said.

"And you." He looked angry. Sulking. "What do I have to do to make you see sense?"

"Come with me."

"Will we come back?"

Her heart leaped. She kept her face impassive. "I've told you we will."

"Well then," he said. "If we come back, and you promise—on your solemn word—that we will live in Alexandria, and build it, and make it beautiful—"

"And be as kings in it?"

"Plain good citizens will do," he said. "Will you promise?"

"By my name," said Meriamon.

"Then I'll go," he said. His anger was gone. His smile swelled, bloomed, blazed. "We'll be the greatest army that has ever been. Our king is the greatest king who ever was. We'll stride from horizon to horizon. We'll conquer the world."

Or at least, thought Meriamon, a goodly portion of it.

She closed her fingers over the memory of pain. She had not seen the last of it. Oh, no. When that day came, she would have come forth into another day than this which brightened the sky of the living earth, and stood in another Great House than this, in the Hall of the Two Truths, and the judges would be weighing the purity of her heart.

She was smiling. Broadly, she noticed. Grinning, for a fact. "We'll conquer the world," she agreed. "Tomorrow. Tonight—or what is left of tonight—"

"Tonight," said Nikolaos, "we conquer Egypt."

Fair was fair, Meriamon thought. Egypt, after all, had conquered Macedon. And would again; and years to do it in, and worlds to wander as they did it.

Even the Weigher of Hearts would be pleased to call that justice.

• AUTHOR'S NOTE •

I • ALEXANDER

The life and achievements of Alexander III of Macedon (356–323 B.C.), with the exception of Mary Renault's trilogy, *Fire from Heaven*, *The Persian Boy*, and *Funeral Games*, have inspired few recent novels in English. There has, however, been a plethora of monographs, biographies, and popular histories. Perhaps the best of the recent crop, with its summaries of prior scholarship and its meticulous recording of dates, events, and sources, is A.B. Bosworth's *Conquest and Empire: The Reign of Alexander the Great* (Cambridge, 1988). Both Bosworth and Renault draw ultimately from the ancient historians of Alexander's life and times, all of whom are available in English translation: Plutarch and Curtius in Penguin editions (Plutarch, *The Age of Alexander*, tr. Ian Scott-Kilvert, 1973, and Quintus Curtius Rufus, *The History of Alexander*, tr. John Yardley, 1984), Arrian's *The Campaigns of Alexander* in the translation of Aubrey de Sélincourt (New York, 1958), and the histories of Diodorus Siculus (Diodorus of Sicily) in Loeb editions, especially volume 8, ed. and tr. C.B. Welles, and volume 9, ed. and tr. R.M. Geer (Cambridge, Mass., 1963, 1967). It should be noted that, since Renault's assessment of Curtius as an irredeemably silly man with access to priceless sources, scholars have concluded that Curtius, for all his bombast, is in fact more accurate than Arrian. There is also, and significantly for this novel, an odd, highly fantastical, and quite entertaining *Life of Alexander of Macedon* attributed to Alexander's own chronicler, Callisthenes. Elizabeth Hazelton Haight in her translation (New York, 1955) sets its actual composition at about A.D. 300, but adds that certain incidents have been found on papyri dated not long after Alexander's death. Here, in the work of the author commonly known as "Pseudo-Callisthenes," is the story of Nectanebo, last native pharaoh of Egypt, and his attempt to create a savior for Egypt through the offices of the god Amon and the womb of the Queen of Macedon.

This novel adheres closely to actual historical events from the battle of Issus in the autumn of 333 B.C., through Alexander's journey to the oracle of Zeus Amon at Siwah in the Libyan desert, in the spring of 331 B.C. I have made occasional changes in the interests of theme, story, or narrative simplicity. Although some sources, including Curtius, speak of Alexander's crowning in Memphis, this probably does not refer to the native rite of accession. Alexander was not at that point interested in taking on the trappings of the country which he had taken. Most likely he held his Greek games, toured the sights (including the Pyramids and the tomb of the Apis Bull) as numerous foreigners had before him, and left promptly for Siwah. The founding of Alexandria probably took place after his return from the oracle; to avoid an anticlimax, I have chosen to follow the tradition that sets the founding before the journey to the shrine. The story of the sandstorm and the miraculous rain seems to have been commonly accepted by ancient historians, likewise the account of the guides, whether serpents or ravens from the groves of the oasis. Some scholars have proposed that this story was originally told by Ptolemy in his memoirs. Alexander never spoke to anyone of his time alone with the oracle, not even to Hephaistion, who, as Curtius says, was privy to all his secrets.

Although Ptolemy claimed after Alexander's death to be the king's illegitimate half-brother, this was probably a political ploy—a means of laying claim to the kingship of

Egypt. He died in 283 B.C., having preserved his kingdom intact through the Wars of Succession that followed Alexander's death. His family ruled Egypt until the suicide of Cleopatra VII and her Roman consort, Mark Antony, in 30 B.C., when Egypt became a province of the Roman Empire.

The Athenian courtesan Thaïs probably did not join Alexander's army until the siege of Tyre. At Issus the army was still under the regimen of Alexander's father Philip, who mandated that no women or camp followers accompany the troops. Soldiers were not allowed wagons or large trains of belongings. Each company shared a servant, and each man carried his own possessions and armor as he marched. After the capture of the Persian king's women and treasure, the army's discipline slackened, and it began to swell into the ambulatory city that accompanied Alexander on his journeys through Asia. For a short, thorough, and very useful account of the army and its logistics, see Donald W. Engels, *Alexander the Great and the Logistics of the Macedonian Army* (Berkeley, 1978).

It was Thaïs who, the story goes, persuaded Alexander in the midst of a drunken revel to burn Persepolis. She bore Ptolemy three children, but she never became his wife. When Ptolemy claimed the kingship of Egypt, he took a properly respectable—and Greek—queen.

When Alexander died in Babylon at the age of thirty-two, worn out by fever, wounds, and grief for the death of Hephaistion, Philip Arrhidaios, Alexander's half-brother, became King Philip III of Macedon. He was murdered in 317 B.C.—a common fate of Macedonian kings, addlepated or otherwise. Precisely what incapacity he suffered is not known, nor is it known whether it was congenital or the result of an accident in his childhood. He was succeeded by Alexander's son by the Bactrian princess Roxane, Alexander IV, who was murdered in his turn, at the age of about twelve, in 310 B.C. His death ended the dynasty. For a good, brief analysis of Macedon's history in general and Alexander III's effect on it in particular, see R. Malcolm Errington's *A History of Macedonia*, tr. Catherine Errington (Berkeley, 1990).

Likenesses of Alexander were frequent in ancient times. It has been said that he changed the standards of beauty from the austere Classical model to the fuller, lusher Hellenistic image. A particularly interesting portrait, done from life, has been found in the tomb of Philip II at Vergina in northern Greece, and is reproduced in *The Search for Alexander: An Exhibition* (Boston, 1980). Manolis Andronikos' essay in this volume, "The Royal Tombs at Vergina: A Brief Account of the Excavations," pp. 26ff., despite its good grey title, is an archeological adventure story. The Getty Museum in Malibu, California, has on display a marble portrait of the young Alexander, and rather more interesting, a likeness that has been identified by most scholars as that of Hephaistion. Likenesses of Ptolemy can be found in any book of classical coins; his lantern jaw and uncompromising nose are unmistakable.

II · EGYPT AND EGYPTIAN MAGIC

Meriamon, like Nikolaos, is my invention, as is her mission to Alexander. Her father, however, was in fact a pharaoh of Egypt, Nectanebo II, last of the native rulers, defeated by the Persians in 341 B.C. and driven out, probably to his death. Pseudo-Callisthenes makes him a great mage. This is true enough, insofar as Pharaoh (the title means "Great House") was regarded as the living incarnation of the god Horus, the direct intercessor with the gods, by whose health and safety the realm prospered or failed.

Egypt in the fourth century B.C. was regarded as unimaginably ancient and profoundly mysterious. Magic had its source there, and magic pervaded the lives and minds of its people. Its practitioners guarded their secrets jealously, but their purposes were as profoundly practical as the rest of Egyptian culture: magical rituals and practices were designed to obtain specific results through manipulation of natural and supernatural forces. Books on the subject are legion, and most are sheer nonsense. The few reliable sources are to be found, in general, in scholarly journals. I have made use, with caution, of Bob Brier's *Ancient Egyptian Magic* (New York, 1981); in this book, while prospecting for tidbits useful to a novelist, I found the quotation from Pseudo-Callisthenes, on Nectanebo and Alexander, which inspired this novel. A sampling of genuine Egyptian magic can be found in *Ancient Egyptian Magical Texts*, tr. J.F. Borghouts (Leiden, 1978). Words are vitally important, puns and double meanings frequent, and the name crucial to the mastery of the thing, whether god, demon, animal, or human.

There is no single, comprehensive, completely reliable book-length text on ancient Egypt. I have found useful J.E. Manchip White's *Ancient Egypt: Its Culture and History* (New York, 1970), and B.G. Trigger, B.J. Kemp, D. O'Connor, and A.B. Lloyd, *Ancient Egypt: A Social History* (Cambridge, 1983). For the religion of the Egyptians, Siegfried Morenz, *Egyptian Religion*, tr. Ann E. Keep (Ithaca, N.Y., 1973), is sufficiently comprehensive for a beginning. Useful also is Adolf Erman's *Life in Ancient Egypt*, tr. H.M. Tirard (New York, 1971). I have adapted Erman's description of the accession of the king, rather than the version described in White, as more likely to have appealed to Alexander's personality and imagination.

Meriamon herself appears—under the name of Ahmose Merit-Amon, a queen of the 18th dynasty, around 1550 B.C.—in Mohamed Saleh and Hourig Sourouzian, *Official Catalogue, The Egyptian Museum, Cairo*, tr. Peter Der Manuelian and Helen Jacquet-Gordon (Mainz, 1987). Her sarcophagus is listed as number 127.

Although Egypt never again saw the rule of native kings after the arrival of Alexander—all the Ptolemies, including the last and most famous Cleopatra, were Hellenes—its cults and gods thrived under Roman rule. The cult of Isis only failed completely with the triumph of Christianity. Even then, many of the attributes of the Blessed Virgin can be traced to Isis and other mother goddesses of the pagans.

Women in Egypt enjoyed more freedom than did women of the Persians or the Greeks. There was no pre-dynastic matriarchy. Egypt was always ruled primarily by men, but queens ruled and held regencies; even, once or twice, claimed the title of king. Under the Ptolemies, queens ruled often, and sometimes unassisted by kings.

Herodotus is incorrect in his statement that the Egyptian priesthoods were entirely male. The priesthood of Amon, at least, included a female high priestess, the Great Wife of Amon, and women singers and dancers in the temple. Ordinary women, even in Hellenistic times, were sometimes educated, were able to make contracts and own property, and, to some extent, had a say in the choosing of their husbands. Statues and paintings depict over and over an image of marriage as a bond of affection between near-equals. Sarah B. Pomeroy's *Women in Hellenistic Egypt from Alexander to Cleopatra* (New York, 1984) addresses the question of women in pharaonic times as well. A broader spectrum appears in the essays collected by Averil Cameron and Amélie Kuhrt, eds., *Images of Women in Antiquity* (London, 1983).

The Egyptian obsession with death was in fact an obsession with life. Elaborate tombs, meticulous preservation of the body, intricate magical rituals for the passage through the land of the dead, were all aimed at reproducing in eternity the image of mortal existence. The essential literary and magical guide to the afterlife, the so-called "Book of the Dead," is actually and more properly titled "The Book of Coming Forth by Day." That the land of the dead was perceived as lying beyond the western horizon of Egypt, in the Libyan desert, and that Alexander journeyed through these lands to reach Siwah, is one of the happy coincidences of the novelist's trade.

BESTSELLERS FROM TOR

☐ 51195-6 BREAKFAST AT WIMBLEDON $3.99
               Jack Bickham Canada $4.99

☐ 52497-7 CRITICAL MASS $5.99
               David Hagberg Canada $6.99

☐ 85202-9 ELVISSEY $12.95
               Jack Womack Canada $16.95

☐ 51612-5 FALLEN IDOLS $4.99
               Ralph Arnote Canada $5.99

☐ 51716-4 THE FOREVER KING $5.99
               Molly Cochran & Warren Murphy Canada $6.99

☐ 50743-6 PEOPLE OF THE RIVER $5.99
               Michael Gear & Kathleen O'Neal Gear Canada $6.99

☐ 51198-0 PREY $5.99
               Ken Goddard Canada $6.99

☐ 50735-5 THE TRIKON DECEPTION $5.99
               Ben Bova & Bill Pogue Canada $6.99

Buy them at your local bookstore or use this handy coupon:
Clip and mail this page with your order.

Publishers Book and Audio Mailing Service
P.O. Box 120159, Staten Island, NY 10312-0004

Please send me the book(s) I have checked above. I am enclosing $ _____
(Please add $1.25 for the first book, and $.25 for each additional book to cover postage and handling.
Send check or money order only—no CODs.)

Name _____
Address _____
City _____ State/Zip _____
Please allow six weeks for delivery. Prices subject to change without notice.

ADVENTURES IN
ROMANCE FROM TOR

THE BEST IN MYSTERY

☐ 51388-6 THE ANONYMOUS CLIENT $4.99
             J.P. Hailey   Canada $5.99

☐ 51195-6 BREAKFAST AT WIMBLEDON $3.99
             Jack M. Bickham   Canada $4.99

☐ 51682-6 CATNAP $4.99
             Carole Nelson Douglas   Canada $5.99

☐ 51702-4 IRENE AT LARGE $4.99
             Carole Nelson Douglas   Canada $5.99

☐ 51563-3 MARIMBA $4.99
             Richard Hoyt   Canada $5.99

☐ 52031-9 THE MUMMY CASE $3.99
             Elizabeth Peters   Canada $4.99

☐ 50642-1 RIDE THE LIGHTNING $3.95
             John Lutz   Canada $4.95

☐ 50728-2 ROUGH JUSTICE $4.99
             Ken Gross   Canada $5.99

☐ 51149-2 SILENT WITNESS $3.99
             Collin Wilcox   Canada $4.99

Buy them at your local bookstore or use this handy coupon:
Clip and mail this page with your order.

Publishers Book and Audio Mailing Service
P.O. Box 120159, Staten Island, NY 10312-0004

Please send me the book(s) I have checked above. I am enclosing $ _____
(Please add $1.25 for the first book, and $.25 for each additional book to cover postage and handling.
Send check or money order only—no CODs.)

Name _____
Address _____
City _____ State/Zip _____
Please allow six weeks for delivery. Prices subject to change without notice.